The Gravedigger of Bronte

Alexander Lucie-Smith

2

Chapter One

Pio Forcella, known to all his friends as Piuccio, was a youngish man in his early thirties, whose thick head of hair had turned prematurely grey, which made him, he thought, with the help of his smart black suit, black tie and pure white shirt, the very model of a Sicilian undertaker. His habitual expression was one of gloomy efficiency, which was designed to reassure customers. He was originally from Bronte, but he had worked, ever since leaving his native town, out of a warehouse near the municipal cemetery. He had overseen the burial of Stefania di Rienzi, and had also had charge of the burial, some years prior to that, of the unfortunate Turiddu. It was about this matter that he had come to see don Traiano Antonescu.

'The original funeral, the original grave,' he explained, 'was paid for by don Calogero di Rienzi, but I doubt very much that he wants to be disturbed by this matter. I know that the deceased is your half-brother's father.'

'The deceased, as you call him,' said Traiano sharply, 'had parents and brothers and sisters. They no longer live round here. I believe they moved. Why speak to me? Speak to them.'

'That was my first thought, don Traiano. But as you say, they have moved, and they have never visited the grave as far as I can see. No one has. It is in a state of dilapidation. I wrote to the family, but the letter came back unopened. What has become of them, I do not know.'

'And I do not want to know,' said Traiano, with decision.

They were sitting in the study of the new flat, the study that had been don Calogero's. He had moved upstairs. The safe, which had been too heavy to move, was still there. Don Calogero retained one of the keys. He had also left the sofa behind and other unwanted pieces of furniture. But he had taken the desk. The undertaker was perched on an armchair, Traiano sprawled on the sofa; at a little distance, one could hear and sense the domestic life of the house: his wife cooking; the sound of the children; the prospect of bathtime. And here he was speaking to an undertaker. But it would not be good to be rude. Perhaps undertakers, one day, might be useful. He waited in silence, waited for the man to realise he was not interested in Turiddu's grave, and waited for him to stand up, take his leave and go, and leave him in peace.

Pio Forcella understood that he had overstayed his welcome; that he had been granted the favour of an interview, but the interview was drawing to a close. It was necessary to make his appeal now, or lose the chance forever.

'Sir, I need your help,' he said.

Traiano looked at him.

'And how can I help you?' he asked coolly.

'Sir, the grave of the late Turiddu is in a terrible mess. The marble cover is broken, the coffin has been vandalised and the body has been, well, there are bones scattered everywhere. And not just bones, but the clothes he was buried in. It is not a nice sight. I have made the grave as secure as I can, but that can only be a temporary solution. A lot of the graves are in a similar state or worse.'

'Go on,' commanded Traiano.

'This particular grave is registered to don Calogero. Once someone is buried there the grave cannot be cleared for a certain number of years by law, depending on the original terms of the sale of the grave: ten years, twenty, fifty or in some case in perpetuity. This one is in perpetuity. I checked. If we remove the remains, if we remove the old coffin, which is like matchwood, then we can resell the grave, and put a new deceased in there.'

'That is illegal,' said Traiano. Then he said: 'The people who run the cemetery would never allow it.'

Then he realised what he had said. The people who ran the cemetery would soon be out of a job when the new junta took power. And that junta would be headed, he expected, by Volta, their friend. And Volta would appoint new people. The cemetery had been a scandal too long. He was bound to appoint someone new to clean the place up. And that person could clean up, throw out all the old bones, and sell off all the old graves and make a fortune. Double selling. Was that what it was called?

'What are you proposing is done with the remains of the late Turiddu?' he asked. 'He was not big, but there must still be something of him left? And the coffin? What is left of it, that is. Have you thought about that?'

'I have, sir. Don Calogero owns a disused quarry and a fleet of trucks. I gather all the drivers are trustworthy men. All one needs is to send people over the cemetery wall at night and collect what is to be removed, and throw it over the wall into the trucks, and then drive to landfill.'

'Don't they patrol the place at night?'

'No, sir. They do not bother. If I was in charge, I would bother. The other thing is, when the new mayor takes over, the cemetery will be a hive of activity, of construction, of trucks arriving all the time. No one will notice.'

'I see you have thought all this out. And no doubt you want me to put it to don Calogero. And no doubt you want me to put a little momentum behind your application to the new mayor when he is looking for a new cemetery director.' He looked at Pio Forcella. 'No doubt others will approach me with similar schemes for don Calogero's attention. And they will offer inducements.'

'I have recently sold some family property near Bronte, sir, and I can offer you ten thousand euros.'

'That is not how it works,' said Traiano with a sad smile. 'The election is a long way off, still. We have to wait for the new Mayor who will take office in the month of March. That is six months away. Other bids will come in. Yours is the first. But yours is an attractive one. When all the bids come in, we will give the job to whoever we trust the most, and whoever rewards us the most. Yes, yes, I know, perhaps ten thousand is all you have to spare. Do not worry. If you get the job, you give us a monthly contribution from your pay for however long it takes. Five hundred a month for twenty months, that is ten thousand. But others may bid, and you may want to go higher. The monthly contribution goes to the Confraternity or the charity of our choice.'

'I will bid whatever it takes, don Traiano. I need this. Even if I have to mortgage my future for decades.'

Traiano gave him a questioning look.

'My wife,' said the gravedigger of Bronte. 'She is not happy; she is not happy with me. I do not make enough money. Trade is good, things tick over, but our overheads are huge, and the amount of money I am owed, the number of bad debts I have had to write off. She says it is because people do not respect me, because I do not have powerful friends. It's humiliating. Now she has found she is pregnant; it was not supposed to happen. She blames me, and... well, I thought that perhaps I could come to don Calogero, through you, and offer my services. There is a fortune to be made in the cemetery. And it would be a slow process, it would be a good long-term investment. And I know don Calogero says he wants to improve the environment, as does Fabio Volta, well, you know that. And then there is the matter of the crypt of your church. It is a wonderful space, don Traiano, I went there, when I oversaw the signora's funeral. It has real possibilities.'

'For what?'

'Burials, of course, sir. You clear out all the old tombs, empty all the shelves, for most of the people have been there for a long time, and you sell the spaces for a lot of money.'

'Well, Piuccio, you have a mind for business, which I like, but that is a matter for the Confraternity and for our priest, don Giorgio.'

'Of course, sir,' said Piuccio humbly, knowing that the Confraternity would nevertheless do what don Calogero wanted, and that his suggestions were commands, as far as people like the lawyer Petrocchi were concerned.

'Tell me about these bad debts,' said Traiano, suddenly interested. 'How much do they amount to?'

Pio Forcella sighed.

'Quite a lot, don Traiano. You will laugh, but the funeral trade is full of bad debts. People spend way too much, even though we discourage it, and then suddenly, when the bill arrives, it is a different story. I am owed about two hundred thousand euro, and some of these debts go back decades, to my father's time. We have tried everything: payment plans - you name it - but it's like getting water out of the desert.'

'You could give us a list, names, amounts, and the paperwork, most of it, by the sound of it, rather yellow with age? You can? Well, listen, Piuccio, it is a pity that you have to worry about these debts you will never recover. It must prey on your mind. I'll tell you what: We will buy them off you. Name an amount, we will give you cash, and then the debts will be to us, and we will go round to these people and persuade them to pay. Two hundred thousand, you say?'

'At least, sir,' said Piuccio, suddenly amazed that his fortunes were turning, but trying not to show it.

He began to calculate in his head, how much he could reasonably ask for. He calculated too that if the debts became the property of don Traiano, that would mean fewer problems with bad debts in future. But he ought not to sound greedy.

'Name a price,' said Traiano.

'Would twenty thousand be too much?' he asked. 'It is ten per cent of the nominal value.'

Ten per cent of the nominal value, where the real value was nil, he thought.

Don Traiano was impassive. He got up, and walked to the safe, which was open. He bent down and extracted a bundle of notes. They were the sort of notes that Piuccio had never seen before. He watched him count out forty five-hundred euro notes. He handed them to Piuccio, who received them with thanks, and carefully put them into his breast pocket.

'I will send someone over to collect all the paperwork tomorrow,' he said.

Don Traiano politely waited for Pio Forcella to take his leave; but the undertaker hesitated.

'There is something else,' he said.

'Ah,' said Traiano. 'You save the best things till the end, eh?'

Pio Forcella was almost apologetic as he explained.

'I had a phone call from Rome. It concerns the late Beata Bednarowska and her son, the late Pavel Bednarowski. The bodies have been in a mortuary in Rome since August, and it is now October. The mortuary in Rome does not want these bodies, naturally, and they want them removed for burial. They have searched for relatives, and there are none, at least none who will take responsibility. They have been in negotiation with the Poles, hoping to repatriate the bodies. It seems they can compel the Poles to take the mother, but not the child, which is only half a solution. Moreover, the commune of Rome refuses to pay for their burial or even their cremation; that is why they rang around the undertakers of Catania, asking if we had any suggestions about friends, relations, possible sites for them to be buried down here. When I got the call, I thought that don Calogero ought to know, or someone close to him.'

'Why did you think that?'

'Because they came from this quarter, and don Calogero is intimately connected with this quarter, and I felt he would like to know.'

'You mean, he might want to pay for their burial?'

'Yes, he might, but more importantly, he might want to prevent someone else paying for their burial. If he were to pay, then he could choose where they were buried as well.'

'You have foresight, Piuccio. I am sure you have read about this unfortunate woman and her son in the papers, and heard the stories going around. As you know, the poor woman was a prostitute, and her profession was a dangerous one. I don't say this out of unkindness, it is just a fact, and as you probably know, my mother followed the same profession once upon a time, as I am sure no one has forgotten. Beata Bednarowska may have been killed by a violent client. Whichever way, the police failed in her regard and in regard to her son. But as you have discovered, no one wants to bury them, no one wants to be reminded of them. As for me, I can quite see how, if they came back to Catania, there is the possibility that their last resting place would attract the wrong sort of attention. Best not. So, tell me, how much would it cost for you to go up to Rome and oversee their private cremation? It would be good if you went, telling the authorities that all had been paid for by a benefactor who wants to remain anonymous.'

'Five thousand euro would cover everything, sir: transportation, coffins, cremation.'

'And we can trust you?'

'Of course, sir.'

Traiano got up and went over to the safe once more; he took out ten more five-hundred euro notes, which he handed to Piuccio. Piuccio looked intensely grateful.

'See to this business as soon as you can,' he said. 'And then send us an itemised bill, not a round number please, but in the region of ten thousand euros, and send it to the office. The accountants know what to do with this sort of thing, I believe. I am not a numbers man myself. Now come through and meet Ceccina, my wife, and do not get robbed when you get to the via Etnea. And you must make sure your wife hears all about this. I don't mean the business of this poor woman and her son. I mean how you came here; how you had coffee; how you became friends with me, and let that sink into her head. You may have to be firm with her, but I am sure you will be gentle as well. She is pregnant after all. But if you are to be a friend of mine, she needs to realise that she has to respect you.'

He smiled broadly. Piuccio was not sure if this was a joke or not.

'Oh yes, one other thing. Write down the exact location of the grave of the late Turiddu, and I will get it cleared very soon, and you can arrange for it to be made ready for someone else.'

They passed from the study to the kitchen, where the beautiful Ceccina was sitting surrounded by children. She smiled as they entered. She was entranced to hear that Piuccio and his wife were expecting a second child, and asked him many questions.

The internal bell on the big door that led into the building on the square with the monument to Cardinal Dusmet was marked 'Bonelli'. It was new label, marking the legal triumph of the new owner. The dusk of October was gathering, as Traiano rang the bell and announced himself on the intercom. The door buzzed open and he walked up to the first floor. It was opened by Tonino Grassi. He stepped in to a vast dim saloon hung with paintings and filled with antique furniture.

'Hi,' he said, without extending his hand. 'You might as well switch on the lights. I have not been here before.'

'The lights are new,' said Tonino. 'Ruggero came and brought some men who installed them.'

He was impressed. It must have cost a fortune. In addition to the massive chandelier in the centre of the room, there were spotlights on each of the main paintings. It was quite a collection. The variety was huge. He wondered if there was anything he would like to hang on his own wall. He examined the furniture. He placed a hand on a nineteenth century desk and looked at the sparkling terracotta tiles of the floor. Clearly the signora Grassi was in her element when it came to cleaning the place. And the presence of Tonino was in itself a deterrent to thieves.

'You like it here?'

'Yes, boss, very much. So does my mother. There is much more room here. The kitchen is bigger, and there are two rooms, one for my mother and one for me. And the bathroom is wonderful.'

'I have a job for you,' said Traiano in a tone that betrayed a lack of interest in these arrangements.

'Yes, boss?'

'Don't get excited. They are already dead. It involves removing a corpse. We will go soonish. But there is something else.'

'Yes, boss?' said Tonino in a different tone.

'The police have been asking about you,' said Traiano.

'Me?' said Tonino.

'Think back to August,' said Traiano. 'Who knows you went to Rome?'

He did not look at Tonino as he said this, but continued to stare at the paintings, taking in the landscapes, the still lives, the portraits of people long dead.

'Muniddu,' said Tonino. 'But….'

He meant that Muniddu was to be trusted, Muniddu was watertight.

'You see,' said Traiano, 'the police are stupid, but they are perhaps not as stupid as we thought. Or maybe they are, I cannot quite make up my mind. Someone in the station at Piazza Santa Nicollela alerted me to this, and they were doing me a favour. They recognised you, and they recognised that you worked for me, and they thought I should know. Maybe they think I will be grateful, maybe they want to get you into trouble; maybe they are trying to tell us something so we panic. Anyway, they have proof that you were on the train from Rome to Catania on the night, well, you know the night.'

'How, boss, how?'

'You were in a compartment with some Americans, and they were annoyed that you smoked in the corridor of the train, when it clearly says No Smoking. Americans… well. They filmed you on those annoying phones they all have, the film is dated, and they gave the number of the carriage and compartment, they had tickets, and then they went and reported it to the police. Typical Americans, deliberately stirring up trouble. You did not notice? No, I suppose not. The police laughed at the report until one of them spotted it was you, someone they recognised from the Purgatory quarter, someone associated with me, and so they told me. This means two things. Within a day or so, they might come round here and ask you some questions: What were you doing on the train, where had you been, what did you do in Rome, at the very time that Beata and her miserable son met their ends? The second thing is this: the pictures they have are of you and another boy. Tell me about him.'

'I met him on the train. He is called Roberto Costacurta. He lives near or on the via Plebiscito, near the Ursine Castle. He is at the university.'

'They may have already gone to see him,' said Traiano. 'If he bought his ticket with a bank card, he is traceable. You bought yours with cash and perhaps are not. I mean, I know they ask for identity cards, but…. They may find that the best route to you is through him. And they may find their best route to me is through you.'

He looked at him now.

'Boss,' said Tonino rapidly. 'I have got my father's example before me. He has been away for fourteen years. He made a mistake, he took the rap and he said nothing, nothing at all. If they come for me, I will say nothing; I will go to Bicocca for however long they send me there, and I will say nothing, nothing at all. And as for what I did in Rome, they cannot connect me with that at all. We were careful. No blood, nothing. We wore gloves, overshoes, everything.'

'Let us hope so. They can't lock you up just for taking a train to Rome, or smoking in the corridor. To tell you the truth, I do not mind too much. If they think that you may have had something to do with the Rome massacre, and that I was behind it, well, let them think that. But there is no proof, none at all. The rumour, well, that is good for us. It establishes us as people to be frightened of. As it is the death of Beata and her miserable son brought down the minster of Grace and Justice, whoever he was. It has damaged our enemies and shown we are more powerful than them. But I would go and see Costacurta in the next few days, just to see what they said to him, and he to them. If he is from round here, he knows what to say to the police.'

'Yes, boss.'

'Now, show me the rest of the place and take me to your mother. I presume the guys who came in to do the lighting did not bug the place?'

It was a very old-fashioned apartment, he soon saw, essentially an enfilade of rooms, one leading to another. Along one side of the rooms was a service corridor which had a door onto each room, and which enabled the servants of the past to enter each room without disturbing their master's privacy. It made a superb gallery. After the vast saloon, there were five more rooms of varying sizes, and then they came to the servants' quarters: a kitchen, a bathroom and two bedrooms, which all looked out onto an internal courtyard. These rooms were spacious and old-fashioned; there was much Formica in the kitchen. In the kitchen, the signora was eating her supper. An interrupted plate awaited Tonino.

'I disturbed you,' he said genially, putting a hand on Tonino's shoulder, commanding him to sit and take up his fork again. He took the signora's hand and kissed it, and then sat down at the table while the others ate, accepting only a glass of water. He had not told Ceccina that he was passing this way, otherwise she would have sent her regards to the signora, he was sure. (He knew they knew each other, and was glad he had remembered this.) In response to the signora's questions, he said the birth had been easy, it had been her third, after all, and the new baby, Alessandro, was thriving, and a delightful child. The baptism was soon. He hoped they could all come. And then the week after the baptism of Alessandro, it would be the turn of Tino, the baby born on the same day, the child of Gino and Catarina Camilleri. And then it would be Alfio and Giuseppina's wedding. It was really going to be a very busy time. The signora confessed that she was looking forward to the wedding, and she had bought a new dress, which she hoped would do for both the baptisms as well. Though she might buy two new dresses and shoes as well, as she could afford to do so, adding 'thanks to your generosity to my boy, dear don Traiano.' Traiano beamed. He turned to the said boy and asked him if he had bought a suit yet. Tonino said he had gone to the via Etnea to look for one, but had not found one he really liked yet. He thought too that they were all a bit expensive. Traiano said that expense should not worry him, and that he needed quality. Then he told him that he needed to find a respectable young lady, it was high time. Tonino went scarlet. His mother laughed and said there was really no need for that, as he was still too young. Tonino bristled. Traiano advised him to look his best at the wedding, for one never knew what might happen there. And everyone would be there. Everyone. Gino's wedding had been something of a hurried affair, the bride being pregnant, but the wedding of Alfio was being taken very seriously indeed, and the guest list was stupendous. In fact, poor Alfio thought he was losing control of his own wedding, though Giuseppina was thrilled, naturally. Girls loved weddings.

After supper was over, while the signora tidied the kitchen and put the dishes away, the two of them walked to the Purgatory quarter. Traiano and Tonino went to the gym where, in the private room, they changed into dark clothes. From the street outside, they took the motorcycle and went out to the building site that was the Furnaces, which was now all securely padlocked, as darkness had fallen. Traiano had the key. A few moments later, they were driving a small pick-up in the direction of the cemetery. They parked it at as Pio Forcella had advised, by the wall, which was crumbling, and which they had very little difficulty jumping over from the bed of the pick-up. Once in the cemetery, they located the place of Turiddu's burial, and found the smashed marble slab that had failed to protect his remains from the world. The remains of the marble, they removed, throwing them into the undergrowth nearby. Then the remains of the coffin were extracted. The plywood, or whatever it had been made of, creaked under the strain, and rapidly disintegrated, to reveal the remains inside. There was a smell. Each of them swore. And there was Turiddu, seen once more, never meant to be seen again, unrecognisable, shrivelled and black in the darkness, mummified, his identity only given away by his dirty blonde hair. The coffin was ripe for being broken up, and was carted to where the pick-up was waiting on the other side of the wall, and thrown into the back of the vehicle. The body was less easy to manoeuvre because as soon as it was lifted up, in fell apart. For this reason, they had taken the precaution of bringing some rubbish bags, provided by signora Grassi. The head went in one, and the rest in two more. The clothes were soiled and stained. The remains were thrown into the pick-up, and they returned to inspect the empty tomb. They then leaped over the wall into the pick-up, covered what it contained with a tarpaulin, and then drove back to the Furnaces. Because the place was reputed to be dangerous, there was hardly anyone about; they only encountered traffic when they came to the Furnaces, and then their pick-up looked perfectly innocent. Once there, at the building site, the pieces of evidence from the cemetery were transferred to various trucks used for removing building waste.

'When we have the keys of the place, it will be even easier,' said Traiano, when they were back at the gym. 'But that depends on our getting Volta elected. The boss wants to know how that is going.'

Tonino stopped smelling his hands, and tried not to think of the horror of that corpse.

'It is going well, boss. Right now, we have got twenty or thirty going out every night and tearing down posters of rival candidates. We do not need more. There are not enough posters to tear down or to deface. But it is enough for twenty or thirty boys to do. That costs two to three hundred euros a night, but they are all desperate for the money, and they love doing it, either on foot or on bikes. I could have a hundred doing it; and we have the other boys working as well.'

Alfio and Gino, he knew, were telling the tenants who they had to vote for, and if they did not, what would be the result. That was taken care of. The more sophisticated part of the operation was being handled by the boss and his sisters and his wife. This was the television and radio angle, the making sure that their candidate, Volta, got the air time he deserved, and his opponents, what they deserved as well. But of course, it was easy, as the candidate of the main party had been told by Rome not to campaign, not even to visit the city. He was a paper candidate alone. As for the Greens and people like that, were they even worth intimidating?

'Everyone who says they are voting for Volta gets a free pizza,' Traiano remarked laconically. 'We have got someone on a radio phone-in show soon. Do you ever listen to radio?'

'Never, boss.'

'You might like to hear this. When it comes.'

There was something in the way he spoke that made him stop what he was doing.

'Boss?' he asked.

'The autopsy report has been leaked; the report of the autopsies of Beata and Paolo. You know what is in it, don't you? I have seen it. The government wanted it kept quiet, but it was leaked by people who are not friendly to the government, shall we say. Or not friendly to the Interior Ministry or the Ministry of Grace and Justice. It could have been someone inside government who wanted to score some sort of point, or get revenge. Anyway, it will reflect badly on the previous junta, though it was nothing to do with them. There is a certain horror to it that will produce a wave of disgust that will help Volta gain power on his anti-corruption ticket. You should be pleased that your animal instincts proved to be so useful.'

'Boss, it was Muniddu,' said the boy.

'You just watched, did you?' he asked with contempt.

'Boss, I did it. I had to do it. He told me to do it. I had no choice.'

'So, you did it twice. No choice. Twice. And the boy, what did you do to him?'

'If you know what is in the report, why ask?' asked Tonino angrily. 'We shoved something up his backside. It may have killed him, if we hadn't choked him. Then we killed the mother. Right? Why ask?'

'Don't question me, unless you want the belt,' said Traiano.

'You told me to do everything Muniddu told me to do, to obey him, to learn from him,' said Tonino accusingly.

'Well, you certainly did that,' said Traiano with a laugh. 'You are a good worker. I just wouldn't want you near my sister, if I had one. Are you still seeing that girl, Lydia?'

'No. She reminds me of Paolo and his mother,' he said. 'I am sorry, boss, I should not have answered back. It is just that some things make me ashamed.'

'There is no room for shame in this business. You are not the sort of person who can afford the luxury of shame. The only thing you have to live off are your wits and your ability to do the things that others are ashamed to do. Take up shame, and you starve. Take up shame, and I will no longer employ you. Remember the point of origin. You will never get anywhere unless you remember where you came from. You cannot afford shame. That is for them, not us. You raped Beata. Live with that fact. You killed her son. Live with that too. Forget about it. Do you think for a moment that I care anything about Turiddu whose remains we disposed of tonight? I have better things to worry about. Like my wife and children, and paying the bills. Anyway, you did a good job in Rome, so be proud.'

'Yes, boss.'

'One day you could be like Gino and Alfio,' he continued, as he tied up his shoelaces. 'You will hear sooner or later. The boss has decided, perhaps it was overdue, that both of them are going to be admitted to the honoured society. They are both nearly thirty, after all, they will soon both be married, and Gino has a child. They have earned the right; they have done everything asked of them. Alfio is going to be the children's uncle, and Gino is married to Alfio's cousin, so…'

'What will it mean, boss?' asked Tonino curiously.

'It means they will get a bigger cut of things; it means more money; they have responsibilities, so they need more money; it means that they will be my equals, and I will have to ask their advice, and they mine, rather than me giving them orders. It means I will no longer hit them with my belt when they screw up. It means that they will expect you and the other boys like you to respect them and fear them more; it means they will be able to give you the taste of their belts should they feel like it, so you had better watch out. It means they will feel important. And they are important; Alfio related to the boss, and Gino the friend of don Renzo. It means you will call them boss and refer to them as don Gino and don Alfio. But it is good news for you, by the way. Gino gave up the mobile pharmacy to you because he was promised this. And he knew you had to be rewarded for your work in Rome. But my advice to you is not to get pushy. You have proved yourself at a young age, as did I, but don't get ideas above your station. You are rich, aren't you? How much do you make?'

'Three or four hundred, boss.'

'On a good night?'

'Every night. The demand is so great. I sell as much as Doctor Moro can supply. Sometimes, he can't supply what people want. I suppose it is because the people who steal, steal what they steal, and not always to order. Some of the things are in very high demand, so I can sell them for a lot; but everything goes. I have to pay the doctor, but then what I make is split between me and don Gino.'

'And what do you do with what you make?'

'I give most of it to my mother,' he said. 'She has had a hard life, boss.'

'Hard lives - haven't we all,' he remarked. 'The wallets, how is that going?'

'I get about ten a day from the kids. The others must be doing the same, I suppose. Alfio does not tell me. But none anymore from the quarter; there were a few guys I would poke in the ass with my gun while their trousers were round their ankles and their thoughts otherwise engaged, but there are none of them anymore. Word gets out.'

'Don Calogero will be pleased. The pills you sell - are any of our guys using them?' he asked almost casually.

'Don Gino, boss,' said Tonino quietly. 'But not don Alfio.'

'And the other stuff, the white powder?'

'Don Renzo, don Gino and even sometimes don Alfio,' said Tonino. 'They do it down here. You don't come down here much, do you, boss, otherwise you would see it for yourself.'

'Perhaps if I came down here more, they would do it less. Or they would just do it somewhere else.' He yawned. It bored him, the way his associates lived: the drink, the drugs, the girls. 'You can go,' he said to Tonino.

It was not late, it was not even ten o'clock in the evening, and the gym was still open, and would not be closing for another hour to its normal paying clients; the special members used it at all hours; Tonino knew there would be people waiting for him in the changing room, wanting to buy pills, wondering why he was late, so he went upstairs with his backpack, the mobile pharmacy. Before he entered the changing room, the guy on the desk gestured to him and told him that someone had been wating for him for hours, and when he entered the room, he saw whom he meant. There was Roberto Costacurta, sitting on a bench with a book. He acknowledged his presence, and then took up his usual position. One by one, the clients approached him, like penitents approaching the confessional in Church, each seeking his own personal desire for pills and other things. Relieved, their long wait over, their desires now fulfilled, they scuttled away with their precious purchases. Then, all clients satisfied, Tonino put the money safely in the pocket of his jeans.

The room was empty, it was near closing time, there were only the two of them. Roberto did not look up from his book. Slowly, Tonino approached, and tapped his foot. Roberto looked up and shut his book.

'You have been waiting. You now have my full attention,' said Tonino.

They had seen each other many times since August, but not spoken. Roberto had waited, as he had known he ought to; waited to be noticed; waited to be addressed by the younger man, as he knew he had to. The waiting had been painful, but now it was over.

'The police came,' said Roberto.

'I had a feeling they might,' said Tonino. 'What did they ask, and what did you tell them?'

'Those Americans....'

'Yes, I know about those Americans.'

'They asked me who you were, and I told them your name was Tonino, but I did not know your second name, and that we just met that night, and that we talked about the Elephants as we smoked; but the rest of the time we were asleep, and in the morning, we had coffee and we talked about the view from the ferry and how nice it was. They asked where you got off, and I told them it was before Catania, because they showed me pictures from CCTV of myself getting off at Catania. They asked me if there was anything unusual about you, and I said there was not, not in the least, and they asked me whether you had told me what you had been doing in Rome, and I said you had not. And they asked me what I had been doing in Rome as well, and I told them.'

'And what were you doing in Rome, Costacurta?' asked Tonino.

'I was seeing my father. He went there for work two years ago and he decided to stay. He is living there with a woman. I went to ask him for some money, to pay my university fees.'

'And he refused. Because he is spending all his money on his new girlfriend. The bastard!' said Tonino, guessing the end of the story.

Roberto looked up at him in mute misery.

'The police took my laptop and my phone,' he said. 'They had a warrant to search the house. They did that and found nothing. Luckily, my mother was out and my sisters were at school. There was nothing to find, and they did not make too much of a mess. But they took the computer and the phone, and….'

Once more he was overcome by mute misery.

'Costacurta, listen to me,' said Tonino, sitting next to him on the bench, idly taking up the book that Roberto had laid aside. 'You think perhaps you are unlucky. The police are investigating me, not you. They only came to see you because of those stupid Americans. They have nothing on you. More importantly, they realise that you are a dead end. From now on they will leave you alone. The computer and the phone contain nothing interesting to them, because you and I have not communicated by phone or by text message or by email. What are they going to find there? The people you have been talking to, messaging, the amount of time you have been spending on the website of the Elephants, and as for the other things that I can guess about, well, they have seen all that before. They will dismiss you as a typical student type. And they will forget about you. You see, Costacurta, you have passed your first big test, and you have passed it well. And now that you have passed the test and can show that you can meet the police and not give anything away, your luck is changing. I suppose their warrant allowed them to look into your bank account, where they found what?'

'Only cobwebs,' said Roberto with a smile.

'Listen, who were the police who came to see you?'

'There were police in uniform who searched the flat, but the two in charge were a man and a woman with northern accents. I asked to see their badges. One was Silvio Pierangeli and the other Chiara di Donato. The warrant was very comprehensive, the sort of thing you use to investigate very serious criminals. Later, I went to the University library and used a computer there and searched for their names. That is when I realised how serious it was.'

'What do you mean?'

'They do not exist.' He saw Tonino's puzzled expression. 'I looked for the names online. There are lots of people in the north of Italy with those names, but none of them with the same faces, or the right date of birth; they were either too old, or too young, or just not the right faces. These two are using false names.'

'Are they really police, or magistrates or whatever?'

'Oh yes. They can't have been otherwise as they had uniformed police with them, who looked and acted genuine. I mean, you think they were criminals themselves? No, they were police who have authorisation to hide their identities. They are police who are sent to deal with the greatest threats in organised crime. The sort of people that they would send to investigate the massacre of Casal Bruciato.'

That was the name, they both knew, that the newspapers were giving to the murder of Beata and her son.

'I saw the gun,' said Roberto. 'I mean, it was hidden, but I saw that there was something hidden under your tee shirt. It can only have been a gun.'

'So, you know all about me, and you have been coming here every day more or less since August, hoping to see me, and to speak to me. And when I ignored you, you persevered; you did not give up. And if you know all about me, Costacurta, I know all about you, or what I do not know, I can guess.' There was a pause. 'I cannot claim to have any special powers of perception. I got people to ask questions about you, your family, and they brought me answers. I know the family situation, I know about your father, I know you have no money, and that you are a very good student with a bright future. I know you have been looking for a job and have not found one. I know you are desperate. But that covers so many people. Desperation is in the air we breathe. But now I know the final bit, that you know who I am and you still want me, you want my help, you want my friendship. You want my friendship, not despite Casal Bruciato, but because of it, and you have shown you know about Casal Bruciato, but can keep quiet. Well, then, you have calculated and so have I. We can be useful to each other. It will be profitable. But I warn you, I don't have any soft feelings.'

'I don't expect any,' said Roberto.

'Good,' said Tonino. 'Did you bring a sports' bag with you? Yes? Get it.'

Tonino went to his locker. He came back with a plastic bag which contained, Roberto could guess, a quantity of bank notes.

'The police won't be coming round to see you again, if ever. They have better things to do. I am giving you this, it's only fifteen thousand, all of it in fifties. That is three hundred notes in all. Maybe you want to count them. I have been wondering what to do with them. I don't need them now. What I want you to do is put this money in the bank, your bank account, bit by bit, not arousing suspicions, OK? It would be a good idea for you to open another account with another bank, and perhaps a third one - after all, who trusts banks? - and then move the money between accounts. Understood? And if you need any money, use it, but remember I will ask for it back. So that is what you are going to do for me right now. The next thing is that I am going to get you a job; I will speak to don Traiano about you first. Maybe he will speak to you. But remember, from now on, you are hiding your true self from not just your mother and your sisters and the neighbours, but the police too. The only person who knows about you is me. And the only person who knows about me is you.'

He took the money and put it in with his sports gear. He nodded. He felt a curious sense of dread as he did so. He knew he had gained a friend, and he had longed to have a friend, someone who would help him, look out for him, someone who would alleviate the misery of being so poor. He had gained a friend, and at the same time he knew that there was a price to pay. He was losing his innocence, lying to the police, keeping silent about what he knew. His mother might not approve, his sisters might not either, but they were young. His father… what did he care about his father? His father had left them, and if he had to be dishonest, then it was his father's fault. He hated his father. Well, this would be his revenge on his father, and on the world. It occurred to him that he had never had so much money before now; not that it was his money.

'You look so serious,' said Tonino. 'Don't worry, nothing can go wrong. Trust me.'

He held out his hand, and Roberto took it. Tonino smiled, and pulled Roberto towards him in a brief embrace, then pushed him away.

'I will see you again soon,' he promised.

'Where?' asked Roberto, a touch more anxiously than he had meant to.

'Here, or there, or somewhere in the quarter. I will find you. Make yourself easy to find.'

With that he was gone, and Roberto was left, with his book, his sports gear and fifteen thousand in cash.

Chapter Two

The business of debt collection, Traiano reflected, was a psychologically satisfying one. It pleased him to be able to sort out the yellowing paperwork that the gravedigger of Bronte had sold him and classify which documents were more likely to yield some hard cash more than others. The shopkeepers, he identified as particularly open to persuasion, and that is where he decided to start, calling in during business hours and mentioning the small matter of the debt to the undertaker, presenting them with the paperwork, mentioning the sum, and giving the impression that he was open to reason. The first place he chose was an ironmongery on the upper part of the via Etnea, where they knew who he was (most people did, he reflected) and where he pointed out that they owed two thousand to Pio Forcella, a debt that he had bought. No doubt they had forgotten it, though the file was full of reminders. Two thousand, outstanding for two years, with interest.... He had his gun under his jacket, and his knife in his pocket, but there was no need to use either. The owner of the shop was pale, apologetic, clearly frightened. He could pay at once, he said, pay the entire two thousand. Traiano nodded, not mentioning the interest and, within a few minutes, was once more on the via Etnea with the money in his pocket in the form of a cheque made out to the Ancient and Noble Confraternity of the Holy Souls in Purgatory. At this rate, he would cover the outlay of twenty thousand very quickly. He might rake in about a hundred thousand, all told, which, after giving don Calogero his cut, would be a tidy profit.

The low hanging fruit was easy to gather. The ironmonger must have warned his friends, because several people paid up, and in full, with little difficulty. One or two even approached him, asking to pay fifty percent, which he accepted, knowing this would accelerate the stream of payers. A bar owner out by the airport said the he would not pay. There were very few clients in the bar when he said this, and when they saw the gun, they rapidly and silently left. Traiano shot the man in the leg, and told him he had a week to pay, then mounted his motorcycle and rode away. The man paid, like all the others, by transferring the sum into the bank account of the Confraternity. Another man, who also refused to pay, and who was quite indignant at the thought that anyone could ask him to pay, found himself facing a man on a motorcycle in the midday traffic, who put a gun up against the window, and then, only when the traffic lights changed, rode away. These were warnings. There was no need to go further.

Now that he had three children, Trajan Antonescu had promised his wife Ceccina, whom he loved dearly, and whose every wish was his command, that he would try to adopt more conventional hours, going to bed earlier and getting up earlier. This had been something of a success. Debt collecting was a daylight pursuit, so he was sometimes even in bed by midnight, and often enough up by nine. When the eldest, Cristoforo, went to nursery the following year, he was hoping he would habitually be up in good time to take him. Today, it was not the youngest who woke him, though the newborn did have a very powerful pair of lungs, more so than his elder brother and sister; rather what woke him was the sense of silence, punctuated by silvery laughter, coming from some rooms away.

The flat he now inhabited was larger than the previous one by a considerable extent, and had belonged to the boss of bosses, don Calogero. The possession of this flat was the sign of his favour in the boss's sight; one sensed the laughter as being distant, coming from the huge kitchen several rooms away. He hauled himself out of bed, went to the en-suite bathroom and splashed some water on his face, then put on his dressing gown over his pyjamas and made his way to the kitchen, thirsty for coffee.

There were five people in the kitchen: his sister-in-law Pasqualina, his three children, and Gino's brother, Corrado. He greeted them all, kissed the children warmly, kissed his sister-in-law's cheek, and then turned to the relative stranger, Corrado.

'This is a surprise,' he said, with a touch of irony, extending his hand. 'Nice to see you.'

'And you,' said Corrado.

'You have come for the baptism?' he asked.

He meant, of course, the baptism of the child that Catarina had given birth to, Gino's supposed son, who had been named Tino. But of course, there was a baptism before then, that of Alessandro, this coming Sunday.

'Of course,' said Corrado. 'But the truth is that I have a bit of a break in work; I have finished one job, and I'm not starting the next for a bit, so I thought I would come to Catania. After all, you said that I ought to come. So, I came. I take your advice seriously, but I had motives of my own as well. And the baptism is coming up, as you rightly say.'

'Well, you must come to our baptism as well, this Sunday, and stay for Alfio's wedding as well. Three things in a row. Mind you, it is not my place to invite you to someone else's wedding.'

'I have already been invited, as a matter of fact.'

'He is coming as my plus one,' said Pasqualina, a little defensively.

'Oh,' said Traiano.

It occurred to him that he had not missed anything at all, and that his previous suspicion was now clear, namely that Corrado and Pasqualina, ever since the wedding of Gino and Catarina, had been interested in each other, and were perhaps well on the way to becoming permanently attached.

A little later, Traiano was in the shower, when his wife put her head round the door, and smiled at him. For a moment, her smile endured, and then she was serious.

'What?' he asked, stepping out and reaching for a towel.

He extended his lips for a kiss. He knew there was something wrong, and he thought he knew what. He dried himself and waited for her to speak.

'You encouraged him,' she said, not accusingly, just as a statement of fact.

'Corrado does what he likes,' he said, knowing what she meant. 'Without reference to me. He is not that sort of person. He is independent, proud even.'

'Pasqualina said that Corrado said that you met up when you were last in Agrigento and that you got on well, and that made him think, well, she thinks; I am not sure what he thinks; she thinks that you think it is a good idea, a good match.'

'I wonder why your sister cares what I think?' he asked, as he dried himself carefully. 'Does she need my permission to marry? No. Does she need yours? No. But she would want your approval. Are you saying you don't like him?'

'I am not saying I do not like him,' said Ceccina carefully. 'It is just that….'

'You don't like him,' said Traiano. 'Why not?'

He went into the bedroom and started to put on his underwear.

'Well, I am sure he is nice and that he is the sort of man she likes, and he likes her, but he does not like us. And he will take her away from us.'

'Oh. I see. Has something come out that makes you think this?' he asked, as he put on his socks, sitting on the edge of the bed.

'He does not have any money,' she said. 'And his next job is on the continent, in Verona. My fear is that soon he will say he wants to marry her and take her away to Verona. And we will never see her again. And the other thing... I made it clear to her that, if ever she were to find someone, not mentioning any names, not wanting to put ideas into her head, that you would help. I mean, you have helped all the family. But she said that she did not want any help.'

Traiano was thoughtful.

'Corrado refused Gino's help, and he told me that in Agrigento. He must have told her that. I suppose if he refuses Gino, he would refuse me. You know, you think this not a good thing, but as far as I am concerned, it is a good thing. He does not want to be dependant. We are rich, but we are dependant. We depend on don Calogero, and that means we depend on him and his whims and his wife.... Corrado and Pasqualina will depend on no one but themselves. They may be happier than us. But I think we may be getting ahead of ourselves. There's no indication as yet....'

'But I can sense the way things are going,' said Ceccina sadly. 'I can sense how it will end. Don't you see, we will be rich, they will be poor, and she will resent it, and wonder if she made the right choice, and she will blame me, blame us... And I do not want her to go to Verona. I want her to stay here. She is my sister. I don't want him to take her away. And his brother lives here. It is just so wrong.'

He appreciated her distress.

'Look, I will speak to him. I will try to choose the right moment. I will try to find out what he wants. I may even try to persuade him to stay. After all, he does not need to go to Verona, does he? He can have a job here. I like the guy, I have to say. I prefer him to his brother. I think if he wants to go somewhere else it may be to get away from Gino. If Gino were my brother, I would probably want to get away from him. Forget I said that, but I hate the guy. And you know he is being promoted by don Calogero. Now it is don Gino and don Alfio. What people I have to work with! Look, I will speak to Corrado. Try not to worry. If it is possible, I will make it happen. Now, I have to wear a suit - which one? Which one goes with this shirt?'

She sighed.

'Look, this Corrado thing has taken me by surprise. I confess I suspected it; I saw it coming. I thought you did too, but I don't have your sense for these things. But I will speak to him, see what can be done, what can be arranged. OK? Just leave it to me. I don't like to see you upset. I will deal with it. Trust me.'

And he would. But first he had to put on his suit and go and see the lawyer Rossi. And while he was there, he would look around the office, see what was happening, and see what Assunta di Rienzi was getting up to. It was partly business, and partly scouting out the land. He did not like Assunta overmuch and he doubted she cared for him, though since the boss's second marriage, the boss's sister had thawed towards him a little. After all, a new threat, or possible threat, had entered the arena, and she might need allies.

When he came up to the topmost floor of the building that contained the gym, the beautiful open plan office, the design of which the late Stefania had overseen, where the potted palms still proclaimed her absence, but where the view was eternal, the view of Etana, the city and the sea, which would be there long after they were all dead, when she saw him enter, Assunta smiled, and when he approached, she extended her cheek, which he kissed.

'So, tell me.' she said. 'Is Volta really going to be elected? My brother says so, but I can hardly believe it....'

'Yes, he is really going to be elected. We are all voting for him, by which I do not mean just you and I, but all our friends, and it's gaining momentum. Have you seen election posters for any other candidates? Me neither. But it is not until February and we are only in October, so things will develop. We need to see what crowds Volta collects, and what crowds go to listen to his rivals.'

She smiled.

'If Calogero wants it, it happens. And my new sister-in-law will make a difference, won't she?' she added with a touch of irony. 'But we are doing our work here too. Which of these lovely people do you wish to see?'

'The one who has been here longest,' he said, meaning the lawyer Rossi.

The lawyer Rossi, shabby, middle aged, going to seed dramatically, but well paid and prosperous, with a happy wife who no longer reproached him, sighed as he approached.

'I have been collecting for the Confraternity,' he said, 'and there will be more to come. I have not written out names and figures, it is all in my head, but here are some cheques, and the rest were direct payments which I oversaw. So far it comes to about sixty thousand. I want you to get the Confraternity to put thirty thousand into my bank account and the same amount into the boss's.'

'Understood. What for? What services rendered?'

'I leave the paperwork entirely to you. You arrange the invoices. Either something to do with the Church at the Furnaces, or something to do with the properties the Confraternity owns. You know what to do. You are good at fake invoices.'

'I certainly am,' said Rossi wearily. 'I have done so many. But after a time, a note of repetition begins to creep in and you start to long for new ideas.'

'You will manage,' he said. 'You always do. And you get paid for this sort of thing.'

'Don't remind me. Our accountants are good, but one day the Financial Police may come round and look at stuff, and then I will end up in Piazza Lanza and you will not.'

'I hope you will not end up in Piazza Lanza. That is where the stupid people go. You are better than that, dear lawyer Rossi. Ah, I have thought of something. Divide it up into small amounts and say it was for supplies for the canteen: coffee, bread, orange juice, treats, and clothes for the immigrants. Stuff transferred from the trattoria, the bars, the pizzeria.'

'The imaginary money merry go round,' said Rossi wearily. 'Round and round it goes, and we cling on, until the time it throws us off.'

This business done, he went back into the office to sit with Assunta. She raised her eyes from what she was doing, and wondered at this evident desire he had to talk to her, to confide in her.

'Is Federico here?' he asked, thinking this would be a good way of starting.

'He has gone to Palermo. To see the people who work for Anna Maria. Very important. I like your suit. Did you put it on specially for me?'

'My wife chose it. She chooses all my clothes. She has my measurements and then she goes and buys stuff and I never have to do so.'

'Convenient. But she has good taste. That is important. You do not want to dress like a pimp or a gangster, do you?'

'I most certainly do not,' he agreed. He hoped he did not. 'It seems there is going to be another wedding. Not just your sister and your ex-sister-in-law, but my sister-in-law. Pasqualina.'

'A pretty girl,' said Assunta. 'I know her. I suppose you mean this new man, Corrado. I have seen him. He is the sort of man one notices.'

'You have noticed him? Why didn't I notice him as well? I did see it coming, but only when it was too late. I don't really like the way this Corrado, this man from Agrigento, has come all this way, to our quarter, in pursuit of Pasqualina, surreptitiously, without asking, deceptively and, presumably, won her affections. It's not exactly that I have rights of ownership over Pasqualina, and that he needs my permission to court her; it's something less easy to put into words. Corrado, polite as he is, seems not to know how to do things correctly. He should have made his intentions clear to Pasqualina's family first. Or maybe it is worse than that; he does know the right way of going about it, but is determined to ignore the usual protocols. Pasqualina is my sister-in-law, and he is ignoring this and treating me as if I did not matter. The more I think of it, the more insulting it seems. Tell me this, Assunta. When Federico wanted to marry you, he came to your father and made his intentions clear, didn't he?'

'My father was dead,' said Assunta.

'Well, he came to Calogero, just as in the same way Renzo approached Elena, knowing Calogero approved? I mean they did it the proper way, didn't they?'

'You are old-fashioned,' she said. 'Just like my brother. Well, no surprise there. But most people like to do it the modern way, you know, without consulting the boss.'

'I understand that,' he said. 'But when the boss is me, the one who pays for everything… Pasqualina and her family, my family now, they have had everything, and once they had very little. One expects a little deference in return. What if everyone else were to do the same? Deference is like magic, and when people stop believing in it, stop doing it, suddenly everything will change. I need to teach Corrado a lesson.'

'You need to teach him a lesson, but he does not strike me as a good learner. He's Gino's brother. He knows how things work, and has chosen not to follow the proper way of doing things. What are you going to do? Punch him? Challenge him to fight?'

It struck him that Assunta was laughing at him.

'Of course not,' he said.

But it was true. That, after all, was the usual approach with people who were problems, people who represented challenges to his authority.

Because Corrado annoyed him, because Corrado was, in a sense that was barely detectable, but nevertheless real, defying him, and because of the danger of contagion, he had to do something, he reflected, when he left Assunta, that was clear. But could he simply teach him a lesson through the power of his fist? It did not seem a very elegant solution. Others could be dealt with this way, but he had the impression that Corrado was not merely strong, not merely stubborn, but strong in a manner he had not really encountered before, morally strong, the sort of man who would not be moved.

Perhaps he should tell Pasqualina that he could not approve of this budding relationship and that she ought to make sure it went no further. Pasqualina had always acknowledged his pre-eminence as the guarantor of her extended family's prosperity. But she had not mentioned Corrado to him, she had not sought his approval, let alone his permission, as if she saw Corrado as his equal in strength and worth.

But the truth that gave him pause was this: he liked Corrado, and he wanted Corrado to like him. Years previously, when he had first seen his wife, even before he had spoken to her, he had been transfixed by the desire that she should like him; that strong desire had lasted but a few days, because it had rapidly become apparent that she had liked him, as much as he liked her. The liking was mutual, the attraction was mutual, the love was mutual. And the love had never wavered from that moment, and it had shrugged off the storm that had broken over them when it was clear to her parents what had happened, that their beautiful daughter had not only slept with this obviously bad boy of fourteen, but was having his child. He had not given a damn about their disapproval, and sure enough they had fallen into line when they realised that no apology would be forthcoming, but great rewards would follow if they accepted the situation. In himself, he knew he did not really care what anyone thought about him, as long as they did what he told them to; the only exceptions were his wife and children, his stepfather Alfonso whom he loved, and who loved him, and don Giorgio, the priest, the one good person he knew, whose approval he lacked, which made him, sometimes, a little sad.

These thoughts took him down to the level of the street, and there he paused. It was early afternoon, and the gym was busy. The place was beginning to make money, he knew, which was good. There were lots of members, and quite a few ghost members, people who paid in cash and who never came, and who did not exist. In the gym he paused to speak to Ceccina's cousin who was on the door, and he soon spotted Tonino, clearly desirous of an interview. After a pause, they went down to the private room without a word being said.

'Well?' said Traiano.

He heard the report, what the police had said to this Roberto Costacurta, and what he had said to them. On the whole it was very reassuring. They had nothing, nothing at all. He heard with great interest about the research that Costacurta had made with regard to the woman Chiara di Donato and the man Silvio Pierangeli. He was not surprised that these were assumed names.

'If the police come to see you, and they may well do so, now they have placed you on that train, even if they do not know your name yet, do you have a good story to tell them?'

'I have worked something out, boss,' said Tonino. 'I will tell them I was in Rome for twenty-four hours, seeing the sights, you know, going to the Vatican.'

'And you trust this Costacurta?' asked Traiano, trying to keep the amazement out of his voice. 'Who is he?'

'Just someone I met, but someone I trust,' said Tonino with a touch of stubbornness.

Traiano considered.

'Trust no one except your closest family,' he said at last. 'As for this Costacurta …. Let's hope that he does not give anything away, or you do not end up going into Bicocca and then Piazza Lanza for a long time, just when your father is supposed to be coming out of jail. Your mother loses one, and gains another. And all for a cigarette on a train with your friend Costacurta. What sort of name is that, anyway? Well, I suppose he is one if us, if not from this quarter. But, don't you realise that by having that cigarette, by getting yourself noticed, you endangered the whole enterprise and you endangered us? You were told not to smoke by me. But it is worse than that. You need discipline, and it has got to be complete, to avoid mistakes like this. Perhaps this time we have got away with it. But the whole enterprise could have been lost for a single cigarette, a single moment of stupidity. You need to be taught a lesson.'

Tonino was silent.

Traiano took off his belt.

After some thought, he decided to invite Corrado to dinner, just the two of them. Corrado accepted this invitation. He was a little surprised that he accepted so readily, and a little pleased as well, though perturbed.

He decided that they would not dine in the quarter, but in a small restaurant he had always wanted to visit by the Opera House. The Opera House always had a rather decayed look to it, he thought, which he liked, and the square in front of it was rather shabby, just like the rest of Catania. He had arranged to meet Corrado here at 8pm, outside the Opera, and as he was a little early, he amused himself by reading the posters advertising the coming season. Later in the month, they were doing *Tosca* by Giacomo Puccini. Maybe he should take Ceccina to the opera. He had never been; she had never been; no one they knew, except perhaps Anna Maria Tancredi, and perhaps Colonel Andreazza, had ever been to an opera, as far as he knew. Perhaps Ruggero Bonelli had, along with his sister and his corrupt carabiniere friend. Perhaps things were changing, and perhaps he now knew more potential opera goers than he had done in the past. Of course, his stepfather might know about opera. He might suggest they go together. He wondered what *Tosca* was about. The poster did not give any indication of who or what Tosca was, whether a name of a character or some sort of word he was unfamiliar with. Did it mean something like fate or destiny? Was *Tosca* comedy or tragedy? That was the trouble of going to an opera. One's ignorance might be cruelly exposed. And the sort of people who went to operas might look at him, his clothes, his shoes and, God forbid, his wife, and find them all wanting. Perhaps he and his type were simply not meant to go to operas. This thought made him a little angry; after all, the people who went to operas were the sort of people who only had the lives they did because of the dirty work done by people like himself.

But he drew himself up short. One should not feel sorry for oneself. There was no room in his life for the luxury of regret or for the self-indulgence of repentance. To see oneself as a bad man would be ridiculous. He had done what he had done and regretted nothing; he had chosen to do it. That was that. And if he had not done what he had done, then nothing he had now would have been his. And what he had now was lots of money, and the prospect of much more to come; and a wife and children; that was the most important thing of all, his love for his wife and his children, and theirs for him. How he loved them; how he loved her! The birth of little Alessandro had been difficult, and he and Ceccina had not made love since then, but the time was coming… but then this morning's conversation had happened. She had not told him what he had dreaded hearing, that she did not want any more children; but she had told him that she did not want any more children just yet. He was hurt and disappointed, two feelings compounded by the realisation that right was on her side. But the thought of not making love in the way that came naturally, and not having a baby next year, this hurt him. It meant a change, a change he had known was coming, but had hoped was not coming just now.

Leaving the façade of the Opera House, he walked idly round the square. It was a large square, much larger that the square outside the Church of the Holy Souls in Purgatory. There were numerous posters attached to the walls, including signs that stridently proclaimed the illegality of fixing posters. The election posters were everywhere, and all of them for the same candidate, Fabio Volta, the honest man who had entered politics to clean it up, or so his posters proclaimed. Of the rival candidates there was no sign at all. The vote was months away, on the first Sunday in February.

He was conscious of Corrado standing next to him.

'They have touched up his photo,' he remarked.

'Volta's?'

'Yes, I have met him, and it is true that he looks like that, but they have made him look a little younger, a little better looking. Maybe his marketing people insisted. Maybe he insisted. These politicians are very vain, you know. Ah well, we all have our faults.'

'We do,' said Corrado. 'Wherever I have been in Catania, I have seen Volta's face, and only Volta's face.'

'Well, he is the best candidate by far,' said Traiano without interest. His eyes surveyed the square. There were people around, and he could tell that they were looking at him. He knew that wherever he went, when people realised who he was, that he became the focus of attention. He could now feel that attention on him. It thrilled him a little, this sense of being someone. The people hanging about in the square, all predominantly male and young, were looking at him with longing, he could tell, the man who had power and patronage. And he also knew instinctively that they were wondering who the stranger was, the lucky stranger.

'We have not shaken hands,' observed Traiano.

'We can rectify that,' said Corrado, holding out his hand.

The handshake was done. Did Corrado realise, he wondered, what it meant? For the people in the square, it meant that they were friends, that Corrado was someone. Of course, he was the brother of don Gino, but to be a friend of don Traiano counted for more.

They began to walk towards the restaurant.

'I was really looking at the posters outside the Opera House, not the election ones,' said Traiano by way of conversation.

'*Tosca*?' he asked.

'You know it?'

'Wish I did. I like music and a lot of my work is solitary so I listen to it as I work. *Tosca* is good. But I have never seen it. But some wonderful tunes. You know…'

He whistled something. He was a good whistler. The tune seemed familiar, perhaps from some advert on the television.

They walked over to the restaurant on the other side of the square. They went in and were shown to a table; after a few moments, Traiano was aware that their arrival had caused a minor disturbance. He had booked under Corrado's name, Fisichella, and a young waiter had ushered them in; but now the manager came forward with the menus, for they had realised who it was who was under their roof. The manager proffered two menus, spoke of what was the best thing to have, suggested which wine, and insisted he bring them two glasses of prosecco to start the evening. This was not what Traiano wanted, but he indulged them.

Besides, as he told the manager, they were celebrating. The manager beamed and asked about don Calogero - was he well? Very well, said Traiano, and his wife was about to give birth any day now, though she was in Palermo and he was with them in Catania, ready for the baptism of Traiano's new son this Sunday. The manager was profuse with congratulations.

The prosecco came, and they were left in peace.

'Ceccina knows that you are interested in her sister; naturally, she is concerned; and if she is concerned, so am I too,' said Traiano, raising the glass to his lips and taking a cautious sip.

Corrado took a sip before replying: 'So that is what this is about.'

'You are clever. You realise that here in Sicily it is not what it looks like at first sight, it is what it really is under the surface. I invite you to dinner, and the real reason is.... Well, do you blame me for inviting you? Perhaps it is not so complicated as you think. Perhaps it is just that I do not know you, that you are interested in Pasqualina, or at least Ceccina thinks so, and I thought it might be best....'

'What does Pasqualina say?' asked Corrado. 'Why not speak to her?'

'Ah,' said Traiano, 'That goes to the heart of things. She has not spoken to her sister, and before this they shared everything. There have never been secrets between them before now. So, a sort of gulf has arisen between them. And I wonder why? They talk about everything; I am sure they talk about me; but they do not talk about you. Why not?'

'Have you called me here to warn me off?' asked Corrado. 'To warn me off before it becomes serious? You may have left it too late. Besides I am very stubborn. When I get an idea in my head, I never abandon it.'

'Well, I am very stubborn too, and I always get what I want,' said Traiano, with a smile. 'Perhaps you misjudge me, though. I just want things to run smoothly. The truth is that my wife is very attached to her sister, very soft-hearted, and perhaps panics at the prospect of change. I am more pragmatic. I am more dispassionate, as she is my sister-in-law, not my sister, after all, though I am very fond of her, as are my children. The truth is that Pasqualina is unattached, and has been unattached for too long. She needs to find someone, and if she finds someone we can all like, then I will be happy. The others take their cue from me. That is just the way it is. Her mother, her grandmother, her sister, all these people will be looking at me, seeing if I approve. And if I do approve, it will make things so much easier for everyone. And I am keen to approve; but you have to show that you want my approval.'

'You are keen to approve?' asked Corrado.

'Of course, familial happiness counts a great deal to me. Ceccina must be kept happy. And then there is the question of your brother. He and I would be brought into a closer relationship, if you and Pasqualina were to marry. You come, you see, with baggage, as does she. I am her baggage and Gino is yours.'

'You and Gino are friends,' observed Corrado.

Traiano looked into his glass. Only the other day, he had told Ceccina that he hated Gino. Well, that wasn't true. He had no real feelings about Gino.

'I have known him for years,' he said. 'Ever since they let him out of Bicocca, which is some time now. We see a lot of each other, so, yes, we are friends.'

'I knew him before he went to Bicocca,' said Corrado, with a touch of bitterness. 'He was a nice boy then.'

'Nice boys do not get sent to Bicocca,' said Traiano sharply, more sharply than he had intended.

The manager returned and the order was placed. When that was done, and while they were waiting for the plate of mixed fried seafood to arrive, once the bottles of Falanghina and fizzy mineral water had been brought and poured by the nervous boy waiter, their conversation resumed.

'Sorry, what I meant was....'

'I know what you meant. What I meant was that Gino was a nice boy until he was about nine or ten. Then he started to do bad things, steal, get into fights, things like that. By the time he ended up in Bicocca, he had done plenty to deserve it. We are very close in age, and I can remember it all. It makes me sad, because I can remember not just the bad things he did, but the way he was before he did bad things. We were very close, but....'

'Not anymore?'

'He went in a different direction. He lacked discipline. He wanted things without having to work for them. It broke my parents' hearts. But maybe now, they think, I am not so sure, now he is married, now he has a child…. maybe now he will settle down.'

Traiano tasted his Falanghina. He remembered that he did not like wine; every time he had a sip, he thought it would be different, but it was never different, always the same. Nothing changed. The same with Gino: violent and selfish at the age of ten, violent and selfish for life. And now married to Catarina, who would, he was sure, make things worse. While it was true, he mused, that he did not hate Gino, his assumption that he felt nothing for any woman apart from his wife was not true. He did not like Catarina. He resented her. She was the one Rosario had perhaps loved the most, and the one who had taken advantage of his inexperience. She was a schemer, and she was clever. She was perhaps dangerous, and she knew that he did not like her but saw her as a threat. One day he might have to settle with her if she did not rein in her ambitions.

'He is happy with Tino?' he now asked, as it seemed the natural thing, the discussion of babies and domestic matters, the sort of conversation that dominated the quarter. 'Is Catarina happy?'

'Well, of course….' began Corrado slowly. 'But you know what I know, or at least I think you do…'

'I know nothing at all,' said Traiano with a seraphic smile.

'Bicocca ruined him,' said Corrado. 'You know that.'

'Yes, I know that,' said Traiano. 'But does he know that?'

'How can he not?' asked Corrado impatiently.

He knew what he meant.

'It is hard for a man to admit it to himself. It is hard for Gino in particular. The boss has five children, I have three, don Carmelo in Messina is rumoured to have thirteen. Men should have children, and not to have children is not to be a proper man. But I understand you. How can he deceive himself like this? He must know. He can read the signs. I know that Alfio must. They were together in Bicocca. But he prefers to deceive himself rather than face the hard truth. Yes, you are puzzled, though I understand it. But I am worried. One day the truth will become inescapable, and what then? He will realise that Tino is not his, and that Catarina was not faithful, and when that happens, I dread to think what he will do. He will realise that we all realise the truth, and have known it for some time. He will find that hard to live with.'

'You are worried about the future?' asked Corrado.

'I try not to think of the future. What will be, will be. Why worry about what we cannot change? But Gino, he is not a future problem, he is one we can see already, here and now, in our midst. It's an unexploded bomb. And I worry about her. She may want to take action before Gino becomes problematic.'

'What can be done?' asked Corrado.

'Nothing,' said Traiano glumly. 'I don't think anyone can speak to him. I don't even think it would be wise to try. What can be done is perhaps send him to Palermo, a new place, where he can be with don Renzo all day long. He spends a lot of time there at present. But if he were to move there permanently, take his wife, take the child… If they were away from here…. If he were to ask your advice…'

Corrado nodded.

'I don't see why he shouldn't move to Palermo,' said Corrado.

'It would be a promotion,' said Traiano.

But he was not convinced. The wife, he was sure, would not want to co-operate. Perhaps Gino would force her to do as he wished, but even there he was not hopeful.

'Is my brother in any danger?' asked Corrado.

'From what?'

'From the police, to start with.'

'No, of course not, not in the least, why should he be?' said Traiano.

'There you see,' said Corrado. 'Friends tell each other things. They do not have secrets. You know what I mean. The case of Fabrizio Perraino. When that happened, I spoke to him about it.'

'You did? What on earth did you know about it?'

'I knew that Gino had been locked up by the man, and that he hated him; when he disappeared, it was easy to work out what happened.'

'Perraino had lots of enemies.'

'Of course he did. But none quite like my brother. He never forgets a wrong like that. It humiliated him. We talked about it. We had a fight about it. He broke one of my ribs, but in the end, he told me it was true, that he had killed Perraino and cremated him in the pizza oven.'

'Look,' said Traiano mildly. 'Your brother says things that are not true; he wants to make himself important in the eyes of the world, and in particular in the eyes of his little brother. He may even think he killed Perraino, just as he thinks he is the father of Tino, but he is a bigmouthed boaster and a fool. Goodness knows what happened to Perraino, and no doubt Gino would like to claim the credit, but I doubt it very much. So, he broke your rib? Nasty! His own brother. He is a simple playground bully. You don't look convinced, but trust me, it is true. But there is one other thing. We may all have broken the law at times. But you see, if I tell you something that is secret and illegal, and murder is certainly both, there is always the danger that you might blurt it out, by accident, of course, or that you might one day be called in for questioning and have to lie about it; or else that the knowledge you had could put you in danger. But if you know nothing, when you say that you know nothing, you are convincing, and no one thinks you are a threat either. So, you see, Gino has not done you a favour by making this absurd claim.'

'Everyone knows and no one knows. That is how it works. Your wife does not know and your children do not know. But Pasqualina knows. I know.'

'She thinks she knows, but what does she know? And you, you think you know, but you know nothing really. But it is interesting that you and she discuss it when you are alone.'

'We are not meant to discuss things? Not to think?'

'Correct. And why fill your minds with such horrid thoughts, anyway? Why ruin your illusions? Why destroy the ignorance that is bliss? Have you told Pasqualina how many women you slept with before you met her? And all the other things you get up to? Of course not! And would she want to know? Of course not. She would be horrified. Maybe you have never slept with a woman or done anything, being the good Catholic boy you are. Let her think that, though she cannot be so naïve. She has chosen not to know, whatever her suspicions are. Wise choice.'

'Actually, we have discussed it,' said Corrado. 'We are getting married, so we wanted to know everything about each other.'

'I think that is unwise,' said Traiano. 'But it is your choice. Congratulations, by the way. When will you marry, and where will you live, and what will you live on?'

'Soon. In Verona. And we will live off my work.'

He sensed that anything further he said might be counterproductive.

'We will come and visit you,' he said brightly. 'I have never been to the continent. I am sure Verona is beautiful, if a bit cold. She wants to move? You have discussed it? Of course you have. It is just that she seemed so happy here, and she has never said anything about wanting to leave, though lots of people do.'

He knew what this meant. Pasqualina wanted to escape, from Catania, from the quarter, from himself. He felt a momentary stab of anger. He had thought they had been so close. He had thought that Pasqualina had accepted things as they were. But maybe not. Would it make Ceccina question things too?

'You have got your path,' said Traiano. 'And I have got mine, and Gino has his. We do things, or things happen to us, and then we realise only after we have done them or after they have happened, that we have made a choice that is irreversible. We have to carry on, we cannot turn back. What happened to Gino in Bicocca, what happened to me, when I am not sure, whatever it was, but there is no going back now. When I was a child, we had nothing. My mother, as I am sure you know, worked in the oldest profession. When you live in that environment, you become desperate to escape. Some never do.'

'Like the Polish woman and her son murdered in Rome?'

'Like them. That boy was unfortunate to say the least. I was luckier. Being the child of a prostitute, you know the dangers, you have a horror of commercial sex. That boy was perhaps selling himself to someone rather important in the state, who would have wanted him dead. Whoever it was would have had access to the information about where they were hiding. An internal leak, an internal job.' The lie came easily. 'Sex is sacred as far as I am concerned. I love my wife and that is it. And I love my children. I would do anything to protect them. My mother did not do enough to protect me. Of course, we all blame our parents. And I should not complain to you, as you know what poverty is.'

The platter of deep-fried mixed seafood came. It looked wonderful and it tasted just right.

'I want to talk about my wife, rather than your future wife. She adores her sister. She does not want her to go to Verona. She wants you both to stay here. It is understandable, so I said I would speak to you, not to try and change your mind, but to try and understand your decision. There are further complications. Pasqualina has been very good to us both. She cuts my hair, and she helps with the children. She has been a huge help with the children. We have three, as you have noticed, and I want more; Ceccina wants to pause, and I naturally respect that, but I don't know how long the pause will be for. If her sister leaves us, I fear the pause will be longer than it might be if she stays. Of course, Pasqualina will marry and have children of her own, but… well, you see my point of view. Of course, there are other relations who can help. But… The other thing is this, it would be nice if you stayed, from Gino's point of view too, I am sure, not that that is my chief concern, but from my point of view, I would like you to stay here.'

Corrado ate in silence. At length he spoke.

'I understand what you are saying, but it is impossible, and I will explain why. I am sorry it is impossible. I live a very solitary life, or at least I did up to now; when you work with stone, you get used to working with a material that does not answer back. One chooses to be solitary, I suppose, and Pasqualina has got me out of the bad groove I have been in for some years now. I would like to stay in Sicily, where my parents are, but she has other ideas. Going to Verona is her idea. You look surprised. But, you see, she feels that she would like a new life completely. She loves her sister, but she lives in her shadow. She lives in your shadow. If we were to live here, she would always be Ceccina's sister, your sister-in-law. You are very rich, and we would not be, or worse, we would be dependent on you. We would have no independence. She likes you, of course but - how can I put this? - there are certain things about you that she does not like. Of course, she does not say it to you, because she knows she would sound ungrateful for all you have done for the family. And you have done a great deal for all of them. But she thinks that you have done this not just out of the kindness of your heart, but because it makes you look good. I sympathise with her position.'

Traiano was silent for some time.

'I am sorry you think I am the sort of person who casts a shadow. As for your brother, I hope you don't think I have been a bad influence on him. Don't forget he is ten years my senior. He was in Bicocca long before we met. The thing is, I admit, thanks to the fact that he met me when he did, he got everything he wanted, and that, well, is not good. One should beware of getting what one wants. I have always tried to be fair with Gino, but he is an adult, and he is strong willed, and in the end his choices are his own. In truth, I would never myself do the things that Gino does. I try to live a good life, a clean life. Ceccina and I have been very happy. The children are a great consolation. Though I sometimes think she worries about the future. As do I.'

'You mean the police, the magistrates....'

'No. They are the least of my worries. I mean the jealousies, the rivalries. It is worse among the women. Your brother has been promoted. So has Alfio. The reason is because they have worked very hard, and they need to move up a bit, so others can take their place, as in any organisation. But it is also because Alfio is marrying Giuseppina, the aunt of the boss's first three children, so that makes him important, and your brother is married to his cousin, and one cannot promote one without promoting the other. And they are both sick, I am sure, of taking orders from me. I won't be able to lay down the law with them anymore, as I have had to do in the past, and which they resent because I am so much younger. But I was at this game longer than them. I was doing things while they were still in the university of Bicocca. And I was more disciplined than either of them, and more single-minded. The boss trusted me in a way he did not trust them. You need brains as well as brute strength. That is why the boss is a boss, and they will never be. The boss is clever, and he realises that Alfio and Gino need to be recognised and flattered. But even with those two fast friends, Alfio is cleverer and more ambitious than your brother, and he sees that your brother is great friends with don Renzo, and that makes him a little jealous. As for Catarina, the cousin, I think she prefers Alfio to her own husband. And as to the rivalry between the women, let's not even think about it. Even Ceccina is not immune. She does not care much about clothes and shoes and bags, but about houses. We have the second best house in the quarter, but she was terrified that it would go to someone else. Guiseppina is nice, but Catarina, and then the boss's new wife, well, she is hardly ever here, and so much higher than any of us that she may not be susceptible to jealousy. Or so I hope and pray. And then the children, in twenty years' time, how will that go, I wonder? - My children; the boss's children by his first wife; his children by the second wife; then any children don Renzo may have with Elena. And this little boy Tino, your supposed nephew. When he finds out, what will happen then? The real father is dead, luckily. But the wife…. I just hope it never occurs to him. But it has occurred to Alfio. Have you discussed it with Pasqualina? About the mumps? Ceccina has asked me.'

'It has occurred to everyone, except him,' said Corrado bitterly. 'Even my parents, even they know. Everyone knows, except him, I sometimes think. It's not stupidity that insulates him, it is pride. It is sad. I just hope he never finds out. If he does, it will be a catastrophe. His drinking, his snorting of that vile white powder, his taking of pills, all that is quite, quite terrible.'

'He lacks self-discipline,' said Traiano evenly. 'He is like a child.'

'Unlike you.'

'I grew up young, very young.'

'Too young.'

'Yes, far too young. But there's nothing to be done about that now. The next generation are the ones to worry about. You are going to be the uncle to my children, so that is nice. When they are older, they can come and stay with you and, well, see that things can be different.'

The plates were removed and the wine glasses were replenished. They spoke about the wedding. They were planning to marry without fuss in Agrigento, given that his parents were not young, not well, and not used to travelling. Gino would come over, perhaps to be best man. They had spoken to don Giorgio this very afternoon past to ask his permission for Pasqualina to marry outside the parish, to sign off the necessary papers. He had been full of congratulations. Traiano knew why. Because Pasqualina, unlike her sister, was not marrying a criminal. Corrado spoke of the work waiting for him in Verona, a long restoration project on a famous church. Traiano asked what there was in Verona, a place he had barely heard of. He was told about the amphitheatre, the famous summer opera performances, the site of the tragedy of Romeo and Juliet. Just as he had never seen an opera, he had never read or seen a play by Shakespeare. Romeo and Juliet were famous. Juliet was a nice name, he reflected, if he had another daughter.

'I would like to visit Verona. I have never been to the continent,' he repeated. 'Too busy working. I have never been on holiday. I know that Ceccina will want to see her sister too…'

'I hope you will come,' he said.

But he knew this would not be enough for his wife.

'One day,' he said, 'Catania may have bad memories for Ceccina. In that case, even though I would not be here anymore, I would want her to move, to leave, to give the children a new life far away. In Verona perhaps. Do you understand?'

Corrado understood. He nodded.

Over the next few hours and days, on the matter of Pasqualina and her future husband leaving Sicily, going to Verona, Traiano began to think that this was, in some ways, a good idea. If something should go wrong, if his blood should end up on the cobblestones of the Purgatory quarter, then Verona would be a refuge for his wife and family. But Ceccina, he feared, would not see reason. There were two things she would not contemplate, two matters that he could not raise with her. The first was the thought of his premature death. Quite reasonably, from her point of view, she thought talking about such a thing would somehow make it possible. In addition, why talk about something that was not going to happen, why depress yourself, why rush to meet the thought one should most avoid? His body was covered with scars of one sort or another, but she steadfastly refused to think of him as anything but immortal.

The second thing flowed from the first: because he was going to live a long time, they could afford to wait until they had another child, in her view. But for him, the prospect of mortality, its very possibility, spurred on his desire to create new life, to leave a legacy of more children. But there was no chance of that at present. She would, he was sure, come round, and see things his way, particularly about her sister, but until then, he was banished from the marital bed. Not only was Ceccina so cross that she was not speaking to her own sister, she even subjected her husband to the silent treatment. Not unnaturally, the news of this double breach, between sisters, between husband and wife, was soon the news of the quarter, along with the now overshadowed announcement that Pasqualina was getting married to Gino's brother, Corrado Fisichella.

No one much cared for the idea of this wedding, particularly as it was also clear they were to marry in Agrigento and live in Verona. What then was in it for them? Pasqualina, it was thought, having been unmarried so long, could perhaps have stayed that way; but of course, she had to marry someone eventually, that was clear, but to marry this man, from Agrigento, a stranger, a man with a trade but no money, to go and live far away and be poor, when one could be poor in Sicily and at least have sunshine, it was all too hard to comprehend. Perhaps she loved him. Perhaps he loved her. At this, many shrugged. Of course, love was love, but did it entail leaving the people and the place you had always known?

As for Pasqualina, she seemed not just to be marrying a man with little to recommend him, but also opening herself to the charge of ingratitude. Don Traiano had done so much for her family, and now she was showing her appreciation by going away. He would have done a great deal for her had she stayed, and so would don Gino, no doubt about that, but it seemed that this was not something the couple wanted. They wanted no favours, and as such they marked themselves out as different from the rest of the quarter, which lived for favours. They noted the way that the visitor from Agrigento, not content with carrying off one of their women, seemed to find himself under no obligation to them, and certainly seemed not to realise that it was his role to ingratiate himself. He was aloof, arrogant, withdrawn. Most unlike his brother, don Gino, for whose sake they would tolerate him, but no more.

These were the things that Traiano Antonescu discussed with don Calogero di Rienzi on the day before his son's baptism. It was a perfect cloudless day, and they were both standing in the carpark at the Rifugio Sapienza. The view was spectacular, and the place was busy, full of tourist buses, and people in hiking and biking gear, and crowds waiting in a patient queue to ascend the mountain by the funicular. It was the ideal place for a discreet meeting. They had arrived in good time, and were waiting for Volta. Before leaving Catania, having endured his wife's displeasure for three days, Traiano had spoken to her and given her his instructions. She was to become reconciled with her sister; she was to show some favour to Corrado that indicated that she was happy to have him as a brother-in-law, and when he came back that afternoon, he was going to make love to her whether she liked it or not. The law thus laid down, he had departed for Etna with the boss.

The boss took no interest in the prospective wedding of Corrado and Pasqualina, though he was intrigued by the surreptitious way that had carried out their courtship, having first met at Gino's wedding. Well, if that was the way they wanted to play it, so much the better. He had enough to worry about. Don Gino and don Alfio were not quite the people he wanted to work with or be related to, however tenuously. He hoped that he would have very little to do with them in the future. They looked at the view, and then suddenly Volta was there, dressed in hiking gear, and wearing a woolly hat and dark glasses, his idea, perhaps, of a heavy disguise.

They nodded to each other.

'Don Traiano will explain what we are doing,' said Calogero conversationally.

'Every night we are sending people out to every quarter of the city, and they are pulling down or obscuring or defacing the posters of your rivals,' Traiano said. 'Each one is paid for this, naturally, and they get ten euros for bringing back the right-hand corner of each defaced poster. We get rid of several hundred a night, so that costs us several thousand a night. So far, we have kept an account, and it is 76,540 euro in all. People are queuing up for this work. In addition, we have made numerous payments to the website you set up, the crowdfunding, and we are donating several thousand a day to that, all in small amounts, which is great publicity for you, I am sure, as it makes it seem you are the head of a popular movement which, of course you are. We have reached almost 200,000 euros so far, and more will come. By the time of the election, we will have given you a million, all nice legal cash from unimpeachable sources, which will mean you will be far ahead of your rivals. By the time the election comes, we will have spent two to three million on you. Maybe more. We want you to win, and we will spend whatever it takes to outgun your rivals. That is what we are doing at present. It may be that later, we will use strong arm tactics as well, to scare off the other side, but I doubt it - I doubt that we will need to. From our angle - the local angle - the bill will be between two to three million.'

'As for the national angle,' said don Calogero, 'I wish I could be so exact. Our sponsors in Rome have been most helpful. The former mayor, who is a complete and utter fool, and utterly pig-headed, wants to run again, and so our sponsors in Rome have made sure that none of his party colleagues stand in the way. No one will vote for him, we hope. In addition, the opposition parties are putting up, shall we say, weak candidates, because words have been spoken that you are the chosen one. One of the opposition candidates is a paper candidate only; another is the sort of person who is calculated to alienate people, in my humble opinion, and has no chance of winning. The race yours. You will win. This sort of political influence in Rome is priceless, but I can put a price on it, you will be glad to know. I am making a contribution to party funds of twenty million, all declared, all legal - not all at once - over the next ten years. This is to the party of your rival, so no one can connect it with you. But that is twenty million you owe me.'

'Jesus, Mary, Joseph,' said Volta under his breath.

'And finally, there is the forensic report,' said Calogero, 'in case anyone should have any doubts about who to vote for. This report has already caused a headache for the government, though they have survived that with a little rearranging of jobs in the Interior ministry and the ministry of Grace and Justice. But the report is so lurid, so disgusting, it will sweep you to power. What is the name of this guy, this gravedigger of Bronte?'

'He is called Pio Forcella, and he has brought us something very interesting,' said Traiano. 'A secret benefactor, that is to say, don Calogero, paid for Piuccio the undertaker to go up to Rome and oversee the cremation of the bodies of the late Beata Bednarowska and her son Paolo. No one else wanted the bodies. They were an encumbrance, and the state should have paid, but there was an unseemly tussle between Rome and Catania: They lived here, they died there, but neither commune would take responsibility. The callousness of the state is remarkable when it comes to dealing with the poor and the destitute and the dead. Piuccio will go public with this. At the same time, the forensic report will be leaked and there will be a drip, drip, drip of revelations as to how they died. Anna Maria has seen to all that. How the state failed and, of course, how you are going to usher in a new era.'

'You hypocrite!' said Volta.

Traiano smiled and made a gesture with his finger.

'Now, now,' said Calogero. 'Let's not talk of hypocrisy. We are doing this for our mutual benefit. There are no hypocrites in this game, just sensible people, and us running Catania rather than the Romans. We all get what we want. You, dear Volta, get to be the mayor; and if you make a success of it, as I hope you will, you will have ten years to transform the city, after which, no doubt, a national career will await you. But the day after the election, if you are successful, you start paying your bills and rewarding us for the risk we have taken in betting on you so heavily. No, don't worry, nothing very dramatic, no bill for millions in hard cash. We are reasonable people. Very reasonable people. The first thing is this: every planning permission we ask for, we get. You can make sure that it all goes through the right motions, but what we ask for, we receive. And, from those building projects, you will get, shall we say, one percentage point of the value of the whole project, either for you personally or for your political party, if you decide to found one. And our building projects are going to be nice, just like the Furnaces, you will see. As for requests about zoning, Rome has dealt with the Furnaces, in that they are moving the flight paths; other zoning requests will come to you, and we expect favourable answers. The other thing is, you are going to appoint this Pio Forcella to be administrator of the municipal cemetery. He will have a free hand, but you will not regret it. The place is a mess, and we will clean it up. Other requests will follow. Apart from that, we require nothing except the knowledge that we have a firm friend in the city hall.'

For a moment, Volta wished that he could lose the election. But he knew that in his heart he did not want to lose, and that his wife wanted him to win, his mother wanted him to win, his child, if he could think of it, too; but above all, he wanted to win, desperately, and win at almost any cost. If the cost were doing business for these people whom he hated and despised, then so be it. But he was not going to work for them; they were going to work for him. He tried to calculate the value of one percentage point of the cost of building projects in one year. He couldn't, but he knew it was huge.

'I agree to what you say,' he said. 'But, this report, no doubt it will discredit the former regime and our opponents, and give the people the idea that we need a clean broom, but are you sure its publication might not have unforeseen consequences?'

'Tell me what you are thinking,' said don Calogero quietly.

'The report makes clear that the woman and the boy were both raped. By two men. These two men may have left their seminal fluid inside the woman. Forensics can work with that. No one has been arrested, we know that, which proves something, namely that the men who did this are not on the national DNA database. So, they are not known to the police, they do not have records, there is no exact match. But it may be the case that their relatives are on the database. It may be the case that the DNA points them in a certain direction, points them south, to Catania or to Palermo. What I am saying is that every time they pull someone in for a driving offence or something minor, they will take a DNA sample, surreptitiously if they must, and then run it through the records, until, hey presto, they win the lottery. And if they find one or either of these men, one or either might lead them back to you, don Calogero, by a chain of acquaintances.'

'And from me to you, dear Volta, and I am sure that is what worries you. I myself am not worried. These murders happened in Rome and had nothing whatever to do with me. I did not know the woman or her son.'

'But he did, I am sure,' said Volta, indicating Traiano. 'Of course, you didn't know them, but you knew someone who did. Of course, you did not know the murderers, but you knew someone who knew someone, who knew someone....'

There was silence for a moment. Calogero considered.

'Boss, shall I knock his teeth out for you?' asked Traiano quietly.

Volta ignored this.

'Shut up, Traiano,' said Calogero. 'Volta, you seem to be under two impressions. The first is that this murder in Rome was somehow messy. Now, I doubt that. These people were under police protection. You know that. The whole Italian state was guarding them. The people who got to them did so because they were professionals. And as such, they would not have made mistakes. The woman was raped, the boy was raped. These were messages sent to the people of the world telling them not to trust the Italian state which, given its incompetence and inefficiency, is a friendly warning to all who might go down that path. But you also have this idea that everything bad that happens can somehow be placed at my door. I am a respectable businessman, and you would do well to remember that. Because that is what you are going to tell people if they ever ask how you know me, and why you know me.'

'I know what I know,' said Volta. 'I knew that woman, I knew the son; she told me she was frightened of him,' he said, shooting Traiano a look of hatred. 'The boy was a fool because he thought he liked him. That's what he told me.'

'You saw them?' asked Traiano. 'In the Castle of the Women, wherever that is? The safe place they were kept, the safe place that was not after all so safe?'

There was silence. Volta realised he had made a mistake.

'You see, Volta,' said Calogero easily, placing a commendatory hand on Traiano's shoulder. 'This Traiano who you so despise, who just threatened to knock your teeth out, is someone you should make friends with, because he Is far, far cleverer than you. You knew the boy, you knew the woman, you saw them after they left Catania. You have numerous contacts in the police. The obvious conclusion is that it was you who betrayed their hiding place. Never mind the DNA evidence left inside the woman by the men who raped her, if it in fact exists. Much more important is the way the whole operation to protect them was compromised from the inside. By someone like you, if not you yourself.'

Volta sighed.

'Very soon, Volta, you will be the mayor of Catania, and everyone will run around doing your bidding. You will be on the television every night, and people will be beating a path to your door. But please remember, I got you the job, and you will owe your position to me; and you will work for me. And you will treat don Traiano here with respect. He has threatened to knock your teeth out, but let us all hope it never comes to that. You work for me. Now, do not look sulky. This is going to be very profitable for both of us. Now you can go, and do whatever it is you are dressed to do up here, and we will return to Catania.'

He pulled Volta towards him, and kissed his cheek. Volta submitted to the indignity, and then, realising it was necessary, kissed the cheek of don Traiano too.

Chapter Three

The baptism of little Alessandro Antonescu was a most important occasion. Ceccina had been preparing for it mentally more or less from the first moment she had realised she was pregnant. So, when the second Sunday of October came round, she was determined that nothing would go wrong, and nothing at all would ruin the occasion for her or anyone else. Naturally, there were the clothes to be considered, and the shoes as well, for the three children, herself and her husband. There was the hair to be seen to as well. It was through this matter, the seemingly straightforward matter of the hair, that she was able to banish the cloud that had appeared on the horizon between her sister and herself. Naturally, she and Pasqualina had to meet and to plan her - Ceccina's - hair which, it was decided, after much consultation of images on their phones, would be a modestly upswept loose bun. Then there was the question of what to do about Traiano. She had selected his suit (he had denied he needed a new one, but she had overruled him); and now she thought that as he was suit-wearing type, he ought to have something neater to go with it, and that he should lose his long unkempt curls. Eventually, she decided on a crew cut, a short back and sides; this was agreed by the two sisters. Then Ceccina broached the question of her sister's intended. What should be done about Corrado? A long conversation ensued, at the end of which the two girls were perfectly reconciled about Pasqualina's wedding to Corrado, and it was decided on just what sort of haircut and beard trim Corrado needed.

So, the question of Corrado was settled. It was not what she would have wished for in the least, but she could see that Pasqualina was determined, and if that was the case, it was pointless trying to dissuade her. One would have to make the best of it, and that was all there was to it. She and her sister had always been very close, but they were rivals as well. She had chosen Traiano when she had been very young indeed, too young perhaps to make an informed choice; but she had been lucky: not only was she passionately in love with her young husband, she had three lovely children by him, a nice house, and they were very well off. She was, of all women in the quarter, the most fortunate. It was at moments like these, the evening before the baptism, when her husband came back from the Rifugio Sapienza, when she studied his flushed face and his long hair, when she felt his arms around her and hers around him, when the flat was deliciously quiet and the children at last asleep, that she felt supremely happy. But it was at moments like these that the worm of doubt gnawed at her. Pasqualina would leave; she would go to Verona; she would live a different life, and her departure seemed to indicate a withdrawal to safety, an avoidance of risk.

A sister in Verona, so far away, and yet, to her surprise, the others in the family were not as doleful about the prospect as she. As for Corrado himself, he seemed nice enough, but she could not quite see whatever it was that her sister saw in him. And she was frankly surprised by the way her husband had even suggested that Corrado be the godfather of their next child, which, she thought, given their very short acquaintance, a sign of great and perhaps undeserved favour. Well, there was no fourth child as yet, a third still to baptise, and they would make that decision when the time came.

The godparents this time were carefully chosen. The godmother was Anna Maria Tancredi, the boss's wife. She liked and admired Anna Maria, and who better to be godmother when one considered that she was one of the most important women, if not the most important, in Sicily? Her husband had had the idea, and she had been pleased by it; and Anna Maria had accepted, which was very kind of her, given that she was pregnant herself and had a great deal to do. As for the godfather, there was a certain symmetry in the choice, and again it had been her husband's idea, one she knew, calculated to please her. They had asked don Renzo. He had been absolutely thrilled. Of course, Traiano had calculated that no one could object to don Renzo, and this avoided the necessity of having to choose someone else, and in particular to make a choice between don Gino or don Alfio, a choice that would have been sure to alienate at least one of them.

Don Renzo was the only member of the Santucci family active in the honoured society. If anyone deserved, or felt he deserved, the extravagant compliment of being a godfather, it was surely him. He might be useful in future; he was going to be the boss's brother-in-law, even if few had confidence in his abilities. Of course, Traiano did not like don Renzo Santucci; he did not like him at all, but that was irrelevant. Don Renzo Santucci was spoiled and had inherited his position. He had not worked for it. But it was more than that. Don Renzo was a drug user, a drinker, a fornicator, and did no hard work, all things he disapproved of. But of course, personal feelings had nothing to do with anything, he knew that. One must not let personal feelings sway one's judgement. As it was, he restricted his liking to his own family, to his wife, his children, to those attached to him by blood. They were the people you could trust.

The great day came. The party after the baptism was to be held in the new flat, and served as a way of showing off this vast new residence, formerly the property of the boss. There would be thirty or forty people present – the guest list was fluid, and so many of the people attending would be children. The food was being provided by the trattoria. As with any event of this type, there were people invited because they *had* to be invited. Amongst them he included his own mother; one could hardly not invite her; besides he liked her husband to the point of distraction, and one had to have him.

Anna, the former Romanian prostitute came with her husband Fofò, her child, now five years old, golden-haired Salvatore, whose father Traiano had helped rebury, and heavily pregnant with what would be her last child. For once, she was on time at the church, her husband trailing behind her with Salvatore and with a heavy bag containing his camera, which he set up as soon as he could before the ceremony began. Anna sat with Salvatore and surveyed the scene, taking in the Spanish Madonna, always a favourite of hers, surrounded by her nimbus of golden rays, waving to don Giorgio, her favourite priest, and accepting the congratulations of all the women who came up to admire Salvatore and to make enquiries about the progress of her pregnancy. The godmother, Anna Maria Tancredi, entered, also heavily pregnant, and even older than Anna, being at least forty-five. The two women smiled at each other. Her husband, don Calogero, scowled. One never met don Calogero; one confronted him. It pleased Anna that the boss was so annoyed to see her. Her own daughter-in-law obediently kissed her as she entered, and allowed the new baby to be admired. The two other grandchildren were delighted to see her, her son less so. She commented on his hair cut, and he went to talk to his stepfather. Other guests arrived, and then the ceremony began.

She was glad that she had left Purgatory for the haven of Syracuse, where there was fresh sea air, more space, more light, more beauty, and where, if truth were told, she did not carry round with her the reputation she had gained in Catania. All the people here treated her with great respect which, in some of the men, was tinged with embarrassment. The respect came from the fact that they knew don Calogero feared her, and he feared no one else; in addition she was the mother of don Traiano, who was wary of her; as for the embarrassment felt by the men, they had all at one time or another slept with her, or had wanted to do so, and they thought she remembered them, though, in fact, she had forgotten almost all of them. That had been another life, a life in which she was no longer interested, a life to which she had no intention of ever returning.

In this, she stood with them all. All of them, nearly, had a past; all of them sought respectability. This was the holy grail; this was the prize. None of them wanted to be reminded of the men they had beaten or killed, the women they had abused, the things they had stolen. If they were to dabble in theft and extortion now, they would do so at one remove. But the younger generation, her grandchildren, who would grow up, not as criminals, but as the children of criminals, rich and entitled, what did the future hold for them? One could perhaps tell in looking at don Calogero's eldest daughter, now ten years old, who was clearly in advance of her years. And one could see it in don Renzo Santucci, a spoilt character if ever there was one and, if she judged rightly, one who drank and took drugs far too much.

She was interested to see that Ruggero Bonelli and his sister Gabriella were there. She had heard a great deal about them. Did they realise just whom they were associating with? At the after party in the new flat, her husband was in huge demand to take pictures of the new baby with his parents, and his extended family which, of course, included herself. Then, after those who most had the right to be photographed, came the rest of them, all wanting their pictures taken, which meant that poor Alfonso had virtually no time to enjoy the party, and which was a sign too of all these people wanting something for free. But that was how it worked here; you did favours, and one day these favours might be returned. Alfonso was very good at photographing children, of which there were a great many, all of whom submitted themselves to be photographed with ease, so good was he at handling them. But his chief interest, she knew, was character: he liked to take pictures of people who were trying to hide things, and yet at the same time giving them away before the camera. Naturally he was delighted to photograph the four young men: her son, don Gino, don Alfio and don Renzo Santucci, all of them standing side by side in their suits, trying to look normal which, of course, none of them were, either singly or together, particularly not together.

She was far more interested in the new people who were present. Signora Grassi was there, she noted. Poor signora Grassi, an unhappy lady, married, with a son, and with a husband in prison for a long, long time, forever in debt to don Calogero who supported her on a pittance, and who ensured that her worthless husband came to no harm in prison, thanks to his contacts. But it seemed that the signora's misfortunes had ameliorated of late. Her son was growing up, she said, which implied that the boy was earning money, though one dreaded to think how, and one dreaded to think what would happen the moment he ceased to be useful. Moreover, the family had moved to a much nicer place, a palatial residence, near the monument to Cardinal Dusmet, where they were living in what had been the servants' quarters and keeping an eye on Ruggero Bonelli's gallery of treasures.

'And where is Tonino?' asked Anna. 'I don't see him.'

Tonino was talking to the boss. He had been examining the wine in the kitchen, looking at the various bottles which one of the waiters from the trattoria had charge of. He was examining each and reading the labels. They were all Sicilian. He had heard of Nero d'Avola, and knew it was a grape. He had seen road signs marked Avola and knew it was a town to the south, which was where the grape was cultivated. He quite liked drinking wine, and he found the way each wine was described interesting. You could say so much about a drink. It was while he was reading the labels that the boss found him and put a hand on his shoulder.

He had known the boss all his life, there had never been a time he had not known him, but nothing prepared you, he felt, for this sort of approach. Sometimes you approached him, like a pilgrim to a saint, but sometimes, more rarely, he approached you, and you never knew what for, though you knew it would be important, even life changing. He noticed the waiter, someone he had also known all his life, withdrew, to allow a private conference. He felt the blood pound through his veins, and the colour rush to his cheeks.

'You are interested in Nero d'Avola?' asked the boss, looking at the bottle.

'Yes, boss, I mean no, boss, it is just that I would like to know more. I mean it is interesting that they say such different things about different wines. I was reading the labels, wondering who writes this stuff....'

'You know we export wine to America now? I mean don Renzo and myself. One day, I should visit some vineyards, see what they are doing, check up on things. It is part of the business that is not doing so well.'

'Do we, I mean you, own some vineyards, boss?'

'I am not sure. My wife will know. I will ask her. If you are interested, I can send you to some vineyards. Though really you could go and do one of these courses on viticulture, when you stay at a vineyard, it is sort of like a holiday, and they teach you all about wine. Have you ever been on holiday?'

'No, boss.'

'You might enjoy it. The vineyard, I mean. We shall see. Right now, we are thinking of our men, and the ones who could do useful things in the future. Lawyers, and of course, doctors. Doctor Moro, whom I have never met, is growing old, isn't he? Can you write as well as read?' he asked.

'Yes, boss,' he answered, not offended. It would have been offensive from someone else.

'How did you learn?' he asked, curious.

'When I watched television with my mother, we would put the subtitles on, and that taught me.'

'You read books?'

'Sometimes, boss.'

'Are you reading one now?'

'I am, boss. A history of Italy from 1815 until the present.'

'Do you like Garibaldi?' asked the boss.

He knew this was a test. He thought briefly. He could say that he had not made up his mind, but he knew there was no progress without risk.

'I hate him, boss. He was not even a proper Italian. He came from Nice. He spent years abroad. He had no business invading Sicily. And he would not have succeeded if it had not been for the English interfering, that man Palmerstone.'

He hoped he had got this right. He hoped he had pronounced the English name correctly. The boss was looking at him with interest.

'You are right,' said the boss, and smiled.

He pulled the boy towards him and kissed his forehead. Tonino thought for a moment he would faint.

'Did you leave your DNA in Rome?' asked the boss, quietly.

'No chance, boss. Muniddu was there, and I did what he did. There was no chance of any clues being left in that flat.'

'Or in that woman?'

'None at all, boss.'

'Good, you are clever. I am pleased with you. That report, when it is leaked, will win the election for our friend Volta. I gather Traiano was annoyed you smoked on the train, and the police traced you?'

'He was right to be, boss, but there is no harm done. The guy I was with is my alibi. He will swear we were together the entire time we were in Rome if it comes to that. If anyone asks. Boss....'

'Yes, you want a favour. Ask.'

'This guy, Roberto Costacurta, he is becoming a lawyer. Can he have a job in the signora's office?'

The signora was Assunta, his sister.

'Take him along there. I will tell her to expect you. What is he to you?'

'Nothing, boss. He is older than me, but he has sisters my age. They have no money, his father has left them, and he needs to pay his university fees.'

The boss nodded.

'Your father,' he said. 'I am going to get one of the lawyers onto that. He has been in Ucciardone so long. Your mother mentioned it to my mother. We shall see what can be done. Tell me, did don Traiano beat you? With the belt? Which end?'

'The buckle end, boss. It hurt like hell. I am covered in bruises and I bled a bit. But it has happened before and will happen again.'

'I am sure it will,' said don Calogero with a smile, placing his hand on the boy's shoulder. 'Did you enjoy it?'

Tonino looked modestly at his shoes.

'You are like God Himself, boss. You know everything about me.'

'Ah, there is Tonino, or so I assume. He has grown!' said Anna, when Tonino came into the sitting room, having left the kitchen. He was carrying a glass of wine.

Tonino approached, kissing his mother, and respectfully greeted Anna, as well as Assunta, who had joined them. These two women, Anna and Assunta, he noticed, radiated power. Of course, don Calogero did too, and so did his wife, Anna Maria Tancredi, but the young men, the dons Traiano, Gino, Alfio and Renzo, were insubstantial compared to these two women; he felt suddenly that they would be here long after the young men were gone.

Anna Agostini, Traiano's mother, was smiling at Tonino; Assunta, the boss's sister, by contrast never smiled, but you could not but feel her looking at you. Tonino listened as his mother explained to Anna how tall her son now was, and how he now had to shave every day.

Tonino groaned softly to hear her speak like this, but knew he could not and should not stop her. He saw Anna smile, and was aware how Assunta, who did not seem to care for these fripperies, who was made of sterner stuff, was listening with attention.

Assunta sighed. She hated these baptisms. She herself had no children, and was never likely to have any. She did not want any, at least not yet. She was still only thirty, though her weight made her look older. Across the room, she caught sight of her husband, Federico. She felt a momentary wave of pleasure. Others did not value Federico the way she did. But the others did not know him as well. The others were not married to him. She was. She knew. She loved him, and he her.

The party was a long one. Tonino wandered from room to room, enjoying being a guest, sampling both the red wines, trying to make out which he preferred, noting that the boys from the pizzeria and the trattoria were there overseeing the food and drink, but not him. He had risen, and perhaps would rise further. He found himself in conversation with Gabriella Bonelli. She had seen him before this, of course, at the gallery, her brother's gallery. He explained that he was signora Grassi's son. They spoke of the paintings in her brother's collection, and she asked if he liked any in particular. He had paid them some attention, she was glad to note, and he mentioned one or two which stood out. There was a picture of an early nineteenth century lady which he liked very much. She knew the one; it was in the manner of (but perhaps not by) Elisabeth Vigée le Brun, and probably one of the more obviously attractive pieces her brother had inherited from the late professor. He confessed he did not like the pictures of fruit and dead creatures but preferred the landscapes. These, she knew, were the French paintings, the products of various French artists who had lived in Rome at the academy there. As a gardener, she liked them too. She detected that he was not much of a Sicilian, liking stuff from abroad. This was confirmed when he said, in response to her question, that his favourite artist was Velasquez, the one who had painted the Spanish Madonna in the Church of the Holy Souls in Purgatory. He had never been to an art gallery, but he had been to the museum in Messina and seen the two Caravaggios there and had not thought much of them. Too dark. But he wished he knew more about it.

'In the end, it all comes back to Caravaggio, though,' she said, noting his reference to the museum in Messina where his paintings hung. 'I wonder why? Perhaps because he did some of his best work here? Perhaps because he was the sort of person we secretly admire?'

'Do we admire murderers?' he asked, with a smirk.

'Do you?' she answered.

He reflected. There had been a time when he had not known anyone who might fall into that category, but that time had long passed.

Tonino was now distracted, looking across the room to where don Calogero's eldest daughter was, the one they called Isabella. That was the girl he was going to marry, he thought to himself, one day, in about ten years' time.

'Who is she?' asked Gabriella, who had observed the direction of his gaze.

'It is don Calogero's eldest daughter, Isabella,' he said.

'The one whose mother died so tragically,' said Gabriella sympathetically.

Isabella knew he was looking at her, and, to his delight, she approached. He was very pleased. She liked him; he was sure of that. The only disadvantage was that she brought her sister Natalia in her wake, Natalia who was so much younger, but saw everything, observed everything, and doubtless reported it to her stepmother, her aunts and her grandmother. But, reflected Tonino, his mother was a friend of their grandmother, which was a help. Their grandmother was one who more or less brought them up. Tonino's father had known her grandfather, before he was blown up, before his father was put away. He knew don Calogero, and don Calogero knew him and liked him. There were so many connections. Why shouldn't he be the one to win the prize? And what a prize she was, even if she were only ten years old. What a prize she would become.

The children had been put to bed, and the other children had been taken home by their mothers. Isabella and her sister and infant brothers had been removed to the flat above. Anna and Alfonso had left with little Salvatore, for Syracuse. Pasqualina and her beau, Corrado, were in the kitchen with her sister Ceccina.

The male part of the company was in the study: Calogero, Traiano, Alfio and Gino, Renzo, and Tonino. Ruggero and his sister had just left. The whiskey bottle was open, mainly for the benefit of Calogero; Traiano was drinking nothing, but the rest were drinking wine. Tonino too had nothing, having had his fill of Nero d'Avola, but was content to be there in the presence of such important people. It was a privilege. They were talking of two things among themselves, but Tonino was pretending to be only half listening. First of all, the gravedigger of Bronte, this man, Piuccio Forcella. He represented a good investment, a good long-term investment, once the investment in Volta came through. Once they got their hands on the cemetery, they could redo the whole place and make a fortune and sink tons of dirty cash in the process. Just like the Furnaces, where the foundations that no one could see – they were underground, and besides they did not exist – had enabled them to wash millions. They were also talking of the art business, that of Ruggero Bonelli. Getting into the art market was an excellent idea. Bonelli was a great find. They were grateful to the sister, beautiful Gabriella, for the introduction. And at the mention of her name, at the thought of her beauty, there was a palpable silence in the room. The day's activities had reminded them of their domestic duties. Traiano alone had no thought of ever committing adultery, though Gino and Alfio, Renzo and Calogero certainly did, but two of them had either a newborn or one on the way soon, and Alfio and Renzo were both engaged to be married and would both be procreating as a matter of urgency very soon afterwards. Gabriella represented an impossible dream for all of them: she was too refined for Gino and Alfio, and too dangerous for Renzo, about to marry the boss's sister, and as for the boss himself…

'Bonelli is so keen to work with us, I am sure he would throw in his sister for free,' said Traiano. 'And I am sure she would throw herself in. But only to you, don Calogero.'

The others acknowledged this. Calogero smiled and shrugged. There was a moment of calm, succeeded by a moment of restlessness. Renzo caught Gino's eye; Gino looked at Alfio; the womenfolk at home, the children asleep, the place to go was the room at the gym, where some of the other boys would be gathering before midnight, and where the cocaine and the pills could be consumed in peace and quiet. Gino had the former and Tonino had the latter. The restlessness centred on Renzo, who could not stay still for very long, ever; and recognising this, the others, who saw in Renzo the one who had to be placated the most after don Calogero himself, stood to go; and Tonino stood as well. Only Traiano had not the slightest intention of accompanying them; and don Calogero himself was content to leave and go home. Traiano went to join his wife, his sister-in-law and her future husband in the kitchen, for peaceful conversation followed by bed.

Tonino knew what was expected of him, and he read their thoughts. He was there in the gym at about 9pm, in the private room, putting out the various pills on the bench for the men to help themselves; at the other end of the bench, don Gino prepared the white powder for himself and don Renzo, offering some to don Alfio, who declined, but not to Tonino. Then they stripped to their shorts and the fighting began.

At midnight, Traiano was wide awake. This was often the case; his sleep patterns were disrupted by years of staying up all night and sleeping all day. Sunday nights like this one were particularly hard. On Sundays one had to spend the day with the family, and then go to bed at the normal time. This he had done. His wife lay sleeping next to him; the children were asleep, and so was the baby, Alessandro, thankfully. If he awoke, he would tend to him and leave Ceccina to rest in peace. But at moments like these, lying silent in the darkness, aware of his sleeping wife and children, he would think of what was going right, and what might go wrong. The worrying thing was that everything was going right, everything: the vast project at the Furnaces, the art business, the election of Volta, the debt collecting, the friends who were not really friends but were as yet no real threat. But this was worrying because he knew that it was in perfect moments like these that disaster struck.

It was with a degree of nervousness that Tonino ascended to the top floor of the gym building the next day, with Roberto, to call on the signora. Assunta sat in her glass office, at her computer, and only looked up when she had finished whatever she was doing.

'Well,' she said. 'I was expecting you. My brother told me.' She looked at Roberto. 'It is always nice to see Tonino. His mother and my mother are old friends. Has my mother been round to see you in your new place? No? Not yet, anyway. She will, I am sure. I believe Calogero spoke to someone to look into your father's case only this morning. He promised you he would, and he has. What will result, we cannot tell. Is your father away from home?' she asked, turning to Roberto.

'Yes, signora, but he is away in a different sense.' He noticed her raised eyebrow. 'He ran off with another woman and they live in Rome.'

'Men!' said Assunta. 'But luckily they are not all like that.' She looked through the glass towards her husband, Federico, assiduously working at his desk. 'How is my future brother-in-law?' she asked.

'Don Renzo is well,' said Tonino. 'I was with him last night.'

She did not look convinced, and he did not sound convincing. She turned her attention to Roberto.

'It is an easy job, and it needs to be done by someone trustworthy and discreet, particularly the latter. One of the girls has been doing it, but I can move her to something else, as we have tons to do, and when the Furnaces are complete, then we will have even more. I am my brother's gatekeeper, and you will be mine. The emails come in, and you read them, get rid of the time wasters, and then pass on in summary form to the right person the contents of those that demand action. Some will be asking for rent reductions; others looking for properties to rent; others hoping to move from one place to another; others requesting repair jobs; others making excuses about not paying their rent, and so on. We are also getting people asking about future properties, not yet available, and we have someone curating the waiting list. As you are a law student, you will know what to do. And you can do it at any hour of the day and night, so it won't affect your lectures. One of the girls will show you what to do.'

She raised a hand, and one of the girls presented herself in the office, and was given instructions. Roberto left with her.

'I like him,' she said to Tonino, when he had gone. She spoke with decision.

They came for him, as he had known they would, on Saturday morning. He had gone to bed very late, as usual, and his mother had to wake him by knocking loudly on his door at about 9am.

'There are some people here to see you,' she said.

He struggled into his clothes, and on the way to the bathroom, his mother pressed a cup of coffee into his hands, and gestured toward the main apartment, where the visitors were waiting. He brushed his teeth, he combed his hair, and then stepped out into the enfilade of salons. Several rooms away, he was aware of a man and a woman. They were looking at the paintings with interest. The woman seemed particularly taken with a series of eighteenth-century views of Italian cities. He approached, and the woman turned to him with a friendly smile.

'You have a nice place here,' she said.

'It is not mine, signora,' he answered, accepting the handshake, adding: 'Unfortunately. It all belongs to signor Bonelli. Are you hoping to buy something?'

'We came to see you, Tonino,' she said. 'I like pictures, but neither of us are here for that reason. Shall we sit? I am Chiara di Donato, by the way, and this is Silvio Pierangeli.'

There were three upholstered antique armchairs in the middle of the room, marooned in the centre of the polished floor. They sat down.

'You know why we are here,' stated Silvio. 'The police are investigating the deaths of two persons, Beata Bednarowska and her son Pawel, which happened in August, in Rome. We are members of the magistracy and we are running a parallel and discreet investigation. We know that you were on the night train the very night of the murder. We have evidence.'

'I was on that train, sure,' said Tonino. 'I smoked in the corridor and those Americans saw us and filmed it on their phones. I know you spoke to Costacurta about it. He told me.'

'He said he had only just met you, and did not know your surname,' said Silvio.

'That was stupid of Costacurta, but that is the way he is. I will explain. It was my idea that we go to Rome together to see his father. He has a very bad relationship with his father, and he wanted me to go with him, besides it was my idea. Costacurta needed money, and was going to ask his father who, as you probably know, has abandoned his family - the bastard - and left them with nothing. He is embarrassed by this; he hates his father, and he needed some persuasion to go. As it was, he was right. The father did not want to see him and was not helpful. He is not a nice man. Costacurta is very upset that you took his computer and read all his emails between himself and his father.'

'And throughout this time in Rome you were with Roberto Costacurta all the time?' asked the woman.

'Yes. I can tell you where we were and what we did if you like.'

'I am sure you can, and I am sure you have spoken to Costacurta about it and your stories tally exactly,' said Silvio.

'They do, because our stories are true.'

'Where did you spend the night?'

'We went to Testaccio and went to several bars. We met some girls who invited us back to their flat.'

'And you cannot remember their names or their address?'

'Valeria and Monica. It somewhere off the via Appia Nuova, and we stayed with them. It was near the Furio Camillo station. But I did not note the exact address. I was too distracted about what was to come next.'

There was silence.

'A good story,' said Chiara. 'As you probably know, when a story is so good, so perfect, it is because it is made up, crafted. But we know what really happened. You killed Beata and her son.'

'Signora, that is ridiculous. How could I kill two people all on my own? And so far from home? And why would I do that? Are you saying I was paid to do so? If so, where is the money? I don't have an overflowing bank account. And there is no cash hidden here, you are free to look. I have read about this crime, but I did not know Beata, though I did know her son, as we played football together in the square. But everyone knew her son. He was a good player. But we did not like him. Everyone knew that he was one of those boys.'

'Explain,' said Silvio.

'He would drop his shorts for money. With men. That is disgusting. It is not the Sicilian way. The boys who do that are disgusting, and the men who do that with boys are disgusting too. That is why they left, because people knew about it, I am not sure how, but we knew. And that is why someone pursued them and killed them, because they wanted their silence. Someone important.'

'Why don't we stop this elaborate game,' said Silvio. 'I am sure your friend Costacurta will say anything you want him to say. You have leverage with him, don't you? You have just got him a job, haven't you? But the truth is that picture that places you on that train is bad news for you. We know. Of course, you did not do it alone, you did it with someone else. And you were paid. Naturally, you have passed the money to someone to look after. Naturally you claim to be a simple waiter in a pizzeria. But we know you are not. When we circulated your photograph, everyone claimed not to recognise it. These people are using you. And when they have used you, they will throw you aside. Don't you understand that?'

'Which people?' asked Tonino.

'Trajan Antonescu, Gino Fisichella, Renzo Santucci, Alfio Camilleri, and Calogero di Rienzi.'

'Calogero's mother and my mother are friends. As for the rest of them, I barely know them. Apart from Renzo. I have never heard of him.'

Silvio sighed. On cue, the signora entered, carrying her shopping basket. Greetings, polite and effusive, were exchanged. As soon as she was gone, Chiara made a phone call. A few moments later the bell sounded. Two policemen in uniform appeared.

'We have a warrant to search the premises,' said Chiara.

He shrugged, as if he did not care. The gun and the knife, he knew, were safely stowed in the gym locker in the private room.

As he sat with the woman, the man Silvio and the two police, who were wearing rubber gloves, went into the apartment he shared with is mother. He and Chiara looked at each other and said nothing. A moment later, Silvio was back.

'The locked drawer,' he said. 'Unless you want us to break it open.'

He took a set of keys out of his pocket, detached one, and handed it over. Silvio left them. There was another uncomfortable pause, in which he did his very best to remain nonchalant, or at least try to appear so. He looked at the pictures, one by one, all the time conscious that she was looking at him, waiting for him to say something. At last Silvio returned and beckoned him to follow him into the apartment. He wondered if they had found what they were looking for.

He was led into his bedroom. There, spread on the bed, were the contents of the locked drawer, all the things he did not want his mother to see.

'Well?' asked Silvio.

'Well, what?' he replied.

'Why was the drawer locked?'

'Why not?' he answered. 'I was not hiding anything. I gave you the key.'

'This money....'

It was about two hundred euros.

'The pizzeria pays me.'

'These magazines, are they yours?'

'Of course they are. And they are none of your business. They are certainly not illegal.'

'Where did you get them? They are in Hungarian. Do you speak Hungarian?'

He shot him a look of venomous contempt.

'And these?' asked Silvio, indicating various pills and packages. 'Can you see what it says on the packaging? Not for resale. In several languages. Including our own and, I see, Arabic. Not for resale. That means that they have been stolen, and from an American army base as well. Now it is not very much, but it is still illegal to receive stolen goods. I could have you arrested here and now. Do you understand? Where did you get them?'

'One of the waiters in the pizzeria gave them to me. People pass these things around. The magazines. The headache pills, the other things. They were locked away because my mother might find them otherwise, and that would be embarrassing. But as for what it says on the packages, I have not got a clue. I can't read. And as for who gave them to me, I cannot remember.'

'How would your mother feel if we showed her all this?'

'Upset. But I think if you are looking for leverage, you will need more than that. You have made various threats; now, arrest me or leave me alone.'

'You are being very foolish,' said Silvio. 'Think of what we can offer you.'

'I have thought. Nothing, nothing at all.'

'How long has your father been away for? Thirteen years? And how many more to go? Quite a few. It must be hard living without him. We can get him a presidential pardon. He could come home. Think how happy your mother would be.' He paused. 'We could find you a new place to live, where the three of you would be happy. And please do not say you are happy. Your mother needs your father. You need your father. Just think what could happen to him in Ucciardone. Imagine what could happen to you one day. Well, you do not need to imagine it. You have seen what happens. You saw what happened to little Paolo.'

Tonino, by an almost superhuman effort, managed to suppress a smile. He had loathed 'little Paolo'. He had no regrets on that score. Moreover, he did not care that his father was away, and he had no desire for him to come back and interfere with his freedom. He had no memory of him at all and did not lament his absence. He had no desire to share his mother with his father, none at all.

'I know what happened to Paolo,' he said. 'You failed to protect him. That is what happened to Paolo. Everyone knows that. And now you are offering to protect me? From what or whom?'

A third person had entered the small bedroom. Behind him were two flustered police and an even more flustered Chiara.

'What are you doing here?' asked Silvio angrily.

'No. What are you doing here?' replied Calogero di Rienzi calmly. 'This young man is a family friend. His mother knows my mother. Signora Grassi came and told me you were here, and she gave me her keys. I don't know who you are and why you are harassing a teenager. Has he done anything wrong? Have you any evidence of criminal activity? I doubt that very much. Why have you not allowed him to have an appropriate adult present, or to call a lawyer? And why,' he asked, glancing at the bed, the pornographic magazines, the packaged contraceptives, 'why have you humiliated him in this way? The boy is fourteen, for God's sake. Tonino, put those things away. No, don't. Put them in a rubbish bag and I will throw them away for you. You may not be in trouble with the police, but you are in trouble with me for having such stuff. You can expect a punishment. Your father may be away, but…. As for you,' he said, turning to the strangers, 'Please leave. Now.'

A moment later, they were alone. They heard the outer door close.

'They won't be pleased,' said Calogero. 'Your mother is sharp. She realised there was something not right about them. Luckily, I was here. I am supposed to be going to Donnafugata this morning.'

'I am sorry you were disturbed, boss.'

'Who were they?'

'Silvio Pierangeli and Chiara di Donato. The same two who came to see Costacurta. He says they do not exist, that they are assumed names. It was a fishing expedition. They failed with Costacurta and they failed with me. They said they would get my father out of jail early.'

'You want that?'

'Of course, boss.'

'What would your father say if he were here and saw this?' said Calogero who was now leafing through the pornographic magazine, mentally comparing it to his own collection, which he kept safely locked away.

'He would give me a good beating, boss, which I would richly deserve.'

'With which end of the belt, do you think?'

'Oh, the buckle end, on my bare flesh, and he would make me bleed,' said Tonino thoughtfully.

It was a good half hour before the signora came back. She found her keys, which she had given the boss, on the kitchen counter, and took them without comment, and then started unpacking her shopping.

'Who were they?' asked the signora without curiosity.

'People wanting to look at the pictures, sent by signor Bonelli,' he answered, gratefully accepting another cup of coffee.

'So early,' she remarked without real interest. 'Soon, we have the baptism of the little Tino, don Gino's baby. I will wear the same dress as last time, and you, the same suit, but I doubt anyone will notice.'

Chapter Four

He heard the sound of the door close behind them and he knew that his wife and his children had left the flat, on their way to church. He lay in bed and he sighed. He had decided that he would not go to Mass with them, as they would all have to be in church later anyway for the baptism of Gino's child. He was not looking forward to that; he did not like the idea of Gino's child; it was not that he disliked the baby Tino, but rather he disliked the lie that the child was Gino's. He did not like Gino. He did not like Gino's ambitious wife. He feared what would happen. He did not like Gino's friendship with Renzo. But today, the day of the baptism, he would have to pretend that he did like, or at least did not mind, all these people.

Because Gino and Catarina had married in some haste, today, the day of the baptism, was a huge day, to make up for the lack of size with regard to their wedding at Easter. Everyone was going to be there. Even the boss, the birth of whose own child was supposed to be imminent, was coming back for the day. He counted the months since Easter. Only eight, surely? Not quite imminent, then. But in her last month of pregnancy, Anna Maria, now over forty-five, would want to be in Donnafugata or Palermo, near the familiar doctors and hospital, and she would want him with her. Was there something she knew? Did she want him not merely with her, but apart from his friends in Catania, apart from other women? He would of course be back and forth, he was bound to be, and he ought to come for the wedding next Sunday as well, the wedding of Alfio and Giuseppina. He could hardly miss this baptism, where he was the godfather, and he could hardly miss the wedding of his own former sister-in-law as well.

He heaved himself out of bed, put on his dressing gown, and hobbled to the kitchen. He had expected to find the place deserted, but there was their house guest, Corrado, sitting in the kitchen with a cup of coffee. He pulled his dressing gown tightly around him, feeling a bit exposed.

'Why aren't you in church with the others?' he asked. 'Sorry, that sounded a bit accusatory, and I am not really in a position to be so.'

'I went earlier,' explained Corrado. 'Fewer distractions. Would you like some coffee?'

He gratefully accepted a cup.

'How's Gino?' he asked. 'All ready for the big day?'

'If only,' said Corrado bitterly. 'He decided that as it was such a big day, such a major occasion, that he would take something to calm his nerves, as he put it. As a result - I was just with him - he is glassy eyed, and I am afraid people will notice. Well, that is not all that worries me. It is not good for him. He will kill himself like this. I am not sure which is worse, the pills that Tonino gets for him, or the cocaine that he takes with Renzo. Between them, he will be a dead man, and soon. And it is not just the physical effects. He is paranoid, I think. He said I was spying on him.'

'Are you? Spying on him? And for whom?'

'I wish I were. I would if it would help.'

'It used to be my job to try and instil some discipline into him, but that is no longer my job. I would have thought Alfio or the wife would be able to… but perhaps not. Gino…. Well, he is your brother, but this does not surprise me. He is like a child, greedy, eats pills as if they were sweets. No self-discipline. I wish I could say I am sorry for him, but I am not. I am sorry for you and your parents. It must be sad for you, and shaming. Maybe he should see a doctor, a proper doctor, not that man Doctor Moro.'

'That is what I suggested. But he won't. He does not want to confront it.'

'I don't blame him, really. Who does want to confront their true nature? Not me. Maybe you do. In which case, you are lucky. Looking in the mirror is not very enjoyable. It is not something I want to think about, the way Gino is destroying himself. You blame me, don't you? But truly, it is only Gino who can cure Gino. Let me tell you what to do. Go to Verona and forget about him. You have done everything you can do, and what more can be done?'

Corrado looked at him.

'You don't think people can change?' he asked.

'Perhaps they can, but they tend not to. Particularly not here. Or if they do, they change for the worse. But repentant sinners, the sort of people you come across in the Bible, you tend not to meet in real life. That is the way it is. Please don't look at me like that. I am being practical. Tell me this, Corrado, why is it every time I talk to you that you bring out the worst in me? I want to be charming and polite but you make me rude and aggressive.'

'Well, you are rude; you are aggressive,' said Corrado.

'I am not,' said Traiano, aggressively. 'You have done it again,' he said, sadly.

'There can be no friendship without truth,' said Corrado. 'You can't accept that I am right and you are wrong.'

'Well, that means I am condemned to have no friends,' said Traiano. 'Thanks for being so blunt.'

Corrado was silent, unable to say anything more.

'I must go,' he said at last, 'to see my parents. I said I would spend some time before the baptism with them. I will see you at the baptism?'

'Of course.'

They both rose. There was an awkward pause. Then they embraced, and a moment later Traiano heard him leave the flat, and the front door click shut. After a moment to gather his thoughts, he went to the window and opened it. Below in the square, he could see several small boys, all of whom turned to the window the moment they heard it open, as if they had been there, waiting for just such a moment. He gestured to one of the boys. A moment later the buzzer sounded, and the boy was in front of the door to the flat. He gave him his instructions and a ten euro note. He then went to brush his teeth and have a shower.

Ten minutes later, just as he was dressed, Alfio arrived, already in his smart suit, ready for the baptism, still some hours away. He gestured him to come to the open window, where they would not be overheard, in case anyone was listening. Alfio was attentive, and he got straight to the point:

'You know Anna Maria is about to have the baby. Well, she is, but not just yet, I think. Whichever way, the boss, our boss, still has time for other business. I mean Tonino. The magistrates came round to see him yesterday. They got nowhere at all. Tonino is loyal to the boss, and the boss loyal to Tonino. Tonino is a good boy, a clever boy, but this is a mess, potentially, do not doubt this for a moment. They placed him on that train. Potentially that can link us to the crime in Rome. And then there is this man Costacurta who is supposed to be watertight, but I wonder.'

'What could he possibly know?' asked Alfio.

'Whatever Tonino tells him. Whatever he observes. He is in the office now, and I am not so happy about that. On the recommendation of Tonino. Well, the boss allowed it.'

'Boss, the thing is, with Tonino and any friend of Tonino, we are on solid ground. Tonino's father is in Ucciardone, and he is alive and comfortable because of us,' said Alfio. 'We owe him a debt, and he owes us a debt too, and that way the ties are strong. As for Costacurta, what is he going to observe? In the office, everything is legal. Besides, I asked around as you asked me to. He has a mother and three sisters. He won't want to do anything to put them at risk. The family are more than just poor; the father ran off leaving them destitute, so they need this job that Tonino got for Roberto. It's all as it should be.'

'They are a respectable family?' he asked.

'Very. No one in jail, nothing like that. All the kids going to school, and the eldest, the boy, at university. Everyone speaks very highly of this Roberto; they say how good he is to his mother and sisters. They do not like the father, running off like that, abandoning the family, leaving the son to take his role. A bad father. As for the family, the main challenge is a sore lack of cash. When this Costacurta is a lawyer, he will work for us. Just like the others we are paying for. I believe we are paying for quite a few, aren't we? Roberto is nice and clean: educated, charming, ambitious, respectable, just the sort of friend Tonino needs to cover up all the deficiencies of Tonino himself.' He laughed. 'He is beautiful to look at as well,' added Alfio. 'Giuseppina was saying that Assunta was saying.....'

'Really?'

'Yes. All the women in the office like him. He makes himself agreeable.'

'That is nice for him, but how does it benefit you and me? - Not at all. I confess that much as I like Tonino, the best thing would have been to have put him on a boat and then dumped him overboard with a weight tied round his neck. But of course, now that the police have him on that train, we have no more choice about it. If anything happened to Tonino, it would look very suspicious. Besides, he will not talk. I suppose I am being paranoid. Calogero likes him. You know, Calogero listens to his mother more than he would have us believe. And signora di Rienzi is signora Grassi's friend. So, there it is.'

Alfio nodded.

'As for Gino, that is another problem. I have been speaking to Corrado. I can see for myself that the situation is not good. After speaking to Corrado, I can see that it is even worse than I previously thought. You are his friend. You are his wife's cousin. Have you spoken to him? Can you get him to see sense?'

'Boss, I have tried,' said Alfio. 'But I am not sure he is capable of listening to anyone at all. And don Renzo encourages him.'

'I despair,' said Traiano. 'Perhaps Gino is paranoid. Worried about the past. He is worried about the baptism as well, perhaps. But try and get him to be a little less paranoid, will you?'

'I can only try, boss,' said Alfio.

'Tonino is a problem, and we don't need more problems. We certainly do not need a Gino problem.'

'I can't control him, boss, you know I can't. If you can't, how can I? Is Gabriella coming, do you think? He invited her, and the brother too, not that he knows him well, but whether they will come or not....'

'They will be there. He and I are meeting, and she provides cover.'

Alfio nodded.

'Did you hear about the baptism on Sunday?' asked Assunta.

Roberto was taken aback by this question. It was now Thursday evening. She and he were alone in the office. She sat behind her desk, and he sat in front of it, with the laptop computer in front of him, reading out a summary of all the emails that accrued during the last few days. They were sent to this special account, that was not really special at all, but a sort of garbage dump. It was his job to comb the garbage to make sure nothing had been missed. He read out who had written in, what their name was, and who, if anyone, they referenced as a friend or relation. As he worked through the list, Assunta was attentive, dismissing name after name with a wave of the hand. There were a few that gave her pause: people wanting rent reductions, or protesting very gently against rent increases; people she knew, or her brother knew, people who were related to someone she knew; people who had someone in jail, people who were working for the family, or had worked for the family. Roberto's instructions were clear: polite refusal to those whom she dismissed by the wave of her hand, and a quarter or a half of what they wanted for some, and all of what they wanted for one or two. Her memory was encyclopaedic, and she knew who deserved favours and who did not, who needed to be rewarded and who did not; and, above all, she knew that the currency of favours had to be used sparingly, lest it be debased.

'The baptism, on Sunday?' he asked, sensing their work was done for the evening, the list complete. 'I heard it was very nice, very grand. They must have spent a fortune. Not that I was invited.'

He enjoyed these opportunities to gossip about the people of the quarter.

She pushed the packet of cigarettes towards him after lighting one for herself. He gratefully accepted.

'They have both got a great deal to prove, those two. He is from Agrigento, he is stupid and ugly, well, I think he is ugly. A big muscular man turning to fat. Ever since he got out of Bicocca, it is as if he was trying to cram in as much pleasure as he could. Now he wants to show how rich he is. And he wants to show off his son who, if rumour is to be believed, is not his son. And she, well, she is ambitious. You should see how she looks at her husband! As if she really regrets marrying him, which, because she is sensible, she must. And they have not been married very long. He tries to impress the quarter, but the person he needs to impress, and fails to impress, is her. She is a good-looking girl, but I noticed how she looked at my brother! My goodness! And he was there just to be godfather, then get back – and I know why too – but I saw the way he noticed that she was looking at him. I am surprised he did not take her round the back and screw her in between the dustbins. She would have been delighted, the trollop! But perhaps he is not that stupid. Though he is stupid enough to be flattered by her admiration. As it was, he had to leave early.'

'Why? Was he in a hurry to get back?'

'He didn't tell me, but I guessed. She - Anna Maria - does not trust him out of her sight for too long. After all, he strayed when he was married to Stefania, and now he is married to the woman with whom he strayed, well, she knows the dangers. And she is twenty years older than Stefania. But there was another reason. Tonino. He was interviewed by the magistrates, as were you. What on earth can they be investigating, I wonder? While that is live, he wants to be far away, so no one associates him with anything to do with that. The murder, my dear, of that woman and her child.'

She looked at him. He shrugged.

'But now that the magistrates have drawn a blank, a complete blank, he does not have to be so cautious,' she continued.

'They have?' he asked innocently.

'Oh yes, I have heard the whole story. He was with you the whole time he was in Rome, and you spent the night in via Turno with two girls you picked up in some bar. At least you have the grace to blush. Via Turno, a nice touch. I always liked the *Aeneid* of Virgil. Are the other streets around there named after other characters in the poem?'

'They are. Via Turno, via Evandro even. They are not nice streets, though they have poetic names. I like that.'

'Well,' said Assunta with decision, 'Invoke all the poetry you like, but you do not fool me.' She smiled brightly. 'I know.'

'I didn't go anywhere near Casal Bruciato,' said Roberto.

'I know that. But someone else did. And everyone knows. Even you.' She sighed. 'In ten years' time, Tonino will be all grown up and very important, you watch. Quite a few will not like that. Don Traiano for example. Don Alfio. As for don Gino, there will be no need to worry about him, the way he is going. In ten years' time, he will be either dead or in a madhouse.' She sighed once more. 'You should have seen him on Sunday. And the same goes for his friend don Renzo, my future brother-in-law. My poor sister. Well, she must know what she is letting herself in for. A lot of money, true, but a lot of trouble as well. Finding a nice dependable husband is not so easy. I managed, but I was lucky, I now see. Have you heard from your father since you went to Rome?' she asked, changing the subject.

'No,' said Roberto shortly. 'I don't expect to. I am not going to phone him or message him, and he is not going to do so either, I feel. We had some harsh words. Or more accurately, he had some harsh words about me, about my mother, and even about my sisters. As you say, finding a good man to marry is hard. I feel most sorry for my mother. I can do without him, but she never expected she would have to do so. Even though he has been bad, I fear she would prefer a bad husband to no husband at all.'

'Some bad men are attractive,' she reflected. 'My own father was not ideal, always away, but my goodness, my mother adores his memory. Tonino's father has been away for so long, but the signora Grassi speaks highly of him and always has. He will be back soon,' she said. 'He will be up for parole, and my brother's lawyers will be very helpful, you see. And as soon as he is back, he and the signora will present Tonino with a little brother or sister. Don't look surprised. Signora Grassi can't be more than forty. It can be done. Look at Anna Maria. I wonder how your friend Tonino will like that? You will never guess. My little niece, Isabella, spent her whole time after the baptism talking about Tonino this, Tonino that. She is only ten but, my goodness, what taste the child has, already! Of course, my brother likes Tonino in so far as he likes anyone, which is to say that he does not like him at all. But he wants his daughters to meet the right sort of people, eventually, not the sort of people you meet round here. The sort of people Anna Maria knows. Now, tell me all you know about Gabriella.'

'I have not met her, signora, but I have heard people talk about her.'

Assunta cackled with laughter.

'Men! They cannot talk about anything else! The world is divided into two unequal portions. Those who seek love and those who seek power. Well, there is another group: those who are haunted by demons. But the rest of us….. My brother and my sister seek to be important. So do they all, even your Tonino. But people like myself and signora Grassi are content to love others and leave it at that. If you want someone to love, Gabriella would be ideal for you. And if you want to get on in life, the same would be true. So…'

'She is at least five years older than me, signora.'

'A problem for you, or for her?'

Assunta lit another cigarette and once more pushed to packet towards him.

'My mother mentioned you the other day. I was surprised she even knew who you were, but she does not miss much, I suppose. 'That nice boy from via Plebiscito' was how she referred to you. And she likes Tonino. She tries not to show it, but she does. I think it is because she is friendly with signora Grassi. She is like Calogero: she does not like anyone officially, but every now and then the mask slips and she admits to some human affections. Calogero.... He is a cold man in most ways. I think Stefania found that, and that Anna Maria will find out in due course. He married her out of ambition, not love. Just like Elena is marrying Renzo.... Well, I married for love, and talking of which, he will wonder why I am so late home. I sent him home hours ago to cook, and he will have something nice for me when I get there. Always nice, the smell of a good meal when you open the door.'

She drew on her cigarette.

Roberto smiled. His mother and sisters would be waiting for him when he got home, he knew, and they were used to the idea of him working late. But before he went home to the via Plebiscito, he would visit the gym, in case Tonino wanted to see him.

He entered the gym rather later than usual, and found the place not as crowded as it usually was. Tonino was there, evidently waiting for him, though concerned, he could see, that no one should notice this. He was selling something from the backpack and he raised his eyes briefly as Roberto came in, and looked away without the slightest flicker of recognition. Roberto continued as if nothing had happened and a moment later, as he was standing at his open locker, he sensed Tonino next to him, handing him a roll of banknotes. Not a word was exchanged, and a few minutes later, he was leaving the gym, having made the desired pickup.

He walked back home towards the via Plebiscito, and he was dawdling in the University square when he realised that Tonino had followed him and caught up with him.

'I was thinking,' he said, 'that you should use some of that money – don't worry, you can repay it all in time – to buy yourself a suit in the via Etnea. The shops are still open.'

'Now?' said Roberto, thinking of his mother and sisters at home. 'And why do I need a suit?'

'You need more than one. To impress the signora, that would be one reason. And for the wedding.'

'What wedding?'

'This Sunday. You are invited, along with the whole of the signora's office. Didn't they tell you? Don Alfio, remember, is marrying Giuseppina.'

'I hardly know them. If I were not to turn up, no one would notice. Besides….'

'You are going,' said Tonino. 'So, you need a suit. But you can get that tomorrow. But don't leave it too late. Right now, I thought you could invite me to meet your mother and your sisters.'

Roberto shrugged, as if to indicate he did not understand things at all. Mostly Tonino ignored him. Now he wanted to meet his mother and his sisters. It was inexplicable. They walked towards the fish market, then past the Ursine Castle, until they came to the ordinary street where Roberto lived with his mother and sisters: the buildings were run down, the rubbish overflowed, and the cars were parked in a haphazard manner. The rubbish stank, even if summer was over, and so did the drains.

One understood something as soon as one entered, Tonino thought: one saw and one smelled the poverty and the lack of hope that suffused the building. It was the usual sort of building; the staircase and the communal areas showing a degree of neglect that was common; that was normal. Behind the front door, the flat was revealed as grim, shabby, dark and cramped. No wonder the father had fled abroad, he thought, sensing the disloyalty to his friend that this thought contained, and to his mother, who greeted him kindly and said almost at once that she was so pleased to meet him and that she owed him a debt of gratitude for finding Roberto a job. She said this with genuine feeling, and she said it as soon as she could, because she knew she had to, she knew it was expected, and the sooner she said it the better.

'I am always happy to help my friends, signora,' said Tonino to signora Costacurta, while Roberto stood by, embarrassed. 'Anyway, it was not really me, it was don Calogero di Rienzi.'

'I am always happy to meet friends of my son,' she said gravely, looking at her son with a mixture of pride and sadness. 'He is a good hardworking boy.'

'Mama….' remonstrated her son, full of embarrassment.

'My mother says the same about me, signora,' said Tonino with a smile. 'And I have learned to put up with it. She is always boasting about me to the neighbours, as I am her only child and all she has to boast about. But I am just a waiter in a trattoria, whereas Roberto will one day be a lawyer.'

'God willing. He is a clever boy. But come in, come in, we are about to eat.'

Supper was being served in the tiny kitchen that could barely hold the six of them. Another place was swiftly laid and they all sat down. The girls, all three of them, were still at school, the eldest seventeen years old. Her name was Luisa, and he looked at her with appreciation. As for him, the stranger in their midst, he felt all three girls look at him and weigh him up. He had told Roberto to tell them he was a bit older than he really was, and he could imagine what they were looking at: a well-built youngster, a bit on the short side, with a pronounced jaw and short bristling hair. Not good-looking in the conventional sense, but he exuded, he hoped, the power and authority of someone much older than his years. They liked him, he sensed. He was smartly dressed, his clothes looked new (they *were* new) and he had a smart back pack. His arm muscles, the girls could surely could tell, were well developed, as were his thighs. Yes, they liked him. He could tell from the way they looked at him. And he could sense at the same time that Roberto had noticed this too.

The food was better than he had expected: the usual minestrone, followed by a variety of hams and cheeses, with plentiful bread. The flat was certainly not large, and the street outside, just off the via Plebiscito, was noisy and dirty, and some of that noise penetrated the kitchen. It was not a nice flat, and he noticed that there was mould on the walls, and that there were all sorts of odd hanging wires to do with the lighting and the water heater, as there had been in the place he had lived in before he and his mother had moved. If Roberto, who hardly spoke, was ashamed of the family home, he did not blame him.

The signora, pleased to meet the youngster she now instinctively categorised as her son's friend, was, like most mothers, hungry for information, the sort of information with which perhaps her own son was not very forthcoming. Noting the way that Tonino interacted with her three daughters, she thought that he did not have a young lady, not yet, or not at present, but was looking for one, and where better to look than here, where Luisa surely commanded attention, as did her two younger sisters, Cosima and Petra? She had noted the way he had heard these unusual names, as if storing them for future use. As for her own son, there had been young ladies in the past, and they had all been most unsuitable, and signora Costacurta assumed that her son had struck up this friendship in the Purgatory quarter, so far from their own, with some romantic sideline in mind. Expressing, once more, her pleasure that Roberto had become friends with Tonino, she asked, not directly, but unmistakeably, about who else he had met. Tonino was generous with details. Roberto was working for Assunta di Rienzi, the sister of don Calogero, and he was going to come to the wedding of don Calogero's former sister-in-law on the Sunday. The signora was wide eyed at this piece of news; even her daughters were interested.

'What sort of person is don Calogero?' she asked.

Of course, she had heard of him; he was a celebrity; she had seen him on television; she had heard the stories, such as the tragic loss of his wife and the sad loss of his brother; and she knew about the man they called the Chemist of Catania. But the man himself, what was he really like, she wondered?

Tonino considered.

'He is very nice,' he said at last. 'I mean, I know him well, because I have known him all my life, and my mother is a friend of his mother. He's much older than me, but he is still not thirty, and he has always been very kind to me, as well as to my mother. In fact, to be honest, it was because of him we were able to live, ever since my father went away. He made sure we did not starve. Because my father has been away, don Calogero has been like a father to me. He got me a job, for example. And he gives me good advice. You know, how to behave properly. His own behaviour is impeccable, really impeccable. He does not like swearing; he does not like smoking - he really does not like smoking; he hates drugs, and he disapproves of people who drink too much. If you break any of those rules, he can be quite strict. He is perhaps a little reserved, because he has had so much tragedy. His first wife was very beautiful, so it was terrible when she died. His second wife is an older lady and rather different from us, but don Calogero, though he moves in that world easily, will always be one of us. He is immaculately turned out, very smartly dressed, and he is, as you have probably seen for yourself, the most handsome man in Catania. His suits, his shirts, his shoes, they are all perfect. He does not like beards.'

'Roberto, you must get rid of your beard at once!' cried his mother in real distress.

'Oh, mama,' said Roberto, agonised and embarrassed.

His sisters laughed.

'Well,' said the signora, 'I am really glad that, thanks to you, dear Tonino, my son has got a bit of the recognition he deserves.'

Tonino nodded. Roberto sighed crossly. It was almost time for the news, and he went and switched on the television. It was his prerogative to control the television, something he had inherited when his father had disappeared. Tonino recognised the action for what it was: the assertion of control, the reminder that he was man of the house now. It wasn't rude to cut the conversation short like this; it reflected rather that Tonino was here not as an honoured guest, but as one of the family, and this is what the family did. They sat at the table and watched the television news on RAI One.

The news hardly ever changed. It reminded one, thought Tonino, that the world was fixed on its trajectory and would never get better. It was pointless waiting for change, hoping for amelioration. The signora shared these feelings, for she sighed and looked sad at this nightly chronicle of Italian decline. The parliament had rejected the budget and it looked as if very soon the Prime Minster, Silvio Berlusconi, would resign. The signora liked him. Roberto liked him too, and muttered imprecations at those who were making like difficult for him as they appeared on the screen. After the political news, there was news of all the crimes, and the family was impassive. Then there was the sport, which was the bit that Roberto had been waiting for with great patience. After that there was Sicilian news, mainly road accidents and homicides, and something about the election in Catania, with a very brief clip of Fabio Volta. It was all, Tonino thought, very boring.

After the news was over, the girls cleared away the plates and began to wash them, and signora Costacurta once more turned her attention to Tonino. She asked what he did for don Calogero. He explained that he was a waiter in the trattoria, and that soon don Calogero was sending him on a course so he could learn about wine. The signora felt a little sad at this: they had only had water with their supper. Tonino averred that Sicilian wine was undervalued and that don Calogero exported it to America and needed people who would know what to buy. The signora agreed with this. Whenever she saw wine in a shop, she had no idea what was what. But he could sense, as he listened to the signora, that her son was impatient at this conversation, and he asked her if she would allow him to take the three girls out to the via Etnea for an ice-cream.

This innocent suggestion seemed, in the circumstances, almost daring. He had only just met them, and why should he pay them any attention at all? But he was paying them attention, or was this simply a matter of politeness to their mother, or a compliment to their brother? Luisa was pleased, so was Cosima, so was Petra. And was he really paying attention to them all, or was he paying attention to one in particular, and just asking the others along out of politeness? And if so, which one? The girls looked at their mother, and the mother looked at their brother, and seeing he consented, she said they might, but that they should not be back late.

Chapter Five

The wedding of Giuseppina, sister of the late Stefania, aunt of the boss's first three children, and don Alfio Camilleri, was a most magnificent occasion. The Mass was celebrated by don Giorgio at the Church of the Holy Souls in Purgatory, which was all very nice, though sparsely attended; signora Grassi was there, and Tonino, and Roberto, so was the boss himself, and don Traiano and his wife and children; so too was don Renzo, and his girlfriend Elena, who were the next couple to be married, and so was don Gino Fisichella who was acting as the best man. His wife too was present. Don Calogero's wife, soon to give birth, and don Traiano's mother, in a similar situation, were both absent.

Tonino had always found the practice of religion rather alien, even though he had been surrounded by it all his life. He did not understand this desire some people had to go to church. He was not sure that God existed. Perhaps He did. But even so, why go to church? It was such a funny way of passing the time. Don Calogero did not believe in God, or so he had heard, yet went to church all the time, being a member of the Confraternity that paid signora Grassi's pension. He and Roberto never really talked much except about the most banal things; sometimes they discussed football, for Roberto was a very strong supporter of the Roma team, unusually for a Sicilian, whereas Tonino obviously favoured the Elephants, the Catania team; but they talked about such banalities without ever touching on more important things. There were more important things, Tonino knew, and Roberto knew, Tonino supposed, but these were things that could not be mentioned, and could not be mentioned even to oneself in one's innermost private thoughts.

When Roberto had said he would come to the Mass, Tonino had been taken aback. He himself was only going to please his mother, who liked these sorts of things. He supposed it would be a good opportunity to introduce Roberto to his mother. But it struck him as odd that Roberto should want to go, and he would have liked to have discussed it with him, though he did not know how.

Sitting in church, feeling the terrible boredom creep over you, after you had looked at all the things there were to look at, the gold, the marble, the Spanish Madonna in her elaborate frame above the high altar, the candles that burned in front of the picture of Saint Rita of Cascia, to whom his mother was particularly devoted, when you had taken in all these things, you were left with your own thoughts, and driven to reflect. He burned with ambition, the constant flame of which had consumed him from within from his very earliest years, from the first moments that he had become conscious of himself as a person. This ambition was fuelled by a very simple emotion; that of shame, compounded with the envy of what others had and he did not. He wanted to get ahead, to get not just ahead, but to the very top, to wipe out the knowledge that his father was a failed criminal, that his mother, whom he loved obsessively, was a woman held in little regard despite her many virtues. He wanted to be respected and feared, and he wanted people to look up to him as they did to don Calogero and to don Traiano, don Gino and don Alfio. These men, whose backgrounds were similar to his own, seemed to be men who enjoyed limitless success and prestige. That was what he wanted for himself. And the way to have that was to have money, and you got money because people feared you and because they knew you could be cruel in your dealings with them.

He knew he had already proved himself, and longed to prove himself more. He had no remorse about the killing of the woman Beata and her son Paolo. Why should he? What were they to him? They were simply a job, a test, something he had passed. He had proved himself. He had proved himself in front of Muniddu, too. He had no soft feelings. And yet he knew this was not true. He loved his mother, and resented the fact that she had until recently been slighted by all the other women, knowingly or not. He wanted her to be comfortable. The idea of his father coming back and his parents having another child did not immediately please him. But this was allowed, he knew: to have soft feelings for one's own mother; that was normal; that was admired. Everyone knew that a Sicilian boy should look after his mother, especially when his father was away. Even don Calogero was good to his mother, difficult as she was reputed to be. Even don Traiano was respectful to his mother, impossible and wilful as she was supposed to be. His own mother worshipped him, so he had no difficulty in worshipping her in return. Of his father, he knew nothing at all at first hand, though he knew that the day of meeting him could not be put off forever, and this was something he dreaded.

But he knew, or he feared, that soft feelings could derail ambition or make one weak. He had felt nothing, nothing at all for Lydia or any of the other girls he had had anything to do with. As for Roberto's sisters, they were nice girls, and that was important. He needed to find a nice girl, one who would add to his respectability; he needed eventually to marry a nice girl, just as don Traiano had done, and have lots of nice sweet children. That was the way forward, to be a respectable married man. He was of the opinion that men who posed as Casanovas, like don Renzo and don Gino, were fools. And their foolishness was across the board: girls, pills, cocaine, drink. That sort of indiscipline could not end well. He despised them, and one day would overtake them. Of that, he was sure. As for don Alfio, he could not tell; and as for don Traiano, he feared him, because in him he recognised the same steely discipline and ambition that he felt in himself.

And then there was Roberto. He liked Roberto and was sure most of the time that Roberto liked him in return. The trouble was that he was not used to liking people, he was used to seeing them as rivals, possible threats, or underlings to be kept in check. It was his job in the quarter, among other things, to dole out threats and punishments, and to maintain discipline. He was not allowed to use the belt, but he was allowed to use his hands to slap, smack and punch whoever did not do what they were told. Most of those he punished were younger than himself, but quite a few were the same age or older, and he knew, because he could hurt them and because he had hurt them in the past, that they feared and respected him and wanted to win his favour. No one minded these punishments any more than he minded receiving the belt himself, which he had on numerous occasions. This was because the one who punished was also the one who dispensed favours. He himself was the one who gave out the ten euro notes for each corner of a destroyed election poster for example, and woe betide someone who attempted to cheat on that. He was the one who dispensed the pills and other stuff which many of them sold on. And he was the one who organised bigger jobs like the hijacking of buses and the burning of cars. These sorts of transactional relationships he was used to. But Roberto was the nearest thing to a friend, and that was different.

Friendship was dangerous. He treated Roberto with a calm indifference, almost with contempt, as if he were a person he was used to, someone who was always there, someone he hardly noticed. But he did this, not to be unkind to Roberto, but to convince himself that Roberto was no one special to him, no more special than anyone else. But he knew this was not true, and that Roberto could derail everything.

He was looking at Roberto right now, who was sitting on the opposite side of the church, his eyes fixed on don Giorgio, presumably listening to whatever don Giorgio was saying. Perhaps he understood religion in a way that Tonino simply could not. His hair was neatly brushed, his suit looked good, and his beard was sleek, he thought. Of course, Roberto was intelligent, a university student, not someone like himself. Tonino could read, it was true, though he had never actually read a book from cover to cover, despite what he had said to don Calogero, but he could read things like road signs and newspaper articles and things in magazines. That was quite an achievement for someone who had never really been to school. But it was nothing to what Roberto had achieved: university, books, a profession to come. Of course, his family was poor, dirt poor in the same way as he and his mother would have been without the help of don Calogero. But they were a different sort of family, as they had a different approach, and had poured all their meagre resources into the education of the children. This, as far as Tonino could see, was misguided. You could become educated and still not progress if you did not have the right friends. You could become educated, and when your father abandoned the family, find yourself marooned, unable to finish your education. Well, he had saved Roberto from that. He had got him the job with the signora, Assunta, in her office, where he would be useful to her and make some much-needed cash. And where he would also be useful to Tonino.

He was attached to Roberto and had been so since first meeting him, but he was also determined to use him, and to keep him at a certain distance. They needed each other. Roberto needed the sponsorship, whilst he needed the respectability. They both needed to get on and could help each other, be allies. It would be mutually beneficial unless something went wrong, but that was the condition of everything: unless something went wrong.

It was gratifying to see how other people liked Roberto; people like the signora, Assunta di Rienzi, who was an important person. She had really taken to him, if Roberto's conversation was any indication. This was good. It was nice to know that people found him agreeable. His mother, too, who had met him when he had come round to the gallery, so they could set off to the wedding together, had commented on how nice he was and how pleased she was that her son had such a nice friend.

After coffee with his mother at the kitchen table, and while she fussed with final arrangements for departure, he had detached Roberto for a moment and primed him about what to expect at the wedding. The Mass would be boring, but people would be looking at him, and he should sit separately from Tonino and his mother. The party afterwards would be very nice, and the food and drink plentiful, but he should not overdrink or overeat, as that created a bad impression. There would, he was sure, when the evening dragged on into the early hours, be lots of drinking. And there would be girls galore, most of whom would be keen to end up in bed with the right boy, and every boy there would be desperate to end up in bed with a girl. But one had to be careful. One must not look too desperate, and any conquest one made must be worth having. Most of the girls were trash, but there were one or two who were not, though the few worth having were the least likely to allow themselves to be had. But people would be watching, and it was important to remember that; one's reputation would be enhanced or diminished according to what people observed. Not finding the right girl would not be good, but not finding anyone at all might be even worse. They would look out for each other. Moreover, he had been to the hotel and hired a room for the night for sitting out and for other activities.

Part of his great plan for self-advancement involved getting married, and getting married young to a nice girl who would be a virgin on her wedding night. He had met Roberto's sisters and thought that the youngest of them, Petra, would be perfect for him. But there was a long way to go before then. He had told himself on numerous occasions, but told no one else, he would marry the eldest daughter of don Calogero, Isabella, who was surely the greatest prize; but she was still far too young, though he could not help thinking that perhaps in ten years' time he would be well positioned to marry her, and she him. Then he would be made. But in the meantime, he had to safeguard his reputation, establish himself as a proper man, but not someone who was promiscuous. He needed to find the right girl at the wedding and sleep with her, just to make his mark. So too did Roberto, as he had made clear to him. These things mattered.

He thought about Isabella di Rienzi and her sister Natalia. They were still little girls, but Isabella would not be so for much longer, and she was alert to the boys around her, he could tell; and her sister too was alert to the fact that her sister was alert. But Isabella was the ultimate prize. She might look at him, but would her father ever allow it? The boss had always been kind to Tonino (he overlooked the fact that he enjoyed beating him) but one assumed that the boss wanted someone important for his daughters, especially now, as they were under the influence of their rich stepmother. The rumour that he had heard was that his eldest daughter was destined for the youngest son of don Antonio Santucci, to cement the alliance further between the families. But that alliance, if it ever came about, was years away.

He turned his mind from future marriages to the marriage in front of him. The current alliance was right now taking place. Don Alfio marrying Giuseppina, the boss's former sister-in-law, the aunt of the boss's children, this was the matter in hand. Watching them take their vows, Tonino wondered at it. He had known don Alfio all his life. Don Alfio's background was similar to his, a father in jail, and don Alfio had done time in Bicocca as a teenager. Don Alfio had a bad smell about him, and yet he was marrying the boss's former sister-in-law, and his children, if he had any, would be the first cousins of the boss's children. If he had any.... One heard all the rumours. And one heard all the rumours because one listened out for them, because one wanted to know, because such knowledge was power. That was why silence, even among themselves, was a cardinal rule. But he had heard people talking. They thought he did not have ears, but he did. He had heard don Renzo talk, boast even, of the girls he had banged up, and had heard don Gino admit that it had never happened to him before he had got together with Catarina. He had heard don Alfio talk of the mumps epidemic at Bicocca where he and don Gino had shared a cell. He had asked his mother about this, and from the way she had told him, he had realised that the women of the quarter knew all about it. Don Alfio was infertile; don Gino was infertile too; his child was not his child. What had Catarina done, and what would she do, if her husband ever found out, as he surely must? She was now in church, looking like a proper wife, but the pretence could not last forever.

The party, as expected, was magnificent; held in a huge hotel, the same hotel where the boss had married his first wife, and where the current bride had been a bridesmaid all those years before. The buffet groaned with food, there was endless drink, and there was a band. It was just as a wedding should be; don Alfio was rich, after all, and needed to show people how rich he was, and he also needed to underline his new status as don Alfio, a boss, not an underboss anymore; his wife, a kind, reasonable and nice person, needed to lay to rest the one less than attractive part of her character, the fact that she had always been in her late sister's shade, and so she had to have a wedding that outdid the one where she had been bridesmaid. Moreover, there was the wedding in Palermo, in a few months' time, to think about, and one had to set a high bar for them. Nothing could be skimped; no corners could be cut. It was this part of the wedding that Tonino's mother liked so much; the observation of the food, the drinks, the dresses, the bridesmaids' outfits, the bridal gown, the shoes, the flowers - all the things that bored Tonino no end. For his part there were better things to look at: the girls, the boys, to see who was getting friendly with whom, to see who disappeared from the festivities and came back looking guilty or flushed, or both. All the boys from the pizzeria were there, and all the boys from the trattoria, and all the employees from the building site that was the Furnaces (all the ones from Catania, of course, not the immigrants); the private army, but not the foreign legion. With them had come their sisters and their girlfriends, girls attached and girls not attached. The older men flocked around don Alfio, the groom, and don Gino the best man, for these were the providers of jobs; and don Traiano too, the dispenser of patronage, and don Calogero, the sun around whom everything orbited, and who was here without his wife. But the younger ones and some of the older ones had time for Tonino too, because they had been recruited by him to tear down election posters by night, or to set fire to cars, or to hijack buses. Tonino felt important, and he was important, after all; they all knew about him, they knew of what he was capable. His importance was at this moment underlined by the fact that don Calogero himself was talking to him alone.

'The election campaign,' he was saying. 'It is going well. In a couple of weeks, we need to have a few buses hijacked in the suburbs, to put the fear of God into people and to make sure that Volta has something to talk about, and a stick with which to beat our current politicians. So, start next week in the suburbs. One a week. Different places, and come in bit by bit to the city centre. Create the impression that Catania is ungovernable.'

'Understood, boss,' said Tonino.

'As to where to make a disturbance, I think you know what to do,' said Calogero agreeably.

He did. When one planned a disturbance, one consulted one's friends in the police first, and one chose an area not covered that night. The police, after all, could not be everywhere. And he knew how to get in touch with the police, he knew who could deliver and receive messages to and from Colonel Andreazza.

'Your friend is enjoying himself,' added don Calogero, with a glance towards the friend he meant.

There was Roberto talking to Gabriella. Of course, Tonino knew Gabriella, as she often came to the gallery with her brother, and he had introduced her to Roberto only a moment ago.

'Well, let them enjoy themselves,' said Calogero. 'And you too, you enjoy yourself,' he added.

The boss had seen someone who made him frown. It was Catarina. Shortly afterwards, they found themselves together in the melée of people and spoke in low voices to each other as they looked, not at each other, but at the people around them.

'They say you are clever,' he remarked, 'though I don't see it particularly. You have my little nephew and I hope you are looking after him. And maybe you have fooled your husband, who is not the brightest of men, we all know, but you will not fool him forever. And then what will happen? Who will protect you then? You are brave, I give you that. I would not like to see Gino angry.'

'If he finds out....'

'When he finds out,' he corrected her.

'When he finds out, there are people I can rely on. There is you, for a start. You would not like your little nephew to be left motherless.'

'Is that your only bargaining chip, or do you have others?' he asked. 'I imagine you have others. You have annoyed me, but as you have the child, yes, I agree, I will not do anything to hurt the child, and as the child grows up, I may feel it my duty to help him. A tribute to my late brother, if nothing else. But I see no reason to help you, my dear. The child, yes, but you, never. You hurt my poor brother, I imagine.'

'And you did not?' she asked.

'Do you honestly think,' he asked calmly, 'that I would consider, even for a moment, what you have in mind?'

'What I have in mind? You mean what you have in mind, because it has clearly entered your head. But why not? I think you would like to enjoy what your brother enjoyed. You were always so jealous of him, weren't you? He was so nice, people liked him, they even loved him, but you they only fear. He had me, and I gave myself willingly, and that must annoy you, because I represent what you do not have and may never have. Besides, from my own point of view, I would like to have another child one day, and I have always found you very attractive, because, I suppose, you are so dangerous.'

'If I am dangerous, you should watch out for yourself,' he said. 'But I am not dangerous at all to you, because if I were, you would not dare speak to me like this. But leave aside whether I am dangerous or not. The real question is whether I am a total fool. All the men you have been with, my dear - and please do not frown like that, it makes you less than pretty - all the men you have been with have had poor judgement; they followed their passions; they lost their heads, and it did them harm; it would have been better if none of them had ever met you. But I made choices, deliberate choices. I weighed things up, and I saw advantages to myself. That is why I chose Stefania, who was, all things considered, an excellent wife; that is why I chose Anna Maria, whose advantages are obvious. It is true they chose me, but I chose them too. I was in control. No one controls me.'

'Did you choose Anna the Romanian prostitute?' she asked.

Now it was his turn to frown.

'I was a child at the time. It didn't count.'

'Oh, but it did,' she said. 'The fact you so furiously deny it counting is proof that it did. It is a terrible reminder to you of what you were and still are. Oh yes, I know, you are so terribly important now, but it was not always so, was it? You need me, as your nephew's mother, and you may need me later when you are bored with Anna Maria, and when you realise, indeed as you must already, that you cannot have any more children with her. I will be waiting for you.'

'He will kill you,' he said to Catarina, meaning her husband.

'Unless someone kills him first. Or he might die of natural causes. But I am sure you will agree it is a risk worth taking. I do. There's no advancement without risk, you know that. Besides, he is stupid.'

'Of course, he is stupid,' he said. 'But even stupid people sometimes get the right end of the stick. When everyone will know, and he is the only person not to know, what then?'

'You underestimate the power of the ego. Don't you realise there are things that people never dare mention to you, but which they all talk about? It is the same with Gino. They are all talking about it, but when he comes into the room, they would not dare mention it in his presence. There's no real reason why anyone ever should. It is a secret, though a very public one. Anyway, you are sending my dear husband to Palermo to be with don Renzo. Then I shall see more of you, perhaps.'

'Never,' he said.

'You say it so fiercely it is as if you are trying to convince yourself.'

'Never means never,' he said.

He left her.

Tonino spotted Roberto sitting with Assunta, her husband, and several of the employees from the office. Roberto was rather flushed, partly because of the heat of the room, it seemed to Tonino, and partly because he was drinking a beer (he had not known him drink much before now) and partly because he was surrounded by adoring females, amongst which he counted Assunta, as well as the various girls from the office. As Tonino approached, he looked up and caught his eye with almost a look of apology. Assunta saw him look up, and seeing Tonino, called him over, making room for him on the sofa. He found himself squashed between Federico and Assunta, neither of whom were slim.

'If you have nothing good to say about anyone, come and sit down here next to me,' said Assunta with a laugh.

Her husband chuckled. They had all been drinking. It was a wedding after all.

He had never really spoken much to the signora before now, and was slightly overwhelmed by her friendliness. He saw quickly that it was Roberto who had enchanted her. His red cheeks, his disarranged hair, the way the top button of his shirt was undone and the way his tie hung down, all this gave Roberto, a perfectly normal if good-looking and athletic youngster, the look of a god, a young Bacchus. He felt something stir within him, and he knew it was the thrill of ambition on the cusp of fulfilment. The signora was important, he knew, and if she liked Roberto, that would help him. It was a step in the right direction, he felt. It gave him the same feeling he had had when he had killed the woman Beata and her son Paolo. These moments were risky, but there was no progress without risk.

'How is the art business?' Assunta was asking.

'I know nothing about it, signora,' he replied, with a trace of embarrassment, not that Assunta could know about it either. 'That is all the responsibility of signor Bonelli. Maybe Roberto knows more as he was talking to his sister.'

'We were talking about her garden projects,' said Roberto. 'The things she has planted at the Furnaces. But she did mention the gallery too. She said I should go and look at it soon.'

'She likes him, you see,' said Assunta in triumph, as if this had been generally contradicted, which it hadn't. 'What do you all think of that?'

'She is very nice and very interesting, but she is a bit older than me, signora,' said Roberto.

'Well, you should not let that stop you,' said Assunta. 'Be ambitious.' She turned to Tonino. 'As for the art business, you will soon know all about it, or at least more about it than you do now. Oh, they haven't told you? You are going to Rome. My brother tells me nothing, but occasionally he lets something out. You are going to Rome to buy some paintings, or so I hear. You and signor Bonelli, and our friend don Traiano.' Her voice was lightly ironic as she mentioned that name. 'That is the plan, anyway. Bonelli will fly, naturally enough, but you two boys will go by road. It was my brother's idea. He thinks you are useful, and I am sure he is right. He is nervous about his wife giving birth, but he still makes all these minor decisions. My sister and my mother are looking after the children, the two girls, and Renato and Sebastiano. It seems that Giuseppina was making herself useful by taking the girls to school and bringing them back. Every weekend after the birth, they will go to Palermo. Either my brother will drive them, or they will all go by train. He needs to get a nanny, someone he can trust, but my mother does not like that idea. She prefers to keep an eye on things herself.'

She was drunk, or at least drunker than she had ever been, and certainly garrulous.

'I sometimes go to Palermo, but I usually go on my bike, though I sometimes take the train as well,' said Tonino.

'Maybe you could escort them. Though the train is so slow. They like you, don't they?' she asked. 'I might suggest it. It is just the girls, as the two boys will be there all the time. But the girls have to go back and forth to school.'

'But of course they like me, signora. My mother is a friend of your mother, and my father was friend of your late father, so naturally they have known me all their lives.'

'Good,' she said with a laugh. 'You can keep an eye out for ambitious strangers.'

'She does not like ambitious strangers,' said Federico, with a chuckle. 'That is not a situation I would like to be in.'

Federico and his wife were both sufficiently drunk to find this very amusing, and so was the rest of the company; but Tonino had not been drinking at all, and he could feel the tension in the scene: the way the new favourite, Roberto, attracted attention, and the way the girls were behaving. They were drunk, or at least drunk enough to look at him without embarrassment, and Roberto returned their stares. But it was still early. Tonino's mother was there somewhere, enjoying herself, and Tonino knew that the real fun would only start when people like his mother went home. He would take her home, obviously, when she wanted, and then come back; by that time all the children would have left and all the respectable girls as well.

'Your father is coming back,' Federico now said. 'Do you know when?'

'I don't, sir. But don Calogero says his lawyers are looking into it. It has been a long time, but I have no idea when he will come back exactly, but it must be within a year or two at most.'

'Your mother will be thrilled,' said Assunta. 'And she is young enough...'

Tonino understood this. He did not like being reminded of the prospect of sharing the house with both his newly returned father and with a baby.

'By that time, I might well be living somewhere else,' he said. 'Not far away, but somewhere else. People do nowadays.'

'But you are needed for the art business,' remonstrated Assunta.

There came a point in every wedding - Traiano knew this as he had been to so many - when the nature of the gathering changed. It happened when the food was all consumed, or the remains removed, but the drink continued to flow. It happened when the children left, and the older, more respectable ladies took them home. It happened when the hardened men all retired into huddles to speak about business, and (this was a new development) to take cocaine; it happened when all the younger men and all the slutty girls, as he thought of them, that is the girls who were not taken home by their mothers, began to look at each other with lustful eyes. It was at this point, when the party changed, that don Traiano got seriously bored. This was not to say that the first part of the party was not boring as well: it was. During the first part of the party he had to shake as many hands as possible, and kiss as many cheeks, and ruffle as many heads of hair as he could manage. He had to remember all the names, who was related to who, what the children were called, what work the men were doing, and for whom, and ask them how it was going. He had to make sure that everyone got their moment in the sun, that everyone could feel the love. He had to recall the last time you had met them, and some particular thing that had happened, to show them they were remembered, they were important. He had to compliment the women on their dresses, their shoes, their new hairdos, and on the healthy and good looks of their children. He had to flatter the men with compliments, and the teenage boys the same, and hint that jobs would be forthcoming, that if there was any problem, any problem at all, they knew to whom they could come for a solution. He had to give all the small children a two-euro coin, or a five or ten euro note, depending on age. The more promising twelve-year-olds were rewarded with a twenty or a fifty. He had to work the crowd, and make sure no one was left out.

He had to be particularly attentive to the women of a certain age, this he knew well, having had plenty of practice with Ceccina's mother, grandmother, aunts and cousins. Ladies of a certain age loved the attentions of a young and important man, and they loved the deference and respect he showed. But he had no illusions. He was for many of them, in private, the prostitute's son, or the Romanian, the interloper, the one who owed his position to the favour of don Calogero alone, the one who, if fate turned against him, few would be sorry to see suffer. But if they did not like him, all the more reason to cultivate them, all the more reason to make a virtuous show of humility, all the more need to rub in the simple fact that he was the one with the power, whether they liked it or not, and that in the end they had to defer to him, however much they might not like him. Their sons, their brothers, their husbands depended on him, and so they had to be polite to him, even friendly, even if it were through gritted teeth.

The signora di Rienzi, Calogero's mother, alone did not need to play this game. He came and shook her hand, and she looked at him through narrowed eyelids. Her daughter Assunta, clearly in a good mood, was more gracious. Elena was almost nice; indeed she was growing nicer by the month. Perhaps Elena knew that in taking on don Renzo she needed friends. Signora Grassi was happy to speak to him, happy to talk of her son and how well he was doing. The signora then spoke of her husband, perhaps coming home soon, and Traiano listened carefully. He had no idea what signor Grassi was in for, but it must have been serious to keep him away for fourteen years; and it must have been serious enough for his silence to be assured by the way they had looked after his wife in his absence. Well, he would come home, and that would change things, it would affect the balance of power, the equilibrium of the ecosystem. He knew why the signora mentioned it. Of course, there would be a job waiting for him, he assured her. The signora smiled happily. She liked don Traiano, even if her friend signora di Rienzi did not.

And now Tonino approached, just as don Traiano was in close conversation with his mother.

'Hi, handsome,' said the boss, with a smile that was never bestowed in private. 'Have you come to take your mother home? It is getting late....'

'Now you mention it, boss, I was just about to suggest that.'

'Good,' said Traiano. 'I wish I could go home,' he added wistfully. 'I will probably see my wife and children into a taxi and then come back. Listen, I have just remembered. Tomorrow, you and I are going to Rome. Can you come to my house at about noon? That way you will have plenty of time to get some rest. Is it alright, signora, if I take this fine young man away from you for a few days? You are very kind. There is no need to bring too much luggage; we are not going for long; and just ordinary clothes, no suits. He looks smart in his suit, doesn't he, signora? I am glad he has kept his jacket on. That is what all our boys have been told to do. It is good discipline.'

'But don Traiano, you are not wearing your jacket yourself,' said Tonino's mother in all innocence.

'Me and don Gino and don Alfio and don Renzo, and some of the important visitors from around the island can take them off. Special privilege, signora. One day, you never know…. Anyway, good night, and see you soon,' he added to Tonino.

He had been completely sincere in saying he wished he could go to bed; in particular, as he joined his wife and children, he felt a strong desire to accompany them home, to be alone with them, with her, and to escape this crowd of people. But that was impossible. There was work to be done, which was why, as the small hours approached, he found himself in the party within a party, the dregs of the wedding. The bride and groom had long left to go and spend their wedding night in another hotel, a wise choice. There was some ribald talk about why they had left so early, what was the hurry, given that they had all the time in the world to live together now they were married. There were various speculations about don Alfio's presumed lack of sexual prowess, his tiny membrum virile which, don Renzo averred, would never do the trick. Renzo, as he said this, was lying on a sofa, his jacket off, his shirt undone and hanging out, his tie lost. He had a bottle of whiskey in his hand, and was drinking straight from the bottle. Next to him was don Gino, his pupils dilated, in an almost catatonic state. At a little distance was don Calogero, looking on in wry amusement.

'My father, Carlo, wherever he went, he found what he liked and they were only too eager to give it to him. I have got brothers and sisters all over the province of Palermo, or so they tell me. You know when you ask why this person is getting paid two thousand euros a month for doing nothing, and someone tells you, oh well, that is a payment we inherited from don Carlo. That is why one day I am going to wipe out the people who killed him.'

'You did that, remember?' said Traiano, sensing that the boss was giving him permission to speak. 'They ended up in the harbour. You were there, I seem to have heard.'

'I don't mean them. I mean the people behind the people who killed him. One person in particular. And his children. And let no one dare tell me what I can and cannot do.'

'No one is telling you what to do, Renzo,' said Traiano mildly. And even if they did, he thought, would you listen?

Gino nodded vigorously, seemingly coming out of his stupor. Renzo, angry at the thought of someone even thinking it was possible that they might give him orders, heaved himself up into a sitting position. Then he and Gino and others settled to snorting some cocaine off the polished table in front of them, while a solitary waiter approached and began to clear away the sea of dirty glasses and plates. Traiano almost felt the desire to smile. If Gino was stupid, what was Renzo? To talk about who you wanted to kill in front of an audience, any audience. It was inviting disaster. And he was all talk. When it had come to killing the trigger men who had killed his father, he had found the process sickening. No courage, no strategic sense, no brains at all. What a man. He felt sorry for Elena who was to marry him. Of course, the boss was using his sister; and when they were married, if something happened to Renzo, the whole Santucci empire would fall into Calogero's hands. Who dares, wins, as he had heard the boss say before now.

Looking up, he saw the boss standing there, preparing to shake hands with the last few departing guests, that is the guests who were determined not to stay till dawn. Having said goodbye to them, he surveyed the detritus of the party with clear brown eyes, his expression giving nothing away. He did not beckon, but Traiano sensed he ought to approach.

'Looking forward to Rome?' he asked.

'Yes. As you know, I have never been.'

'Ah, you would like it. But this is going to be business, isn't it, not time for sightseeing. But one day…. When you go to Rome, I will go to Palermo, and perhaps by this time next week, the new child will be here. I cannot wait. The gravedigger from Bronte will drive you, won't he? You trust him?'

'Yes, he has put business our way, this debt collecting. It is a useful sideline. And he will make us a fortune through the cemetery. You watch. He is not fastidious. He likes business, he does not like missing an opportunity.'

'Good. And Tonino? You trust him?'

'Yes, of course. We have known him since he was a child.'

'Good. These pills he is selling. They make money, I believe. We could make more. I want you to think about that. Doctor Moro, he is getting old. We need to cut out the middle man, I think. But we need to find his source. Understood?'

'Tonino would be only too glad to handle that.'

Outside, Roberto had put Gabriella into a taxi and said goodnight to her; he was smoking a cigarette. He liked Gabriella, and she liked him. She was only three or four years his senior, he reflected. Their conversation had been so interesting. They had discussed plants and trees, and what was already growing in the Furnaces, and how in twenty years' time the place would be a beautiful *rus in urbe*, the most wonderful suburb in Sicily. Then they had spoken of her brother and his art dealing, what he liked, and what she liked; her tastes were firmly anchored in the nineteenth century; his tastes were concentrated on an earlier time, the seventeenth century; he had a particular liking for Italian landscapes painted by French academicians. She was surprised that Roberto understood this, but he told of his trip to Rome and how he had visited some of the galleries, and had seen the Villa Medici which had been, perhaps still was, the French Academy.

After she left, he returned to the wedding, now hardly recognisable as such. Tonino had disappeared some time previously with one of the girls. Assunta had left; the boss had left; the bridal couple had left. All that remained were the young, the dancing and the loud music. There were lots of young couples dancing, many kissing desperately on the dance floor, many doing a little more than kissing. He sat down on one of the armchairs and wondered if he should go home or have a drink. The time it took to consider this was fatal. A waiter was passing with a bottle of champagne – it was a very expensive wedding – and curiosity got the better of him. He took the bottle and a glass. Very soon several unattached females arrived with empty glasses. Names were exchanged. He did not know them, but he knew who they were: friends and relations of the people who worked in the office, as he did, or in the gym, or on the construction site at the Furnaces. The amount of alcohol, the very late hour, the sense that the party was like the last party that would ever be held, end of the world party, all these things, made the conversation pass easily. They all spoke of what they were doing for work, who they knew, what they thought of the bride and groom. Another bottle was supplied and then a third. Then Tonino appeared with a girl, holding the key to the hotel room he had booked.

'I have to get some sleep, I have a long trip tomorrow,' he announced, throwing the key at Roberto. 'The room is free.'

Roberto took the key and stood up.

'I will go and have a lie down,' he said. 'One might as well.'

He stood up to leave, wondering who would stand up with him.

The next day Tonino was at Traiano's flat as instructed, at lunchtime, carrying just a small bag of clothes. He rang the bell and was told to wait below in the street; soon don Traiano emerged and gestured him to follow. He was carrying a large knapsack on his back. He followed him from a distance as he made his way down the road and into a narrow alley that ran behind several run-down buildings. Knocking at a door, they waited for a few minutes, until it was opened by an old lady, who Traiano greeted effusively. She was glad to see him, and was one of the more distant of Ceccina's relatives. They entered the small, neat and clean room in which the old lady lived, and without being asked, she took a key from a hook above the cooker, and handed it to Traiano. This opened a small door in a tiny little outdoor area behind her kitchen. They entered a confined and damp space, filled with what seemed to be the rubbish of centuries. This dark and neglected storage room was crowded with battered and empty suitcases and boxes, which were removed to reveal a metal cupboard. Another key, which Traiano took out of his pocket, opened this. It contained one thing only: money, blocks of five-hundred-euro notes wrapped up in clingfilm. Tonino immediately began to calculate how much money, how much was in each block, and how many blocks there were. He also wondered whose money it was, the boss's, or Traiano's personal savings.

'You have got your gun; you have got your knife? Yes? You use them to make sure no one steals what I am giving you. Empty your bag.'

He did as he was told, taking out the few clothes. Traiano placed several of the blocks of money in the bottom of the bag, and then instructed Tonino to place the clothes on top of them. Then he did the same for his own rucksack; Tonino calculated that they must be carrying between two or three million between them.

'Are we taking the train, boss?' he asked.

'No, you will see.'

They locked the cupboard, replaced the battered cases and boxes, and locked the door to the claustrophobic little storeroom. The signora took the key, and a hundred-euro note was left on her kitchen table. No one saw them emerge into the narrow alleyway. Within a few moments they were back in the heart of Purgatory, the square outside the Church. Parked outside the Church, was a hearse of the usual Sicilian kind, an adapted minibus, with opaque windows and its paintwork distinguished by various Catholic symbols. Sitting at the driving seat was a smartly dressed young man with curling greying hair, in a black suit, a white shirt, and a dark tie. It was Pio Forcella, the gravedigger of Bronte.

'Hi, Piuccio,' said don Traiano.

'Hello, sir,' said Pio Forcella. He nodded to Tonino.

'Hello, sir,' said Tonino respectfully.

Traiano got into the front passenger seat, and directed Tonino to get into the back of the vehicle.

'Where do I sit?' said Tonino.

'On the coffin,' said Traiano.

It took eight hours for the hearse to approach the outskirts of Rome. For hours, he sat on the coffin as the motorways sped by, not that he could see anything out of the darkened windows. He hoped that when on the ferry he might be allowed to get off, but this was not the case; he was here to guard the money, and that was that. Somewhere near Salerno, they stopped for refreshments, and he was allowed out to relieve himself, but had to stay with the coffin while Piuccio and the boss went into the restaurant without him. At least the boss brought him back a sandwich. After that, he lay down next to the coffin and went to sleep, which was the best way to escape the boredom.

When he awoke, it was dark, and it was clear that they were in the midst of the tangle of roads that surrounded the ring road, none of which made sense to him, not that he could see much anyway. Eventually they came to a stop in a carpark, a definitive stop. Don Traiano yawned and stretched, and the gravedigger of Bronte looked towards him expectantly. No word was exchanged, but Traiano nodded. A moment later the pair of them were alone in the carpark, watching the hearse drive away. Then they walked up a slight hill where there was what seemed to be a monastery or convent. Entering at a door, a young man looked up from behind a reception desk.

'Good evening,' said Traiano, placing his identity card on the desk.

Tonino did the same. The young man registered them, gave them a room key and advised that supper was being served, and would be for the next half hour. Without having to ask, Tonino could see where they were, for behind the desk was a reproduction of the famous picture of the Madonna of Divino Amore. They were just outside the ring road of Rome, along the Ardeatine Way, at one of the most famous shrines in Italy. They went up to their room and then, to Tonino's relief, they left the luggage and went down to the dining room, where there was a buffet and lots of pilgrims, all of them Polish, speaking in their own language.

The food, to Tonino's surprise and delight, was good. He had heard that when you left Sicily, the food declined, and the further north you went, the worse it got, but perhaps this pilgrim hotel was an exception to the rule. He looked at the Polish pilgrims, many of them young, the girls all very pretty, and some of the young men the sort of young men who could defend themselves. He thought of his mother at home, and how she was. The wedding seemed a long way away now. He remembered the girl he had taken upstairs. He wondered who Roberto had spent the night with on the night of the wedding. He waited for don Traiano to speak to him, knowing that that was the rule: no questions; only speak when you are spoken to.

'I'll go upstairs and have a shower and keep an eye on the money,' said Traiano at length. 'You hang around and then go to Church, act natural, remember we are pilgrims. So go in and pray in front of the Madonna, and I will find you there in an hour or so.'

He was left alone, which was most strange. He was very rarely alone. He went and got himself a second helping from the excellent buffet (the sandwich on the motorway had been most inadequate) and as he piled up his plate, he was aware of one of the Poles next to him doing the same thing, who smiled and nodded to him. He then returned to his solitary table, and was aware of the convivial Poles at the other end of the room, and more aware than ever of his solitude. As he tackled some really delicious artichokes, he realised he missed his mother, who was always so good to him; and the thought of his father's return came to the forefront of his consciousness, and how that would change everything, especially if they were to have a child, another child; he was the only son, and if that were to change…. He thought of the girl he had been with only last night, in the hotel, at the wedding…. He thought of Roberto and Roberto's sisters who, unlike the girl last night, were nice respectable girls. It would be a nice way of passing the time, going around with one of them, though which one should he choose? Then there was the boss's daughter, little Isabella, but that was a long-term project, something for ten years from now. If he married her at the age of twenty, he would be twenty-four... He really wanted to do that, he realised. But in the meantime, he had the number of Roberto's house, and if there were a public phone, he would ring after he had finished eating and before he went to Church, perhaps to thank the signora, perhaps to have a word with Roberto, perhaps with one of the girls.

He was sitting at a table by the door, and the Poles, in order to leave the pilgrims' refectory, had to pass close by him. They were a friendly bunch, he could see, and several of the girls smiled at him, and some of them smiled at him and looked away self-consciously. The boys, all a little older than himself, looked at him with greater and franker curiosity, and their priest stopped at the table and shook hands.

'You are here on your own?' he asked with friendly concern.

'No, father, thanks for asking, but I am here with my mate, but he has gone upstairs for something; we are meeting in Church later, to pray in front of the Madonna.'

'You're Sicilian?' said the priest, who had been in Italy long enough to recognise accents.

'Where the criminals come from?' said one of the boys.

'Shut up, Tadeusz,' said the priest genially. 'Ignore him.' There was some laughter, and a self-deprecating gesture from Tadeusz.

'I work in a pizzeria,' said Tonino. 'My mate is a bit older than me, and he is the manager and part-owner.' He felt Tadeusz, clearly the most aware of the bunch, raise an eyebrow at this. 'His wife has just given birth and he came there to thank the Madonna,' he added piously. 'We drove up, as we had a lift, and it was too good an opportunity to miss, so I came too.'

'You have an intention?' asked the priest.

He knew this language. He had heard his mother use it.

'Yes, father,' he said. 'I am here to thank the Madonna for a special favour. She has answered my prayers. I have met the girl I am going to marry.' Again, he sensed the raised eyebrow. 'I am nineteen,' he lied, 'and I need to get some money together, so it won't be for some time, but it is what I want.'

All the good Catholic Polish boys murmured their appreciation. Tadeusz alone looked unimpressed. He was aware of this. Perhaps the one they called Tadeusz was more cynical than the others. Perhaps the one called Tadeusz recognised lies when he heard them.

'You and your mate came in a hearse,' he observed.

'We have a friend who is an undertaker and who has business in Rome, so we got a lift,' said Tonino, a touch defensively. He looked at Tadeusz with a touch of dislike which he found hard to hide. 'We are going back the same way. Flying visit. Though, of course, if we had money, we would fly, I mean come by plane. But I have never been in a plane, or indeed outside Sicily until now.'

'Well,' said the priest, 'We are going to see the Madonna now, and say the Rosary, and we will be up most of the night, so do join us whenever you like. And tell your friend to do so. I will be hearing confessions too, all night if need be.'

'Thank you, father,' said Tonino with what he hoped was sufficient gratitude and humility.

The Poles left, and he was left alone. The staff came in to clear away the remains of the buffet, and he finished his food – the artichokes were wonderful – without daring to go for a third helping before it all disappeared. Then he wandered out and crossed the small piazza to the church where the Madonna of Divine Love was to be found. The Poles were there, in profound silence, all kneeling down. He sat at the back, wondering what they were doing, wondering what they were thinking, what they were saying to God and the Madonna, and wondering if either would or even could listen. There was an intensity to the atmosphere of the small brightly lit church that took him by surprise. These Poles had come here for some reason, but the reason to him was unfathomable.

After some time of intense boredom, he felt an arm touch his elbow. It was the one called Tadeusz. His gesture was unmistakeable. Quietly he followed him out of the door, and joined him in the dark piazza.

'Take one,' said Tadeusz, proffering the open pack of cigarettes.

The smell of the raw tobacco was so enticing. How he longed to have a cigarette. Tadeusz, who was clearly being friendly now, perhaps regretting his earlier irony, noted his hesitation.

'Are you allowed to smoke?' he asked, referring perhaps to his age.

'I am grown up,' said Tonino, taking the cigarette, thinking it ridiculous he could not smoke, given that he was old enough to sleep with women and kill other human beings.

They both lit their cigarettes, and savoured the way the nicotine hit their blood streams and the way the smoke rose in the cool night air.

'It's not a sin,' said Tadeusz. 'Other things are, but not this. How old are you really?'

'I am eighteen,' he said, failing even to convince himself. 'You?'

'Nineteen. First year of university. You didn't want to go?'

'No.'

He realised that he was being defensive. He had not liked Tadeusz when he was not friendly; but he liked him even less now he was friendly. He did not quite know how to deal with people like this, people who weren't enemies, but who were not in your debt either, people who were just people. He felt constrained to make an effort. He was supposed to be acting like a normal person, wasn't he? But it was a strain. He realised, not for the first time, that he was not normal, by any standard you judged.

'Is Poland nice?' he asked.

'I suppose so,' said Tadeusz. 'We are from Warsaw, and most of the tourists give us a miss. But it is nice, yeah. There is lots to do. But there are so many Poles in Italy. All of us are living here now, I mean all of us you met tonight. It is a bit sad that so many of us leave.'

'Like Sicily,' said Tonino. 'A lot of my relations, whom I have never met, are in America, which is sad for them, and sad for us. I blame the government. But I am lucky, I have a job and a future. I have friends.'

He felt a bit better all of a sudden. It was true. He had friends; there were people who feared him. He finished his cigarette and put out his hand.

'I must go back into church,' he said.

In the church, they were saying the Rosary, and went and sat at the back and listened to the gentle drone of devotion. After ten minutes or so, don Traiano came in, and he was allowed to go back to the room, where he soon fell into a deep and welcome sleep.

When he woke, he was aware that it was still early, but it was light, and the curtains were open. He could hear water from the adjoining bathroom, and he could see the boss's clothes and the dreaded belt laid out neatly on a chair. He understood at once. The window looked out onto the little piazza outside the Church; the boss had seen him smoking. That was bad luck, he knew. But at the same time not bad luck. They saw everything. He heaved himself out of bed. He must have made an appreciable noise, as his feet hit the floor, because the door of the now silent bathroom opened, and there was Traiano in his bathrobe, brushing his teeth, looking at him with a glint in his eyes.

He stopped brushing his teeth, then he rinsed his mouth and did something unexpected.

He smiled.

Tonino was taken by surprise. He had never seen the boss smile when there were no other people around before now, at least not at him; he had smiled at others but, for Tonino, there had always been the serious business face.

'You slept well,' he observed. 'I supposed you would after that long and uncomfortable journey on sitting on a coffin. We should have asked who was inside, perhaps, and the gravedigger of Bronte would have told us. Never mind. I will go down to breakfast, while you use the bathroom, OK? The gravedigger will be here by eleven, I think. I will be back soon.'

By the time he emerged from the bathroom and had got dressed, the boss re-entered. His first glance was towards the two knapsacks, which contained the money. Then he looked at Tonino. They both sat opposite each other on the two beds.

'Today is going to be very important,' said Traiano. 'You have been chosen for this by don Calogero because you are very trustworthy and you do not talk. Today we are meeting up with Ruggero Bonelli, whom we know, and his friend Pasquale Greco, who is very important to us, as he is the man who is on the inside, who works for the Carabinieri who safeguard art treasures, and who can do the opposite of protecting them, making them disappear, lose the paperwork, not that any of this is on paper any more. But, and this is the important point, we are brokering a deal between Bonelli and Greco and some people from Rome who have been stealing stuff for years and are constantly looking to offload it onto some buyer. With Bonelli and Greco, we can find what is worth buying, what can be washed, and what can be sold on. It is a lucky thing that these Romans were found; well, not lucky. Don Calogero has all the contacts. We are going to be rich. Well, richer. We are already rich, but this opens up a nice new income stream, lots of nice clean money and a way of investing for the future. It will be a bit boring today, as it will be looking at pictures in great detail, something I know very little about, and you, I expect, even less, but it is going to pay in both the long term and the short term. Understood?'

'Yes, boss.'

There was silence between them.

'Everyone was talking about you at the wedding,' said Traiano. 'Or so I gathered. You are getting a reputation for yourself.'

'Thanks, boss,' said Tonino.

'You are a tough fighter, aren't you, and no one would dare take you on. That is good. But you are also clever, which is just as important. Where did you end up after the wedding?'

'In bed with a girl, boss.'

'I think most of our men did. Was she anyone we know?'

'Doubt it, boss. I didn't know her myself. But I made sure she had a good time, and she did. I made doubly sure, in fact.'

'That is the Sicilian way. And did you enjoy it?'

Tonino shrugged.

'I don't care much, boss. I don't want to be immoral, but it was like the sandwich I had on the motorway. It filled a gap. But I do not want to be chasing girls all the time like some men. I want to get married and have children. In ten years' time, I want to be married with my first child. That's what I care about.'

'Ten years' time,' mused Traiano. 'You think ahead. A good sign. You have anyone in mind?'

'Roberto has sisters.'

'Ah, Roberto. And where did he get to after the wedding?'

'I haven't spoken to him since, boss.'

'A very handsome man.'

Tonino shrugged.

'If you say so, boss.'

'My wife says so. The other women as well. Maybe Gabriella too, who knows?'

'She is a bit older, but it would be nice for him. And for me, if he becomes my brother-in-law.'

'More immediate is the question of your father coming home. He will be out soon. We have looked after him, we will continue to look after him. It may be a shock to him to find that the baby he left behind has become a rich and successful man, but we will tell him that he must respect you and defer to you. But we will find him a job, we will look after him. Now listen. Don Calogero is sending don Gino to spend his weekdays in Palermo, to keep don Renzo company. Do you understand what this means for you? This ship of ours, what does it run on? I mean what is the ultimate source of all our money?'

'Cocaine, boss,' said Tonino.

'And that comes from…?'

'Palermo, boss.'

'And Palermo means don Renzo, or more accurately the people who have been working for the Santucci family for years and years; the people who worked for don Antonio and don Carlo. They are not our people. The ship is running and we control the top decks, but the engine room is not ours. Do you see?'

'I see exactly, boss.'

'And when we get the engine room, then we shall be even richer. But that can wait for now. Let us see what don Gino manages, what Elena manages when she marries don Renzo. In the meantime, there is something else: the mobile pharmacy. Doctor Moro is getting old. Perhaps it would be kinder to cut him out of the game altogether. Put him out to grass.'

He outlined the Moro job, and Tonino listened carefully.

At eleven, as promised, the undertaker's van returned, driven by the gravedigger of Bronte. The coffin was no longer in the back, but had been safely buried in the Campo Verano cemetery. The shrine of the Madonna of Divine Love was quiet: the Poles had left in their bus an hour or so before, exchanging cheery greetings with the Sicilian friends. They left an odd feeling in their wake, this idea that there were people who travelled around Italy, visiting shrines, enjoying each other's company, ordinary people.

The hearse took them, somewhat to the relief of Tonino, who had bad memories of the place, not towards Rome, but towards the suburbs. They spent some time locked in traffic on the ring road, and then turned south along the via Pontina, until they came to the outskirts of the anonymous and modern town of Pomezia. The railway station was outside the town, and here they stopped and picked up two men who joined Tonino in the back. One was Bonelli, whom he knew. The other was introduced as Pasquale Greco. Hands were shaken. Then they drove into an industrial estate, where a man was waiting for them and directed them towards what looked like, and indeed was, an abandoned factory. They parked on a concrete forecourt, and entered the building. Tonino carried the money, while the gravedigger waited outside with the vehicle, and read a book. He was happy to do so. He did not want to know what was inside this building.

As they entered, a man with a walrus moustache was waiting for them. He held out his arms to Traiano and embraced him.

'We have never met, but I have heard so much about you,' he said to Traiano by way of explanation.

Releasing Traiano from his grasp, he kissed both his cheeks.

'Wait till you see what I have got for you,' he said.

The man with the walrus moustache looked at the other two, at Ruggero Bonelli and at Pasquale Greco, but no introductions were made. He barely gave Tonino a glance. Tonino supposed he knew who they were and that names were superfluous. The space they were in was large and seemingly empty. At a signal from the boss, he sat down on a chair and placed the money bags next to himself. He noticed a small table, another chair and a counting machine. There was another table too, at which Greco sat, and at which he placed a laptop computer.

Work began. There were several iron-grey metal cabinets along the far wall, and each of these were opened in turn to reveal a mesh on which hung various paintings. Bonelli studied each in turn, without saying a word. Everyone looked at him with expectation. There were two people with the walrus moustache, both young, who addressed him as 'uncle'. There were seven or eight cabinets of pictures. The two youngsters opened the cabinets as directed. Tonino began to get very bored. Bonelli's examination of the paintings seemed eternal. How much was there to see in a picture? He looked at several of them through a thing that looked like a telescope. Occasionally, he whispered to Greco. At last, after what seemed like an hour or so, he made his choice. A dozen canvases were chosen and set aside after being taken down. There was a long trestle table on which they were placed. There now ensued a long discussion between the walrus moustache, Bonelli, Greco, who frequently looked things up on his computer, and Traiano.

The two nephews drifted over to Tonino. They greeted each other with suspicion.

'How's Sicily?' asked one. 'We know where you come from, your accent gives you away.'

He was noticeably taller than Tonino. The other one, who could not be his brother, but perhaps was his cousin, was shorter, but fair haired.

'You have fun there?' the blond asked. 'In Sicily?'

'Have you been?' asked Tonino.

'No.'

'You should come, both of you. You would be dead within five minutes of stepping off the train.'

'You are a ferocious little bastard,' said the tall one with admiration. 'We had better keep away. We are just innocent art dealers, after all.'

Tonino laughed.

'What are they discussing?' he asked.

'Oh, it is always the same,' said the short blond one. 'Money. Your friends will be trying to beat our uncle down. Our uncle has three prices in his head. The asking price, the price he thinks realistically he can get, and the price he is prepared to settle for. And your friends are trying to guess those latter prices, because they don't want to insult him, and they do not want to give him a good bargain either. At the same time your friends are trying to work out what the things will sell for, and how easy they are to sell. The dozen or so they have picked show that they have a good eye, or at least that chap has, if indeed he is the main player. How much money have you brought?'

'Mind your own business.'

'It is my job to count it,' said the blond. 'I will find out in due course.'

'And it is our job to pack things up when you finally make up your mind to buy them,' said the tall one. 'Have you brought any coke?'

'No. Have you?'

Both shook their heads. The conversation then moved onto football.

Ruggero Bonelli did, as the two nephews supposed, have an eye for what was worth buying. He had liked what he had seen without conveying the slightest enthusiasm for any of it. He had maintained the expression of a man sifting his way through a huge amount of pictorial rubbish. For his part, the walrus-moustached seller had done his best to project the idea that he really did not care if he sold any pictures or not, and that he was doing this viewing as a favour. But under the studied boredom, the truth was that he was desperate to sell, and that he had had many of these stolen pictures for years and years and was eager to get rid of them. He had the prices he had paid for each of them in his head, so many times had he shown them to prospective buyers over the years; he had factored in inflation and a reasonable appreciation, and had the prices he wanted too, but he awaited an offer, hoping for the best. He knew too that this man, whose name he did not know, was an expert of sorts, though what in, he was not sure.

Bonelli's eyes had surveyed the pictures, and several had jumped out at him at once, though he had hidden any reaction. There were some that were incredibly bad, seventeenth century canvases that had the distinction of being old, but little else, still lives (a genre he had never warmed to), some in indifferent condition, which made him wonder why anyone had bothered to steal them. And there were some that he had really liked, eighteenth and nineteenth century canvases, for the main part, of architectural subjects. There were a series of six smallish paintings of Neapolitan scenes which he had recognised at once as masterpieces, and by no less an artist than Vanvitelli himself. These he simply had to have; they were exquisite, beautiful. He had whispered as much to Greco, and Greco had looked at his computer, and sure enough these were hot pictures, stolen from one of the many Bourbon palaces in Campania some thirty years previously. Well, not stolen - lost: they were last recorded as hanging in a hunting lodge that had been built by Ferdinand III, and then somehow had dropped off the radar. If Greco could lose them again, they would be valuable; some American buyer would love them. He hoped very much that Greco could; but even if he couldn't, they could hang on his wall forever.

But he did not ask for the six Vanvitellis to be transferred to the trestle tables. He hung back. He pretended to ignore them, which was hard; it was like ignoring the most beautiful woman in the room. On the table, instead, were twelve paintings that he was interested in, but not that interested in, compared to the Vanvitellis: there were several portraits, several religious paintings, and one or two landscapes. One of the portraits was early nineteenth century, in the manner of Angelica Kauffman or even Elisabeth Vigée le Brun, a very nice piece. The provenance was complex. The painting had been stolen by an Italian officer in the Second World war from some residence in Slovenia; it had been sold on illegally several times since then. The picture was not officially 'wanted' as far as Greco could tell, which meant that selling it legally might be relatively simple: it could be launched as a hitherto unknown Kauffman, if that was what it was. In addition, there were two medieval panel paintings of saints on a golden ground, which he liked, and which, because so many panel paintings were of a limited amount of subjects, could surely be 'washed'. Around these, the discussion raged. The twelve paintings were good, thought Bonelli. But given all the difficulties involved, namely their questionable status, he advised an offer of 650,000 euro. Walrus moustache man laughed. He demanded eight hundred thousand. Bonelli laughed in his turn, and so did Greco. There was a long discussion; they all knew that there had to be such a discussion; from the other side of the warehouse, Tonino and the two youngsters watched, knowing that this would go on and on.

There was not much the youngsters could talk about, as there was so much to stay silent on; when the subject of football was exhausted, boredom became intense, and one of the nephews, the tall one, actually lay on the ground on some packing material and went to sleep. They had had a long journey, said the blond one, suggesting that they had come from the north of Italy, though Tonino knew he should not ask where. They began to discuss girls. The blond fellow was hanging around with the boss's niece, which was why he called him uncle. The tall chap, now asleep, was his girlfriend's brother. They were a close-knit family. The boss trusted his relations in a way that he did not trust others. In a couple of years, they would get married. It would be a good move. They both wanted it. She wanted to have children, of course, and so did he. The boss, her uncle, had lots of children and endless nephews and nieces. It was a large family.

Large families were good, agreed Tonino, and he wanted one himself, though he had to wait for a few years at least, but, even so, he believed in early marriage. The boss had married young and had three children already; the boss of bosses had four children, and had had two wives, and his wife was about to give birth again; as was the boss's mother; this was the way things should be. The worst thing, as far as he could see, about not having money, was that one could not afford to have children. That was terrible. Luckily, it did not apply to them and their friends.

Suddenly, everything sprang to life, voices were raised, and hands were shaken. The tall chap woke up. Traiano approached.

'Eight hundred and fifty thousand,' he said to Tonino.

Tonino got the blocks of money out of the bags and began to remove the clingfilm. The blond nephew started to count the stuff using the machine. The tall nephew moved to the trestle table and began to pack up the pictures they had bought, under the supervision of Bonelli and Greco. The price was higher than first offered, and the walrus moustache was pleased; he had thrown in the six Vanvitellis as a sweetener, and Bonelli thought this was good deal. Indeed, for a couple of thousand more, he was even prepared to give Traiano a small Madonna, of the school of Mantegna, which Traino was determined to give to his wife, so that they could hang it over the marital bed.

Eventually, hands were shaken, goodbyes were made, the paintings were carefully stowed in the hearse, and then the party from Catania, along with Greco and Bonelli, got in. This time, Tonino was told to get in the front with the gravedigger of Bronte, while the others got into the back. In the back, Traiano discussed with the two art experts the personal purchase he had made. They thought it was worth two thousand at least, and, as he had no intention of selling it, there was no need to worry about the provenance. The other paintings all had provenance issues, but these, Greco was sure he could fix. They now discussed what they had seen, what they had been offered. There were other pieces that might be worth returning for, and in a few months their supplier would have some new pieces in, that was for sure. But for the present they had a very good haul indeed. Bonelli calculated that they could sell everything they had bought, once suitably washed, for at least three times and in some cases many times more, than what they had paid for them.

They drove to the Line B station at EUR Fermi, where they stopped, and Bonelli and Greco got out; Traiano accompanied them into a bar for a cup of coffee, leaving the other two to look after the hearse and its contents. It was getting late. Bonelli was to spend the night in Rome and then fly down the next day.

'We will be driving all night,' said Piuccio Forcella, a trifle sadly. 'Perhaps don Traiano will drive part of the way. Can you drive?'

'Not really, I mean, I do not have a licence yet,' said Tonino.

'Might be awkward,' conceded Piuccio.

They sat in silence. After all, what was there to talk about? They could not talk about work, because that was secret and illegal, to be buried forever in silence; perhaps most men talked about work, but they could not. It seemed futile to talk about football, with all that art work in the back on the hearse, for how could they possibly relax enough to talk about sport before all that was safely delivered? Tonino wanted to ask Piuccio about the business of undertaking, about his domestic life (he had heard he had one child and another on the way), to make some overture of friendship or even intimacy, but he did not know how to begin this, and even to contemplate it seemed a little presumptuous, given that Piuccio was twice his age. He was not sure even how to address him. As for Piuccio himself, he was in awe of don Traiano, that was clear, of his power, his money and the unspoken assumption that he could always get what he wanted by brute force; of the way he had collected those debts; and he was a little bit in awe of this tough little bastard Tonino, who never spoke but who would, at a nod from his boss, break his neck, if that was what the boss wanted. Piuccio knew he was playing with fire. These people were dangerous and to be kept at bay; but he needed them, and here he was, working with them. He prayed the angels and saints would protect him.

Traiano returned, alone.

'Sicily next stop,' he said. 'But have a cup of coffee before we go. You may need it.'

They left for the bar. Coffee was ordered. While they waited for it to arrive, Piuccio took out his mobile phone to tell his wife that he would be back by the morning, early. He then listened to some long description of what was happening with their son, and with the new baby yet to be born. Across the crowded bar, Tonino could see one of the very few surviving public phones. It was late afternoon, and Roberto's sisters would be back from school. He knew the number of the flat near the via Plebiscito. He went over and dialled, inserting the coin. The youngest sister, the one called Petra, answered. That was providential, he thought. He explained he was phoning from a bar, from far away, and that he was on a trip, in fact a pilgrimage. She seemed very happy to hear this, and to have picked up the phone. He explained that he was ringing to thank her mother for the other evening. She offered to pass him to her mother. He told her that was not necessary, but she could pass on his thanks.

'Could I come and visit you again?' he asked. 'Perhaps this weekend? Perhaps Friday evening? If you mother agrees, of course.'

'That would be nice,' said Petra. 'My sisters were saying how they were looking forward to seeing you again. I will ask my mother, but I am sure she will say it is OK. She said how much she liked you.'

'Did she?' he said, pleased by this, knowing, or thinking he knew, what it really meant, namely that Petra really liked him.

'I am in Rome, on a payphone, and I may have to go soon, as we are driving back soon.'

'What are you doing there?' she asked, enviously, as she had never been to Rome.

'We have not seen the centre of Rome, just the suburbs. My friend don Traiano asked me to come with him, and we went to the shrine of Divino Amore to pray for an intention.'

'That is nice,' she said.

She was really, he thought, a very nice girl, just right for him, the right age; the prettiest of the sisters, and perhaps, which was an advantage, being the youngest, the least sophisticated, for she did not seem to question anything.

They said their goodbyes. He could see that Piuccio had finished his coffee. His was waiting for him on the counter, so he drank it quickly, while Piuccio observed that it was best not to keep don Traiano waiting. They returned to the hearse, and Tonino got into the back with the paintings, and thus they began to long tedious trip back to Sicily.

Chapter Six

'Does he know?'

'That we are meeting? No. I did not mention it.'

'Why not? I thought you were friends,' said Gabriella playfully.

'We are friends. I tell him things, but not everything,' said Roberto.

'Ah, you are learning the ways of Purgatory. Everything must be kept a secret. Everything. But you are not from there, I am not from there.'

'Where I am from is just as bad,' said Roberto. 'Or only a little better. And where you are from… well, that is rather different.'

She smiled.

'Well, if you think I like rough young men from the lower classes, you would be right,' she said.

'You mean rough young men like Tonino?'

'No. I mean like you.'

'I am flattered to be thought rough,' said Roberto. 'I am not in the least, but if that is what you think, I am prepared to go along with it.'

He smiled. His smile, she thought, was beautiful. They had exchanged numbers at the wedding a week ago. This was their first meeting since then, and they were in a bar quite close to the Roman theatre, a considerable distance from Purgatory, which lessened the chances of being spotted. This Purgatory idea that everything had to be secret, everything had to be discreet, was catching.

'So, what happened after I left the wedding?' she said.

'Oh, it was all very disorderly,' he said. 'It went on till dawn. The things they do, or at least some people do.'

He reflected about his trip upstairs. Two girls had followed him. He had had a lot of teasing from Assunta about this, but if the whole Purgatory quarter knew, that was no bad thing, he reckoned.

'Tonino went to Rome with your brother the next day,' he added.

'Not quite. They travelled separately. My brother flew. They met up with Pasquale Greco when there. Did Tonino say anything about that?'

'Nothing at all. That must have been the secret part. He just told me that they went to the shrine of Divino Amore. He told my youngest sister the same thing. He is interested in her. The two elder ones are a little put out, but they are the closest in age, so it seems right.'

'Do you want that, your sister and Tonino?' she asked.

'He won't lay a finger on her, he promised me. That, we have discussed. He knows she is a good girl, and destined to remain so for a long time. Don't worry. I am not worried. Tonino is manageable.' He saw the expression on her face. 'All animals have trainers; all criminals have lawyers. He needs me.'

'Is that how you see him? An animal? A criminal? Your sister's boyfriend? Jesus, Mary!' She sighed. 'Haven't you ever heard of the lion tamer who had his head bitten off? The crocodile trainer who was eaten when the crocodile jumped out of the pool? The lawyer who was killed by his own client?'

He laughed.

'I have got leverage. He needs me. He comes from the bottom of the pile and wants to get to the top. He needs people like me, you know, the veneer of respectability. You may not understand it, but there are as many grades of rank in the working class as there are in the aristocracy. The dukes look down on the counts, who despise the barons… you know. His father is in jail, he and his mother are, or at least were, very poor. He is not quite illiterate.'

'Is he? Is he really? Are there still people like that?'

'Well, he can read, but he certainly cannot write much. Yes, there are people like that. Particularly round here. So, you see, he needs someone like me, someone to cover his deficiencies.'

'And what can he do for you?'

'A great deal. He has already got me a job. It's transactional, you see. But there is more to it than that. I understand him, and that perhaps give me leverage. I understand his character. He likes that in a funny way.'

'He likes that, but does he like you? He may come to hate you.'

'A risk I am prepared to take,' said Roberto.

'It is not really your sister he likes,' she observed shrewdly a moment later. 'Is it?'

'Don't be ridiculous,' he said, momentarily annoyed. 'This is Sicily, not…. Las Vegas.'

She laughed.

'Oh, there is plenty of Las Vegas around here,' she said. 'Or so I am told. But you believe what you like. Las Vegas, my foot! Taormina is just up the road. That is where it all used to happen.'

'Well, it may well do, but I am not interested in that sort of thing,' he said mildly, knowing that too much protest would give the wrong impression.

Gabriella considered this. It was convincing, she decided.

'Is the signora nice?' she asked, meaning Tonino's mother.

'Signora Grassi? Yes, very nice. She adores her son, and she likes me. We met at the wedding. She was anxious I should come round, as he has been to my house and tried my mother's cooking. But…'

'But what?'

'Well, she is not stupid. Far from it. She may look like an unimportant person, someone to overlook, but she is ambitious, ambitious for her son. Without saying a word directly, when I spoke to her at the wedding, she gives the impression that Tonino does everything he can to help her. One can tell that though he is tough, he is sentimental too, and that he feels himself under pressure from her to please her. Before he started working, when he was still a child, they were desperately poor, and he remembers that, so now he does everything he can to make up for the past. They used to live off the charity of the Confraternity, but now they have his income as well, and it is a lot.'

'You mean he sells drugs,' said Gabriella.

'Prescription drugs, at a discount,' said Roberto, correcting her. 'Stuff siphoned off from the Americans. He has lots of takers, as there is huge demand each and every night. But he does this because of his mother, not because he loves money for its own sake.'

'How do you know all this? I mean, if he does not like people asking questions and he does not speak about it…..'

'I have seen packets of aspirin, marked US Army not for resale, things like that. He comes into the gym changing rooms and people queue up to buy stuff. That trade has to be discreet but it cannot be secret. Everyone knows. But you are right, no one says anything.'

She seemed unconvinced by this, but more than that, she seemed disapproving, for she was frowning. He could guess what she was thinking: how had it come to this? Here she was, in a bar near the Roman theatre, talking to someone whom she liked about someone she did not particularly like, and wondering how on earth she had come into the orbit of Tonino Grassi, Calogero di Rienzi and people of that sort.

He looked at her and wondered. Did she even realise what life was really like for Tonino, and for himself as well? Did she understand the desire to get on that burned within him? He had started near the via Plebiscito, but he was determined not to end there. University was the way out, so was hard work, but one needed that extra push that friendship and patronage could provide. What did she know about that? After all, she was rich, she had money: she owned, he knew, a nice flat, no doubt gorgeously furnished, its kitchen cupboards stuffed with food and wine, its bedroom with a beautifully appointed double bed. For her, poverty was unimaginable. No doubt she assumed everyone had at least some money, and she could not picture the way some in Catania like himself never seemed to have more than ten euros in their bank accounts. The idea of not being able to pay for things was foreign to her, he was sure. If you ran out of money, for people like her, you went to the bank and you got some more.

'So, who do you think is going to win the election?' he asked, wanting to change the subject.

There was a pile of flyers for one candidate, and one candidate only, on the table next to them.

'This guy Volta seems OK,' she said. 'The party I always voted for does not seem to be making much of an impression. I used to be more political than I am. What about you?'

'Volta,' he said. 'He seems the obvious one.'

Their drinks were coming to an end. He knew he had to be patient, he had to be clever, reserved, not too keen, or at least not seen to be too keen. He was, of course, enormously so, he could feel it in his blood, even now, as he raised his glass to his lips, but the whole thing needed to be strung out, extended, so that there was no appearance of hurry. He knew what he wanted, and he was convinced that she wanted the same thing, but there were hurdles to be overcome, things she had to get used to: she had to get herself used to the fact that he was younger, that he was not from the same social class as herself, and that, perhaps, he was too ambitious. But he was determined to spin things out, so that her desire for him would grow stronger the longer it was unfulfilled, and would trump all objections her rational mind might have. He was determined to make the most of the chance she represented.

'Have you seen *Tosca*?' he asked suddenly. 'The thing is someone gave Assunta two tickets but she and her husband do not want to go, and she said I might have them, and while I am sure one of my sisters would love to go, I would prefer it so much if you could come instead.'

She looked at him, and smiled, delighted by the prospect.

Later that same evening, he ascended the grand staircase in the company of Tonino and entered the gallery hung with its works of art, now barely visible in the darkness, and then followed Tonino through the open door to the servants' quarters from whence came warmth, light and the aroma of the signora's cooking. The signora took great pride in her culinary skills. It was essential that her beloved son was well fed; besides, having been very poor, and now being much less poor, it was important to be reminded of this on a daily basis, and what better way than by eating delicious food? Oh, the Catania market, what a heavenly place, the object of her daily quest for all the delightful things the land of Sicily and its waters produced. And to know that at long last, once again, one shared in the riches of the land.

He was taken into the kitchen and was greeted by the signora. He wished her a good evening. She smiled back at him with approval. He thanked her for the invitation to have supper, but was at once aware that the mother and son were not quite at ease with each other, and very glad to have a third between them. Supper passed off easily enough. The signora remarked on how signor Bonelli had been round, showing some clients the gallery, and they had made an important purchase, or so she assumed, as Bonelli had looked very happy and, on leaving, had pressed a hundred euro note into her hand. A very important sale, she was sure. In fact, Bonelli had been there every morning of late, (ever since Tonino had brought the pictures back from Rome, though she did not mention that) showing stuff to clients, sometimes two or three sets of clients a day. This afternoon he had been in the storage rooms, picking out new pictures to hang to replace those sold.

That was very interesting, both boys agreed. Tonino said he would show him the gallery after supper, put on all the lights so he could see things properly. There was a catalogue too, which he might like looking at; Tonino himself had been studying it. The signora beamed at this mention of her son's cultural pursuits. It made her happy, as did meeting this charming and handsome young man who was studying law at the university.

The signora then spoke about how they should watch the news after supper, by which she meant the local news which came after the national news. She did not like the national news, which never had anything good to say about Sicily. But last night she had heard there had been disturbances in various parts of the city, streets blocked, burning vehicles, it sounded terrible. The artichokes, said Roberto, were wonderful, which was off topic, but true. They were her son's favourite, she said.

They did the washing up and the switched on the television for the news. The national news was terrible, as it always was. The usual crisis of government. Pictures of the Quirinal, and President Napolitano's car being driven at speed through the giant doors. Pictures of the

Prime Minister, Silvio Berlusconi, entering the Chigi Palace in Rome. Various vox pops, and various experts predicting the imminent collapse of the government. ('But I like him,' said the signora.) Then there were people abroad, predicting, once more, the imminent demise of Berlusconi. There was talk, yet again, of Ruby the Heartstealer, and the signora asked once more what bunga bunga meant, to which Tonino replied he did not know. Then there were reports of bad weather in the north; well, if people wanted to live there, what did they expect, and some very boring stuff from England, but with nice pictures. 'The English are all so good-looking,' remarked the signora, to which her son assented. Then came the sport, and the signora did not speak, knowing both boys would be very interested in this. Francesco Totti, the captain of Roma, was still injured and not playing, and Roma was suffering. This was of the greatest interest to both of them, and even the signora was interested, as she considered Francesco Totti to be the most beautiful man in Italy.

'He is so handsome,' she sighed, when the piece on Totti was over.

'He needs to recover from injury and play a few games,' remarked Roberto.

'It is a pity that our Sicilian teams aren't better,' said Tonino. 'The children in our quarter are all mad about Inter and Milan. And you, mama, need to keep your opinion of Totti to yourself when my father comes home.'

But this conversation was cut short by the local news coming on. There was a report of several murders in the greater Palermo area; murder always had priority. Then came the disturbances in Catania. Every night, for three nights, on the Monday, the Tuesday, and the Wednesday, buses had been hijacked and set alight in one part of the city or another. Tonight, said the reporter, the forces of law and order were on high alert. Every quarter, every suburb was under strict surveillance. There was an interview with the commissioner, the man who had replaced the mayor, who blamed the central government. He had asked for the deployment of more police, and had been refused. A candidate in the forthcoming election came on next, demanding that the government deployed troops. Tonino yawned loudly at this point. Troops, remarked Roberto, would be a cosmetic solution only. Finally, Volta came on. ('I like him,' said the signora. 'Good,' said Tonino, 'Because you and everyone else is going to vote for him.') He was calm and authoritative. He made the simple promise that once a decent administration was in the city hall, led by himself, all this nonsense would stop. The cause lay in the fact that there had been an administration which had not been up to the job, and which no one had respected, followed by a commission that no one had voted for. Once they were gone, and a serious mayor, namely himself, took over, people would behave, and the violence, which was mainly the work of high-spirited teenagers, would cease.

'I hope nothing happens tonight, not that it ever happens here,' remarked the signora. 'They say the weekend was peaceful.' She looked at her son. 'Are you going out tonight?'

'No, mama, I am thinking of going to bed early. In fact, more or less now. After I have shown Roberto the gallery. I have had a long day.'

The two boys went into the gallery. No words passed between them. Tonino switched on all the lights and found the catalogue, essentially a print out, and gave it to Roberto. He began to look at the pictures and match up the numbers with the numbers on the list, reading the brief description of each. There were no prices mentioned, but he knew what that meant. If you had to ask, you could not afford it.

'These are nice,' he said, looking at the set of six by Vanvitelli, the series of Neapolitan views. 'That is nice,' he said, looking at the Angelica Kaufmann.

He was being very attentive to the pictures, knowing that he would have to discuss them with Gabriella when he saw her next. He was memorising the names, so he could look them up afterwards, so he would not seem so very ignorant in conversation.

'What did you do today?' asked Tonino, bored by the pictures, or more accurately, bored by the way they claimed Roberto's attention.

Roberto put the catalogue aside, realising that he should pay attention to Tonino.

'I went to the university, lectures, work in the library, going home for lunch, then more time in the library this afternoon; then I went and met Gabriella in a bar near the Roman theatre.'

'That was quick,' said Tonino.

'No, I am taking it slowly. Don't want to mess things up. I want it to be serious. She is clever and beautiful, and her brother owns all this. It would be a step up for me.'

'He owns all this, but he is cash poor.'

'Still, it is not bad, and he won't be that way forever, I feel. Not with you to help him.'

'Not me, don Traiano.' Tonino paused. 'When I said it was quick, I meant that it was only the other day you met those girls at the wedding. You forgot them pretty quickly.'

'Yes, I did. Do you blame me? It was nice while it lasted, but that was all. What about you and the girl you met?'

'The same. She is forgotten. When are you seeing Gabriella again?'

'Next week. When are you seeing my sister again? And have you made up your mind which sister?'

'Actually, I have. Petra. You know I have. She said she would ask her mother's permission. I am seeing her tomorrow. I am sure your mother consulted you before granting her permission.'

'Actually, she did. If you lay a finger on her, well, not a finger, you know what I mean, I don't care how tough you are, I will....'

'There is no need,' said Tonino. 'I won't. She is your sister, after all, and she is the youngest. But I like her. We are just going out for an ice cream. You can come too.'

'I might have to work, but we will see,' said Roberto.

There was a pause.

'When are you laying a finger on Gabriella?' asked Tonino at last.

'Mind your own business,' said Roberto. He relented. 'Not soon, that is for sure.'

'She likes you?'

'Seems that way. I mean, yes, she does. What did you do today?'

'Mind your own business,' said Tonino, with an edge to his voice.

'You said you had had a long day.'

'I did. I have to go and tell my mother all about it, though I might wait until tomorrow.' He sighed. 'I went to Palermo.'

'On the train, or on your bike?'

'What difference does it make? My bike. The train takes too long. I went to see my father.'

'And?'

'What is there to say?' said Tonino.

Indeed, what was there to say? He had not expected to like the prison. After all, who could like a prison? But nothing had prepared him for the fortress wall, not so very far from the viale della Libertà, in the fashionable and modern part of the city, and the grim building that lay behind it. And nothing had prepared him for the sight of the father of whom he had no memory at all.

He had had the idea, received from where, he knew not, that boys were supposed to idolise their fathers, especially if their fathers were absent. Of course, he knew this could not be true. There were plenty of boys in the Purgatory quarter whose fathers were absent, either in prison, like his, or else men who had simply disappeared, leaving the children and mothers to look after themselves, or men who worked in Italy, far from home. None of these boys had idolised their absent fathers, as far as he could remember. And there were the boys who had fathers at home, fathers whom they hated for their brutality or despised for their weakness. So, fathers on the whole were not admired. But nothing had prepared him for the shock of seeing his own father.

Grassi senior had been there in the room used for visits, sitting at a table, with an air of defeated patience about him, a man of just under forty, but seeming a couple of decades older. He was small, shrunken, diminished, grey-faced, as if the prison atmosphere had eaten him away. He was unmistakeably like Tonino, and it was clearly him, it could be no other, for there was a strong resemblance between father and son, but a cruel likeness which underlined how unlike they were. Tonino, at the sight of his father, realised what he would be like when he was old, what he would be like when placed in his coffin, if he allowed them to defeat him. For his father, he saw, was a man who had rebelled, and been defeated and been kept cruelly alive. Better to have been killed, to have died young, than to survive like this. He felt a terrible shame come over him. How could his father, his own father, have allowed this to have happened to him? Why wasn't he dead? Why hadn't he died in the attempt to be free from these people, the people who had imprisoned him, the people who had betrayed him? A life without honour was surely intolerable. How had he accepted it?

As soon as he saw the hollowed-out shell that had been his father, he wanted to turn and leave. He knew that his mother, in wanting to prevent him coming all these years, had been right. Why hadn't she explained it? Well, she had, he knew that now; but she had not had the words or the ability to convey the horror he now faced: half an hour with this man whose very presence filled him with pity and disgust. The thought that this man was somehow connected to him was deeply repugnant. But he had to go forward. The visit had to take place. It was supposed to last thirty minutes. He had thought that short. Now he realised how long it was. Thirty minutes seemed an eternity. He had to go through with it. He came up to his father, and sat opposite him.

'Hi,' he said softly, not knowing what else to say.

'Finally,' said the man. 'Your mother said you would come when you were able to come. I agreed with her that you ought to come when you wanted to come, not when we thought you were able to do so, but in your own time.'

'Are you disappointed it took me so long?' asked Tonino out of curiosity.

He realised that this was stupid question. The man had lived with fourteen years of disappointment. Everything was disappointing. Disappointment was the air he breathed. Indeed, he did not understand the question.

'Your mother said that you are doing well, that you have done well. But she did not go into detail.'

'Don Calogero di Rienzi likes me,' said Tonino. 'He trusts me. His deputy, don Traiano, trusts me. I have done things for them.' He kept his voice low. 'The things I have done cannot be traced back to me. A woman, a child… they wanted them out of the way, and I saw to it. Of course, mama could not tell you because she does not know. She will never know. I am young, but I am there with the adults. I sell pills and things like that. I organise things. I am strong and not frightened of anyone. I have lots of money, saved up, and mama is comfortable. She has a pension from the Confraternity. You do not have to worry about her. I have had a few women, so I know what is what, but now I am thinking about becoming serious about a good girl in Catania, whose brother is a friend of mine. So, everything is set fair for me.'

The father looked at him, without the ghost of a smile.

'When I was young,' he said, as if he were talking about another person whom he barely remembered, 'I was a friend of don Calogero's father. He was much older than me, of course. I did things, like the things you mentioned. He was blown up, and I was arrested and put on trial and brought here. Because Renato was dead, there was no one to help me. But later the friends you mentioned promised to look after you and my wife. I suppose they did.'

'What are you in for?' asked Tonino.

He looked as if he had difficulty remembering.

'I stabbed a boy in a fight, here in Palermo. I cannot remember what the quarrel was about. I was arrested for brawling, and it did not seem serious. Then, some weeks later, the boy died as a result of his injuries, they said, and they arrested me for murder. But…'

'When did this happen?' asked Tonino.

'Just after the time Renato di Rienzi was blown up. You see, after my first arrest, I thought Renato would help me. But then he died, and they arrested me again after the man I stabbed died. And because Renato was not there to help me, I stayed here. They would not even allow me to be transferred to Catania, to be close to home. Usually, they allow that. But in my case, they were unkind.'

'How well did you know don Calogero's father?'

'Very well. I used to help him whenever he needed things doing. I would drive him around sometimes. I would pick things up for him. He was kind, he was generous. Our wives were friends.'

'Did the police come and ask you about him once he was dead?'

'Never. What was there to tell? Besides, I would never speak to them, ever. And don Calogero was soon looking after you and your mother.'

'When the police were trying to reconstruct his movements…..'

'Who cares about that now?' asked Grassi. 'The younger son, he died, didn't he? What was he called? I cannot remember.'

'He was called Rosario.'

Grassi nodded. Rosario was indeed dead, but one did not ask why he had died, how he had died, what had happened to him. One never discussed the past.

'You have done well,' said Grassi. 'Thanks to don Calogero. Me, not so much….'

'When they let you out….' said Tonino.

Grassi looked at him with his sad, dead eyes.

'I will come back to Catania. Your mother wants me to come back….'

It was left unstated between them that what the signora wanted, her son, who loved her, might nevertheless not want.

'She said that her friend signora di Rienzi has spoken to her son, don Calogero, and that there would be something for me to do when I got out. I don't know what, but something, something to keep body and soul together.'

'You don't need to worry about that,' said Tonino. 'I can look after you and my mother. I have plenty of money.'

'All under the mattress?'

'No! I have a bank account. I have several, in fact. It is spread around, all small sums, in various banks, but it all adds up. Some is being looked after by friends. And yes, a bit under the mattress, a bit of liquidity for when I need it. But I am not stupid. I know a bit about how these things work. I opened a bank account for my mother. In a couple of years, I may want to be here, in Palermo, or some other place; and if you are in Catania, looking after my mother…'

Grassi senior nodded. He understood.

'I mean, Palermo is where the Santucci businesses are based. And they may want me here in a few years' time. We will see.'

'You think ahead, you are clever,' said his father. 'There were lots of things I should have thought of, but failed to think of. When I met your mother, when we married, after you came along, I should not have taken the risks I took. I should have realised that I had a wife and a child, and that I should have been more careful. Others take risks and do not suffer, but I was not so lucky. I am sorry. When they let me out, I shall take no more risks.'

'You won't have to,' said Tonino. 'I will look after you.'

'But you will take risks,' said his father. 'Maybe you are one of the lucky ones.'

'I am clever, you need to be lucky and clever,' said Tonino. 'I am both. I have friends, big friends. You watch. I am going to outwit them all. I am going to wipe the smile off their fat faces. You will see.'

'Can you read and write?' asked his father.

'And count up to ten,' said Tonino. 'I never read books, but I could if I wanted to. I never write anything down, but I can write. I don't have one of those phones either. I don't have a computer. I don't leave a trail of evidence behind me. My friend Roberto, he is at the university, he is clever, but he would be nothing without me. I am the one who can take the risks most people are too scared to take, and win the big prizes. I have already won the big prizes; I have done what few would have dared, and everyone now knows, without knowing the details, that I would dare do anything. Anything. I am brave.'

The older man looked at him without comprehension. He had been in prison too long. His mind had narrowed. He had no ambitions. He was a failure. Worse than that, he was an embarrassment to his son.

What was there to say? He looked at Roberto. He could not put any of this into words. His father had made him sad, but it went further: he had not liked his father either. Did anyone actually like their father? Roberto sensed this inability to speak about his experience. He himself had hated seeing his own father in Rome, on the return journey from which he had first met Tonino.

'Why did you go and see him?' he asked.

'Curiosity,' said Tonino.

The success or otherwise of an operation, Traiano knew, depended on the amount of preparation and research one put into it. He had thought about getting a new doctor for some time; first as a little thought, after all, Doctor Moro was getting old; then as a major thought, one that seemed to take up all his waking hours, always there at the back of his mind. Now at last, he had found what he had been looking for.

His first idea was to get hold of a doctor who liked cocaine; so, he had put the word out among the boys who dealt with the drug, letting them know that if they came across a doctor, a medical one, they were to let him know. But while it turned out that every profession was represented in the users of cocaine of Catania – lawyers, policemen, shopkeepers, accountants, and even, shockingly, several priests – there was one exception to the rule: there were no doctors. Despairing of this angle, he had spoken to the gravedigger of Bronte, the man who now enjoyed the distinction of being able to buy debts from anyone who sought to offload them; and the gravedigger had found someone.

His name was Doctor Adami, and his surgery was in the upper reaches of the via Etnea, near piazza Cavour. He was not in debt, but his wife was. Signora Adami was extravagant, and there were several outstanding debts, though all of them of a certain age, which seemed to indicate that people no longer gave the signora credit. But human nature did not change. The signora was probably running up debts with the bank and on her credit card, if she were allowed one; and the doctor, her husband, was probably in despair. But this was just a hunch, and it needed to be checked out. Accordingly, he set several little boys to watch the place where the doctor lived, which was just round the corner from his surgery, and sure enough they reported that every day the signora went out shopping to the via Etnea and to the jewellery shops in particular. He also sent some older boys to the surgery to join the never-ending queue of patients and to gauge the atmosphere there. The doctor practised general medicine, and the waiting room was full of old men, women and small children. The doctor himself was middle-aged. Old, but not so old as to be without his uses. Old enough not to react badly; old enough to know what was what, and in which direction his own interests lay.

He would tackle Adami himself, he decided. As for Moro, there was research to be done there. For this, he would rely on Tonino.

'You are going to the doctor,' said Traiano, one evening, once the other boys had been sent on their way.

They were alone in the changing room of the gym. The other boys had all been given various bills to collect, yet another tranche of which had arrived that day from the gravedigger of Bronte. Traiano had bought them and now sold them on.

'Doctor Moro?' asked Tonino.

'Yes, Doctor Moro. Has he ever mentioned who his supplier is?'

'Never, boss.'

'Or when he gets his deliveries, or how he gets his deliveries?'

'I once saw someone entering with a box when I was going out. A man of about forty, who looked American. It was in the evening, I remember that, as that is when I usually see him. But it was unusual. They would vary the times, I think. He said nothing about it at the time; I don't think he would ever tell me.'

'Then we have to find out,' said Traiano. 'Look, go to him tonight and tell him we really need some fentanyl. He may have it. If he does, ask him for something until you reach something he does not have. Ask him to get it, as a matter of urgency, then he may say that he will have it in a few days. In the meantime, make sure you have a kid watching his front door and an older boy with a bike who can follow whoever drops the stuff off and get the car numberplate. That is important. It will be boring watching his front door, day and night, but it won't take more than a few days, I hope.'

'And once we know the supplier?' asked Tonino.

'Exactly. Moro will no longer be necessary.'

He dressed with care for his trip to the doctor. He put on a jacket that he did not much like, which he had worn only a few times before, and which zipped up at the front. He wore a pair of jeans and some trainers, both of which he knew would give him the appearance of any other person of his age. Thus, when he entered the doctor's waiting room, and asked who was the last in line, and took his seat, no one paid him any attention at all. The old men were concerned with their ailments, no doubt, the women with their children, and there was only one other young man there, who looked most uncomfortable, thus attracting attention to himself. But Traiano was calm, quite calm, affecting the boredom of the waiting room.

His turn came, and he was shown into the doctor's office. Adami looked at him, gestured him to sit, turned away from his computer and looked at him expectantly, waiting for him to speak.

'I am not one of your patients,' explained Traiano. 'But I am in a position to help you.'

Adami looked at him and frowned slightly.

'Go on,' he said, without emotion.

'Your wife has run up various bills,' he said, taking out the papers that the gravedigger had given him. 'These bills are all old and they have come into my possession, and I wish to return them to you.'

He placed the pieces of paper on the desk in front of the doctor.

'I do not want them,' said Adami.

'I am doing you a favour,' said Traiano. 'Are you refusing to accept a favour from me?'

'Who the hell are you?' asked Adami. 'Actually, I do not want to know. I can guess. I know who you are and what you are looking for.'

'I don't think you do,' said Traiano calmly and politely. 'If you did, your tone would be polite. I hope, sir, you will regain your manners. My name is Trajan Antonescu, and I am a friend of don Calogero di Rienzi, of whom you will have heard.'

'Ah, I have,' said Adami. 'You are right there. I know all about him, and you. You people are the scum of the earth. Your don Calogero is a crook, a thief and a murderer, the son of a murderer, and you, Antonescu, are the son of a prostitute and a murderer and a thief as well. My contempt for you is total. All of you, and all your associates.'

'Well, now that you have told me what you really think, do yourself a favour and tell me that you are only too happy to work with us. We do not need you for much. If one of our men is hurt or injured, we will bring him to you, you will patch him up, and no questions asked. Do not tell me you will turn this down. You need the money. Oh yes, you have your high and mighty moral posturing, but you need us the same way as you need the men who take out your rubbish, and the same way you need the men who unblock your drains. Be reasonable, we need each other.'

'Maybe we do, Antonescu, but I would rather die than admit it,' said Doctor Adami. 'I know about that man, Moro, who calls himself a doctor.'

'He is a doctor.'

'But he is not a good man.'

'Agreed. I do not like Moro myself, at all. But this is not about him, it is about you. Your other patients are waiting. I had better not take up any more of your valuable time. Can we rely on you?'

It was a mild question. Traiano looked around the room. Behind the place where the doctor sat was a clean white wall, perhaps recently painted. He waited for an answer. Under his jacket, he could feel the gun. The doctor surely knew it was there, if he had any sense. If he had any sense, which he was beginning to doubt. He looked now at the doctor, questioningly. He saw he had misjudged him. Of all the doctors in Catania, had he stumbled on the only honest one?

'No,' said Doctor Adami.

Traiano frowned, as if puzzled.

'Are you quite sure?' he asked.

In the waiting room, the wait seemed interminable. Thank goodness it was winter, nearly, and the room was cool. As the afternoon advanced, so did the state of somnolence that seemed to embrace the waiting room. Some of the old men had nodded off; some of the children were fast asleep in the arms of mothers and grandmothers, all of whom looked from time to time at the clock with weary resignation. Another embarrassed young man, recently arrived, looked at the clock as well, feeling the agony of waiting drawn out to an almost unendurable extent. Then the boredom ended suddenly, as the two shots rang out from the other room. There was a sharp intake of breath and a feeling of horror, a moment of paralysis. And then, without a word, silently, swiftly, the mothers and grandmothers picked up their children, the old people got up, the agonised young man forgot his agony, and all headed for the door and were hurriedly gone.

He had not intended it to end like that, but he was not sorry that it had. Every now and then, an example had to be made, and this man Adami, with his absurd posturing, clearly needed to be made an example of. There would be less posturing among doctors from now on. He walked through the empty waiting room, not hurrying, and out into the piazza Cavour, and towards the via Etnea which, as he headed south, grew more and more crowded. In fifteen minutes, he was back in Purgatory, back at the gym. He went into the underground room, and went to the cupboard that contained the shaft, the oubliette. The first thing he disposed of into the silence was the gun, then his shoes. Afterwards, he patiently took off all his clothes and disposed of them one by one. Then he went to the shower, and stood under it for some time, taking particular care to wash his hands and his face thoroughly, again and again. That over, he returned to his locker, where he always set a fresh set of clothes. As he got dressed, he smelt his hands, which smelt delightfully of soap.

Afterwards, as dusk was falling, he went to the bar in the square outside the Church of the Holy Souls in Purgatory and had a Cinzano and shook hands with a lot of people. The news was not good. There was traffic chaos everywhere, as the police had blocked off the piazza Cavour, as there had been a murder there late that afternoon. Before going home to have supper with his wife and children, he saw Tonino briefly, who looked at him questioningly.

'I have a feeling that something might happen tonight,' he said. 'But I am prepared for it. If it happens, unleash chaos.'

They came for him that evening at about nine o'clock, just after the children were in bed. He made no resistance to being cuffed or having plastic bags put over his hands, or being taken to the police station, not the local one, but one out in the suburbs a short distance away, by car. He kissed his wife before going and told her not to worry. He told her he would be back, but he could not be sure when.

When they got there, he recognised the place, the same police headquarters where he and Gino and Alfio had been taken years before by that awful man, may he rest in peace, Fabrizio Perraino. He was taken to a large interview room where the cuffs were removed and the plastic bags as well, and where his hands were swabbed. The swabs were bagged and sent off to forensics. Then he was told to strip, and each item of clothing was placed in a separate bag and also taken away. He stood there stark naked, staring boldly ahead, the police around him, impassive. He was told to lean forward, and they ruffled his hair with a stick. He was told to stand upright and they pushed aside his testicles with another stick to see if anything were hidden there. Then they told him to bend over and he was subjected to what he knew was called a cavity search. At last, this done, they allowed him to put on a white jumpsuit, and then they marched him to a cell and locked him in. There was a bench there. He lay down and shut his eyes; despite the bright light, within a few moments, he was asleep.

A few hours later, he was woken by a visitor. It was the lawyer Rossi.

'I am sorry they woke you up,' Traiano said apologetically.

'I had barely gone to bed. Your wife called Calogero, and he called me. She, Calogero's wife, is actually now giving birth, but he only took a few moments to call me.'

'That was nice of him, and nice of you to come.'

'What has happened?'

'I have no idea,' said Traiano. 'No idea at all.'

'It took an age to get here,' said Rossi a trifle querulously. 'Lots of streets are blocked, and the traffic, for this time in the morning, well, it's like rush hour.'

'Maybe that is why they have not interviewed me,' said Traiano. 'They have other things to worry about. But they may be waiting for the forensics to come back with the results on my clothes and my hands.'

'Your hands?' said Rossi, alarmed.

'No need to worry at all,' said Traiano, calmly.

The presence of Rossi galvanised the police. Outside, while Catania burned, they began the first interview.

He was asked to explain his movements that day. He did so calmly and reflectively. He had risen late. He had had something to eat. He had played with the children. He had then gone out. His mother was about to give birth, and his best friend's wife as well, and that made him a little nervous. So, he had gone to the gym and spent the afternoon there, where he had seen lots of people. He had then left the gym, gone to the bar and had a Cinzano. Then he had gone home, had supper and put the children to bed. The rest they knew. When asked who he had seen at the gym, he said that there were too many names to mention; but he had a long conversation with Tonino Grassi, who was a close friend of his. They did not ask what about. The police looked bored by this information.

'Were you at any time in piazza Cavour?' he was asked. 'Do you know Doctor Adami?'

He shook his head to both.

The police sighed. He was sent back to his cell, and the lawyer Rossi was sent home.

Hours passed. He asked for something to read. They gave him a Bible. He settled down to read it. More hours passed. Then they came into his cell and returned his clothes. He knew what this meant. The clothes were 'clean', they were forensically useless. They told him to put them on and stared at him with great hostility as he did so. But they were not letting him go, not just yet. There was the identity parade first. Who had they got? He wondered. He assumed none of the children or the old ladies in the waiting room, or even the old men. It must be the embarrassed looking man of his own age. He was taken into a room and made to stand in front of an opaque window. Four other men joined him shortly, all his own age, his own height, his own colouring. Instructions were given: two klaxons were to sound, at the first they were to stand to attention with their hands behind their backs, and the second klaxon would announce the end of the parade. It seemed interminable. During the silence he withdrew his right hand from behind his back as if to scratch himself, but in fact to make a shooting gesture with two fingers, just briefly.

It was clear that he had not been picked out, for the police officers' expressions were now thunderous in their discontent. But still they did not let him go; he was returned to his cell and to his sacred reading. Every now and then, he had the idea that someone was looking at him through the spyhole. He was completely calm. He assumed it was the nervous young man who was to have picked him out from the identity parade and who had failed to have the guts to do so. He had his watch now and noted the hours as they slipped by. He was fed, given water, given coffee, allowed to go to the loo. But he knew they had to charge him or release him. The clock was ticking. Rossi would be back soon to demand his release. But they were waiting for something, and he could guess what.

It was late afternoon when the cell door opened, and Silvio Pierangeli came in.

'You took your time,' remarked Traiano levelly. 'Where is the lady? Chiara di Donato? Though of course, that is not her real name is it, any more than Silvio is yours?'

'I had to get here from far away,' said Silvio. 'They called me last night; I got the first plane I could, and here I am. I would have been earlier, but the traffic in your city is in gridlock still.'

'Well, you have had a wasted journey, as Chiara must have realised, otherwise she would have come too.' He put the Bible aside and looked at him. 'We are not friends, but it is nice to have someone to talk to after spending so much time here alone.'

'You killed Doctor Adami,' said Silvio.

'Did I? That is an interesting thought. I have never met him, I did not know him, and most murdered people, as you know, are killed by people they know. What one earth would my motive have been?'

'Some sort of extortion or blackmail,' said Silvio. 'But you know and I know that you have impunity. No one would dare pick you out of an identity parade. They do not want to suffer the same fate. Of course, one of your associates may betray you, but that is many years in the future. Until then…'

'Until then, I continue,' said Traiano with a hint of bitterness. 'As do you, tracking me like a revenging Fury, though not a particularly effective one. You want me to give up. But perhaps you should give up, get a proper job. You are no good at this one. I am very sorry you had such a wasted journey, and even sorrier for the tax payer who foots the bill.'

Silvio shrugged, and sat down next to him on the bench.

'How is the family?' he asked.

'Growing. My mother is having her third, today probably. May already have had it.'

'But your children, how are they? And your wife? Cristoforo is what, four now?' He paused. 'Boys grow up to be like their fathers, you know. He is entering an impressionable age. The whole Purgatory quarter will hear how you killed Adami and got away with it. He will hear about it. The man who shoots innocent doctors. He will hear about it, and as he grows up, he will want a gun of his own. You are a monster, but do you want to be the father of monsters? Repent before it is too late.'

'I am not who you think I am. Oh, I know you despise me. I saw the way the police looked at me, the way they spoke to me, the way they reacted to my answers. You know, I would make a good policeman, because I have some understanding of human nature. Contempt is an ugly thing. It is not enticing. Why would I want to join those who hold me in contempt and betray those whom I love? As for repentance, well that is a religious virtue. I go to church on Sunday, I know about repentance. And I know that it never springs from fear or ambition, but only has one source, and that is love. Only love redeems. Surely you know that?'

Traiano smiled.

'Your hypocrisy revolts me,' said Silvio.

'I am no such thing. I have never claimed to be a saint. Now, are you going to let me go? What reason do you have for holding me?'

He came through the front door as quietly as he could, without making a noise, and took off his shoes as he did so and then, on silent feet, made his way down to the kitchen, from whence he heard the sound of the television which was on a local new channel. As he opened the door, he saw how she was concentrating on what was a on screen: the murder of the doctor in his surgery in piazza Cavour, the disturbances the previous night, the number of cars and buses hijacked, the blocked streets. It was all bad news. She sensed his arrival and turned, surprised and delighted. He gestured with a finger to his lips not to say anything, motioning with his head towards the other door, the room where the children were watching television. She went to the door, saw that the children were rapt in attention before the screen, and then closed the door gently. He took her in his arms. Their kiss was intense. There was no need for words.

Chapter Seven

The boss, don Calogero di Rienzi, had a new son. The news arrived in Catania, in the Purgatory quarter, as evening came on the last day of October. The first to hear it was his mother, by telephone, and she communicated it to her two daughters. It seemed that the birth had been difficult and prolonged, but the new son was safely here at last, and he was to be called Romano, which, in his grandmother's opinion, was a most unsuitable name, and, she assumed, the choice of her daughter-in-law. Elena, her younger daughter, would take the four other children with her to Palermo in the morning to see the new baby and to see his parents, and perhaps stay there some time. Assunta, her elder daughter, running the office, with no children of her own, had no intention of haring off to Palermo, and would see the baby in due course. Her mother, Romano's grandmother, took the same view.

The birth of this new child was of enormous interest to the other women of the quarter, as one would expect. Where would the baptism take place, in Catania, in their own Church of the Holy Souls in Purgatory, or in Palermo, which was, after all, the place where the mother spent much of her time, where she was from too? And was she not a friend of the Cardinal of Palermo, a rather more prestigious cleric than their own much loved don Giorgio? If she chose Palermo over Catania, they would know what to think. Indeed, it was a sensitive subject and one that led to a lively argument between don Calogero and Anna Maria Tancredi, his wife.

The news soon became even better, for a few hours after the birth in Palermo, Anna, Traiano's mother, gave birth to another son, the child whom everyone knew would be her last. She was forty after all (though Anna Maria Tancredi was older, forty-five.) She now had three sons by three different fathers, though the first two fathers were both long gone and forgotten. The new baby was called William, which everyone agreed was an appropriate if unusual name, as it had been borne by one of the Norman kings.

At ten o'clock that night, the bar in the square opposite the Church of the Holy Souls in Purgatory was full, and the prosecco was flowing, all of it on the house, to celebrate the double birth. While the women put their children to bed, spoke on their phones to each other, or settled down to watch television, the men gathered to celebrate the boss's latest triumph, and the latest triumph of don Traiano as well. The first had another son, and the second another brother. That, of course, was the outward reason for the celebration, the focal point of which, in the absence of the boss, and the absence of don Alfio, on honeymoon, and don Gino, in Palermo with don Renzo, the focal point of which was don Traiano himself. But, behind it, was another reason: he had been taken away by the police, and the police had let him go; the first piece of news had been greeted with consternation, the second, thirty-six hours later, with jubilation. He was untouchable. He was what they all aspired to be, immune to the interferences of the forces of law and order, the people who had for centuries oppressed them.

Oh, how they hated the men in uniform and the women in uniform too! How they despised and loathed them and their interfering ways; the way they stopped you parking your car where you wanted to; the way they stopped you leaving your motorbike or scooter where no reasonable person would object; the way they stopped you and asked for your identity card; the way they looked at you; the way they asked offensive questions, whether you were at school, whether you had a job; the way they frisked you, searching for weapons and for drugs; the way they made you turn out your pockets, and even take off your shoes; the way they threatened you with arrest; the way they spoke with their horrible sounding northern accents. Of course, some of them were alight, some of them understood the way things were done, but most of them, no!

And here was don Traiano, returned from the purgatory of unjust imprisonment, where he had been subjected to the full battery of humiliations (they had all heard the stories of what happened in police stations) but it had not broken him, and here he was, and what could they do to him now? And as for this story of the murdered doctor in piazza Cavour, shot dead while his patients waited to see him, what was there to link that to don Traiano? No one knew this doctor, and there were plenty of indications that this had been either a robbery that had gone wrong, or else a case of blackmail, or else (the favoured theory of many aired on the television over the last few days) the man had been shot by his wife's lover. But how could don Traiano have had anything to do with it? Besides which, they had all seen him at the gym where he had been all afternoon, just when the unfortunate doctor was meeting his fate.

Standing in the door of the bar and pausing for a moment, Tonino surveyed the happy scene. He saw the men looking at don Traiano, the source of all their happiness and security; he saw the younger ones look at him with unfeigned devotion, with the deepest admiration possible for one human being to feel for another. One day that would be him, he swore to himself. He would be the centre of attention; he would command. He saw too why Traiano commanded. He was reserved, in command of himself, therefore able to command others. The boss saw him and gestured him to approach. He smiled at him, a smile, Tonino knew, that meant nothing. He took his hand.

'You did well while I was away,' he said. 'They say the traffic was at a standstill; the city was in chaos. So much disorder for our friend Volta to sort out. Good. Now, you see all these boys? An army is only as good as its commander. I am sure they all do what you tell them, and they all get the reward they deserve. But if anyone annoys you, or anyone does not do as they are told, well, use your fist, as in the past, but use the belt too.'

'Can I, boss?' asked Tonino, surprised.

'Yes, you can, from now on, because I say so. It is a useful thing to have. It hurts more.'

He kissed Tonino's cheek, a special favour. Then he pushed him away.

'I am hoping you have a message for me,' he said. 'You do? From Doctor Moro? Good. The answer is no. I will not see him tomorrow. Let him stew. He is worried, you see. Let him worry, it will help us. Tell him we will see him next week. The second half of the week. And tell him to make sure the person we want to meet is there. No need to tell him that tonight. Let him wait, let him worry.'

'You are brown,' said Catarina.

'The beach,' said Alfio, her cousin.

He was just back from honeymoon.

'Was it nice?' said Catarina.

'Delightful. White sand, palm trees, nice hotel, nice food, all run by Italians, so really nice food. We spent all our time on the beach.'

'Well, I hope Giuseppina was not disappointed. I am surprised she has not rung me to tell me all about it.'

'She is still unpacking. We only just got back.'

'And you came round here as soon as you could?' asked Catarina.

'I told her I was coming to see Gino.' He paused. 'I think you should be a little nicer to me.'

'If you think…' she began, then stopped. 'Are you still thinking about that? Well, it was a long time ago. You went to Bicocca and that was that. I told you at the time it was a bad idea, as we were first cousins. And I also told you that I did not enjoy it or find you physically attractive.'

'It was over ten years ago,' he said.

'And nothing has changed. I have not changed my mind about you, and you have not become more attractive, despite your superior dentistry. Anyway, you came to see Gino. He is not here. He is in Palermo with don Renzo. So, you can go home now.'

Alfio sighed and sat down.

'What are we going to do?' he asked.

'We?' she asked.

'You know what I mean. What are you going to do about Gino when he finds out; and he will find out; Renzo will tell him. And he will wonder why Renzo told him and I did not. And he will wonder about that child in the next room. And he will wonder about you. Not that he is much given to wondering, as you know. He is a man of action. If Renzo does not tell him, someone else will. Giuseppina knows. She knows I cannot have children. I have told her that. She thinks there may be a miracle, but I do not believe in miracles. And I do not think, and neither does she, that Tino was a miracle baby. So, what are we going to do? How long has he been away?'

'A week,' she answered.

'Will he come back for All Saints? For the feast of the Dead?'

'I doubt it.'

'There, you see. He prefers to do whatever he and don Renzo do in Palermo, far away from you. So, what are we going to do?'

'You know what I want,' said Catarina.

'I know who you want, and it is not me,' said Alfio.

'I want Calogero,' she said.

'You are married, he is married,' said Alfio in exasperation. 'Even if, even if, he would not want to offend his wife, the mother of his children, and his banker.'

'He likes to show he commands. He would like to show her that though she is his banker, he is the one in charge.'

'He is his own man, he does what he likes, I can't push you towards him.'

'You would not have to. Just leave him to me. I can take care of him. You see, I have his nephew, the child of the brother he was obsessed with, and I have the ability to give him further nephews and nieces should he want them.'

'Listen, there are rules. No man in the honoured society can touch the woman of another man in the honoured society. He can't break that rule.'

'That rule will not apply forever,' she said. 'The way Gino drinks, the way he takes pills….' She paused. 'The way things are going… He would only need a little push.'

'He is my best friend,' said Alfio.

The tone in which he said it told her all that she needed to know.

There was no more to be said. He would do whatever was necessary, because his own interests were the only interests that made any sense to him. Indeed, the argument, which did not need to be made out loud, because it was so obvious, was unanswerable. She was his cousin, and he had to protect her, he had no choice about that; and then there was the question of the ultimate prize. If she fulfilled her ambition, and clearly it was a long-term plan, then he would benefit enormously for having smoothed the way for her, and for him. She would be grateful, the boss would be grateful as well no doubt, and then perhaps, with Gino out of the way, he might even dislodge Traiano in the boss's favour.

Of course, Gino was his best friend. They had been friends since their time in Bicocca. But already that friendship looked dated, it felt dated, it felt like something from a past age. And Gino had made choices since then that separated himself from Alfio: the drink, the drugs, these were things Alfio did not share. And his friendship with don Renzo. That too excluded him. He did not like don Renzo. He did not like in particular the way that Gino had taken up with Renzo to the detriment of a previous firm friend, himself. He felt that a resentment was building inside him, and that it was directed at Gino. Gino made things so damn difficult.

He looked at his cousin with something like dislike. She was forcing him to do this. But it was decided. It had to be done. They should never have sent Gino to Palermo, to help don Renzo, he thought, overlooking the fact that Gino had wanted to go. It was all their fault. They were forcing him into doing this.

It was, Renzo said, necessary to visit the new baby, Romano. He himself felt no compulsion to see the new child, but Elena, his intended, was staying in the flat near the Politeama with her brother and the children, and she reminded him that it was incumbent upon him to visit. And if had to go, then Gino could not be left out.

They were there at ten in the morning. The new child, Romano, was brought in, looked at, admired, and several things were said about him; Renzo was even invited to take him in his arms; the older children were delighted, it was clear, by the whole business of having a younger brother. It seemed that Isabella, the eldest, was now thrilled to have a younger sister, Natalia, and three younger brothers to order around: Renato, Sebastiano and now Romano. It was, Anna Maria conceded, a little exhausting, but she had help, smiling at the nanny as she said this, and at Elena too. Elena had been so wonderful taking all the children out every day to see the sights of Palermo, rather than leaving them cooped up in this poky little (in reality, enormous) flat of hers.

Coffee was served.

'What have you been doing?' the boss asked Gino.

'Tastings, don Calogero.' He noticed the very slightly raised eyebrow. 'We have been visiting the suppliers in the hills, the farmers, the vineyards. We have been sampling the products, the wine, the cheese, checking things are up to standard.'

'Do you like cheese?' he asked.

'Very much, don Calogero.'

'And if the cheese is no good?' he asked.

'Then we tell them it has to improve. But mainly it is to make sure they are not selling to our rivals. You know, when you are on the telephone they tell you one thing, but when you go in person…'

'It sounds fun.'

'It is. We have been visiting places around Montelepre, where don Renzo's great-grandfather came from.'

'And mine too,' said Calogero. 'Not that I have ever been there. I may, one day. Is it nice?'

'I am more of a city man, don Calogero.'

'Well, I am sure they do not give you any trouble in Montelepre,' he said. 'And if they do, you know how to deal with it. But tell me, how is your brother? He carried off one of our women, didn't he?'

Gino frowned. This clearly was not a subject he liked.

'He and Pasqualina are in Verona. They seem happy. But….'

Don Calogero's enquiring look invited confession.

'He should have stayed with us. We were once very close. But he went away. I did not want him to, neither did don Traiano. But....'

He noted the tone of anguish. It seemed that Gino had a heart, something he had not suspected until now.

'If your brother is being stupid, we should talk some sense into him,' he said. 'I am surprised that Traiano did not succeed. I do not mean with your brother, but with Pasqualina, as I am sure he will do what she tells him to do. Someone should explain things to them. You need your brother. I will speak to Traiano. He has never been known to fail before now.'

'Thanks, boss.'

Somewhere in the room it was decided that they should all go out: that is, Elena and the four older children, along with the nanny, and, the children insisted, with Renzo too, and Gino, leaving the baby Romano with his parents. Gino hesitated, but he could see from the pleading look that Renzo did not want to be left alone with so many women and children, but needed an ally, and feeling he had to go because of Elena, felt too that Gino's presence would make the thing more bearable. They were plainly being urged to go out for as long as possible, and the idea was to go to Monreale, which none of them had ever visited before; and so, the procession of two boys, two girls, two men, two women, left the flat to decant themselves into two cars and drive up the hill to the ancient cathedral.

Elena and Renzo, being an engaged couple, went in one car with Natalia and Renato; Gino found himself with the nanny, Isabella and Sebastiano. He had assumed correctly that the nanny was foreign, and was surprised to find she could speak correct but accented Italian. Her name was Henrietta. He had never met an English girl before now, and was rather unsure about how to speak to her; neither had he ever met a professional nanny. Natalia, from the back seat, ever forward, informed him that she and Henrietta were instructed by her mother (she meant Anna Maria) to speak together in English in order to prepare her for an English boarding school in due course. The signora, of course, spoke English, and that little Natalia should do the same impressed Gino.

As for Henerietta, she could not quite, in her English way, place Gino. He was clearly not in the same league as Mr di Rienzi who was, despite his youth, still not thirty, one of the most important businessmen in Sicily; he was not in the same league as Mrs di Rienzi, a highly educated woman, a banker, a clever woman. She was puzzled to some extent by his relationship to Mr Santucci, who was to marry Miss di Rienzi; these two were obviously very close, but not close in the way Englishman sometimes became close; but she had seen them looking at each other, and sensed the secret understandings that were between them. She liked her employers, Mr and Mrs di Rienzi, who were smart people, the sort of people she liked. She thought well of Miss di Rienzi, her charges' aunt, but she had her reservations about Mr Santucci. He was badly dressed, for a start, unlike his future brother-in-law, Mr di Rienzi. Quite often, as today, his shirt hung out, or partially hung out, which was even worse that hanging out entirely. He was, according to Isabella, who must have gathered this from the adults, extremely rich, with immense holdings, lots of companies that he had inherited after his father's early death. Presumably, this money made him attractive. It gave him his sense of confidence. But he was not good-looking at all, Henrietta thought. He had nice auburn hair, though it was ill-combed and unruly, but he had freckles and his eyes were too close together and his nose was too big. Like a lot of unattractive men, in her mind, he was almost good-looking, which was worse than not being good-looking at all. She was rather glad that she was not in the same car as him.

Instead, here she was with the 'friend' of Mr Santucci, as she thought of him, Mr Fisichella. She had been struck by him the moment she had seen him, and he too had been struck by her, she had been pleased to notice. He was not in the least bit good-looking, and there was something a little sad about him, an interior sadness, she noticed, though what its cause was, she had no idea. He was a giant of a man, and he moved into the room carefully, as if knowing he might knock something valuable over. He sat in his seat with care, lest he break it. In the car, he got into the driving seat with more ease, though aware of her next to him, aware that he should not crush her or inadvertently hit her when he grasped the gear stick. His hands, she noticed, were enormous. The car was not large and their physical proximity was pronounced, slightly awkward, and yet, she sensed, in a way, enjoyable.

The traffic was terrible. It always was in Palermo, but today it seemed worse than ever. Mr Fisichella tried to make conversation with her, listening attentively to her replies, as if paying special attention not to their content, but to their enunciation. They spoke of the traffic. Yes, London was as bad. Paris where she had worked, worse, perhaps, though they went everywhere by metro there. Vienna as well, where she had worked for a couple with six children. Discussing traffic was boring, but the point was rather different. She felt this man's interest and he felt hers. Natalia interrupted from the back seat. She wanted to know about Tino. Tino, he politely explained, was his son, the same age as Sebastiano. She took in the fact that he was married.

'Uncle Gino is married to the cousin of our Uncle Alfio,' Isabella explained.

Gino explained that he had not seen Tino for a couple of weeks, as he had been here, in Palermo, away from home, helping don Renzo. He clearly missed his son; his wife, not so much, so his tone conveyed.

They ground on through the traffic and at last began the climb to Monreale. None of the adults had been there before and were taken aback by its beauty. After the Cathedral, they walked in the cloisters where the two girls ran around, and where they remembered vaguely that they had been before with their deceased mother and their equally deceased uncle, Rosario. This thought remained private to the girls, who never spoke of either mother or uncle, not knowing quite how to broach the subject of the dead, the ghosts in their midst; a subject furthermore that neither Renato nor Sebastiano would understand, one being too young, the other not the son of their mother; a subject, because never spoken about, they imagined more or less forbidden; this thought of the dead created a slight sadness over the gathering which only lifted when they left the cloisters behind and went to lunch in a neighbouring restaurant. Here, not for the first time, the talk was of the wedding, Elena's and Renzo's; for the two girls, who were to be bridesmaids, the wedding was an almost unimaginable distance away, being fixed, at long last, for the Saturday before Ash Wednesday.

Elena spoke of all the logistical problems, all the difficulties with getting the right church, the right hotel, the right caterers. She had chosen a small ancient church in the centre of the city, Saint Mary of the Admiral, and the reception would be at the Grand Hotel, which, luckily, Renzo's family owned. Henerietta was an attentive audience to these details, as were the girls; the dress, the shoes, oh the shoes, always such a difficult choice. She had been to endless fittings of shoes. And her dress: she was flying to Rome soon for the second time to see about that. This time Renzo must come, as he had to be fitted for a suit by the very best Roman tailor available. She had found just the place, though it had taken an age to find. And the expense, the expense of everything. Renzo adopted the expression of the man who was paying for everything, though of course he wasn't; her brother was paying for most of it.

'The thing is, if uncle goes and mucks it all up for us,' he said, intervening. 'No,' he continued, cutting her off, 'Just mentioning it will not make it happen. My uncle,' he explained to Henrietta, 'is very unwell with cancer and he could get a lot worse between now and February. Back in August, it really did seem that the end was near, but his treatment seemed to work, and he has rallied since then. Naturally we hope for the best. Actually, as Elena will point out, he is not my uncle; he is… what is he exactly? He is my grandfather's first cousin, but he is also my aunt's father-in-law, because my cousins are my cousins twice over, as my uncle, my aunt's husband, is her cousin. Oh, it is complicated. But never mind the blood relationship and the marriage relationship, Uncle Lorenzo is a very important person, so… and Elena knows that, I know that, and Calogero certainly knows that. So, we must all hope that he hangs on till after the wedding is over. But whatever happens, Gino here is going to be the witness, what you call in England the best man. He is the best man.'

Renzo beamed.

Elena frowned and outlined the challenges of dressing Gino for the occasion. His chest measurements were enormous, she explained. Henrietta listened with grave attention, sensing Gino next to her.

In Palermo, lunch was served. Veronica had cooked, and she brought the pasta into the dining room, and then withdrew until the little bell should summon her once more from the kitchen to clear the plates. He poured them both a glass of white wine, just one. Little Romano was asleep in his nursery, and the thought of his new child, the thought of all his children, filled him with immense satisfaction. Two daughters, three sons, how blessed he was. He had not imagined when he had first met her that winter evening in Noto, that Anna Maria would ever give him sons. It had been hard enough having a son with his first wife, for various reasons that he no longer dwelled on; but she had, despite her age, given him two sons, effortlessly, it seemed. He could not be more pleased.

To have sons was the greatest victory. His own father had had two, one, himself, a worthy successor; the other, his brother Rosario, not at all worthy. Look at the Santucci dynasty, now dying on its feet, the two old men past everything, and the only young man, Renzo, completely hopeless, and soon to be his brother-in-law. His own sons would inherit the earth, and the Santucci family would either be allied to his family or extinct.

'It was nice of Renzo to come round,' said Anna Maria, as she played with her spaghetti al pesto, specially prepared, blandly un-Sicilian, but ideal for a new mother.

'He came to see my sister,' said Calogero. 'He is very devoted to her, and she to him. As she was here, he could hardly not come. She will make him an excellent wife. She is an accountant at heart, just like dearest Assunta. She has the heart and soul of a cash machine.'

'Don't I?' enquired Anna Maria. 'I am your banker after all.'

'You are, but much more than that.'

He smiled. The others were all out, and provided Romano did not wake up, they could lie down this afternoon and resume married life. He was looking forward to it. Immensely. Oh, the sheer joy of being married to an older and experienced woman, and one as beautiful as Anna Maria. What hard work poor Stefania had been, by contrast. But with Anna Maria, it was not just the pleasures of the flesh that were so enjoyable, it was the other pleasures as well: living in this flat, in the house at Donnafugata, in the flat in Catania that she had made so lovely, luxuriating in her good taste, feeling that everything around you was just as it ought to be, perfect, judged exactly right, beyond criticism. The joy of being guided by an expert! Of course, he had grown up knowing that he was amidst people who had no taste at all; then he had developed his own taste, and he had let Stefania guide him, but he had always felt a little uncertain whether they passed, either of them, for the real thing. But now he knew what the real thing was: her instincts for what was right guided him, and had become his instincts. It wasn't simply that she chose his clothes, or that she had thrown away several bits of tasteless jewellery he had owned; but she had changed his behaviour, his facial expressions even, his way of holding himself, his way of sitting, his way of talking, even his way of thinking. She had made him into a socially confident man, into the Renaissance prince he had always thought of himself as being.

'Are you worried about Renzo?' she now asked.

'Worried? Not in the least. Oh, you mean about his drinking, his drug taking and his hanging around with Gino? That might well worry my sister, but me…. No. Why should I be worried? The drink, the drugs, those things neutralise Renzo. And Gino and my sister will keep him in order, you will see. As long as his head is full of cocaine, he will not make trouble, he will be too busy enjoying himself. Are you worried about Renzo?'

'Not really,' she conceded. 'The cousins, what about them?'

'They are too young,' said Calogero. 'We will cross that bridge in due course. Meanwhile, it is the old man we should be worried about. Lorenzo, your father's friend. When he dies, what changes? Perhaps very little.' He smiled. 'But we must think about our own children.'

They had been talking about the children for some days now. The idea under discussion had been that of sending the girls to an English boarding school. His wife spoke English, he wanted to learn it, and the nanny Henrietta obviously spoke it. It would be good for the two girls to be placed somewhere abroad, especially as they were now growing up. This last was his huge concern. Isabella was not yet eleven, but she was forward for her age. Sicily was full of predatory boys, he knew, from which she had to be protected. To place her in some nice cloistered school in England seemed a perfect solution, and then, when the holidays came, to spend them in Donnafugata, away from the noise and heat of Catania, away from the distractions of Palermo, that would be a good solution too. They loved Donnafugata. They were already growing interested in the prospect of England. It seemed the perfect solution. As for the boys, they were still too young, but an English school might suit them very well too when the time came. His sons, he was determined, were going to become little gentlemen, not like the sort of boys one met in the Purgatory quarter, not like the sort of boy he had been. Just as the girls needed protection, the boys too needed to be detached from potentially bad influences; they needed to be kept away from Traiano and his children, from Renzo, and above all from Alfio and Gino.

'I wonder why,' he now said, 'the Santuccis, Carlo and Antonio, never sent their children abroad to be educated.'

'It might have helped Renzo,' she agreed. 'As for Angela's children, she was too fond of them to let them go.'

She rang the bell, and Veronica arrived to remove the plates, and to return a moment later with the scallopine alla marsala. She herself had the tiniest portion. Of course, their children, their five, the three she had inherited from his first wife and the two they shared, were going to turn out rather better than the younger generation of the Santucci family. She was determined about that, and so, she could see, was he.

Lunch was over in Monreale; it had lasted a very long time, and the children had enjoyed themselves. The adults too; for the two women, for Henrietta and for Elena, it was nice to be out of the flat for such a prolonged time. Henrietta had been delighted to see the splendours of Monreale, which she had read about, and had found lived up to expectation. The splendour of the mosaics surpassed anything she had ever seen. And it had also been pleasant to be with Renzo and Elena, who were to her mind rather more relaxing company than Mr di Rienzi and Doctor Tancredi, as she liked to be called. Both were, as her employers, somewhat forbidding, beautiful, remote, surrounded by a forcefield of perfection. Of course, she would never dream of discussing her employers with anyone but her own family back in England, but she sensed too that Elena and Renzo visibly relaxed when away from Mr di Rienzi and the Doctor. She quite liked Elena, who was friendly, and Renzo who, though very unattractive, had a pleasant air about him, and never seemed to get his shirt to stay tucked in. Of course, she could tell that Renzo was rich - one only had to look at his watch to see that - and from a good family, but at the same time something of a tearaway. This explained his friendship with the big guy, Gino, who was not from the same background. As an Englishwoman, she was sensitive to matters of class. But Gino, though from a different social background, behaved carefully and well, which she liked. He was a little shy and unassuming, which she also liked, and he gave off a friendly air. It was a pity he was married, though she had picked up the hint that he and his wife did not get on. He was by no means classically handsome, in fact far from it, but she liked him.

A glance at watches told them that it was time to go back, as the children were tired, and the parents of the children would have had a sufficiently long interval in which to enjoy themselves. They drove back in a different order from that in which they had come: The two women and two girls in one car, and the two men and the two male children in the other. The children were soon fast asleep, tired out by their day, which enabled the adults to speak.

For Elena and Henrietta, the talk was of the forthcoming wedding, and in particular the bridesmaids' dresses. The two bridesmaids were asleep in the back while Elena outlined what she had planned, and the forthcoming visit to the dressmaker and fittings for the little girls. Then she spoke of her own dress and described it in detail. Henrietta was rapt in her attention. She loved a wedding. There would be so many people there; Elena explained how the whole Santucci family had to be invited, all the employees of the Santucci companies, all the people from each subsidiary, how they all expected it. This meant a lot of people, from all walks of life, and all the people from Catania as well, so it would provide Henrietta with a kaleidoscopic view of Sicilian life. She was very excited by the prospect. She asked how the couple had met.

'Through work,' said Elena, without elaborating.

Gino and Renzo were wedged in the traffic, and the children were fast asleep. Gino took out the cocaine and a magazine from the glove compartment and, as soon as it was ready, proffered two lines for Renzo and two for himself. There were the usual expressions of relief at the sweetness of the hit, not the first of the day, but the first for some hours. The second hit confirmed the initial wellbeing conferred by the first. Then Gino took the bottle of mineral water from the footwell of the front seat and ingested some pills.

'When are you going back to Catania?' asked Renzo.

'Never,' said Gino, without emotion. 'Why are you asking? You want me gone?'

'Not at all,' said Renzo. 'I like having you to stay. When I am married, I will move to the new house, and you can stay in the flat if you like.'

'Can I? It is a nice flat.'

'I will sell it to you for a nice price then,' said Renzo.

'That would be good,' said Gino, thoughtfully. 'I mean, I am not from Catania. Why should I spend the rest of my life in Catania? I like it here. And if you need my help…'

'Of course I do. I would not have mentioned it otherwise,' said Renzo quickly. 'Would Catarina want to live here?' he asked.

'I don't know. I don't know what she wants. I have not asked her. I have not spoken to her for days. Our conversations….. But the real question is not what she wants, but want I want.'

'Quite so. Tell her you are moving to Palermo, and that will be that. She will have no choice.'

'She is not the problem,' said Gino. 'Catarina is irrelevant. The real problem is Alfio.'

He spoke as a man who had suddenly made a discovery.

Alfio, back from honeymoon, was contemplating a trip to Palermo to see the boss, to visit the centre of power. He knew that he ought to wait for a few days, and that to rush to see the boss as soon as one returned would look not just undignified, but desperate. Well, he was desperate, but it was important not to look desperate, not to look too much like the humble suitor he in fact was. The boss was the source of all power, and one had to see the boss, one could not keep away, but at the same time, one had to preserve the appearance that one could do without him, that one had some autonomy.

His newly married wife was of the same opinion, though they did not discuss the matter. There was no need. They both understood and communicated, in a way that was wordless, their shared understanding of the centrality of Calogero in their lives. He needed to go to Palermo to see the boss, Giuseppina knew, but she needed to go just as much as he did. She had to see him, she had to see Anna Maria, she had to stake out her position as the children's aunt, as the dead wife's sister, and she had to do this soon, in case she was viewed as surplus to requirements, or squeezed out by the boss's sister or mother. If her husband was hungry, then so was she.

She had lived so long in the shadow of her sister, and her sister had been in every way more fortunate than she, except in the manner of her early death. Stefania had been prettier, more desired, cleverer, more ambitious, more pushy, more successful. But dearest Stefania was dead, and now it was up to her to make up for lost ground. Of course, like all women in the quarter, she would have liked to have married the boss himself, but Anna Maria had carried him off before she or anyone else had had a chance. Perhaps Anna Maria had known just how desired a prize Calogero was. But, in his absence, she had done the next best thing by marrying the underboss, don Alfio.

The honeymoon had been enjoyable, as it should have been, and in a further and unexpected way, a revelation, indeed, several. She had had no idea that Africa could be so beautiful. That was the first thing. She had never been aware of beauty, she realised, until now, but as soon as one landed at the airport, one was aware of a world of difference. This beauty was not purely in the sea, the beach, the animals they saw on safari, the lovely hotel, the colour of the sky, the wide, open grasslands, the distant mountains, the lakes or the flamingos, it was also in the people, in their way of being. She was enchanted by the people, their gracefulness, the way they moved, the beauty of the children.

The other revelation was her husband. They were alone together for the very first time; her parents distant, Gino the same, and far away from Catania. Alfio had said, as they took off, that he was leaving work behind, and this was a promise he kept. He did not mention work or home, even once. Moreover, he was very attentive to her needs and very deferential to her wishes. Every day, he asked what she wanted to do; every time they surveyed a menu, he asked her what she wanted to eat, and what she wanted to drink, as if he had to know first so that he could order his own food in the light of her choices. She had not expected this. He came with her to church, he came with her to visit the orphanage (something the Italian priest at the church had suggested) and to meet the Italian nuns who looked after the orphans; he made a substantial donation to the orphanage, knowing it would please her; not just a single donation, but a pledge that he would send them something every month. Moreover, he was everything a new husband ought to be when they retired for the night to their cottage in the grounds of the hotel. The bedroom was full of the scent of sweet tropical flowers, of hibiscus and bougainvillea growing beneath the windows. She had made him so happy, he told her. She believed him; she felt it was true.

They flew back from Africa, happy, contented, holding hands in the darkness of the plane, and yet each aware of the one cloud on the horizon. He had told her that it was most unlikely he would ever be able to father a child. She had declared that this would not matter to her, while privately thinking that there was still a chance, however slim, and miracles were possible. This idea was one that he became aware of on honeymoon, and he thought it best to remove this delusion. He had told her that Gino's child was not Gino's child, and that miracle babies did not happen, at least not to people who had caught mumps in Bicocca.

Clouds, they both knew, had the habit of growing bigger. That they could not have a child was at present, given they were freshly married, not that important. But ten years from now, twenty years from now, it might poison everything. He dreaded her future reproaches. He dreaded the idea that she might one day raise the topic of adoption; he had a horror of strangers' children in his own home, and preferred the idea of no children at all. But a child, one even only tangentially related to him, would be different. He knew too that she was not discontented, but that she wanted him to do something to compensate for this lack of a child; she did not explain what; there was no need for words, for he understood. Whatever needed to be done needed the consent, tacit or otherwise, of the boss. And so, just after a few days after their return, they went to Palermo.

It was a nerve-wracking trip in the car. Naturally they telephoned first, asking to visit, saying that they wanted to see the baby, but, as everyone knew, this was a threadbare excuse, at least on Alfio's part. What was his interest in babies? Giuseppina was interested in babies, but more interested, both the boss and his wife could see, in establishing her claim to territory, as the children's aunt. And what could Alfio want, except to extend his power, at the expense of Gino, and the expense of Traiano? It was a social visit, but both Alfio and Guiseppina felt exposed, felt that their real motives were too apparent.

Their motives were indeed apparent, but Calogero was determined not to show that he saw through them. He greeted them with something approaching enthusiasm. Anna Maria was all graciousness, and the children were delighted to see them. Indeed, the presence of the five children and their nanny made the whole occasion go smoothly; any awkward silences were covered up, any adult unease was disguised. Calogero delighted in paying attention to Giuseppina, a woman who, if she had not been the late Stefania's sister, no one, he was sure, would ever have noticed at all. He was solicitous about her parents, for whom he had never cared much, and whose judgement, ever since he had married Stefania, despite their misgivings, he had despised. They were venal and grasping people, as far as he was concerned, though he acknowledged that their grandchildren loved them, and he did not begrudge his children that, any more than he resented their devotion to Giuseppina. Giuseppina was a pawn, he saw that. Alfio had married her because she had opened the way into the inner circle and because he had to marry someone; and she had married him because she had to marry someone, and she had seen Alfio as a way into the inner circle. Their ambitions coincided.

She, he thought, was better at covering up her ambitions than him; she reacted naturally to Anna Maria's charm, which was to be expected. She wanted to show that she did not resent Anna Maria taking her deceased sister's place; and Anna Maria wanted to show that Giuseppina had a guaranteed and privileged place as far as the children, her sister's and Anna Maria's, were concerned. But Alfio was clearly on edge, Calogero noted with amusement. His ambition tormented him. He wanted the boss to provide him with absolution for this sin of ambition, to tell him that the pain gnawing away at his insides was not going to kill him.

They did not know the signora, they had never been before now to the enormous flat by the Politeama, and they both tried their very best not to show the awe they felt. A glass of champagne was served, and all four looked at the baby, which was the reason for the visit; the supposed reason. Then the boss indicated that they might leave the women with the baby and the other children, and he and Alfio withdrew. They went into the drawing-room, and the noise of the children and the women became but a distant sound.

'So, you are married at last,' said the boss. 'Congratulations! The honeymoon was nice? I remember mine with your late sister-in-law' – it took Alfio a moment to realise that he meant Stefania – 'in a hotel in Taormina. I swam in the pool and read books. It was very strange being so alone with someone.'

Alfio nodded.

'There are quite a few things I want to tell you, boss.'

Calogero raised an eyebrow.

'The hotel we stayed in is owned and run by Italians. I got talking to the manager, you know, as one does. A man from Lombardy, but friendly, you know, nice. I got the impression he was checking me out. From the questions he asked. He mentioned not your name, but the name of a friend of ours.'

'Who?' asked Calogero, now genuinely interested.

'Don Carmelo. At least he was mentioned. But the one he spoke about more, in strictest secrecy, of course, which I told him I would not break, was the son.'

'The one in that university in America?'

'No, boss. The illegitimate one.'

'Be more specific. He is supposed to have thirteen children.'

'The eldest one. The one called Costantino. The one whose mother was a Serb.'

'Him,' said the boss, with distaste. 'The sweepings of the Balkans. I know the man you mean. He drives the car for don Carmelo sometimes. Is he really his son? He's got an interesting history. Or so I imagine. But how on earth does this hotel manager know about Costantino?'

'It seems that Costantino wants to invest, and they need investors. But you see why he was telling me? Perhaps they would prefer an investment that is more, shall we say, ethical? Anyway, Giuseppina liked it so much that she wants to go back, and I have promised her we shall.'

'Is Costantino investing on his own, or is his father behind him? This is interesting. Look, we will look into this more, find out more. Perhaps we should get involved. We are always looking for new outlets, aren't we? Maybe I should go to Africa and see. But there is something else you want to talk about, my old friend Alfio, I can tell. The bit about the hotel was the easy part.'

'Boss…. My cousin Catarina. She wants to talk about the child's future. With you.'

Calogero was silent for a few moments.

'Are you seeing Gino?' he asked.

'I have no plans to see Gino.'

'Is he going back to his wife? What is happening?'

'I don't know what his plans are, boss. We have not spoken. But she has spoken to me, and she has asked me…'

'The child is my brother's?'

Alfio nodded.

'I need to think about this,' said Calogero. 'Tell her I will think about it in my own time and without any pressure from her.'

He looked at Alfio. They were the same age. They had been at school together. He did not dislike Alfio. He preferred not to let dislikes cloud his judgement. Alfio had been useful to him. But he remembered something now, from when they had been teenagers. Not the numerous occasions when he had made Alfio cry with pain, but the occasion when Alfio, aged about fourteen, before his imprisonment in Bicocca, had boasted about sleeping with his cousin Catarina. It had been the talk of the quarter, or at least the boys of the quarter, for about a day, given that Alfio's horrible teeth seemed to have precluded sexual congress of any type, and for the sheer unusualness of the claim. Catarina was his cousin, and a very beautiful girl; it was as if, almost, he had slept with his own sister. Why on earth had she done it? Curiosity? Had she been worn down by his persistence? Had she despaired of getting anyone better? Well, she had, eventually, if Gino were in fact better. But then she had moved onto his brother, with a financial inducement to do so, and the child was the result. And now, what did she want? Was it revenge, or, more accurately, vindication? Did she want to be recognised, by him, somehow?

There was no time to say more, which was good, as what could he say, except that the thought of Catarina annoyed him, disturbed him, as did anything to do with his late brother? But his wife and children and Giuseppina were returning from admiring the baby, and the family party was resuming. In the midst of it all, the boss Calogero realised that he had much to think about.

There were internal threats, he knew, and there were external threats. There were also the sort of threats that no man really wanted to confront, personal threats. He felt that in this brief conversation he had identified all three.

Very soon, his children, those who went to school, the eldest two, the girls, would be going back to Catania, and his wife and the three youngest, the boys, would be going to Donnafugata, where, when Christmas came, they would all be reunited for a week or two; in the meantime he and the girls would go to Donnafugata every weekend; during the week, Isabella and Natalia would be looked after by the Black Widow Spider, his mother, and Elena, his sister, with, no doubt, Aunt Giuseppina not far away. All this suited him. He did not feel the need to see his wife more than at weekends.

He had never suspected Alfio was clever; of course, he had known him to be cleverer than Gino; and the truth was, he was clever, but not clever enough. Naturally, it was supposed by many who considered themselves to be good judges of character, his character, that very soon, in a year or less, he would fix himself up with a mistress. His wife was twenty years his senior, and she could not have any more children, the two she had already had being great surprises. Naturally, he would want a younger woman and perhaps more children, illegitimate children, but nevertheless, children. Alfio's offer had been subtle: he was putting forward Catarina for the role; beautiful but scheming Catarina – was it his idea, or hers? It was a good idea, for she already had his nephew, but it represented a miscalculation. He did not like being manipulated or tempted in this way. That displeased him; indeed, it offended him. But there was something worse than that at work. He did not want Catarina or anyone like her for that matter. He was content with what he had, his wife, who was also the mother of two of his children, and who was also his banker. His wife, who was almost as old as his mother. His wife who knew so much. He valued her. He did not want to upset her, though, he was sure, if he did take a mistress, she would probably accept it. But he did not want to take a mistress, at least, not yet.

He remembered his first wife, dearest Stefania, with something bordering on distaste. Of course, she had been in every sense the perfect wife, and just right for him. She had been one of the best-looking girls in the quarter; she had been smartly dressed, clever, ambitious; one could take her to places where one could not take the usual sort of girl one met in the quarter, that was for sure. But at the same time, she had been so demanding. She had developed the nasty habit of telling him what to do, which, given that his mother, and to a lesser extent his sisters: had the same habit, was not welcome. Moreover, though the first pregnancy had been without complications, in that she had welcomed it, and marriage, the subsequent children had only come along after much difficulty. He had wanted children much more than she; she had wanted something entirely different: love, sex, whatever one wanted to call it. Her appetite for that sort of thing had been greater than his, he reflected. She was attractive, but he had always felt that she had regarded his attentions to her in that department as somewhat lacking, which, in truth, they had been. She had done something that neither Anna the Romanian prostitute, with whom he had first slept as a lad of thirteen, or Anna Maria later on, had never done: perhaps they had both flattered him, perhaps being older they had realised that a man needed to be caressed; but Stefania had made him feel inadequate.

Now that Stefania was dead, now that her story was completed, he was able to interpret it, helped by the lapse of time. He remembered all those nights he had spent on the sofa in his office, while she slept in the marital bed. He remembered the relatively few times when he had slept in the marital bed and enjoyed, if that were the word, the purpose of the marital bed. Those occasions had been somewhat fraught, in his recollection. He had tried his best, but been left with the idea that his best was not good enough for her. He remembered the time they had spent in Taormina on honeymoon, and the time they had gone to New York on holiday; that had been less trying as the children had been there with them, but the truth was he had not liked being alone with her. She was an uphill struggle.

Compared with this, were the examples he had all around him of the way the other men in the quarter acted. Traiano, who he loved and hated in equal measure, was always eager to get back to his ever-pregnant wife; he radiated an uxorious satisfaction. He himself had never felt the eager anticipation of going home in the same way. As for the others, they all slept with as many women as they could, he knew that, and then discussed the matter when they met up in the gym afterwards, a place that he had never once visited. He had a horror of that male banter, that camaraderie. For their sexual profligacy put his own timidity into perspective. Of course, every woman wanted to sleep with him, he knew that, but he did not want to sleep with every woman - far from it - and he did not want to be reminded of it.

He was sure Stefania, with her strong sexual appetites, had strayed in their marriage. He was not quite sure how this certainty arose, but he was sure of it, and though there was no proof, the certainty had become fixed by something Volta had said to him once, a throwaway remark which was nevertheless significant and meant to be so. Whenever he met with Volta, which was necessary for business, the fact that hung heavily in the air was that he had leverage over Volta, ways of making him cooperate; this they both knew. But something that Volta had said about his own wife, about her slavish devotion, which hinted that this was something Calogero had never known, hinted that Volta perhaps knew something. Volta had been the friend and confidant of that hypocritical milksop his brother Rosario; for that betrayal he had disposed of his brother; but what had Rosario told Volta about his marriage? And why had that stupid awful boy Maso been so keen to kill Volta and ended up getting killed himself? What had Rosario known? Had the hypocritical milksop, not only enjoyed the embraces of the foul Catarina, also.... Had that boy Maso....? These were his suspicions, but he was damned if he were to ask Volta to elaborate on his assertion that signora Volta would never commit adultery. He suspected, but he did not want to know the truth. That time Rosario had stayed with Stefania and the children in Cefalù... That boy Maso with his bold handsome stares....

He had thought that by disposing of his brother, the boiling passionate hatred he had felt for him would by now have evaporated and disappeared, leaving only the bare outline of a memory of what had once been. Sometimes, you walked through Catania and you noticed that a building had been knocked down and replaced by something else; but you felt no affection for the demolished structure; you merely noted it and moved on. Sometimes you could not even remember what the old building had looked like. So, he had supposed it would prove with his late brother. He had been there, then he was gone, and that was all there was to it. He assumed that this was what his mother felt, and his sisters too. They never discussed Rosario, never mentioned him. They had made a pact of oblivion with each other and with him. They felt, perhaps, they had failed their brother and son, but what could be done about that now? How sensible they were not to regret the past. He regretted nothing of course; he could not afford regrets, but he resented the fact that there had been some who had loved Rosario and some whom Rosario had loved, and above all he resented the fact that Rosario had not loved him. This scheming girl, this Catarina, had he loved her? Enough to sleep with her, certainly, betraying his intended wife the lawyer's daughter. And this child of his; she thought that he should show the child some affection, do something for the child. The child, his brother's child, was an object of loathing to him, just as his brother had been.

The person closest to him, apert from his wife and children, was Traiano, and Traiano had been close to Rosario, he knew that. When he had given the order, he had done so on the understanding that the deed was never to be mentioned again, nor indeed was Rosario. This pact of silence had been strictly observed. Traiano had never mentioned him; but he was not privy to what Traiano thought on the matter. When Antonescu senior had been disposed of, hadn't Traiano gone to see Rosario and sat on the end of his bed and wept? Hadn't they seen each other and spoken almost every day? So, what did Traiano think now? He had no way of knowing. But he was sure of this: in his developing plans, he would not call on Traiano to help him, but leave him out. What he had in mind was too close, too personal. Traiano would understand too well. Besides which he feared that if he told Traiano what he had in mind, Traiano might refuse to do it. He was sentimental that way. Renzo was eager to please and stupid; he would use Renzo – Renzo and his great friend Gino. As for the African story that Alfio had brought him, for that, before else, he would consult the person he trusted the most, his wife.

He chose his moment carefully.

'How well do you know don Carmelo?' he asked.

She looked up from the book she was reading.

'Well enough,' she said. 'Well enough to form a judgement. He is fat and old and lazy. Or rather that is the impression he gives. But he is pretty sharp underneath.'

'Sharp enough to be a threat?'

'Of course,' she said. 'He did not get to where he is today without being sharp and deadly to his enemies.'

'Would he turn against us?' He paused for a moment. He knew the answer. 'If it were to his advantage, I suppose he would. I mean, is he ambitious enough to do so?'

'He might,' she said, laying the book aside. 'Has something happened that has alerted you to danger? You have sensitive antennae, I know.'

He explained what Alfio had told him. She listened attentively.

'This Costantino is the supposed son of don Carmelo. You may have heard of him. They call him the Serb. His mother was – is - Serbian. She lives there and he was brought up there, but when he was old enough, he came here to work for his father. He has been well paid and I have invested money for him. If he really wants to pour money into a hotel in East Africa, then he may well approach me. I mean, he is a client. But….'

'Precisely. But. This is not the sort of thing one expects. If Costantino is doing well here, why would he think of moving continents, not just countries? The investment would be a big one; and he has not spoken to you about getting his money out? You see, this was some sort of message; they were betting on it getting back to me via Alfio. At least that is what I think. Is Costantino jealous of the legitimate children, the real children, the ones Carmelo spoils so much? And the other illegitimate children he is supposed to be so good to? Is Costantino making an approach to us, or rather, hoping we may make one to him?'

'You had better send Alfio to find out,' she suggested.

'A dog is barking,' Calogero said, a few days later.

His future brother-in-law Renzo looked at him, awaiting elucidation.

'Alfio,' said Calogero. 'A person I never paid much attention to, but now someone demanding my attention. But my attention, which he has certainly gained, may not be entirely beneficent. It may cost him something, in a way that he does not yet realise. But first tell me about Gino.'

'What is there to tell, boss?' asked Renzo.

'A great deal. He lives with you, he and you spend all your time together, don't you?'

'He is not happy. He and the wife are not happy. He is not happy with Alfio. The two are connected as she is Alfio's cousin. The reason Alfio has tried to attract your attention, boss, is because he is jealous that Gino has mine. They were friends, now they are rivals, fast becoming enemies. He blames Alfio for the fact that he married Catarina. Of course, that is ridiculous, but that is how it feels to him. She is his cousin; she might have brought them closer together, but she is driving them apart. As you have noticed, he has stopped going back to Catania to see her and to see the child, which he was originally supposed to be doing every weekend. He says he prefers it here.'

They were in the Santucci office; Calogero looked out of the window onto the viale della Libertà.

'I know he does,' he said. 'He likes it here with you. All the food and drink and cocaine and pills he can consume, and no one to disapprove. He thinks I do not notice; and you think I do not notice. Well might you look at me like that. And has he found a girlfriend?'

'Boss, I....' Renzo quailed. 'Yes, he has,' he admitted.

'And you were going to keep that secret from me?'

'Boss.....'

'My wife told me, and the girl herself told my wife. There is no accounting for taste. I mean, he likes her, sure, but she probably has no idea what he is really like. All that cocaine, all those pills. And you, does my sister know what you get up to? Sometimes I wonder if you need another taste of my belt. You need discipline, Renzo, and I can provide it. For you and that fat fool Gino.'

'Boss, I....'

'I what? What is your excuse now?'

For a moment he raised his voice. Then he made a gesture that conveyed that Renzo was to follow him out of the room, out of the building and onto the pavement of the viale della Libertà below. There was something he wanted to ask him that no one must overhear.

'You look worried,' she observed.

Alfio had been back in Catania for some time, but had only now slipped away once more from home to see his cousin Catarina. Giuseppina knew where he was going, he neither needed to tell her or deceive her; she could guess. Well, what was wrong with seeing his cousin?

'I am not worried,' he said.

'Did you see my husband?' she asked.

He shook his head.

'And you used to be such friends,' she observed.

'Then he met you,' said Alfio, accusingly.

'No, then he met don Renzo, and met the joys of drinks, and cocaine and pills,' she retorted, correcting him. 'You know that is true. You have abandoned him as much as I have. And our own dear don Calogero uses him to neutralise don Renzo. Two cokeheads are no worry to him.'

Alfio sighed.

'Don't you realise that he might wake up from his coke-induced stupor and actually start to wonder what had happened to him, and apportion blame?'

'His mind will be dark forever, long before that happens.'

'I don't know what you mean,' he said. 'If you think….'

'I don't think anything at all. I leave that to you.'

'You are ambitious for Tino and for yourself. I understand that. But don't you realise that there is no ambition without risk?'

'Of course I understand that. It is something I learned from you,' she said. 'You want to get on; I want to get on; our interests coincide. Gino is blocking your path, just as he is mine. Besides which, he is useless. With him gone, just think how much don Calogero will rely on you.'

'It can't be done,' said Alfio.

'It must be done,' she said. 'It is an insurance policy. You need to realise that he may well come after all the men I have slept with, you included.' She looked at him hard. 'You know what you did. Now you have to pay for it.'

'For goodness' sake, I was fourteen. Am I going to have to pay for this forever?'

'Yes,' she said. 'I tried to push you away, but you insisted. The only thing that got you away from me was Bicocca. One day, someone will tell him, and he will kill you. Now, be sensible. Weigh up the possibilities and act accordingly, and act also to ensure peace of mind.'

'I should kill you,' he said bitterly.

'That is one thing you will never do,' she said calmly.

'Look,' he said. 'Let us be reasonable. What you are suggesting, if I read you right, and I think I do, is not how it is done. It is an unnecessary risk. You need to go to Palermo with the child and be reconciled with him. That is what he wants. He feels unloved. A little love from you, and he would feel better. He likes you; he always did; he loves you. But if you are going to shun him, let him go to Palermo and never ask him back, he has his pride, poor man. He just needs to be won round. You know that. You need to massage him.'

'You may well be right, but you overlook one thing. I despise him, I loathe him and I could not bear to let him touch me ever again.'

'You only think of yourself,' he said bitterly.

'Someone has to. But I am thinking of you too. Think of the gratitude of the boss, think of how don Calogero will love you.'

Once more, Alfio sighed.

The holiday weekend was approaching. The feast of All Saints, and the feast of the Dead, and the successive Saturday and Sunday beckoned. Renzo knew that Elena expected him in Catania, so she could show him off to all her friends, now that the wedding date was fixed for Saturday 18th February next year, before Lent began. Her brother would be there with his wife, with the new baby, and taking part in the various ceremonies associated with the feast of the Dead at the Church of the Holy Souls in Purgatory. Naturally, Renzo wanted to go to Catania, to please his future wife, and also to please his future brother-in-law; but there was the question of what to do with Gino. At first it had been assumed Gino would stay behind in Palermo, but then Gino surprised him, saying that he had decided he would go to Catania too.

It could, Renzo saw, be no longer put off. He wanted to put it off, but he knew he could do so no longer. Besides which, the boss would, sooner or later, start breathing down his neck, asking why he had not acted. This idea, that Gino should come to Catania, acted as a catalyst.

They sat at the kitchen table of his flat, the two of them, a bottle of wine between them, along with the detritus associated with an hour or so of cocaine ingestion. Gino had just spoken, saying he would come to Catania.

'What? Because of that girl? Henrietta? Because she will be there?' asked Renzo.

'You were the one who said that she liked me,' said Gino accusingly.

'Calogero and Anna Maria are employing her, so you have to be careful. Besides…. Does she know you are married?'

'She does.'

'And?'

'It is a problem,' conceded Gino. 'She says she does not want to sleep with a man who is married.'

'It has gone that far, has it?'

Gino took a slug of wine to try and clear his thought processes.

'It is not that she does not want to sleep with me. She does not want me to be married.'

'Has she…? Have you….?'

'We have.'

'That was quick,' said Renzo.

Gino raised his chin slightly. It was his way of saying that he did not care what others thought.

'Look, I am glad for you. She seems a nice girl, and she may not be from Sicily, but perhaps that has its advantages. And I was the one who spotted she liked you. We all want you to be happy. The truth is that Catarina is not right for you, she is not nice, and she does not make you happy. It is not your fault; it is her fault. She has been with other men.'

'What other men?' Gino asked sharply.

'One dead, one still alive. Don Calogero's brother, when you were in Hungary. And before she met you, she was with Alfio on one occasion, but she never really liked him. Rosario was the one she liked.'

Renzo watched him closely.

'When I was in Hungary?' he asked.

There was silence.

'Are you saying…?'

He did not reply. It was precisely what he was saying. They both knew it.

'How long have you known?' asked Gino quietly.

'Not long. Calogero told me.'

'He knows? How?'

'She told him, I think, that the child was his nephew, and that she had been Rosario's lover. She wanted him to know so that he could provide for her. But that is exactly what he does not want to do. He does not want to provide for her. He does not want a nephew. He does not want her. He is funny about his brother, and he does not want reminders of him. I don't understand it, but that is the way it is. Look, listen to me. Calogero has made a decision.'

Gino looked at him, his face pale. Renzo was not sure he understood. Unsteadily, Gino rose from the table, and left the room. Renzo heard the bedroom door shut.

There was, Alfio realised, a strange atmosphere in the quarter that night. For a start, the boss was still away, though returning for the weekend, with his wife, and with his younger children, so all five of them would be together. It would be the first time that the quarter would have the chance to see the new baby, and no doubt the boss would come down to the square outside the Church of the Holy Souls in Purgatory, and to the bar, and the pizzeria and the trattoria, and show off the new child so everyone could admire him. It would be good to have him back. There was always a slight and unwelcome change in the air when he was not there. People liked the assurance of things being the same. His father had counted for much, the late Chemist of Catania, though that had only become apparent after his death; Calogero counted for much more. Indeed, Calogero was everything. All his calculations were based on this: the centrality of Calogero and his needs, the centrality of Calogero as the holder of all power.

Moreover, tonight, being Friday, and being before a long weekend, given that Tuesday was a public holiday, the day of All Saints, and that no one would be working on Monday, that too created a special sense of freedom.

If the boss was coming back, at the same time Traiano and his family were going away. For the first time ever, they were taking a holiday. Of course, Traiano was not bound by the fact that it was a public holiday at all, as he worked when he pleased. But his brother-in-law Corrado was, as was Pasqualina his new wife, and therefore, if his wife wanted to see her sister, this was the time to go to Verona. Given that he was a completely fearless man, who feared no one and nothing, not even death itself, not even eternal damnation (a subject which was unavoidable in early November), he was nevertheless nervous about going on holiday, going somewhere unfamiliar, being surrounded by people who spoke in a funny way and would regard his accent and his appearance as somehow foreign. It got worse: they were going to fly, and he had never been in an aeroplane, and was frightened of making a fool of himself, of throwing up (he had heard this happened), of quite simply not knowing what to do or where to go. They would be staying in a hotel, which was another ordeal: they had lots of money, but he was aware that it was not having money that made you acceptable, but knowing how to handle money, how to spend it, how to tip, how to treat staff. Then there was the question of what to pack, and what to wear, how smart one should be, how casual one ought to be. But he resolved to put all this aside, as his wife wanted to see her sister, and that was all that mattered. He was doing it for her.

And at the same time, he admitted to himself with a feeling of guilt, he was doing it for himself. The hotel had been booked via computer. One of the boys had a brother at school who had a computer and who had brought it round, and booked everything from the kitchen table, flights, hotel, everything, all he had needed was the rarely used bank card. Three nights in Verona, in a lovely hotel, with a nice room and a huge bed, and the children, whom he loved dearly, far, far away. For the first time ever, they would be alone at night, in a strange city, able to enjoy themselves. For the plan was to leave the children with their grandparents.

But there was opposition to this plan from his wife. She could not bear the thought of being away from the children for three days. Of course, she trusted her parents, and the children loved their grandparents, but she wanted them with her, and Pasqualina would want to see them as well… and she felt she could not enjoy herself if they were not there, as she would always be wondering what they were doing without their parents.

He did his best to persuade her. It was only three days. Besides, the two youngest were far too young to be taken on an aeroplane, and they would not enjoy it, and they would enjoy staying with their grandparents. He told her that she too would enjoy herself, be able to get a good night's sleep without them, and not having them coming into the bedroom and getting into the marital bed. She frowned at this; she liked being with the children; well, so did he, he protested, though she said it did not appear that way. He wanted to go all the way to Verona without the children, she said accusingly, all so that they could make love and have another child, when he did not even want to spend time with the children he already had.

He was deeply wounded by this. He loved the children, he spent lots of time with them, fed them, bathed them, put them to bed, much more than other fathers did, and she implied that he only cared about making love, not the products of the lovemaking. It was untrue. He loved the children, and he wanted more children. Did she? And if he wanted to make love to her in Verona or anywhere else for that matter, that was because he loved her to the point of madness, in case she had not noticed. He loved her more than any husband loved a wife, more than any husband had ever loved any wife. Didn't she understand?

Didn't he understand? Were they to have a child every year, like their great-grandparents? Didn't he realise that nowadays people did things to prevent that happening? He realised that he had walked straight into the one conversation that he had dreaded having with her. He tried to explain. He had done what she said, she knew he had, but not always. He did not like it. It was not dignified. (She looked at him very curiously as he said this.) It was not natural. It was not moral. It ruined the pleasure and the spontaneity. It did not seem like much, but it was a lot to ask, and the thing was that if they did not have children now, later, there might not be a later. They might one day find that too late came upon them rather suddenly.

'You want me to feel sorry for you,' she said, feeling sorry for him as she said it.

'No,' he said, with feeling. 'We are the lucky ones. We should feel sorry for people like my mother once was, people like Piuccio who, when his wife was pregnant for the second time, was in despair, because of their debts, because he worked all day and all night and never seemed to have any money at all. We should feel sorry for all the people in the quarter who want to make love freely but simply can't because they live in poverty and squalor. We are lucky. But one day my luck may run out. The money might dry up, or else those magistrates will fit me up for something.'

'What magistrates?'

'The ones I do not talk about because I do not want to upset you. The police took me in the other day, remember? One day, no doubt they dream of it, they will take me in and never let me go. But I do not care about going to jail or ending up dead. I just care about not being with you and the children. It would be torture, the idea of seeing you in prison, through bars or through a glass barrier.'

The prospect horrified her as well.

'Is it likely?' she asked, worried by the prospect, of course, and at the same time shocked by the way he had revealed himself to her, showing a side of him she had never seen until now.

He could tell the argument, if that is what it had been, was over.

'The magistrates, the police, they are complete fools, don't worry about them,' he said lightly. 'I should never have mentioned it. I want you to have a good time in Verona.'

They embraced.

But with one argument over, another was about to begin.

Cristoforo was four years old, and quite capable of understanding what was being proposed – being left behind with his grandparents, aunts, uncles and cousins, and his brother and his sister, while his parents flew off to Verona for an interminable weekend. His protest was vocal and loud. He wanted to go in an aeroplane too.

The child moaned, wheedled, screamed and wailed. His father spoke to him and tried to reason with him. His father then grew stern, and told him not to complain. His father made threats. The child cried the louder. Traiano gave up.

Things got worse. Tearful Cristoforo took his case to his mother, and she, rather than seeing her husband's point of view, was sorry for the boy and told her husband that he had to come; if he didn't come, neither would she. He realised that with both of them against him, he had to accept defeat. Cristoforo would come, while the two youngest children, still too young to protest, were left behind. Cristoforo was still tearful, but now triumphantly so. Traiano felt he had been put in the wrong, and unjustly so. He had never treated his firstborn harshly, unfairly or badly. The fact was that he loved Cristoforo, perhaps more than he ought, certainly more than he loved the others, and that meant, he knew, that the little boy could manipulate him and exploit him in this way. Cristoforo had clearly learned the value of sulking.

It struck him that in the world outside the home, when he did not have to be kind and gentle, in fact the opposite, things were easier to manage. He had been don Calogero's enforcer so long that he hardly had to enforce anything anymore. People did as they were told. And here was his own son refusing to behave as he ought. But the whole matter was complicated by his deep, obsessive love for his wife and his almost as deep, obsessive love for Cristoforo himself. Contemplating this, he began to feel sorry for himself. His mother had never loved him as a mother should, that was clear; he had fallen in love with Ceccina as a child of fourteen, and he had readily submitted to her family, partly to atone for the crime of making her pregnant as soon as he met her. He had been more than respectful to his parents-in-law and his grandparents-in-law. He had been friendly and respectful to all the cousins, uncles and aunts; he had been very good to her sister, Pasqualina, in particular. Moreover, the entire family had had very little before they had met him. He had provided them all with jobs, with pensions from the Confraternity, with the status of being related to him. He adored all his children, his eldest in particular, on whom he had lavished love and all good things, the sort of things he had never had at that age. He was now beginning to see that he had spoilt him, and this was beginning to torment him.

He was reasonable, and he tried at first to reason with the little boy. He tried to talk to him. One morning, when they were alone, he pointed out to the sulky and uncommunicative child that he was better off than any other little boy in the quarter; he had everything he wanted and more; no one forced him to do anything he did not want to do; he was never disciplined or punished; indeed, his parents exercised no control over him, and Traiano himself had allowed him to do whatever he liked.

Cristoforo looked at him with venomous discontent.

'You need to work out who really cares about you,' he continued. 'And you need to stop making things difficult for Mummy and Daddy. You need to start being reasonable. We are going to Verona tomorrow, and you need to behave in a way that is not going to ruin it for everyone else. After all, you wanted to go to Verona, didn't you?'

The boy nodded. He wanted to go on a plane badly. He sniffed, then he managed a weak smile, only partly to please his father. It was really a smile of victory.

The two women had gone back to the flat to cook the lunch for the feast of All Saints, and Cristoforo had gone with them; the two men, Traiano and Corrado, sat out in the open air in one of the bars in the Piazza Bra, even though it was cold, certainly much colder than Sicily, and had a drink before going home to lunch. They would be flying back tomorrow. On the whole, the trip had been a great success. He liked Verona, though not enough to want to live there. But maybe one day he would. One never knew.

'Well?' asked Traiano, his usual glass of Cinzano before him.

'Well, what?' countered Corrado.

'You want to speak to me, I know. I can read you, to some extent. So, go on then, speak to me.'

Corrado smiled.

'If you know what I am going to say....'

'I think I do. I read you, and you certainly read me. You are the only person who makes me feel guilty. It is an almost enjoyable sensation. You think I am a bad father. Well, I am, but not in the way you think. I have loved Cristoforo too much. I have spoilt him. I never tried to discipline him. He is still very young, but it is already too late to instil discipline. It depresses me. He has had too much, too young. He thinks the sort of life we have is normal.' He reflected on what he was saying. 'Does every father think he makes mistakes and is a bad father? I never knew mine.'

'Probably,' said Corrado. 'My father felt he had failed with Gino. He tried his best, but he always thought that Gino going to Bicocca was somehow his fault. I told him it wasn't, but he has never really believed me, nor stopped blaming himself.'

'Well, he should not blame himself,' said Traiano. 'Gino went to Bicocca because Gino was stupid, because Gino got caught. Gino is a nice guy, but he is easily influenced, first by Alfio, then by don Renzo. He is a herd animal. He ought to spend more time with his family, but he thinks you do not want him. There, I have said it. I never thought it would come to this, but I am feeling sorry for your brother. He feels no one wants him, and that is why he latches onto people like don Renzo, people who he thinks want him. That was why he married her; he so badly wanted to be wanted, but she does not want him, she married him because it suited her right then to get married. Poor Gino. He is unloved. That is why I think he should spend more time with his family. You love him. It would be nice for him to be loved for a change, to be really loved.'

'You should speak to him.'

'We don't speak,' said Traiano. 'I mean we speak, but…'

There was silence between them for a few moments.

'I want Cristoforo to be different. I want my children to be different,' said Traiano. 'I don't want them to be like Gino and me. I don't want Cristoforo and Alessandro to grow up fighting, drinking, smoking, taking pills, thinking about money all the time, and spending time with bad women. At least I do not drink, or take pills, or go with bad women; ever since I met Ceccina, I have known what love is. Maybe Renzo will settle down now that Elena and he are getting married. But I want my children to be settled from the start, to go to university, to become lawyers and doctors and things like that. It is possible, isn't it? Don Carmelo, who you won't have heard of, his eldest son, or rather his eldest legitimate son, is at some American university, studying astrophysics. Well, if that is what it takes for the children to have a good life, then I would happily see them in America. Anything, to be normal. If only Gino could speak to you, but he can't, because he cannot abandon the lies he tells himself. Besides, these things are hard to express: what if he were to tell you the truth about her, about Catarina? What could you possibly say? It has all gone too far for truth now. Anyway, I am blessed, Ceccina is happy. We have ironed out our difficulties.'

'You are having another child?'

'In due course. Not just yet, but one day. But for the moment, a pause. You guessed?'

'She was talking to her sister, and her sister was talking to me, naturally enough.'

'You and Pasqualina can wait; you can afford to wait. I can't. For me, a pause is a bit of a gamble, a risk. One never knows when one will depart this life. But one can be sure one will. It is the timing alone that remains uncertain. I don't want that for my children. If anything happens to me, Ceccina will have the children to look after her, and she will have you and Pasqualina. She will come here… It is nice here. Though they do not like Sicilians, do they?'

'There are all types here,' said Corrado. He changed the subject. 'About my brother; it is very strange, yesterday he rang me up.'

'If he does not ring you as a matter of course, then that is strange indeed. He must know I am here, and that whatever he told you, you would tell me,' said Traiano.

'It was a personal thing.'

'Nothing is personal,' said Traiano. 'Whatever he told you, he wants me to know. I wonder why.'

'He has left the wife,' said Corrado. 'Or more accurately, he told her to leave, with the child, and that he would never see either of them again. He paid her off, I don't know how much, but she has taken the car, the child, her clothes, and left, to go where, I am not sure, perhaps she has left Sicily all together. You see, he knows: she was unfaithful to him, and the child is not his. He says it is unforgiveable, the deception, and she is dead to him. She made no protest, but cleared out. He sent don Renzo to tell her to do so – he is his friend after all, and he could hardly send don Alfio – and said to her that when he got back to Catania, if he found her there, he would kill her.'

'He told you all this?' asked Traiano after a pause. 'My word. I must say, she did the right thing. Gino, angry, would not be a nice sight. He gave her a chance and she took it. She is not stupid. I never liked her. Manipulative. Any idea where she went?'

'I asked that. He does not know and does not want to know. Somewhere in the north, I imagine. I think she has relatives in Milan or Brescia or Pordenone; maybe relatives even in Germany. But if she has any sense, she will never cross his path again. I can't say I liked her either. The child was sweet.'

'Like his father, his real father. What an unlucky child.'

He sighed.

'How did Gino seem to you?' he asked.

'Subdued. He was deluded so long, I am a little surprised at how well he has taken it, how reasonable he is being.'

They were both silent.

'Your brother is stupid in more ways than one. Marrying that girl, when she was pregnant with someone else's child; I wish I had told him; no wonder it lasted less than five minutes. But he has hitched himself to don Renzo Santucci. That is not a good idea. Renzo is not solid, not dependable. That whole family…. The drink, the women, the cocaine, I hate it all. Yes, I do. But I have to live in that world. I know no other. At least you can escape the wedding. I can't. Then there is his great friend Alfio. I don't trust him and I wonder how he will take this Catarina business.' Someone had left a newspaper on the table, and Traiano glanced at it casually. 'What is the IMF?' he asked. 'The government is in trouble. When was it never in trouble? And the news from Catania: It says that there's been a weekend of things burning. An inflammatory headline!'

He laughed.

It had been, on the whole, he reflected, a most wonderful weekend, his first proper trip to Italy, the trip to Rome and its suburbs hardly counting. His first time in an aeroplane as well. It was his first sight of what a beautiful Italian town could look like, and the sights of Verona had silenced him, and made him think that the new mayor Volta, when he entered office, would have so much to do. Catania was beautiful, but Catania was a mess, compared to fair Verona, this lovely city. It was also his first time alone with Pasqualina and Corrado, without the extended family, without his brother Gino, without the boss, without the dark and oppressive atmosphere of Purgatory (or so it now seemed), without being in a place where everyone knew him, everyone wanted his attention, and where everyone feared him and perhaps, he suspected, disliked him. Here, life was anonymous; here one could sit at a café and be ignored by everyone, and find that even the waiters were less than attentive, for no one knew who you were. It was a novel sensation and a pleasant one as well.

Of course, he missed the two younger children, never having been separated from them before now, and so had Ceccina, but he more so, he thought. They had phoned Catania twice a day, and spoken to Ceccina's mother, and all was well. One almost had the impression that this phoning up was regarded as excessive. But he loved the children excessively, so that was that. Of course, not having them present was an advantage in some ways. It meant that the capacious hotel bed belonged to him and Ceccina alone, though at the bottom of the bed was a smaller bed for their eldest, so they had not been entirely alone. But it had been a glimpse of what normal married life might be like. He would always, from now on, think of Verona as a city of romantic love. His lips were sore with so much kissing, though solicitous Pasqualina had put that down to the cold air that came from the nearby Alps.

The holiday, then, was a great success. But the return to Catania was a reminder that life was not holiday, but work. The first thing on arrival was to go down to the square and to survey the scene. The boss was there, Gino was there, so was Renzo, and so was Alfio, and no doubt he would see them soon. However, the first important message, brought by a little boy, who was rewarded with a fifty euro note for his trouble, was that Piuccio, the gravedigger of Bronte, wanted to see him; he sent the boy off with the indication that he would see Piuccio at six that evening in the church of Saint Agatha in Terpsichore Square.

Piuccio was there, at six precisely, as the church was growing gloomy, looking serious, but not dressed in black: he was wearing jeans and trainers and a Barbour, over the collar of which trailed his longish, greying and curling hair.

'You were away?' he asked.

'A holiday. Verona.'

'Nice,' said Piuccio. 'By contrast, sir, here in Sicily, and in Catania in particular, it is all bad news.'

He gave a little smile, and indicated a brief case by his feet.

'But not bad news for you, Piuccio, I think,' said Traiano.

'No, sir, by no means. Since you first bought my debts, as I am sure you remember, debts totalling more than two hundred thousand, well, word has got about. There is so much bad debt about. Not just the undertakers, all small businesses, shops, even the professions. Dentists, would you believe it? Even doctors and lawyers. Anyway, I have been approached by various friends and acquaintances, and friends of friends, and acquaintances of acquaintances, you know what a small community we are; mainly from Catania, but also from Bronte, and they have told me that they know I can solve this problem of theirs. To cut it short, sir, as I do not want to bore you, you paid me twenty thousand for my own debts, and you gave me two thousand for driving you up to Rome with the coffin, and with a little bit of money I was able to scrape together… in the bag, sir, is the paperwork for bills totalling three hundred thousand euros in nominal value, for which I paid about twenty-five thousand.'

'Twenty-five thousand for worthless paper, that is quite a lot.'

'Agreed, sir. But you can turn them into hard cash. They won't be valueless then.'

'Agreed. If you paid ten percent of the nominal value…'

'Actually, sir,' said Piuccio, 'I beat some of them down. Some I gave only six or seven per cent to. My total outlay was twenty-two thousand, not twenty-five, just so you know.'

'Good, you have done well, dear Piuccio. You are turning into a real businessman. I will take this useless paper and I will spin it into gold. You paid twenty-two, I will give you thirty.'

Piuccio allowed himself a sigh of relief.

'Thank you, sir, that is generous.'

'My feeling is that more will come in. As they do, sell them on to me, and I will pass them on to our boys. You said it was all bad news in Catania. What are they saying?'

'Well, sir, all weekend, there have been cars burning in the suburbs, and buses as well; it is a disgrace, and the police and the people who are running the city cannot or will not do anything about it. They say they are all off on holiday. The traffic has been worse than ever with so many roads blocked, and the bus drivers are going on strike. Then there was this doctor shot dead, but they do not have a description of the man who did it, and there were no witnesses, and now they are saying this Doctor Adami was engaged in something illegal, selling unlicensed pills, that sort of thing.'

Traiano sighed. 'How is your business, your other business?' he asked.

'Very good, sir. Now people assume I am your friend, I get fewer people trying to cheat me or trying to get away without paying. It is wonderful. My wife is happy.'

'The new child?'

'Going well, sir. I gather don Calogero has a new son?'

'Yes, called Romano. An odd name, some people think. And I have a new half-brother, called William, which is unusual too, I suppose. What are you thinking of calling yours, if a boy?'

'The first is Gianni, so maybe the second will be Paolo,' said Piuccio. 'And is the signora well?'

He meant Ceccina.

'She is very well,' answered Traiano with a trace of caution. He knew when people asked this question it usually meant a reference to Ceccina's pregnancy. Well, there was none, nor was there going to be for some time, sadly. 'Don Renzo is marrying don Calogero's sister in February, so there is going to be a huge celebration, and Ceccina is very pleased about that. You know how women enjoy weddings. It is going to be in Palermo, but it would be nice if you could come, Piuccio. I will make sure your name is on the list.'

'I would be honoured, sir.'

'And then we can meet your wife and little boy. I know she may not know many people there, but we are a friendly bunch, and so… When are you next doing a burial on the continent?'

'They come up regularly, sir. I do quite a few a year, sometimes Naples, sometimes Rome, sometimes as far afield as Bologna or Venice.'

'Good. Keep me informed, as I may want to come along.' He smiled. 'Thanks, Piuccio.'

He stood up, and they shook hands, and he could feel in this simple gesture something he had come to recognise, namely the tremble of desire in the hand of the other. How badly Piuccio needed him; how desperately he wanted to be his friend; how he craved the help that only he, and his friends, could give. Poor Piuccio, condemned to such a dreadful life as an undertaker; a despised gravedigger; one of the common herd; one destined to live and die poor and disregarded, unless, thanks to a miracle, Traiano should have pity on him and help him. It was like the people who prayed in front of the Spanish Madonna, asking for the impossible, asking for graces and favours. How many went away comforted, he wondered? And here was Piuccio, longing for a sign of favour, like someone on their knees before the Madonna. But the Madonna could help everyone, he knew, because she loved everyone; he was more practical: he helped those who helped him. Piuccio was useful, there was no doubt about that, so he was inclined to reassure him. He dropped his hand, and touched his cheek with his right hand, as a gesture of reassurance, but without smiling. He felt a certain pleasure in doing this, knowing that he was torturing Piuccio as he did this. Piuccio wanted reassurance, love, certainty. But what he was giving him was a mere crumb. But what more did he have to give? Piuccio was a minor player, unlike Bonelli, unlike Volta. He was one of the little men.

'Send me a message when you are next going to Rome,' he said. 'I will send someone with the money to you very soon.'

'Thank you, sir,' said Piuccio humbly.

Traiano picked up the briefcase, genuflected and crossed himself before the altar, and then left the darkening church.

He deposited the briefcase in the changing room on the gym, in one of the lockers he used, and then went home to have supper and put the children to bed. After that, having said goodnight to his wife, he went down to the square and called in at the bar. To several of the people, he indicated that he would see them later, and so it proved. At midnight, he was in the changing room at the gym once more, where he pushed the various scattered and malodorous bits of clothing off the central bench and made it into an impromptu desk, where he spread out the bits of paper. He had paid 10% of the nominal value, so he knew he had to sell them on for between 15% and 20% in order to make a good profit, and some of them would render more profit than others. The overall nominal value was three hundred thousand euro, and he sorted the debts in order of value. None were above twelve thousand in value, and there were thirty-two bills in all, some rather modest, such as the fool who had refused to pay his dentist for work done to the value of 350 euro. Well, that was quite a lot for a dental bill, but why run up a bill you either could not pay or had no way of paying? Whoever had done that was fool. He looked at the date on the bill. It was only a few months old, which made it unlikely that the debtor had died in the meantime.

The boys had come in and were all standing at a respectful distance. He looked up at them, and he gestured slightly towards one, a big tough fifteen-year-old called Marco, who approached.

'I can sell you a way of making up to 350 euro for 80 euro,' he said. 'Have you got 80 euro?'

The boy nodded.

'Can you read?'

'Not really, boss.'

'Look, this man, a signore Ermengildo Tucci, that is his address right there, can you see, owes the dentist 350 euros. You take this paper to him, you will have to find out where best to confront him, and tell him he must pay. He may offer half the sum, or slightly less. See what you can get out of him. He might refuse altogether, in which case you ask again, and you make him pay. Every cent over 80 euros is pure profit for you. Got it?'

The boy nodded.

'When he pays, you give him the bill, OK? He should be easy to persuade. Do you know how to use pliers? Yes? Good. And if you do well with this, there will be more to come.'

The boy took the bill and handed over the money, which Traiano put in the briefcase. And so it went on for several hours. Boys came and went, bringing back with them the money they needed, with which to buy the bills. The hardest bills to collect, which were the oldest and the biggest, he would entrust to Alfio and to Gino. Both were for over ten thousand euro, and both represented a gamble, but Gino and Alfio would be eager to pay for both. He would make sure he got the money there and then.

He found Gino and Alfio in the bar. They were not together, but at separate ends of the bar, both surrounded by their little coterie of particular friends. He approached Alfio first and explained the nature of the bill he proposed selling him, saying he had saved it especially for him. It was for a supermarket in Bronte that owed a supplier 12,000 euros, going back years. He had paid 10%, which meant he had to recoup 1,200; he was quite prepared to let Alfio have it for 2,000; he was doing him a favour. A supermarket was an easy target too.

'I hear your cousin has disappeared,' he said by way of conversation, in sympathetic tones.

'What do you know about it?' asked Alfio a trifle more sharply than he intended.

He noted the tone.

'I was in Verona with my brother-in-law Corrado. He told me. Said she had gone to the north to be with some relatives, people you know, I suppose?'

'Not relatives of mine,' said Alfio. 'She is my mother's sister's daughter. These would be people I do not know, relatives of her father. The other side of the family. But I know nothing about it, just like you,' he said with meaning. 'How was Verona?'

They spoke of Verona, and then he went to the other end of the bar to see Gino, grim and triumphant, back from his long time away. The bill he sold him was also for 12,000, this time for a supermarket in Catania itself. It was clear to him that Gino was determined to be happy. He had fallen out with Alfio, but was determined not to let that depress him.

By the time he had finished his business, the briefcase he held was stuffed with cash. He felt no need to take it out and count it, as his arithmetical brain told him just how much it contained, all in low denomination notes: forty-two thousand euro. He had made a profit of twelve thousand euro for doing very little. More importantly, he had managed to sow the seeds of crime and disorder throughout Catania, Bronte and beyond. The boys would go out and intimidate the debtors, and in some cases set fire to their houses and shops, their cars too, and, in cases where fools refused to pay, make then pay with their lives.

'Have you got anything for me, boss?' asked Tonino, who now appeared at his side.

'Sold lots of pills?' asked Traiano, not answering the question.

'All gone, boss,' said Tonino.

He looked at him questioningly.

Tonino detailed what he had sold and who had bought it. He himself collected the cheaper stuff from the doctor, things like ordinary painkillers, and passed these onto other boys. There was a lively market for pills like paracetamol which were sold for about a tenth of the price they fetched in shops. Other things too went for one tenth of their shop price, as and when the doctor supplied them. But Tonino was restricting his own activities to the one pill everyone wanted, the opiate. This was easy to carry and commanded an excellent price. And its users needed it. Each pill cost fifty euros; or rather there were people who were prepared to pay that much. It was very expensive. Don Gino, of course, got his at cost price, namely twenty euros a pill.

'And how many is he taking a day?' asked Traiano curiously.

'Four or five some days. It is hard to tell,' said Tonino. 'I don't know what he did when he was away in Palermo. Though on one occasion he called me over and bought the entire supply.'

'These other things, the paracetamol, things like that, they are just a way for children to make pocket money. The opiate is the way forward. We need more of it. It seems a harmless enough sort of thing, not something likely to embarrass Volta, at least not yet. The doctor gets it from the Americans, doesn't he? Well, when are we meeting the supplier?'

'Soon. He suggested it. What happened to Doctor Adami has made him very nervous. You know, someone going round and shooting doctors, it's not good from his point of view. There is some guy,' said Tonino. 'They call him the Major. That is all I know. The doctor is secretive, but he has promised to talk to the Major and allow us to talk to the Major.'

'So, this is what I have got for you, Tonino. I want to meet the Major, whoever he is, and soon. And I want you to arrange it. When you do, you will be rewarded.'

Tonino considered.

'Yes, boss,' he said. 'I will let you know when I have fixed it up. It may take a bit of time.'

'I am patient, as you know. And in a few months, we will be going to Rome again with the gravedigger of Bronte. What did you think of the pictures we bought last time? We will be buying more.'

'To tell you the truth, boss, all pictures look alike to me. I don't really look at them. I see them every day in the gallery when I walk through to go home, but they don't make much impression. I don't really see the point of art. Don Calogero and the signora, signora Tancredi I mean, not the signora his mother, they like art, don't they?'

'How do you know that?'

'Something Isabella told me one day.'

'How is your girlfriend, Roberto's sister? What is her name?'

'Her name is Petra, boss, and she is very nice, very well, it is all going well, all with her mother's permission, boss.'

Traiano felt a tiny stab of annoyance. When he had met his wife, at the same age Tonino was now, there had been no parental permission at all, and a corresponding big fuss, at least for a few weeks.

'She sounds just right for you,' said Traiano, in a manner meant to be friendly, but which in fact sounded dismissive to Tonino's ears.

As they left the bar and emerged into the square, the bells were sounding eleven over Catania. He saw the boss's light was on. They parted, each to his next destination: Tonino to his mother, Traiano to Calogero, to pay him his share of the profits from the newly sold bills.

Chapter Eight

The announcement of the date of the wedding of Renzo Santucci and Elena di Rienzi was not received with unalloyed joy in Palermo.

Weddings, weddings were tedious beyond belief, reflected don Antonio Santucci, in his more sober moments. The wedding itself would be painful and boring, he was sure; but the preparations for the wedding would be extremely tedious as well. So, he resolved, even if it were the wrong time of year, to stay put in Castelvetrano for as long as he could and let his wife Angela deal with the whole matter. After all, she was the groom's aunt, and he was just the groom's cousin. She presumably liked her nephew (he had never asked) while he loathed him, and loathed the brother of the girl he was marrying. Yes, he would be there, he promised her, and yes, he would be sober, but apart from that he wanted nothing to do with it at all. He would pretend to enjoy himself, he told his wife, but further than that, she could not reasonably ask.

Angela Santucci sighed, and put down the phone. Ever since her husband had given up responsibility for the family, the matter of dealing with the children had fallen exclusively on her. The children, four of them, were, it had to be said, of varying difficulty when it came to managing them. Sandro, now about to start university, hated his father, and his father could not stand him, but Sandro was more or less all right with her, provided that she did not ask any questions about what he got up to. In truth she did not ask any questions at all, in case he gave her honest answers, which, she suspected, would distress her. Best not to know. Sandro had already done a lot of things of which she heartily disapproved, but she had taken refuge in silence. He knew, surely, what she felt about these things, and he was not inclined to listen, so why muddy the atmosphere by trying to engage with him? Best to let him be in the hope that one day he would grow up into a pleasant human being. And he might. She had not yet despaired. A devout Catholic, she prayed for him, almost as much as she prayed for her husband. His ear stud displeased her. The bleached hair as well. As for the tattoo, she tried not to think about that.

Things were not made easier by the way her two daughters, Emma and Marina, both idolised their brother Sandro. They thought he was cool, they thought he was beautiful, whereas his mother secretly lamented his hideous appearance and his poor choice of clothes. He had a generous allowance – was that where they had first of all gone wrong, by giving him too much? - and she was forever picking up bits of designer gear off the floor of his bedroom. When she plucked up courage to ask him what he was going to wear for the wedding, she was relieved to hear that he had decided on his Dolce and Gabbana suit, the one with the very loud checked pattern which was, she hated to admit, rather a fine outfit; that and the Ferragamo shoes that he had bought on his last trip to Rome. He had worn the suit once before, and this would be its second and final outing, he said. She noted this. A charitable woman, her own old clothes, none very old, were always sent to a charity shop where they fetched good prices, raising money to help the rehabilitation of drug addicts.

As for the girls, they were in fact looking forward to the wedding, even if they did not like to admit to anything so uncool. They were the cousins of the groom, the daughters of don Antonio Santucci, and all the employees would be there. This was, as far as they saw it, a tribal occasion, a gathering of the entire clan, and all of these people knew them, even if they did not know them in return. All eyes would be on them, after the bride. And here there was a matter of pride to be considered. They did not really care much about Renzo, but they cared even less for anyone from Catania. These girls from Catania gave themselves airs. They overdressed. They were common and vulgar. They needed to be shown how it should be done. It was true that neither Emma or Marina would talk to their father (though they considered it their right to keep on spending his money) but they still resented the way Catania had treated him. It was necessary to reassert the supremacy of Palermo.

While they despised the bride and the girls from Catania, the men who would be present, wherever they were from, were a different matter. Of course, they knew what the Santucci group of companies did: import, export, that sort of thing. Most of the employees were boring men in suits, the fathers of boring boys they met at parties and dances. But there would be some of the more old-fashioned element there, people who worked for the company, and whose families had worked there for generations. Amongst these would be some boys of their own age, and, though they had never discussed this, both Emma and Marina, Emma even more than Marina, had an interest in the rougher elements of society. The sort of boys they met, boys from their own background, these were the least interesting boys on the planet, as far as they were concerned. Sandro, who was not given to delicacy of statement, just said that they both wanted the same thing, to be screwed by a gangster. This annoyed them and exasperated them both, for they knew there was some truth in it. Sandro was lucky, they retorted. He was a boy. He could do what he liked. He had defied their father, and their father had tried and failed to shoot him. This meant that Sandro had complete freedom to do as he liked from now on. And he used that freedom. Marina and Emma were not so lucky: they had to behave and, at least outwardly, conform to what polite society wanted of them.

Of course, Angela Santucci knew nothing of her elder three children's sex lives, nothing at all. She did not want to know, she did not dream of asking, and she tried not to think of it. Consequently, she had no idea of whom Sandro slept with, or whom Emma and Marina had slept with or were sleeping with or wanted to sleep with. She buried her head in the sand. She had known all about her late brother Carlo, who had never been faithful to his wife, but who bedded every girl he liked the look of; she had heard her sister-in-law say that Renzo, thank goodness, was settling down at last, suggesting that he had been a great worry. She sometimes thought that the whole Santucci family was sex mad, with the sad exception of her husband, who had lost all interest in that sort of thing years ago.

The only member of the family that gave her unalloyed delight was her youngest, Beppe, the afterthought, as the others rather cruelly termed him. She adored him, and not just because he was the youngest, but because he was the sweetest and most lovable. It pained her that while the elder three all seemed to get along quite well with each other, they had little time for their youngest sibling. They regarded him as spoilt; and, despite the fact that they never reined in their own spending, they became quite angry and resentful when any money was spent on Beppe. For the wedding, she had decided to have the child properly dressed in a proper adult suit; so, she decided that they would fly to Milan to visit a tailor there, to have him measured up; she had wanted to go to Milan for some time, to visit the shops on her own account; it seemed a harmless little jaunt, but the other three had been furious at what they claimed was the waste of money. (She had spared them several details, such as the hotel she wanted to stay in, or that they were planning to fly first class.)

Oddly, Beppe himself had said that while he was always happy to go anywhere with his mother, and loved her company, he did not see why he needed so many new clothes, considering there were so many poor people in the world. The boy was a very serious Catholic, just like herself, and what he said was true, but she reassured him that though they were spending this money on themselves, they (by which she meant herself, as her husband paid no attention to these things) gave a lot of money to charity, and, because one could give, just to assuage one's sense of guilt, she herself also spent a lot of her time in charitable activity. As a major donor, she sat on the board of directors of several charities that helped drug addicts; she was also involved in the diocesan Caritas; moreover, on certain days she herself worked in the kitchen of the diocesan Caritas and served in the canteen. She had promised Beppe when he was older that he too could volunteer to help at the diocesan Caritas.

Her husband, wisely, had never commented on her religious commitments, her endless going to church, her charitable endeavours. In this he showed a restraint and a generosity that he did not often display. He knew his wife was a disappointed woman. He was a disappointed man himself, so he recognised all the symptoms; her disappointment was assuaged by religion, his by drink. His was mainly to do with the way he had mismanaged the business, and been outfoxed by that bastard from Catania. For her, it was the family. Her brother's death – did she know that he had given the order for that? He hoped not. He assumed not. Perhaps she simply did not want to know. The children – well, he shared her disappointment there, though they had never discussed it. His elder son was a spoiled child, a disgrace, an embarrassment. The girls refused to speak to him. Only Beppe was on good terms with both parents. But Beppe was on good terms with everyone.

As for the other children, they despised their mother's religiosity, and did their best to ignore it. Sandro hated religion, hated Catholicism, and saw it as something aimed personally at his right to have a good time. It was hypocrisy, a provocation, an act of hatred. Emma and Marina subscribed to the same view, more or less. The girls knew about the family business, or thought they did. Sandro knew more, and viewed his mother's work for drug addicts as the supreme act of hypocritical self-deception. He loved her, of course, but she was so stupid. Did she not realise, did she not see, that the Santucci family fortune was based on drugs, and these drug addicts were the collateral damage? If she was really against drugs she would confront the family, but that was surely something she was too afraid to do. Of course, he knew it all, being eighteen years old; and his mother knew nothing at all. And Beppe, the despised youngest child, he was just too stupid for words. When were these people going to wake up?

Sandro's feelings about the family were, like those of his sisters, conflicted. He hated the family name because it was so constricting, because people knew who you were, they knew you were rich, and they acted accordingly. And yet without the family name he would be, he suspected, nothing at all, and he would not like that. He despised the family name, but he was more than happy to exploit it. His mother, who had been born a Santucci and married a Santucci, and lived her whole life under her brother's shadow or her husband's, felt a pang of despair when she heard him speak in these terms.

Contrary to what everyone supposed (or so she assumed) she knew the nature of the Santucci family project. From girlhood, she had listened to the stories of the original two brothers, the way they had built up the lemon business, and how they had done so. She was not stupid. She had never seen it happen, but she had felt its effects, the fact that power came, in the end, from the barrel of a gun. She had loved her brother Carlo with passionate devotion because of his charm, his sweetness, his good looks, his spirit: but she had known of his immorality, sleeping with every girl who would have him, and most would, and she had known that he was, from an early age, a murderer. Men who killed other men had an aura about them, and Carlo had gained that aura young. But she had still loved him. He had known, and she had known, that he would die young, though when he had, it had been hard to accept. And she knew who to blame, but she also knew the futility of holding grudges. She did not forgive her husband for what he had done – she knew it was him. Who else could it be? – she merely felt sorry for him. She despised him for the cowardly act of murdering her brother; but more than that, she despised him for his failure to follow through, to seize power. She despised him for losing power to the people from Catania. But she knew that having lost to the people of Catania, one had still to make peace in the end.

She had seen this don Calogero and seen his aura, seen the way he commanded, and knew that, for better or for worse, the security of her children depended on this man. She had known his wife, slightly, for years, and was on friendly terms with her, but the wife, she knew, though playing an important part as the banker, and the money woman, was not that important. The man who wielded the knife and the gun, he was the one who counted. But he was not just a brute, he was a very clever man, as one could tell from this dynastic marriage he had brought about, this marrying off of her nephew Renzo to his sister Elena. Of course, Renzo was a fool, rather like her own son, his cousin Sandro, though one always hoped Sandro would grow up, she remained confident Renzo never would. But with this in mind, she determined on a bold course of action.

As soon as Anna Maria had had her baby, she waited for a decent interval to pass, and then rang to congratulate her; what could be more natural than to call on her in person and wish her well, and see the child? She went when she hoped he would be there too. And what was more natural than taking her children with her? This, she had judged, would be a good overture to peace.

As it turned out, the visit, which was a mere matter of twenty minutes, went extremely well. The girls had been charming, and the boys surely appeared to be no threat, and she herself thought that perhaps she had won him over, if only a little bit, and convinced him she was no threat at all either.

The children had not been difficult to marshal, as she had at first supposed. Beppe, of course, was always biddable; the two girls, even though they might not have chosen to admit it, still cared about babies, but she had been a little surprised that Sandro assented. He had heard about the boss of Catania and was curious about him. Of course, he had met him, the day his father had tried to shoot him, though he had no real clear impression of meeting him that confused day. He wanted to meet him again.

'Your aunt,' Calogero was now saying to Renzo, 'She thinks she is clever. She came to see me, well, ostensibly my wife, in order to win me over.'

He had been describing the visit to the flat in Palermo, when Angela Santucci had come with her children. Into this conversation, Traiano had just walked, bringing the money. It was getting close to midnight. Renzo was sprawled on an armchair, all arms and legs, his shirt hanging out as usual, his eyes dull, a whiskey glass in front of him. Calogero was opposite him on the sofa, more alert, wide awake. He absently took the money that Traiano offered him, and told him to put in in the desk, giving him a key. It was an elaborate desk, always kept locked. A single key opened all the drawers, and turning it, he put the cash in the one drawer that seemed least full. Then he locked the desk and returned the key. Calogero took it without looking, and gestured for him to sit next to him.

'And did you allow her to win you over, boss?' asked Renzo, barely acknowledging Traiano's presence.

'I did not,' said Calogero. 'I think your aunt thinks she succeeded in making a good impression. I did not disillusion her. Why should I? Let her feel comfortable. But I am no more sentimental about these people than you are. Yes, we will keep the money flowing in her direction and her children's direction while it suits us to be generous. But this is our thing, not theirs; we are not going to work hard at making a fortune only to share it with them. They will not starve, the girls I mean; they count for nothing, nothing at all. The two boys and your uncle, well, I know what I owe you on that score.'

Renzo looked for a moment uncomfortable, Traiano noticed.

'I invited Sandro to your bachelor party,' said Calogero.

'You did?' asked Renzo in disbelief.

'I did. He is old enough to come. He will come and we will keep an eye on him. He was pleased to be asked. He is, I think, a worthless boy. The younger one, Beppe, wanted to come, but I told him he could not, as he was far too young. He was very disappointed. But Sandro is interesting. He hates his father almost as much as you do, and he also loathes the little brother. I could tell.'

'Beppe is not a bad kid,' conceded Renzo. 'But, you know, it is best to be sure.'

'Of course it is,' said Calogero. 'When the time comes, we have friends we can rely on.' He looked at Traiano and smiled at him. 'I owe you so much,' he continued, directing his eyes at Renzo. 'And you are my future brother-in-law, the one who is going to provide me with lots of legitimate nephews and nieces.'

'I will try my best,' smirked Renzo.

'Where is Gino?' Traiano now asked.

'Right now?' said Renzo. 'By my calculations entering the gates of paradise.'

'Don't be vulgar,' said Calogero.

'He's found a girl, or rather she found him. A very nice girl too. English.'

'Oh,' said Traiano, understanding. He looked at the boss. 'You don't mind? You are employing her.'

'What people do in their free time is their business,' said Calogero. 'And there is no accounting for taste, is there?'

'None whatever,' agreed Traiano.

'I need to speak to Alfio,' said Calogero. 'Can you go and find him for me and send him here? We need to talk about the Furnaces and Africa, this hotel business. I am not going to bed. Find him and send him up.'

'Sure, boss,' said Traiano getting up from the sofa. He looked at Renzo, still sprawled on the armchair. 'Look,' he said, 'If Gino is off enjoying himself, why don't you and I go to the gym and have a fight, and you can show me how good you have become.'

He leaped to his feet.

There were two ways, he knew, of getting things out of Renzo: one was to hit him repeatedly with a belt until he bled; the other way was to be nice to him, to give him what he wanted. He knew that the first way would, from his own perspective, be much less unpleasant. Indeed, he relished the thought of beating Renzo, of banging his coke-filled head against a hard surface repeatedly, of kicking his ribs, but on the whole, he thought this the less productive way forward. Better to give him what he wanted, even though that went against the grain. He didn't like Renzo, he did not like anyone apart from his own wife and children; and what Renzo wanted was love and friendship, indeed intimacy, things that he clearly craved, that he had perhaps found with Gino, things that Traiano did not have to give, but was resolved to pretend to give. They would all have to put up with Renzo for some years to come; it was best to make him think he was a friend, a true friend, even if he was not; and it was necessary for him to find out what had really happened with Catarina. He had sensed a favour had been done, by Renzo, for the boss. He could guess what that favour was. He was perturbed that he had asked Renzo, not himself. Of course, the boss knew, but one could not ask the boss questions. He resented that. And he would resent to the point of murderous fury any questions about Catarina. Of that, he was sure. For Traiano knew the truth about the boss - there was no accounting for taste – which others had no idea about. But Traiano had guessed. The boss feared and loathed beautiful ambitious women like Catarina. He was only really comfortable with dominant older women like Anna, Traiano's mother, and Anna Maria, his wife. That had to be true. He had never really liked his wife Stefania, though he had thought her an asset; he had spent most of his married life sleeping on the sofa, and he had never once looked at any young woman, though they all would have liked him to have looked at them.

Oh yes, he was a big powerful man, but no great lover, and Catarina's mistake had been to remind him of the fact that he did not desire her at all. If Catarina was dead, which he imagined she might be, it was because she had made the boss feel like a sexual inadequate. As for the child, if he were dead, and he imagined he might be too, he was dead because of his parentage, the child of the hated murdered brother. What had he said about legitimate nephews and nieces? The illegitimate one was a reminder of someone, his own brother, whom he was determined to forget. But he had to be sure.

It was a long night. From midnight to about three in the morning, he and Renzo sparred, each trying to hit the other. Traiano was agile and could avoid most of the punches. Renzo less so, particularly as he took frequent breaks to numb himself with cocaine, with pills and with drink. They fought until Renzo was exhausted, until it was clear that Traiano was a fighter who could not be beaten. The sweat poured down Renzo, his untidy hair was wet, his shorts soaked, and every muscle was aching, which filled him with the deepest contentment.

'Have I hurt you?' asked Traiano, with solicitude.

'I can take it,' said Renzo.

He was sitting on the bench and looked up at him with an almost slavish devotion. Traiano grabbed his greasy hair and pulled it playfully. Renzo laughed.

'The boss never comes down here,' he said regretfully.

'You just have to make do with me,' said Traiano.

He sat down next to him on the bench, and tried not to mind the acrid smell of sweat emanating from Renzo.

'How is your sex life?' asked Renzo.

'Perfect,' said Traiano. 'How is yours?'

'She is OK. She is nice. She is clever, you know? She thinks of things. I like her.'

'Good.'

'Once we are married, we will have a baby, I hope, pretty soon, and, well, she will be busy… Have you…? What I mean is, how long do I have to wait before I can find other things to amuse me?'

'I don't think there is a fixed period,' said Traiano. 'I am not interested in anything like that, but other people have different needs. Gino has got this girl now…'

'Yes, she likes him. Not many liked him before now. I mean, he had money, he was important, he was my friend, the boss's friend, but he wants to be liked for himself.'

'Didn't Catarina like him for himself?'

'Not in the least. He found out, you know, and he was very upset by her betrayal.' Renzo frowned. 'Poor Gino. I feel sorry for him.' He frowned again. 'Do you like me for myself?'

'Of course I do,' answered Traiano, without a moment's hesitation. 'I mean, we work together, don't we? But it is more than that. I have watched you; I have seen you. You are brave, you are clever. You are just like your father don Carlo, not that I knew him, but I have heard the stories. You are your father's son. A real man. The sort of person other men will follow.'

Renzo beamed.

'And I am glad that you taught Catarina a lesson,' added Traiano.

'How do you know that?' asked Renzo.

'You are Gino's friend. Who better to avenge his honour than you? Though what Alfio may say or think….'

'Alfio can say and think what he likes, but he cannot do anything. The boss authorised it; he ordered it. That is final. He wanted it. Gino was happy to go along with it. And Alfio must go along with it too. That is all there is to it.'

'All?' asked Traiano.

Renzo hesitated.

'Can I trust you?'

'Of course.'

'It didn't quite go to plan. I drove to Catania through the night and woke her up at about two in the morning. I told her that she needed to get out as soon as possible, with the child. I told her that Gino knew, and he was planning to kill her, and that she needed to drive to Messina as quickly as possible and take the ferry to Villa San Giovanni. Once she got to Italy, she should just keep driving. But we had agreed that Gino would meet her at the ferry… but she never turned up.'

Traino was thoughtful.

'Gino wanted to kill her? And the child? Was that his idea or the boss's?'

'The boss said he wanted her out of the way, her and the child, and that he never wanted to hear her name or hear from her or about her again. Gino thought that this meant…. She thought that this meant her life was in danger, at least I think she did. She may still be in Sicily, or else she went some other way, not via Messina. Maybe Gino wanted to confront her, to upbraid her, not to kill her. But with Gino, you never can tell. One moment he is gentle, the next, he is quite harsh.'

'But where has she got to?' asked Traiano. 'I suppose Alfio will know, but Alfio will not say. She will be hiding with the child somewhere like Enna or Mussomeli, somewhere quiet. But Alfio will know that you were behind it. But don't worry. He knows you would only have acted because the boss told you to.'

'Should we be worried about Alfio?' asked Renzo.

'What can Alfio do?' asked Traiano. 'Of course, he will never forgive Gino. That is finished forever now. But Catarina and the child, wherever they have got to, will not be returning. She is as good as dead. And Gino can enjoy his little English girl in peace. Alfio must be furious, and even more furious, when he realises he can do nothing about it.'

The meeting was arranged. To Traiano's surprise, the Major specified the arrivals hall in the airport, which was regularly patrolled by armed police and soldiers. This gave him an advantage, he realised. He would not come to the meeting armed, not that he had ever had any intention of doing so; but it told him something of the frame of mind of the Major. He was nervous. He was ill at ease. As such, he was easy to spot when he entered the arrivals hall. Not only was he plainly American, he was an American pretending to be sitting there with a newspaper and a cup of coffee as if this were the most natural thing in the world, and making a bad show of it. Traiano got a cup of coffee for himself, and then joined him at the table, after politely asking him if the seat was free.

'I am not in the mood for pleasantries,' said the Major, more petulantly than he had intended.

Traiano raised an eyebrow.

'I am sorry to hear it,' he said.

'Doctor Moro wanted me to meet you. He was spooked, by the murder of this Doctor Adami. He thinks someone is going round killing doctors, and he may be next.'

There was determination in his voice, a determination not to be intimidated.

'Doctor Adami, that was a shocking business,' Traiano agreed. 'But Doctor Moro should not worry. He has friends. We would never hurt him, nor would we let anyone else do so. But I am glad he persuaded you to see us. I appreciate it, and I appreciate your coming. You see, we want to cut out the middle man, in this case the doctor. He knows that. I think he accepts it. You and I, dealing with each other directly, that can be to your advantage and to ours. You and I need to do business. Tell me about the opiates. I am not interested in the other stuff, the paracetamol and the aspirins, for goodness' sake. It is the big stuff I want. You have got the stuff; we can provide distribution. You stand to make much more than you are making at present, Major.'

He saw that he had his got his attention now, by the look that crossed his fat stupid face.

'Depending on how much you can put our way, you will in just a few years have enough money to retire from the Army, with whoever you please, wherever you please. It's a nice prospect.'

He smiled, the Major scowled.

'Explain the opiates to me.'

The major explained. He wasn't really a major - that was a joke of the doctor's - but a mere sergeant. He worked on the airbase, overseeing the landing and the taking off of American planes. Many of these planes were arriving from bases in America, bound for bases in the Middle East; the planes stopped to refuel or to change crew and, often to take off cargo and put on cargo. The airbase in Sicily supplied the commissaries of the bases in the Middle East with perishable items such as fruit and vegetables; some medical supplies were unloaded for the use of American bases in Italy and the rest of Europe. The accounting for these things was slapdash, and a lot was lost in transit. In addition, there were quite a few things in the cargo which were illegal, disguised as personal letters and parcels from home. The entire American army in the Middle East, he implied, was off its head on illegal drugs and prescription drugs, the most prominent of which was the opiate in which he was interested. The amount of these pills that were transhipped from the United States to the Middle East every week was staggering, most to be prescribed by Army doctors. However, a significant amount was not for prescription, but informal distribution, which was tolerated because people, people somewhere, somehow, knew that the troops needed these pills with no questions asked. He was stealing these pills and selling them on to the doctor for ten euros a piece. In a good week, as it all depended on what he could get away with, he managed several blister packs, some 200 pills. The real skill was not in the stealing – this the Army expected, indeed tolerated, knowing that it was a necessary way of feeding the addiction of the troops – but in getting the things off the base. He went off-base once a week and drove to see his girlfriend and passed the stuff onto her, having smuggled it off the base in his car. The people who did the checks knew him, and only checked him when going into the base, not when leaving, or if they did so, they did so in a rather hurried way. They were his friends, but he paid for their friendship. Because of this he was able to leave the base with sometimes quite bulky items, concealed under a blanket. The pills, however, he always hid under the spare wheel. The girlfriend helped with the selling on, and she kept the money from the doctor.

Traiano considered this and then said: 'I need to know where your girlfriend lives.'

'In Catania.'

'Near a bus route?'

'Yes.'

'Good,' said Traiano. 'We will send people round with the money and with our shopping list.'

'Look,' said the Major. 'I don't want her.... annoyed in any way, do you understand?'

Traino looked at him. He was very nervous, he could see, and this was the source of his aggression. So, he was soothing.

'No one is going to hurt her. The boys we will send next will be nice, quiet and gentle boys. Don't worry. Reassure her. If she needs reassurance, give it to her. I am sure you can do that. How long have you and she been together?'

'Two years,' said the Major. 'She was, is, my Italian teacher.'

'You speak well,' said Traiano. 'And your wife, how long have you been married to her?'

'Twenty years. Two children,' said the Major glumly. 'This idea was hers, and we need the money to start a new life.'

'Of course, a new life,' said Traiano.

A new life, the one thing everyone wanted, but no one could have, yet everyone still persisted in seeking.

'Keep on giving us the stuff, and you will have your new life,' he said. He looked at the paper on the table before them. 'Practising your reading of our language? How is the election campaign going?'

'If this guy wins, he will inherit a poisoned chalice,' said the Major. 'This place is worse than Chicago, which is where I come from. We are always warned about going off the base. I mean obviously it is not Baghdad, but… you saw this latest story? The guy who was robbed and had his teeth pulled out?'

He gestured at the paper. Traiano glanced at it.

'Nasty,' he said. 'I guarantee you and your girlfriend will be safe as if you were in Chicago, well, not Chicago, wherever is safe in America. Now where does she live? And tell me a time when she is going to be in?'

She lived by the triumphal arch at the end of via Garibaldi. He mentioned a time and a day the next week. Then, after a few more civilities, they parted.

Don Renzo Santucci was thoroughly bored at the prospect of his own wedding, now the date was fixed. In this, he was like his uncle don Antonio. As soon as the date was announced, he realised that he was now a marginalised figure, given that Elena, the bride, had so much to organise, none of which concerned him: the dress, what he would wear, the bridesmaids, their number and their dresses, the food at the reception, the photographer, the list was so long, that he blanked out as she talked, and made excuses to leave the room and take a restorative snort of cocaine, which was the only way he could bear it. Moreover, it was not just Elena who seemed to obsessed with these arrangements, but a whole cohort of women who joined her: her sister Assunta, whom he had assumed, wrongly, was above that sort of thing, and even her mother, the Black Widow Spider, who seemed deeply interested all of a sudden. His only contribution was to be monetary; the same applied to Calogero. Of course, he had tons of money, as did Calogero, but the appetite of his bride seemed insatiable. Occasionally, he was detected in his lack of enthusiasm, and Elena would ask him if he were not looking forward to the big day. Indeed he was, he told her. He was looking forward to it being over, to these people all leaving them in peace, to their being married and alone, and settling down to the serious matter of making babies.

If Elena's female relatives were not enough to cope with, there were also his mother, his grandmother and his aunts to deal with. They bombarded him with questions about what the women of Catania were doing; they were only the relations of the groom, and thus at a natural disadvantage when dealing with the bride's family. Besides, there were other matters that concerned them, chiefly the health of don Lorenzo Santucci, father to don Antonio, whose cancer was advanced, and who might not be alive by the time the wedding happened. There had been bad news back in the summer, succeeded by more hopeful news, but now, once more, the news was bad. If he were to die beforehand, would that mean the wedding would be cancelled? Quite a lot of people raised this question, the ones from Catania hoping that it would not, as they had waited long enough, the ones from Palermo saying that if don Lorenzo were to die before the wedding, it would look very bad indeed if the wedding went ahead.

Don Renzo himself could not bear the thought of the wedding being cancelled at the last minute, which would mean all this rigmarole having to be gone through yet again, and decided that he would take some action of his own to make sure the February date would not and could not change. His plan was a simple one. He would secure a private interview with the man he thought of as his uncle (actually his grandfather's cousin) and when the time came, if the situation arose, tell people that Uncle had told him to go ahead with the wedding in the event of his death, just before that lamentable event had occurred.

He decided to call at the villa his uncle inhabited in the northern suburbs of Palermo, at about 10am in the morning, reckoning that at such an hour the old man would be at his best; not recognising that he himself was at his best at that hour too, and the hours that followed were always a little hazy as the time passed. He made sure he was showered and groomed, wearing a good suit, and took a present for his aunt, don Lorenzo's wife. He was a little conscious, as he rang the doorbell, that he should have called before this.

The house was, to his surprise, full. One of his female cousins, whose name he could never remember, opened the door, and showed him into the sitting room. There they all sat, all the relatives, all in one place, and he thought for a moment that the old man must have died. But no, this was Sicily, a place where bad news, or impending worse news, cancer and death, attracted crowds of relatives, all for the most part clad in black, like birds of ill omen. One almost had the impression they enjoyed this sort of thing: illness, its eventual termination; the arrival of the undertakers; the removal of the coffin to church; the requiem Mass; the journey to the cemetery; the opening of the family chapel; the burial.

In fact, many of them were thinking of just this, and it was all planned in their heads, what would happen when the inevitable took place: the family chapel was in Montelepre, the village where the family originated. The Mass would take place in their parish church in Palermo. The coffin, that was pictured, and don Lorenzo lying in it surrounded by white satin, looking thin and grey. They had already given orders for the family chapel to be repaired and cleaned, in preparation for its being needed.

Don Lorenzo's wife, soon to be a widow, looked up as he entered. He bent over and kissed her cheek, noting her sad but impassive expression.

'How is uncle?' he asked. 'And how are you, auntie?'

'I am very well, replied the old lady. 'Your uncle is with don Michele.'

She said this with evident satisfaction. He nodded to show he understood, but he did not. He had no idea who don Michele was.

'Could I see him when he has finished with don Michele?' he asked.

'Of course,' she said.

He then went round and kissed all the other relatives: his mother, his grandmother, several aunts, and his aunt Angela, his father's sister whom, if he were to admit it, he liked a lot. Beppe, her youngest, was with her, looking solemn, and her elder boy, Sandro, looking truculent. The latter extended a hand and allowed his cheek to be kissed. He was clearly there under protest, though his bad temper seemed assuaged for the moment by the presence of Renzo.

Sandro could not make his mind up about Renzo. He was wildly jealous of his cousin, because he was older and he seemed to be able to do whatever he wanted. Moreover, he was the son of heroic don Carlo, and not pathetic don Antonio. But there was a good chance he was stealing the family inheritance, so he hated him as well. By contrast, Beppe felt simpler emotions. He liked his cousin, who now kissed him on his forehead, and whom he rewarded by a warm embrace.

'My grandfather is with the priest,' said Beppe to Renzo, thus explaining who don Michele was.

Renzo looked at Angela, who nodded her head. This was by no means the end, she wished to convey, just the preparation for such. It explained as well why there was such a solemn hush in the house. A maid came in and gave the visitors tiny cups of coffee and proffered sugar. Renzo had his without.

'He is going to confession and receiving Holy Communion,' continued Beppe.

Renzo nodded. He understood. That also explained the silence in the house. This was the hour of the women's triumph. For years, they had prayed for his soul, as perhaps had Beppe, and now his soul was just about to be saved; the great work of years was about to be brought to completion, and they held their collective breath until the priest should emerge from the upstairs bedroom and announce that all had been done as it should have been done: the words of absolution; the anointing with the Holy Oil; the reception of the Body, Blood, Soul and Divinity of Jesus Christ the Saviour. For a moment, Renzo understood; this death, unlike his father's, blown up off Favignana by a rocket propelled grenade, this death was not to be dramatic but peaceful; it was to be traditional, a death where the soul floated off on the breath of prayers, to journey to God. He was not sure he believed, but he could sense there was something beautiful about this. Lucky don Lorenzo.

'Have you been to confession recently?' he asked Beppe.

'Yes. You are not supposed to ask, but yes. I go every two weeks.'

'Your mother has brought you up well,' said Renzo, reflecting as he said this that he was implying his father had not. He noticed the scornful look that Sandro directed at his younger brother. 'I will go before I marry.'

'And how kind of you to ask Sandro to your bachelor party,' Angela said to her nephew. 'I hope he behaves.'

'Mama,' said Sandro, groaning in embarrassment.

'Don't worry, auntie, my friend Gino is organising it, and he will make sure that it is all very decorous,' said Renzo. 'We are thinking of going to the country and spending the weekend doing clay pigeon shooting.'

Sandro, not seeing this as the joke it was, looked at him with incredulity, disappointment and anger. Beppe looked mystified and wondered why he could not go as well.

'Clay pigeon shooting sounds lovely,' said Angela. 'We are all so looking forward to the wedding, and becoming relatives of your friend don Calogero,' she said, smiling at her nephew. 'I saw him the other day and the new baby. But I think they are now in Catania, aren't they, and perhaps going to Donnafugata for the Christmas holidays?'

'Anna Maria and the children will be in Donnafugata, certainly, for Christmas, that is what I understood,' said Renzo, 'It is her favourite place, and the children love it, and as she has just had a baby, but don Calogero will be back and forth. He is always so busy. So many calls on his time.'

'So, if we came to Catania, we might see him?' asked Angela.

'Are you thinking of coming to Catania, auntie?' asked Renzo, with a slight tremor of alarm.

'Well, I have not been for a such a long time,' she said, 'And it is such a lovely place.'

'Yeah, right,' said Sandro sarcastically. 'Where people walking along the pavement are jumped on and have their teeth pulled out.'

'Darling,' said his mother, putting her hand on his arm, motioning him to be quiet, while Renzo sniggered. 'No, I have not been to Catania for ages, and it would be nice for me to visit it again, and also to meet your future mother-in-law, she might expect it.'

'Elena would be thrilled too, I am sure,' said Renzo gallantly.

'But really I am thinking, if I am honest, of him,' she said, indicating Beppe. 'He has never been to Catania and wants to see all the churches, and the Cathedral, and the museum attached to the Cathedral which I believe it very good.'

'It is. Elena took me,' said Renzo. 'Where will you stay?'

'Oh, some hotel. We are always flying off to Rome or Paris or London and we never catch the train to Catania, which is ridiculous.' She heard her son Sandro whisper something obscene under his breath. 'Yes, we will perhaps come before Christmas, which is a nice time to go shopping.'

The door opened, and the priest entered, approaching don Lorenzo's wife. There was sense of interest in the room. He smiled a sad smile as he took the old woman's hands in his own, and whispered some comforting words. The signora smiled, listened, and then, without cutting the priest off, looked towards Renzo. She knew that Renzo had come for a purpose, so best to get it over with right now. Renzo approached. His aunt told him he could go upstairs to see don Lorenzo. He nodded respectfully to the priest and left.

He sensed that he ought not to stay long, and somewhat to his surprise he found his uncle, not in bed, but sitting up in an armchair and fully dressed.

'This is a surprise,' said the old man, indicating by his tone, that it was not, that the visit was in some ways overdue, and in others, not welcome, but perhaps necessary.

Renzo drew up a chair, and placed it near his uncle's. He took his hand and reverently kissed it.

'There are lots of people downstairs?' asked the old man.

'Lots. All waiting for a word, I am sure, but auntie let me come up first, which was nice of her. Perhaps she guessed it was important.'

'And is it?'

'No, uncle, no, it is just that I wanted to see you, that is all, to give you my good wishes and my love in person, and see how you were, so, yes, it is important.'

'I am not quite dead, dear Renzo, but give it time. I have, as you will have realised, seen the priest. I have put everything behind me. I did this to please your aunt, my wife, and to please your mother and other relatives as well. I owed that much to them. I am not insensitive. They put up with so much over the years, not least your father's death, but other deaths too. When I die, I want them to think of me in heaven, not in hell. I want them to have a modicum of peace; they have not had so much to date. I wish I could decree peace, and people would listen to me. But I fear that those who are not peaceful will not listen to me now.'

'Uncle, dear uncle, after you have gone, and when that is, I hope it is not for some time, after you have gone, there will be peace. I promise you. I will create no trouble. I know that Uncle Antonio gave the order and betrayed my father and had him killed; and you did not know, and if you had, you would have stopped it. But Uncle Antonio is now out of the picture and will stay out of the picture. As for his children, they are my cousins, my cousins twice over. I love them. Your grandchildren will never be harmed by me, I swear it.'

He looked at don Lorenzo as he said this and held his hand. Don Lorenzo knew he was lying. He nodded.

'How are the preparations for the wedding?' he asked. 'My wife keeps on mentioning them.' He paused in thought. 'Even if I am not there, you must have a wonderful time.'

It was much later that Angela, his daughter-in-law, came to see him. She brought her two sons. They all three kissed his cheek. His cheek, he realised, was much kissed, by these vultures. However, he liked Angela, and he liked his grandsons very much, though Beppe more than Sandro. He noted the absence of the two girls.

'I have been praying for you, grandpa,' said Beppe.

'That touches me,' said don Lorenzo. 'Thank you very much, dear Beppe.'

He noticed that a look of annoyance crossed Sandro's face.

'Have you been praying too, Sandro?'

'I am an atheist, grandpa,' said Sandro.

'So was I, once,' said the old man. 'But I learned the folly of my ways. Now, grandsons, let me talk to your mother alone.'

When they were alone, he spoke again. 'I notice my only son, your husband, is not here. Well, I did not expect him. He has not forgiven me. But what is past is past. There is no need to go over it, and you too are thinking of the future. Perhaps Renzo will try to kill Antonio for killing his father. Yes, yes, I know, we all know, you as well. Let us stop pretending. It is ironic, is it not, that the very first act of daring my son ever undertakes leads to disaster, between me and him, him and you, and delivers us all into the hands of don Calogero di Rienzi and your nephew Renzo. Ah, we should have stayed united, but it is too late to lament that now. This fatal disunity in the family will cost us all a great deal. Of course, I will not be here to see it, and my brother Domenico will also leave the scene before whatever must happen must happen. Renzo, your nephew, my cousin, is neither kind nor intelligent. I do not trust him. By which I mean, I expect him to be just like Antonio, both cruel and stupid. As for don Calogero, my dear, I think he is cruel and intelligent, and in his intelligence is your best hope. Yes, I know what you are hoping for. He is marrying Renzo to his sister, and he has daughters. He may well think that your sons might make husbands for his two girls. He may well decide that your sons are no threat.'

'They are no threat,' she said.

'Oh, but they are, you know they are, even though they may not realise it. It is a pity Sandro is not more amenable to good advice and common sense. It would make saving his life easier if he were. There was talk of him doing studies in America, wasn't there? Maybe in America he would be safer, less visible, less annoying to Renzo. Sweet little Beppe will at least do as he is told, I am sure. Make sure don Calogero sees him, gets to know him, pays attention to him, by which I mean notices him as a chess piece on the board that he can exploit. That is Beppe's best hope of salvation. He must marry Calogero's daughter. The ages are about right. As for Sandro… There is something else you must do. The Romanian, Trajan Antonescu. You must befriend him. He is the same age as Sandro, maybe a bit younger, only a few years older than Beppe. He has young children. He has a nice wife. He has no other relatives. Win him over. He may not be utterly without feeling.'

'You mean as he is young, as he has children….'

'No,' said don Lorenzo with pity in his voice. 'He does not follow his feelings. At least, I doubt he has done so up to now. At least, not feelings for other people's children. And I doubt he cares a jot for Antonio. But he wants to get on in life. He started with nothing, and he wants to arrive somewhere, because of the children. It's a project, just like our family. We were once little better than bandits, but now we are respectable. That is what he wants too, to be respectable, to be accepted. It is what they all want. Well, it is something you can give him. Beppe is innocent, and that is good. I mean, he won't realise what you are trying to do, and that means he will act naturally. See what happens. Beppe is a nice boy, and he comes from one of the richest and most bourgeois, if I can use that word, families in Palermo. They will like Beppe, because they can use him. And if they can use him, they won't kill him.'

'You think it will work?' she asked, anxiously.

'It is your best chance,' he said. 'Don Calogero and the Romanian may well fight over my grandson, if they consider him a prize, particularly if they both do. Antonio, we cannot help, because he does not want to help himself, and all this is his fault. But Beppe has a good chance. Sandro, I am not so confident about. You need to warn him about the danger he is in.'

'He won't listen,' she said miserably. 'He won't listen. I have tried and tried.'

'Keep on trying,' said the old man. 'Then, if it happens, you can tell yourself that at least you tried. I feel for you. Believe me, I do. We take a lot of risks, we men, but the women are the ones who are left to deal with the consequences. Your brother took risks all the time, but you are the one left mourning him, along with his wife, his mother, and his daughters. Renzo is not in mourning, he is angry; well, perhaps he is in mourning too, but it is the anger I notice. You see, my dear, I have come to the end of my life, more or less, and I know it, as you can see, as I have surrendered to my wife, to the priest don Michele who, incidentally, is a good person. I have surrendered, indeed, not to be over-dramatic, to God Himself, if He exists, which on the whole I think He may. It is worth making that bet, and what have I to lose?' he smiled. 'I feel a little hypocritical, which is not a new feeling to me, I admit. If you remember, your brother, Carlo, he enjoyed everything he did. Well, so did I. I have no regrets, or rather I had no regrets at the time. We did what we did. We did what we had to do, and we enjoyed it. But now, now it is all over for me, or nearly, I see where we have ended up, discussing how to protect a thirteen-year-old boy from being murdered, my grandson, a child who has never harmed anyone. Have we come to this? Is this how it ends? Perhaps not. You see, my dear, I have confidence in you. You have the right spirit. You are strong, you're intelligent, and unlike most, you do not delude yourself. Your children have a strong protector. You're like one of those Roman matrons of old. Not Agrippina, but Julia Domna. In different circumstances, if your husband had not been such a fool, you could have ruled, like Anna Maria Tancredi. But I know you do not want power; you just want them to survive. I wish you success.'

He sighed. The two boys were called back. He told them to obey their mother in all things; Beppe took this very seriously; Sandro looked at him with barely concealed incredulity, which, the old man realised, did not bode well for the future. He kissed them all and dismissed them.

The 8th December that year was providentially a Thursday. This meant that in accord with custom, few would work on the Friday, but make an extra-long weekend of it, which meant in turn that these four December days would be a perfect little winter holiday for many people. Angela Santucci thought this an excellent opportunity to pay her respects to the Spanish Madonna of whom she had heard so much, but never seen. Her son, devout Beppe, would like it. As for Sandro and the girls, she was not sure, and put that aside.

Her first idea was to ring Renzo and ask him about the feast of the Immaculate Conception in Catania, and at the Church of the Holy Souls in particular. Renzo confessed that he would be spending the long weekend in Catania with Elena, but that he had no idea what went on in the Church. He had suggested they go away for that weekend, but Elena was far too busy with wedding preparations, and in particular the dress, to be able to go away. So, he was going to her. He suggested that his aunt ring Elena and ask her what the programme for the feast would be.

Elena was rather thrilled to be called by her intended's Aunt Angela. She had found his mother rather aloof and off-putting, and she knew Angela was liked by Renzo as his beloved father's sister, and that she seemed so friendly over the phone was, she thought, a good sign. Moreover, it seemed the right sort of attention, this idea of the signora of visiting Catania, and paying her respects to the signora di Rienzi, a person about whose social skills Elena was sensitive. Yes, she was going to be there over the feast of the Immaculate Conception, and yes, her brother was going to be there, with the two eldest children, who were at school in Catania, and who wanted to go to the feast, and would then go on to Donnafugata the next day to join Anna Maria and the three younger children. Of course, Renzo would be coming too, and he would be delighted to see her. But Angela was chiefly interested in the fact that don Calogero would be there with the two girls and without his wife. The wife, she knew already, and had known for years. It would be interesting to visit Catania, not under her eye. She told Elena she would be there on the 8th December.

There was no difficulty in persuading Beppe that a trip to Catania would be fun. He liked travel, and he had never been before now. He was particularly desirous of seeing the city and Etna up close, perhaps even going up Etna. She knew she would have a harder time persuading Sandro to come, Sandro who never went to church and proclaimed himself an atheist, Sandro who despised people from Catania and the family of don Calogero in particular. But to her surprise, Sandro said yes, not graciously, but at least he said yes. Of course, what Sandro was thinking of was nothing to do with the things his mother had in mind, it was rather to do with the fact that Catania would be, he was sure, a source of endless free cocaine. He was very interested in cocaine.

It was Elena's idea that on the eve of the Immaculate Conception they should have a family gathering, an idea that her mother accepted with stony faced consent, and her brother, with wry amusement. Angela and her two sons were invited to the top floor flat of the boss to meet Elena and Renzo, Calogero and his two daughters and their grandmother, who, as always, was cooking.

Sandro, quite apart from his love for cocaine, was an intelligent, sharp observer, who was aware that this meeting was significant. He was on his best behaviour and determined to learn something about these strange creatures amongst whom he found himself. And they were strange creatures. The flat itself was immense, an enormous sitting room, a huge dining room, and beyond that a vast kitchen. A trip to the loo established four, or was it five, presumably large bedrooms. There was also a study. Well, he was used to large houses and flats, and he knew that most Italian families lived in around fifty square metres or less, and that Italy was one of the most physically crowded countries in the world. So, space meant wealth; he knew that; he knew too that his own family lived in a huge amount of space. But here, in Catania, the space shouted wealth in a way that he had not encountered before now. These people were rich, and not quite used to being rich. The money was as shiny and new as the hideous marble floors. No doubt this was the work of don Calogero and his first wife, not Anna Maria, whose immense flat in Palermo was muted by comparison.

They all shook hands when they arrived, except for Beppe who, being so young, was kissed by all, and hugged by his cousin Renzo. Everyone beamed at Beppe, including his mother. He remembered the trip to see their grandfather, and how Beppe had made such a sweet impression there. He had rewarded that piece of legacy-seeking sycophancy with a kick in the shins when they got back to the house, and he would remember this behaviour today, this toadying to their enemies, and punish it in due course. He himself received a kiss and an embrace from his cousin Renzo, a most unpleasant experience. He considered Renzo to be a physically repulsive specimen: he did not like the roughness of his cheek against his own; the feel of the buttons on his jacket; the smell of the man, which was of some sort of aftershave leavened by an unmistakeable tang of sweat. He did not like the way Renzo was at all. The reddish-brown hair, the watery blue eyes, far too close together, the way his clothes never seemed to fit him. Why was this Elena marrying him? Why would anyone want to marry him, apart from his money and his name? But she, though perfectly nice, was no beauty. He wondered what the financial arrangements were, who was paying whom, who was getting the most out of this alliance.

The children, the two daughters and his brother, went into another room; the signora was busy in the kitchen, and the four remaining adults sat in the sitting room while Renzo poured the champagne. It was clear to Sandro that Renzo was a man in love, so clear. One could tell from the way he looked at the object of his devotion, the way he poured the wine, the way he solicited approval. Renzo was not looking to Elena, but her brother. He was the centre of that particular universe. Could you marry a woman because you were obsessed with her brother? He supposed you could. The brother knew it, though he could tell that the brother despised Renzo. It was that sort of relationship. One adored the other, the other despised him, enjoying his abnegation. Don Calogero accepted a glass of champagne from Renzo without thanking him, and looked straight at Sandro, as if to advertise the fact that he dominated his cousin, and he knew that Sandro knew it, and that he did not care. As for the man himself, don Calogero, the man who filled and dominated the room, and filled and dominated the thoughts of Renzo too, he was sure, there was no doubt that he was a smart-looking, handsome man, but Sandro found him repulsive in the extreme. He was, he realised, the sort of person who played with others, the sort that was cruel. He didn't care about his cousin and what he suffered, but he did not like Calogero, he decided. He felt he loathed him. And this was the person his mother wanted them to be friends with.

The conversation was the usual boring adult conversation about babies. They were speaking about the child that had just been born, called Romano, Calogero and Anna Maria's latest child. All a great surprise, but born safely and without complications. There was lots of talk about the baby's teeth, his hair colour, the colour of his eyes, which parent he looked like the most, all of which was utterly uninteresting to Sandro. But not to them. Clearly, Renzo and Elena were very interested in babies, and straining at the leash. When they married in February, they would have their first child nine months later, in November, he calculated, as did they, no doubt. His mother spoke with some authority on the question of children, having had four, two of each, and she spoke as someone who looked forward to being a grandmother. The very thought made Sandro feel sick. Calogero leaned forward - they were sitting quite close together - and asked him how many children he wanted to have. He answered that he had not thought about it. As indeed he had not. The very question was creepy.

Calogero smiled beatifically. His mother entered just then to announce that dinner was served. The children were called. They all went into the dining room. Calogero made a point of having Beppe on one side of him, and Sandro on the other. His daughters were opposite.

The two girls had been interested at the prospect of meeting two boys, moreover, two boys that they had heard about, and two boys that they were going to be more or less related to, the cousins of their uncle by marriage. They knew without ever having been told, despite their tender years, that they were expected to find mates in exactly this sort of penumbra of relationship, cousins of cousins, relations by marriage, a vast number of people. Grandfather, whom they had never known, had known the grandfather of these two boys as well. One boy, of course, was grown up – Sandro - and the other not grown up at all - Beppe. Sandro was ugly but, in some ways, attractive, Isabella thought; not yet eleven, she had already started to look at and evaluate the boys around her. But he was grown up and would not notice her. Beppe, by contrast, was sweeter-looking, but not at all attractive. He was not worth looking at, even if he was almost fourteen, as she had ascertained. He had nothing of the adult about him. He was, to use her least loved designation, boyish. Moreover, his conversation was dull: things to do with home, mother, going to church and going to school. Well, they did all that too, but one could see by looking at Sandro that he had left all that behind him, and did more adventurous things. What, she could barely imagine.

'Do you have a girlfriend?' she had asked Beppe, when they had been alone, and she had seen him blush. Of course, she knew the answer. 'Does your brother?'

This follow-up question made Beppe blush even more. He did not know the answer. He knew that Sandro never told him anything of interest and constantly accused him over being nosey and a spy. He knew, or thought he knew, that Sandro was sexually experienced, as were his two sisters. His own complete lack of experience in that department made him feel very uncomfortable in front of Isabella and her sister, and her persistent questioning, and her contemptuous smiles. He was quite glad, at the dinner table, to find himself between don Calogero and don Calogero's mother. He had always preferred the company of adults.

Don Calogero was kindness itself, asking him about school, about the house in Castelvetrano, where they had first met, tactfully making no reference to the attempted shooting of Sandro. He asked if he were looking forward to the wedding, and what he would wear; he himself did not care what he wore, but unfortunately, one had to please one's womenfolk, as he was sure Beppe understood. Besides, people would be looking at them. He looked at his daughters as he said this, to convey to them that this insignificant teenager was an object of curiosity to many, being the child of one of the richest families in Sicily.

As for signora di Rienzi, almost in spite of herself, she was delighted with Beppe. She thought him modest and respectful to his elders, which was important (she looked over the table to Sandro and felt less pleased with him). She was even inclined to like his mother, who seemed a nice and attentive lady, one ready to acknowledge the very special position she held as the mother of don Calogero. She too asked her about the wedding in February and whether she was looking forward to it. She was, of course, going, as the bride's mother, and her friend signora Grassi was going too, and she had a special reason for this as her son Tonino was going and looking forward to seeing Muniddu once more, or so she gathered. Beppe admitted to knowing and liking Muniddu, who had been his father's chauffeur, and to knowing his children, Rosalia and her brother Riccardo, very well. He often went to their house, where they did their homework together. Signora di Rienzi heard this with satisfaction. It was nice to know that the boy socialised with his father's former employees and their families, and did not give himself airs. Her own granddaughters were not beyond reproach when it came to snobbery.

The food, as usual, was magnificent. The signora had no intention of letting anyone from Palermo think they did not eat well in Catania. Indeed, her future son-in-law had always been profuse in his compliments, being clever enough to see that that was the way to win her favour. And the signora Santucci joined in as well, paying compliments too, paying the necessary tribute. The signora understood, she felt where the power lay. Everyone had paid homage to her stuffed sardines.

After the meat dish was cleared away – it had been the most succulent of beef olives – it was time to relax, as it was still relative early, not yet ten. They would do what they often did on the eve of a great day: go and walk around the quarter, see and be seen. The signora generally stayed in to tidy up, but on this occasion, she decided that she would join them. From the dining room window, one could see that the Church was still open and brightly illuminated, and it would be nice to see the crowds outside and be seen, and be seen with signora Santucci too.

And so, down they went. Angela felt the humiliation of how she had come here as a suppliant, for she was sure that don Calogero knew exactly what her aim was and was enjoying seeing her as his potential client, the once powerful Santucci reduced thus to begging for her sons' lives, and implicitly saying that she surrendered her husband's life to his power. Let him kill Antonio, just as Antonio had foolishly killed Carlo. He had to pay for that. But let him only spare the two boys. The two boys, for their part, were seemingly unaware of the danger in which they stood, and the humiliation of their mother. They now all stood outside the brightly lit Church of the Holy Souls in Purgatory, the door of which was wide open and from the steps of which they could see the Spanish Madonna in all her glory. Calogero was explaining the long and costly restoration of the Church, financed by the Confraternity of the Holy Souls. The gilded stone that surrounded the Madonna glowed in the darkness. As he spoke, Calogero had a friendly and protective hand on Beppe's shoulder; Beppe listened to what he said with attention, as did Angela.

Renzo leaned over to his cousin Sandro, and said; 'I will take you over to the bar to meet my friend Gino, and he can perhaps introduce the pair of us to our old friend Charlie. Would you like that?'

Sandro nodded. Renzo spoke to Elena, and spoke to the boss, as well as his aunt, saying that he was taking Sandro away. They disappeared in the direction of the bar. Meanwhile, while Angela was engaged by signora di Rienzi and her daughter, someone new appeared on the church steps. It was Tonino. Isabella looked at him, and Natalia looked at Isabella looking at him. Tonino had been a favourite of Isabella's as recently as a few months ago, but now he had lost her favour, ever since she had heard of the girlfriend, the one called Petra, the sister of his friend Roberto. She no longer felt a burning admiration for him; or rather she did; she just wished she didn't. Surveying Tonino with an air of assumed indifference, she took Beppe's hand for a moment, as if to lay claim to this stranger from Palermo. Tonino did not approach the boss's daughters or their visitor, but waited for the boss to notice him, which he did. He called him over, and introduced Beppe Santucci, knowing that Tonino would immediately know how important this guest was. And he suggested that the children go for a walk around the quarter for the next hour or so, under the care and guardianship of Tonino.

Was it possible to have too much cocaine? This question had never occurred to Sandro, until now, the morning after, when he woke up, or rather swam into bleary eyed consciousness, got out of bed, drank some water, washing down the pills that Gino had given him the night before, which he had been told took away the side effects of alcohol and the drug. He looked at his phone beside his bed, and saw the time, then groaned. After a short interval he did indeed feel a little better, and managed to stand up and head for the bathroom where he got under the shower.

He found his mother and his brother in the hotel dining room, finishing their breakfast. A cup of black coffee helped his head a little more. His mother asked how his evening had gone.

'Nice,' was all he managed to say. Then he added: 'Renzo and Gino, and the other one, the one they call Alfio, are taking me to Taormina.'

His brother raised an eyebrow; his mother looked surprised and pleased.

'That's nice,' she said.

It was anything but nice. He had heard that the views from the motorway between Catania and Taormina were spectacular, but as he gazed out of the back window of the car, he felt constantly on the point of nausea. Last night, when this had been suggested, the idea had been attractive, but after all the drink and all the cocaine in that underground room with Gino and Renzo, and later the one called Alfio, he was not so sure. They eventually turned off the motorway and drove more slowly, which was a relief, but only for a moment, as the car then began to take the hair pin bends up the mountainside to Taormina. On the fourth of these bends, he begged them to stop, staggered out of the car, and vomited. It was the most horrible type of vomit, as he had had nothing to eat all day, a sort of greenish-yellow acidic fluid which stank. He was given some water, and some more pills by Gino, and then they drove on in silence. He began to feel slightly better.

At Taormina they stopped and had coffee and met the person who was to accompany them further into the mountains, to the house that they were thinking of hiring for the stag party. This person was Costantino, the eldest son of don Carmelo, who had arranged to show them the house, which was the point of the trip. He respectfully shook hands with all of them, but greeted Alfio as an old friend. It was arranged that Constantino should take them all up to the villa in his car, and Alfio would follow on later. He would be an hour or two, he explained. Business. There was some ribaldry at this, from Gino and Renzo. Alfio admitted the charge.

'Look, she is just beautiful, OK, and it seemed like an opportunity too good to miss,' he explained. 'And it is quite hard doing these things under the radar. Needless to say…'

'Not a word,' agreed Renzo.

'But what about us?' asked Gino.

'You have got someone new, from what I have heard, and you, don Renzo, are getting married, if you have not forgotten.'

'Hypocrite!' said Gino, when they were in the car, and Alfio was out of earshot. 'He criticises me for what I do, and then he himself goes off like this to see some woman. I would like to tell his wife.'

'But you won't,' said Renzo.

Further and further up they drove, until they came to electronic gates which opened before them, and then a long driveway and finally a parking place. Sandro got out, his legs unsteady. Costantino led them up the staircase to a spectacular terrace. There was a view on two sides: towards Etna, now covered in snow, and on the other side, towards the straits of Messina and the mountains of Calabria on the other side of the straits. The cold air of December made Sandro feel a little more alive. He breathed deeply.

'This is all your fault,' she said bitterly.

'Have you got everything you need?' Alfio asked. 'And as for it being my fault, well, if it were not for me, you might not be alive. Not would he,' he said, indicating the child. 'So, a little gratitude to your cousin might be in order.'

She glared at him.

'The car…?'

'It is in a garage and well hidden. I have not used my bank card, only used the cash you gave me. I have followed your instructions.'

'Good,' said Alfio. 'That way you stay alive.'

'He would not dare kill me. Gino is all words,' she said, without quite believing it. 'Do they realise you are here?' she asked, for once betraying the anxiety she felt.

'No. I had an excuse. And I trust Costantino. He owes me. We have a thing going together. Never mind what it is.'

'Am I staying here forever?' she asked.

'No. In fact that is what I wanted to talk to you about. Gino thinks you have disappeared. So does Renzo and so does the boss. It is best that you do nothing to make them think otherwise. Costantino has fitted you up with a new identity, new card, new social security number, new name. He has done this for you, as a favour to me, and tonight he can send you on your way in a new car, with a new driving license, and you can cross the straits, and never come back. You will be forgotten. That is important. You have had one warning, and they won't give you another. They won't give me another either.'

'They?' she asked. 'Is this really about Gino wanting to get rid of me, or you wanting to get rid of me? And why are you so frightened of them, of Gino, of Calogero?'

'I know what they can do. You don't seem to have grasped that.' He paused. 'You are lucky, you know. You are alive; you have escaped that awful man, and you can start again. You have a second chance. The rest of us....'

'Will I never be able to come back?'

'Why should you want to? What is so wonderful about here?'

'Where should I go?'

'Wherever you want. Wherever you choose. I will make sure you have money, you can get a place, you can get a job. You can have a life.' He looked at her. 'Take it, it is a good offer.'

'You want to get rid of me,' said Catarina again.

He sighed.

'First you accused me of wanting to sleep with you, now you accuse me of not wanting to see you again. It cannot be both!'

'You did sleep with me, remember?' she said.

'I can't forget, can I?' he said. 'But you do not want me, and that is an end to it.'

'You are all talk and no action,' she said bitterly. 'You want me to run away. You are a coward. You don't seem to have the guts or the intelligence to realise that you have to take risks in order to advance. Everyone knows that Tino is the boss's nephew. That is not a catastrophe, it's an opportunity. Gino may be annoyed and may have sent his stupid friend Renzo to tell me to leave, but…'

'Are you sure it was Gino, and Gino alone?' he asked. 'Are you sure it was not the idea of someone else?'

'Are you frightened of him?' she asked.

'If you are not,' he answered, 'You ought to be. He is dangerous. People he does not like do not survive. He killed his own brother. He would kill you and the boy without a moment's hesitation.'

'Are you sure of that?'

'No. It is a guess. But I know him. And another thing. You left the quarter. He asked no questions. If he cared a jot about you, wouldn't he have asked where you were? Wouldn't he have asked if Gino had killed his own nephew? Trust me, he is the one behind it. He is the one behind everything. You may have charmed Gino and you may have charmed me once, but you cannot charm him. No one can. He is heartless. You have to go, you have to hide, you have to start again. Have a life, a simple, ordinary life.'

'Is that what you have got, a simple ordinary life? Why should I put up with something you would never, not even for a moment, consider? Listen to me. Gino wanted me gone. Perhaps he even planned to kill me and the child. He cannot be allowed to get away with this. Get rid of Gino. When you do, I will come back and show the world I am not frightened of that man, my child's uncle. If I come back, he would not dare touch me. You think he is so very strong and brave, well, perhaps he is, with people like you. That is because you fear him. But I do not. But people like his mother, his sisters, Anna the Romanian, and me, before us he quails.'

'I hope you are right.'

'It is a risk I am willing to take.'

The villa itself was, as they had been told, luxurious. The main living room, which overlooked the terrace, was a riot of black, pink and red marble. On the terrace itself, was a hot tub, which attracted attention. Gino had never seen such a thing before now. Next to it, there was a wooden door, behind which was a sauna. The place was the property of a Russian who never used it, and don Carmelo's people had the management of it. They looked over the place and examined the bedrooms, then started to discuss the price of having it for the weekend. They asked if they might try the sauna and the hot tub. Costantino switched both on. He spoke of the price of hire, the price for caterers, what they wanted to eat and drink, and any extras they might have in mind. Costantino explained about the extras. Renzo looked at Gino and then at Sandro. It was true he was getting married the next weekend after this party, but... Gino cautioned that the boss was coming, and Traiano, and perhaps they would not approve, especially as Renzo was marrying the boss's sister. And Traiano was such a spoilsport and killjoy, always faithful to his wife. At this talk of extras, Sandro wished he did not feel so bloody sick. The very thought of girls made him want to vomit.

He gradually drifted away to the other side of the terrace to breath in some more fresh air. Then he was called back by the others as it was time for some more cocaine. He felt he could not refuse. They all, apart from Costantino, snorted some more of the drug off the smooth, shiny wooden surround of the hot tub. Then the two of them, Gino and Renzo, went into the sauna, which was now hot. They said it would do them good. Sandro declined, thinking the air outside would be better.

Suddenly he found himself alone with Costantino, enveloped in silence, and he did feel better.

'Not used to it?' asked Costantino with a smile of sympathy.

'Not really,' said Sandro. 'You know....'

He had heard them talking about Costantino last night, and felt curious about him. He was, he knew, one of the disinherited, because he was illegitimate. The eldest son of don Carmelo, he was still a second-class son, only half-Sicilian, son of a Serbian mother. The other children lived in luxury, but Costantino had to work.

'Are you married?' asked Sandro.

'Yes, two children. My wife and I live in Messina, the children are teenagers, fifteen and sixteen. A boy and a girl. What about you, have you got anyone?'

'No. I mean, it would be nice, but no. Do you know my father? Did you know my uncle, don Carlo?'

'I have heard of both,' said Costantino.

The persons that Beppe felt most comfortable with were the people who treated him as if he were a normal, ordinary boy. Chief of these was the old gardener at Castelvetrano who had told him so much about the cultivation of the soil and lemon trees in particular. The old man treated him in the same way he treated everyone else, without favouritism; he sometimes was annoyed with him, sometimes he shouted at him, and even swore; when he saw him after an absence, he made no great fuss about it, but was plainly glad to see him. But here in Catania, it was clear that he was on display, the son of don Antonio, the dreadful drunk of

Castelvetrano, whom Beppe loved, but for whom he felt great sadness and shame. He was old enough to understand what had happened. His father had been flung out of the family business, sidelined, sacked by a combination of his own father, don Lorenzo and his own uncle, don Domenico, supplanted by his nephew Renzo and don Calogero, not even a relative, but soon to be connected by marriage, which was the next best thing. There had been a family coup, and as the child of the fallen boss, what would his role be? His mother, he knew, was fighting his corner. So, he co-operated with her, with this trip to Catania, a place he had always wanted to visit. And he had put up with having to walk around the quarter with Isabella and her sister, while she took his hand, knowing that this parade was meant to mean something. Of course, his mother had plans, and because he was young and he always did what she said, she felt that she was able to make plans because he would in the end co-operate with the plans she made. But he couldn't make Isabella fall in love with him. He supposed he could fall in love with her, if it was deemed necessary. But he had the distinct impression that Isabella did not find him attractive at all; her attention had been fixed, one could see, on Tonino.

They went to Mass, and after Mass, don Calogero and his daughters prepared to leave for Donnafugata, where the three boys would be waiting for them, along with the mother of the two youngest children. They all said goodbye to each other politely inside the church. Then they stayed to light candles in front of the Spanish Madonna and then stepped out onto the square. There was a man holding a baby, whom he recognised as don Traiano, and who was soon joined by a very beautiful woman and two young children, a girl and a boy. He approached don Traiano, as he did know him, and proffered his hand, and was pleased that don Traiano remembered him. He was introduced to the wife and the three children, and he introduced his mother. Don Traiano was all charm. He heard with interest that Sandro was off in Taormina with Renzo, Alfio and Gino, but the sort of interest that conveyed he was pleased to be here with them and not in Taormina. His interests, he implied, were domestic. He made polite conversation with Beppe's mother, and then looked at his wife expectantly. She read his mind, this beautiful young woman; there was a sort of telepathy between them. Ceccina expressed her desire that they join them for lunch. Signora Santucci said she would be delighted. They had a table booked at the trattoria, but there was always room for more. And so, they moved off.

Lunch was interesting. The trattoria had the best antipasto that Beppe had ever seen, the most wonderful aubergines and glorious artichokes. The two ladies spoke of children, for Ceccina had the baby on a high chair on one side of her, and her daughter, Maria Vittoria, seated on the other side of her. This was a very fertile subject for both women, and the two males were at the other end of the table with little Cristoforo between them, who gazed first at one, and then the other, with looks of mute adoration.

'How is your father?' asked Traiano.

The two women called each other 'signora' and used the polite form of address. Their phrases were elaborate, polite, and floated over them.

'He is not good,' said Beppe. 'He is sad, depressed, drunk, alone. I go to see him, but the others don't want to; they do not even speak to him. He does not do anything, and my grandfather is dying, we think, but he does not even want to go and see him. But he is coming to the wedding. Renzo's wedding.'

'What a shame,' said Traiano, with sympathy. 'That day I saw him, I knew then that… well, it wasn't good. It is a shame for him, but a shame for you too.'

'Is your father living here?' asked Beppe.

He was momentarily taken aback by the question. There were three reasons for this. First, no one ever asked him questions, especially not questions of a personal nature. They took orders from him, but they never asked him things like this. Second, no one, no one at all ever referred to his dead father, or to the fact that he was not from 'here' but there, even directly. But Beppe clearly did not know this. Beppe had unknowingly pierced his armour.

'My father was never here, he stayed there, in Romania, in Iasi,' he said. 'I never knew him much. I left there to come here before I was two. Besides, he is now dead. He was in prison and he was killed.'

'Are Romanian prisons bad?'

'All prisons are bad,' said Traiano. 'I imagine Romanian ones are terrible. Though the ones here are pretty bad too. You hear stories.'

'But you are a Catholic?'

On this too, he was sensitive. He remembered that once someone had asked if he were a Muslim or a gypsy.

'Of course,' he answered. 'There are Catholics in Romania. There are in the city I was born in, anyway. My mother was very keen for me to be brought up a good Catholic. And I am for my children as well. With this little one, we read the Bible every night together. Well, I read and he looks at the pictures and asks me questions. And then we say prayers, you know, the rosary.'

'Well, if that is what you do, your mother made a success of bringing you up a good Catholic,' said Beppe. 'My father says he is an atheist and so do my sisters and my brother. I think they say it to upset my mother. I am not sure they really mean it. When your father died, were you sad?'

'Very,' he answered.

'Were you my age?'

Traiano realised what he was asking about: how he would feel when, if, but really when, his father was killed.

'I was a bit older. Maria Vittoria had been born, so I was sixteen, I think, maybe seventeen.' He saw Beppe's puzzled look. 'I am nineteen now. Ceccina and I fell in love when we were very young. We had Cristoforo when we were both fifteen. But I lie about my age and pretend I am in my twenties, and no one questions it. But really, I am the same age as your brother. But when I was your age, I didn't have anyone to control my wayward side. It was nice I met Ceccina; goodness knows what would have happened if I had not.' He smiled. 'Do you have a wayward side?'

'Not as far as I am aware, but I am only thirteen.'

'Don Calogero was like a father to me, and still is. Perhaps he will be the same to you. I know he likes you a lot. He has an affectionate nature.'

'Well, it is nice he likes me. But,' he looked at his mother, deep in conversation with Ceccina, 'the real question is whether his daughters like me.'

'You think that far ahead?' said Traiano. 'You should think whether you like them. Isabella will be a handful in a few years' time. Whether they like you or not is not important. The thing is, it is your money they are after. That is what it boils down to. Love, not so much.'

'That is what I thought,' said Beppe. 'Money.'

Alfio arrived and appeared on the terrace, to find Costantino there, studying the view. They hardly knew each other, but they had become business partners, without quite wanting to. They greeted each other warily, almost curtly. The expression on Alfio's face asked where the others were. He explained: the boy, by which he meant Sandro, was feeling so unwell he had gone to lie down; the other two were in the sauna, trying it out.

'Thanks, by the way,' said Alfio.

Costantino nodded. He knew what he was being thanked for: for hiding the woman. He asked no questions.

'She will cross the straits tonight,' added Alfio. 'Then you can stop worrying.'

'I wasn't worrying,' said Costantino. 'Were you?'

'It is a difficult situation,' said Alfio.

He realised Costantino assumed that Catarina, about whom he had asked no questions, was that forbidden thing, another man's wife. Well, she was. But not quite in the way Costantino imagined. But he was content to leave it at that.

'How are you?' he now asked.

The Serb shrugged. How was he? Did it matter? Did anyone care? Did he himself care about how he felt? He felt nothing except a generalised resentment at life itself, which had been with him for almost his entire forty years of existence. But Alfio knew the story; he would have taken the trouble to find out. Costantino had been conceived in Sicily, but his mother had gone home to Niš to have him, finding that don Carmelo, then a teenager, was not keen on fatherhood. She had married someone else, but always received money from Messina. At the age of sixteen he had grown out of Niš, and come to find his father, who had employed him. But he wasn't the equal of the other legitimate children, some years his junior, or even, he sometimes felt, of the much younger illegitimate children whom he had never met.

Alfio had been there when they had discussed the Africa project; he had noticed the coldness with which don Carmelo treated the Serb, his slighting references to his mother.

'You need to come and see the private army, we must arrange it,' said Alfio, referring to the men who had been working on the Furnaces project.

'Are they any good?'

'Damn good. Better than our own people. Over a hundred, and we can recruit more from their friends and relatives. Disciplined too. One of them misbehaved the other day, was caught stealing. They dealt with him. The one in charge, Omar, he is excellent. Takes no nonsense. As long as the money is good.'

'Oh, the money will be excellent,' said Costantino.

'My wife wants to go back to Africa desperately,' remarked Alfio. 'What does yours say?'

'Oh, she is staying here, with the children,' said Costantino.

Alfio nodded. He knew, because don Carmelo had mentioned it, that Costantino had a girlfriend in Africa.

'Has she….?' asked Alfio, referring to the girlfriend.

'We have twins,' said Costantino proudly.

The lunch in the trattoria dragged on late, but no one seemed to want to bring it to a close. Angela Santucci knew that to make the first move, to signify it was time to go, might give the impression that they were not enjoying themselves, which would be the last thing she wanted. Besides, she was enjoying herself. She liked Ceccina, and after two hours they had started to use each other's names and adopt the informal mode of address, which she thought very cosy. This Ceccina was a very nice girl, she thought, and a clever one, given her age, for it was apparent that they thought alike on many topics. For a start, Ceccina, being a woman, was less enamoured of the boss that one might expect. They discussed Calogero at length, the superficialities at first. His clothes; his shoes; his shirts; his ties; the way his hair was cut; the way he looked perhaps older than his years, being still under thirty. The way when he came into a room, everyone paid attention; the way when he stood in the square, they all looked at him and only at him; the way he carried himself with such confidence. She for her part, confessed Ceccina, she understood what people felt, but she did not entirely share it herself. It was something that she stood outside of, which she saw from a distance. As for her husband, he lived and breathed the boss in a way she could barely understand. Some men, agreed Angela, were charismatic, her brother Carlo being the prime example, which aroused jealousy. But Carlo had been the object of much attention too: they had loved him, they had revered him, they had feared losing his favour. This last, Ceccina understood. Everything they had ultimately came from Calogero's favour. In the end, one had to live with this fact, that devoted as your husband was to yourself and the children, at the same time, part of him belonged to the boss.

'You are going to the wedding? And the bachelor party?' Beppe was asking. 'My brother Sandro has been invited, and they are checking the place out right now. I can't go; I am too young.'

'I wish I had that excuse,' said Traiano, 'But I have to go, and Renzo would be offended if I didn't. But the truth is….' He paused, for her rarely told the truth, and wondered if he should tell it now. 'The truth is that I find the whole thing very boring. They drink a lot, and I drink very little. They take drugs, and I do not. They talk about women in a way that I do not. So, you are lucky to be so young. There is food, which is nice, but the conversation is boring.'

Beppe nodded.

'I thought they were going clay pigeon shooting.'

Traiano laughed.

'I am married and I like staying at home. But every now and then I have to make the effort to go out, and so does the boss. He doesn't touch drugs, or the other sort of thing.'

'My brother….. that is why my father tried to shoot him,' said Beppe, glancing towards his mother, to make sure she could not overhear. 'But I would like to see Etna up close. I have never been.'

'I will take you, tomorrow,' said Traiano. 'With your mother's permission.'

When Sandro got back from Taormina, he went to the hotel and was somewhat put out not to find his mother and brother there. But he was tired and went to his room and slept. He woke up when it was getting dark, and went to look for them, but wherever they were, they had not returned. He texted his mother, but there was no reply. After some aimless television watching, he rang her, to discover that she had turned off her phone. He had Beppe's number but never rang him. It was eight in the evening by the time they returned. He pretended not to notice that they had been gone so long, or that he had missed them. And when he found out that Beppe had been invited to go up the mountain the next day and he had not, his displeasure was deepened.

On the day after the feast, four of them, Renzo and Elena, Alfio and Giuseppina, all drove to Donnafugata to have lunch with the boss, his wife and his children. This was a family party, a noisy one too with five children present, who were delighted to be with both parents, all together, and have two aunts and two uncles in attendance as well.

Lunch was magnificent, and when it was over, when everyone was somnolent, the three men went into the garden to walk it off and have some fresh air.

'How was your trip yesterday?' asked Calogero.

They both had a look of embarrassment about them.

'It is a great place, boss,' said Alfio as easily as he could. 'We saw it. Lovely views. Great terrace. There was a sauna and a hot tub. We had a few drinks.'

Calogero nodded.

'Anything else beyond a few drinks?' he asked.

There was silence.

'You disappoint me,' he said. 'Pills? Cocaine? Did that boy take some too?'

The silence was now deadly.

'Do you want to kill that boy? Is that it?' asked Calogero, looking at Renzo.

'Yes, of course I do. You know I do. His father killed my father.'

The words were desperate but defiant.

'Let me tell you both something,' said Calogero. 'Our position is a good one, but it is fragile. Very fragile. We have internal problems and we have external threats. Don Antonio murdered don Carlo and that means that there is an unresolved issue. At present it is patched up. But one day it will have to be faced. For the moment we will make do with the sticking plaster in place. Antonio stays in Castelvetrano, he does not interfere –'

'But he will!' interrupted Renzo.

'Shut up. It is a risk, but the risks involved in killing his sons, then killing him, are greater. I am worried more about the external threat. I do not trust don Carmelo at all. He is old, he is fat, he is domesticated, he looks harmless, but that is the idea he wants us to have of him. He does not like us. But, and this is the important thing, though I suspect that don Carmelo is the enemy, he is not the entire story. There is someone behind him, and until we know who, we wait. We carry on with this hotel deal, but we are cautious. We wait for him to show his hand. He has people of his own working for us, perhaps; our people who he has turned, though we cannot be sure about this. But to cut down the bad branch without being able to pull up the bad root, that would be futile, and it would also tell our ultimate enemies that we know what they are up to. Are you working on this Costantino?'

'I am, boss. I am gaining his trust, I think. As for our ultimate enemies, do you mean the Romanians, boss?' asked Alfio.

'That is possible. When we dealt with them last time, my idea was that they would always be back for more. It could be the Romanians. But it could be someone else. We have to be patient until they show themselves, then we strike.'

'I don't like that Serb, the one they call Costantino,' said Renzo.

'He is a nobody. He drives the car and he arranges girls and he sells cocaine,' said Alfio. 'He is scum from the Balkans, and his mother was some woman don Carmelo picked up when he was still a teenager, and just as quickly got rid of. He owes don Carmelo everything. He came to Sicily when he was sixteen or so and has worked for him ever since.'

'He owes him everything,' said Calogero. 'But is he grateful?'

They were standing among the lemon trees as they said this.

'His mother was some whore, and we all know how grateful they are,' said Alfio with a smirk.

Calogero gave him a look that drew him up sharp.

'It was hearing things like that that might have made Costantino ungrateful,' he remarked.

'Stop sulking,' said Angela Santucci to her eldest.

'I am not sulking,' he said, knowing that he was, and that in the end he could not lie to her. Sandro looked around him. Beyond the restaurant window he could see the crowds walking up and down the via Etnea. Catania was nicer than he had assumed, but he was sick of looking at churches. 'I am not sulking,' he repeated. 'Or maybe I am. I am just mystified. By you. By my own mother. By what the hell we are doing here. By what my father is doing, but what my grandfather and great-uncle may be doing, by what the world is doing. And how I fit into it.'

'Things are difficult right now,' she said.

'Are they? Well, I am eighteen, so tell me how and why they are difficult, and what I can do to help. Or at least tell me, so I know what the situation is and can act accordingly. The truth is, I want to go to America. I am sick of this island, this family, this… way of life.'

'This way of life can cross the Atlantic, you know,' she said sadly. Your uncle Carlo….'

'Has been dead for ages. I was fond of him. You were fond of him, but he is dead. Renzo was fond of him too.'

'And Renzo is the problem,' she said. 'That is why we are here. Looking for friends.'

'Are these the sort of friends you want?' he asked with disbelief.

'It is not the friends we want; it is the friends we need. Renzo is not stable. But don Calogero is sensible, the young Romanian is sensible, and they will rein him in.'

'Haven't we got enough money?' asked the boy petulantly. 'Are you worried they are going to steal it all? Is that it? Is that what you are worried about? And you let Beppe, who you think is such a little saint, go up the mountain with the Romanian bastard? God knows what bad habits he will teach him.'

She looked at her son with sadness and distaste.

'Beppe has more moral sense in his little finger than you do in your whole body. He can look after himself. The one who is susceptible to bad influence is not Beppe. Besides, you don't understand.'

'Then make me understand,' said Sandro.

She was silent for some time.

'I am not sure you are capable of understanding,' she said. 'Your father is no longer active in the world of business. Your grandfather will not live much longer, sadly, and Uncle Domenico is also old and retired. When your grandfather and great-uncle are gone, your father will have no one to protect him, and many people hold grudges. My brother Carlo was murdered by the order of your father, and your cousin Renzo knows this, has not forgotten this, and will never forget this.'

He was silent for some time, considering this.

'But Renzo likes me,' he said. 'And I am not interested in what they do, their work, their drug dealing, their other things. I just want to be left alone by them. And I am no threat to Renzo.'

'I know all that. But is it enough?' she asked.

He was lost in silence.

'If I were to speak to him…?'

'And show him you were afraid?' she asked. 'That would be a disaster. No. In every dispute, look for allies. Don Calogero, Traiano, the others you saw yesterday, Gino and Alfio.'

'How did this happen?' he asked. 'How did we get into this terrible mess? Why are things this way?'

'Blame your great-grandfather and his brother, blame the founders of the line,' she said. 'That is where it all began. Long before you were born.'

He was on the point of saying that he would change his name and go away, or go to America, or something like that, but he stopped himself. These ideas were pointless, childish. One had to stand and fight. But he was not sure he wanted to do that.

'And you sent Beppe up a mountain with that Romanian? If he comes back saying he fell off the cable car or something, will you blame yourself?'

'Of course. But I observed them yesterday, and I got the impression that Traiano liked him.'

'Liked him? Liked him enough not to kill him, you mean?' said Sandro. 'These people like no one. They are not capable of it.'

The ride along the motorway on the back of the motorbike, holding on to Traiano, with his eyes shut most of the time, had been exhilarating, they were going so fast. Then they had turned off up towards the mountain and the Speranza refuge where they had left the bike and the helmets in the carpark and bought tickets for the cable car. It was a bright day, but there were few tourists, it being December, and they were blessed with clear views. At the end of the cable car, for what seemed like a huge amount of cash, they were driven up to the accessible summit by a four-wheel drive bus, along the black cindery track, through the lava desert, in which a few pathetic plants struggled. Alongside the track were streams of water, melted snow, making its way down to the sea far below. Finally, they arrived at the crater, not the topmost one, but the furthest that could be visited. They walked up the cone, and there beyond them was the final summit, smoking and steaming. The ground beneath their feet was warm. Because of the altitude, they were wearing gloves and scarves and woolly hats, each of them barely recognisable. Traiano was used to being recognised, and was glad of the anonymity, and thought that the others who had come up with them in the vehicle would have dismissed them as a pair of teenage brothers, not that they looked alike, though the woolly hats gave that impression to someone not looking carefully.

Beppe was taking photographs with his phone, and took one of Traiano. Then he took one of himself with Traiano, both of them staring at the screen, close up. This pleased him. Traiano pointed out the various landmarks of this part of Sicily: Catania, spread below them, Acireale too, and on the other side Caltanisetta, and Caltagirone, and far, far away out to sea, the tiny island of Malta. It reminded him of that bit in the Bible, about all the earth and its kingdoms being offered by the devil. He had been made the offer, not that he remembered it, and had accepted it. Now all this was his, he was rich, respected and feared, and his children would never be poor, and yet there was a price to pay, and he felt sad at the thought of it. He had no friends. Somewhere far to the north, Pasqualina was enjoying a new life with Corrado. He had hoped that he and Corrado would be friends, but he had not heard from him at all since his return from Verona. He reflected on this and felt desolate.

'You're cold,' said Beppe. 'The wind is making your eyes water.'

He nodded.

Beppe put his arms around him.

Later, at the bottom of the cable car, there was a shop, where Beppe looked at souvenirs of Etna he could buy his mother, and a bar where they settled down to drink some hot chocolate. It was an ordinary place, a strange place for a theophany, reflected Traiano, a strange place to realise that life had changed, and changed terribly, perhaps for the better, but certainly changed in a way that could not be undone. On the mountain, he had shivered uncontrollably and wept; the physical symptoms had passed, and Beppe had taken them to be a reaction to the extreme cold on the mountain top, and the sight of the snow and the barren black lava. But he was glad Beppe did not know that what had happened up there was something else entirely, a realisation that he had come thus far and he did not want to go further, he wanted to turn back. Turning back would be arduous; climbing down would be harder, paradoxically, than climbing up; but the top of the mountain was so grim, so cold, so desolate, that he knew he had no choice.

What had happened up there? What indeed? It was something completely negative. It was the realisation that while he would usually do anything for Calogero, there was this one thing he could not do. He was not sure why he could not do it. He just knew it was impossible. He knew that if Calogero asked him to do so, he could not kill Beppe. He had killed Rosario. He had killed Turiddu, he had given the order for Beata and Paolo to be killed. But while those murders had been easy, thoughtless, this murder was impossible. And because of that, everything was changed.

'We have got Christmas to look forward to, and then we have the wedding in February, and then it is my birthday – I will be fourteen – and then it is my Confirmation after Easter. My mother has the idea that I should take the name Lorenzo after my grandfather, or Domenico after my great-uncle, and that I should ask Renzo to be my sponsor. She thinks he would be pleased, that he expects it. I don't know where she gets the idea from. What was your confirmation name, and who was your sponsor?'

'I was never confirmed,' said Traiano.

'Aren't you a believer?'

'I am a strong believer. But when I was fourteen, when I should have been confirmed, events had already overtaken me. I had met Ceccina and, well, we were sleeping together and having a child, and there was a lot of anger from her family, and from don Giorgio, our priest, and they wanted us to separate, but I refused and she refused; and then we wanted to get married and they said we were too young, but eventually they gave in. But with all that, I was never confirmed. They said I could be later, but, well, I have never been to Holy Communion since I was married, and….'

'I was going to ask you to be my sponsor,' said Beppe. 'But you have to be confirmed. Looks like I am left with Renzo.'

'Has your mother talked to you about Renzo?' he asked.

'No. Why should she?'

'I suppose she does not want to worry you. But listen to me. If there came a time when… there may come a time when you are in danger.'

'From Renzo?' he asked.

'Maybe. You have one of those phones. Give your number to Ceccina, as she has one as well, and give me your number so I can memorise it. And if there were a time for you to protect yourself from harm, I would warn you, and you would be able to run and hide. Do you understand?'

'What about my father and my brother?' asked Beppe, after a pause. 'And my mother and sisters?'

'No one would harm your mother and sisters. As for your father, he knows what is coming when your grandfather and great-uncle die. Sandro is older than you, but you are a sitting target. You run, and you hide!'

'Run where? Hide where?'

'You go to Ceccina and you hide with her and the children. It is the best place. No one would think of looking there. No one would dare look there.'

'Why hasn't my father told me this?'

'Because he is drunk, and stupid and selfish,' said Traiano. 'Your mother has tried what she is trying, appealing to don Calogero, but…. I know don Calogero.'

'I thought he liked me.'

'Oh, he does. But he is not sentimental. He likes me too. But as I say, he is not sentimental. For him, it is business.'

'But not for you?' asked Beppe. 'Are you sentimental?'

'I love my wife, I love my children; everything I have done, I have done for them. And there is nothing I would not do. Or so I thought.'

'But for him it is business? And what is business?'

'Making money and gaining power. Gaining power to make money; making money to gain power.'

'Two things my father tried to do and failed to do. It is a bit shameful to fail at that sort of thing,' said Beppe. 'I know he killed my uncle. From something Sandro said that day, that day when he tried to shoot him, that day we first met. I suppose you are saying that I should trust no one, certainly not my cousin Renzo.'

'I am saying,' said Traiano, 'that you can trust me. You can trust me absolutely.'

'I am very pleased I can trust you,' said Beppe. He extended his hands, and put them over Traiano's, which were holding the cup of hot chocolate. 'Are you still cold?'

'Less so, less so,' he said.

Chapter Nine

The excess of Christmas was followed by the sloth of January, and on the last weekend of the month, the bachelor party was to take place at the villa above Taormina. There was not going to be a female equivalent at a hotel in Taormina. This was a male thing, and a male thing alone. The women accepted that. Gino, Alfio, Calogero, Traiano, Renzo and his cousin Sandro, were all going to be alone. When first mooted, it had seemed like a good idea, but now most of the participants were not so sure.

The boss and his family had been in Donnafugata for the Christmas holidays, but now, thanks to exigencies of schools, had come back to Catania, at least during the week. This was good news for Gino, as it meant that Henrietta was in Catania too, and given that his flat was now conveniently wife and child-free, they could meet. The little English girl was still as delighted as ever with her huge Sicilian swain; she loved being in his arms and she loved his tender kisses. And if the flat felt empty without Catarina and Tino in it, they neither of them noticed or cared. After all, Henrietta had never known either of them, and had heard of their departure with the thought that it was remarkably convenient. She had also heard that Catarina, so briefly married to her husband, had never been particularly nice to him. She herself felt an overwhelming desire to be nice to him, so she was grateful for the wife's absence, and the child's too. They would not be coming back she had been assured.

In the intimacy of the bedroom, he had told her what had happened. That he had been cursed with mumps as a teenager; that Catarina had become pregnant by another man, now deceased, and had decided to marry him for his money and the child's sake; that she had lied. This had made him sad, and he had, he said, dismissed her. It was so painful, he had done it through an intermediary, his friend don Renzo, who had told her to go, and paid her off. Catarina and her child were now a closed book, a concluded episode.

He explained this to her, and as he was so happy, so contented, so pleased to have found someone so lovable who loved him in return, he almost believed it. Renzo had sent her away, no one would see her again, or the child. He had not asked for details. Occasionally he wondered what had really happened to her. She had deceived him, insulted him; she had chosen to deceive him, it had been her choice. She had no one to blame but herself. But these thoughts were rare. The presence of Henrietta banished them and replaced them with feelings of the greatest softness and delight.

January, the cold month, the month of sharp wind, was such a nice time to spend as much time in bed as possible. The trip to Taormina was happening at a weekend when Henrietta would be in Donnafugata, so he would not miss any time with her. And the trip to Taormina was necessary, as it cemented his alliance with don Renzo.

It was very clear that there was to be no expense spared. This was the first thing that struck Calogero. Not only was the villa that had been hired for the party a place of unimaginable, even vulgar, luxury, with pink marble and black marble and crystal chandeliers, and deep leather sofas; there was a sauna, there was one of those funny things called a jacuzzi, and there was a fine wide terrace which overlooked Mount Etna, Taormina and the sea. It was accessible by a long winding driveway, with a gate and a lodge at the bottom, ideal for security, perfect for privacy. It was to be a small and exclusive party: himself, his brother-in-law to be, don Renzo, don Traiano, don Gino, don Alfio, and Sandro. This last invitation had raised a few eyebrows, as the cousin was not one of them, but Calogero had insisted, and when that was clear, there was no further comment. All the other arrangements had been left to the groom, don Renzo. There were to be six cases of champagne, one each, six bottles of whiskey, six crates of beer. What other entertainment was arranged, the boss had not been told, but he resolved to grin and bear it, whatever it was. He was not going to Taormina to enjoy himself; he hated the place; his honeymoon with Stefania had been spent there. No, he was going because he had to; he had to spend time with his most trusted associates. But he did not like them; he did not like anyone much these days, he thought.

Sandro, for his part, knew that being invited to this mountain top for two days of carousing was, somehow, political not social. They wanted to look at him. He was, after all, his despised father's son, and though he had no ambitions to follow in the family business, being content to live off the money others had won by hard work, while doing no such hard work himself, he knew that if they were watching him, then he too needed to watch them. When the cake was divided it was important to show that one knew what one was entitled to, and that one was not willing to be robbed blind. He was in a den of thieves, greedy unscrupulous thieves; and more than that, he was in the midst of murderers, for each one had surely risen to the top, and outdone his father (for whom he felt no sympathy at all) thanks to a fearsome reputation, and how else was such a reputation acquired? He wondered how many they had killed between them.

His own life was surely not in danger, or so he reasoned. Why should it be? But like most teenagers, and he was eighteen years old, he thought himself immortal. But at the same time, one had to be careful, one had to be cautious. He drove himself to Taormina in his own car, and at the gate to the villa he met the two on guard duty. Costantino he had seen before, the last time he was there, and Muniddu he recognised as the man who had driven him to school as a little boy and had acted as his father's driver on occasion. It cost nothing, so he was effusive with Muniddu, and kissed both his cheeks. He asked about his wife, his children (he remembered them vaguely) and he heard about the new baby on the way, and was warm with congratulations. All the while he was aware of Costantino studying him. Finally, as he prepared to drive up the hill, Muniddu asked him if he would leave his mobile phone with them, and pick it up when he left. He was surprised by this, as he was never parted from his phone, but consented.

'None of us carry phones,' Costantino explained, taking the phone and putting it in sealable plastic bag. 'They allow people to know where we are, which we do not like.'

And they allow people to record things, reflected Sandro, and to take photographs. Don Alfio and don Traiano, he was told, were still on their way, but don Renzo and don Gino had already arrived. As for the boss, he had arrived in good time, and had come from Palermo, or was it Donnafugata, where his family were spending the weekend with the new baby. He replied he had seen the new baby only the other day. To his surprise, the two men seemed quite interested in the new baby. Perhaps in thirty years' time they would be taking orders from young Romano di Rienzi, if they lived that long. Perhaps it was because Muniddu himself was going to be a father again, as might Costantino.

The staff at the villa had been given orders to be silent and invisible and only to leave the kitchens when called for. As a result, there was no one to meet him at the door, and he walked in, carrying his case. He heard the sound of distant voices and followed them out to an open terrace with astonishing view of Mount Etna. The whole place was built in tasteful shades of black volcanic stone. In the middle of the terrace was a sunken jacuzzi in whose foaming waters sat two men, one of whom he recognised as his cousin Renzo, the other as don Gino. Between the two men, on the edge of the jacuzzi was a bottle of champagne and some glasses; there were several empty bottles littering the place too, along with white towels and dressing gowns.

His cousin was loud in his welcome, which he had never been before now, but he was clearly drunk and high on cocaine. He stood up in the jacuzzi and held out his arms, and subjected Sandro to a wet embrace. Gino half stood and offered a hand.

'Do you want some champagne? Go upstairs, grab a room, come back in your bathing suit and get in. Do you need any cocaine?' asked Renzo.

'I am fine for now,' said Sandro. For once in his life, he realised the cocaine could wait. He went upstairs and found a bedroom, and changed into his bathing costume. When he got down, and got into the jacuzzi, he took a glass of champagne from the opened bottle. It was, he noticed, a very expensive bottle. That was what these people did, he realised: they were drinking it as if it were Seven Up; but the only reason they drank it was because it was expensive.

'We have got some girls coming tonight,' said Renzo turning to his cousin. 'You ready for that?'

'I don't know why you got more than one,' said Gino. 'I mean there are six of us, but the boss won't touch one, and neither will Traiano. I myself have given that sort of thing up, thanks to Henrietta, and I do not know about Alfio, but he has not been married long now. It will be OK for our young friend here, but what about you? You cleared it with the boss? You know he can be funny about those sorts of things.'

'It is my party, not his. I can do what I like. If there is one girl left over, so what? A good girl never goes to waste. Have you had a threesome, cousin?' he asked.

'Not yet,' said Sandro, thinking this a clever answer.

'How many women have you slept with?' asked Renzo.

'Don't, he is young, he is shy,' said Gino. 'He may have not got through his first dozen. And you how many have you had, eh?'

'About two hundred, I reckon,' said Renzo. 'What about you?'

'More than that,' said Gino. 'Much more. I am older than you. A thousand or so, I reckon. I have lost count.' He winked at Sandro. 'Your cousin is a beginner.'

'Where are these girls coming from?' asked Sandro.

'Who cares? One girl is just like another. Tall, blonde, from the Balkans,' said Gino. 'They are coming from where they all come from. Some factory produces them. You ring up and you place your order.'

'There's a man we know, he supplies them. The guy down at the gate, Costantino, you met him, who works for our friend don Carmelo. They work in the hotels in Taormina. Nice respectable girls. You would not think for a moment they are prostitutes, but they are,' said Renzo. 'They could be librarians. You will see. They can talk about anything you like. What subject are you doing at university?'

'Literature,' said Sandro.

'You will discuss Tolstoy, you'll see.'

'Tolstoy, my ass,' said Gino. 'He will do what he prefers doing.' He made a gesture. 'That is what we all like doing: drink, cocaine, pills, more drink, and girls, girls, girls. That is the life we have. Nice, eh?'

'That and making babies,' said Renzo. 'But that we do at home. A month after the wedding, and Elena will be pregnant. You watch. The boss has had a new son.'

'I met him,' said Sandro.

'And Muniddu's wife is pregnant,' continued Renzo. 'That is why he is so happy. And don Traiano's wife will be one of these days, as they have had a baby every year since they married, I think. What is it, four or five?'

'Four,' said Gino. 'I think. Or is it three? I should remember. Don Traiano is my brother-in-law now.'

'No, he's not.'

'Yes, he is. His wife's sister is married to my brother.'

'That is not how it works. You are his sister-in-law's brother-in-law. You are not his children's uncle, but your brother is their uncle by marriage.'

Gino looked puzzled by this.

'Look,' explained Renzo. 'Sandro and I are cousins, but I am not cousins with his cousins.'

236

'You probably are, though,' said Sandro, 'Because you are my cousin twice over, as my parents were second cousins. Am I right?'

'Oh, damn it!' said Renzo. 'Let is open another bottle. This argument is too complicated.'

Two people now entered. They were Alfio and Traiano. After the initial greeting, they went upstairs as well to choose rooms, and came back in their bathing costumes. They got into the water and accepted some champagne, poured for them by Renzo. The atmosphere changed, though nothing was said. Alfio had come with Traiano, not with his former great friend Gino.

'We have girls tonight,' said Renzo. 'Are you interested?'

'We have wives,' said Traiano. 'It is a nice thought, but, as for me, I can manage without. You can have mine, or he can,' he said, smiling at Sandro. 'But don't let me be a dampener on your pleasures. It is your party, after all. Your farewell to being a bachelor, your last chance before Elena gets her man.'

'When's the boss coming downstairs?' asked Gino.

'Soon, soon, I believe,' said Renzo. 'He said he wanted to have a little rest. Romano keeps him up at night.'

Conversation, so spirited before the arrival of the newcomers, now stalled. He could see that his cousin Renzo was thinking of the cocaine, and how he could safely leave the jacuzzi and go and have some without making it too obvious. Given that it was his party, given that he loved cocaine and everyone knew it, or so Sandro assumed, he was surprised that Renzo did not simply get up and leave for the purpose of snorting some of the drug. But he understood why. It was the presence of don Traiano. He was in awe of him. He was frightened of him. Don Traiano had the air of a man who was absolutely confident in himself, and this self-confidence filled the jacuzzi. One could see that Alfio saw it; and one could see that Gino acknowledged it. Traiano had arrived, and all deferred to him. The Romanian now turned his attention to Sandro, and Sandro felt something shrivel within him. In the hot pounding water of the jacuzzi, he felt his bowels grow cold.

But Traiano was only asking after his family, his father (whom he surely hated), his mother, his sisters, and his brother Beppe. His manner was friendly and pleasant, and yet it seemed to

Sandro that this was the man with whom he might easily have to bargain for his life; in what circumstances, he was not sure, but the idea of being at his mercy was all too imaginable. Yet don Traiano was speaking very pleasantly about Beppe, and how nice he was.

'He wanted to come,' said Sandro. 'He was disappointed.'

'It might have been a little bit too grown up for him. It's nice that he is young for his age, and innocent. I am very fond of him, and so is don Calogero.'

'He wanted to see you, too, I am sure,' said Sandro, marvelling at how easily this hypocrisy came to him. 'But he will do that at the wedding, won't he, in a week's time?'

'Yes, the wedding,' said Traiano.

The groom, meanwhile, was thinking of the vast amount of cocaine in his bedroom, and how it would have to wait. He must not be seen to be so dependent on the drug with Traiano watching him. But there was a more prosaic problem. He had drunk a huge amount already, and he needed to visit the bathroom, as polite people said. But if he made his excuses and left, he was sure people would think it was for something else. Indeed, as he stood up, he could feel their eyes expectantly upon him.

'I need to piss,' he explained.

He got out of the jacuzzi. Compared to the hot churning water, the air was very cold indeed. It was January, and they were up a mountain, after all. He ran to the edge of the terrace, feeling the biting cold, and began to undo his bathing trunks. Then, with uncharacteristic modestly, thinking he could be seen from there, he moved to the further edge, at right angles to where he had been standing. Here there was a low balustrade, and beyond it, not the terraces of the garden, but a sheer drop down to a ravine, which was clad in various small bushes and dwarf trees. He aimed at the foliage, and with considerable pleasure and relief, emptied his bladder. He then turned and rushed back to the hot water. When he returned, Gino, and then Alfio, followed him, pissing into the void.

'What about you?' asked Traiano.

Sandro shook his head.

'I have not drunk as much as them,' he replied.

'Sensible,' said Traiano.

Then the boss arrived, refreshed from his sleep, and the atmosphere was transformed again. At once all attention was on him. He greeted each one effusively, and there were kisses all round; he remarked on the cold. They told him the water was very hot indeed, but he declined to join them. He helped himself to some champagne, and asked what time they were eating. He had noticed that the caterers were in the villa. Dinner, he was informed, was at seven. It was now a little after six. After a little champagne and conversation, he retired, and taking their cue from him, one by one they left the jacuzzi to go upstairs and get ready for dinner.

Sandro was in the shower when there was a soft knock at his bedroom door, and a moment later, his cousin's head poking round the bathroom door.

'Hurry up,' he was told.

A moment or so later, he stepped into the bedroom clad in his white towelling robe, to find Renzo there with Gino, both wearing the same thing, and both bent over the shiny polished table, dividing up the cocaine. Each snorted a line.

'Oh God,' said Renzo. 'I thought it would never happen.'

The boss, don Calogero, was sitting on his bed, taking off his shoes. As each expensive and elegant shoe hit the ground with a clunk, he wiggled his toes, feeling the freedom from leather, and admiring, he could not help it, his expensive socks. There was a tap at the door, so soft, that he hardly heard it. Then the door opened, and someone came in, shutting the door gently behind him. It was Alfio, who stood by the wall, and waited.

'Brother-in-law,' he said, with gentle irony. 'I was not expecting you. The others, where are they?'

'Don Traiano is on the phone to his wife, and don Renzo and Gino are with the cousin in his room.'

'You're observant,' said Calogero. 'You listen at doors too. You must be wanting to say something important to me. Go on.'

Alfio hesitated.

'Ah,' said the boss.

'I want to do you a favour, boss,' said Alfio.

'Ah,' said the boss again. 'Usually, it is people who ask me for favours, not the other way around. You seem a little nervous, my friend Alfio. You calculate that what you are going to say brings risk with it. But you have gone too far now. You had better speak.'

'My cousin,' began Alfio. 'Caterina.'

'What about her?' said don Calogero coldly.

'Boss, she has done nothing wrong. She slept with your brother and had his child, but that was before she married Gino. Then she got the news that Gino wanted her gone, and don Renzo came to tell her. Well, she did what you might expect her to do. She asked me for advice. I told her what to do. Everyone thinks she has gone, never to return, but ...'

Don Calogero looked at him with cold dislike.

'Why are you telling me this? What is it to do with me? If Gino wants to get rid of his wife, what is that to me? And if he asks don Renzo to tell her to go away, well, why should that concern me?' he paused. 'Do you know where your cousin is now? Has your cousin been speaking to you?'

'She is in Reggio, lying low. I have not spoken to her just recently. I told her that it were best she never came back, but…'

'This is her quarrel with her husband,' said Calogero, 'Nothing to do with me. What do you mean by 'but'…?'

'I understand, boss, that this is not your quarrel. It is between Gino and her; and the truth is, it is between Gino and me, as well, as she is my cousin and she asked for my protection.'

'Are you saying this is Gino's fault?' asked Calogero.

Alfio hesitated.

'To be perfectly honest, boss, I feel ungrateful. Gino and I have been friends since Bicocca, since we were both teenagers. Everyone has always assumed we were very close, like brothers. I was the one who brought Gino to the quarter. I helped him get on; he protected me when we were in Bicocca. But…'

'Ah, but, there is always a but,' said Calogero. 'Tell me about this particular but, this but of yours.'

'Before I went to Bicocca, before I met Gino, Catarina and I were more than cousins, we were friends. But when I returned from Bicocca, she showed that she preferred him to me. Well, they were not suited. But she felt she had to marry him, and now he wants to get rid of her. She is my cousin, boss.'

'Have you other reasons to hate your best friend?' asked the boss. 'Apart from this jealousy? I mean, it must have been very frustrating for Gino to be locked up in Bicocca, with you for company. Did he make you suffer?'

Alfio was silent.

'If I said yes, boss, would you let me kill him?' he asked at last.

The boss was silent, and then made a gesture with his hand, as is brushing this away.

'Did your friend Gino give the order to kill Catarina?'

'No.' Alfio paused. 'He just told her to go away, and that if she came back, he would kill her and the child. I think. She wants to come back. She can't do that while Gino is here. And someone will need to speak to don Renzo as well to remind him that she is not to be touched. She or the child.'

The boss heard this without comment. His face was impassive.

'Why does she want to come back?' he asked at length.

'For the child's sake,' said Alfio. 'I tried to persuade her, but she would not listen to me. She thinks the child needs to have his inheritance, as a child of our quarter. He cannot be brought up somewhere like Milan, somewhere foreign to his heritage. It was impossible to argue with her. And it was clear to me that it went further than that.'

'Was she offering you an inducement if you made her return possible?' asked Calogero coldly.

'No, boss. She has made it plain to me on many occasions that she does not like me that way. She does not want to come back for me, but for the child, and she wants to come back, boss, for you.'

Calogero looked at Alfio, without giving anything away. Calogero made a waving motion with his hand. He needed to think, to consider.

'Now go away,' he commanded, 'before anyone knows you are here.'

Alfio slipped out of the room.

For a few moments, he sat on his bed without moving, while he tried to arrange things in his head. He had told Renzo, that day in Palermo, when they had spoken on the pavement, next to the stream of heavy traffic. He had made himself clear; he had said that Catarina was to be removed from the picture. Yet here she was again, obdurately unfrightened. Renzo had failed. Renzo must know he had failed, but had kept quiet about it, and thought his failure would not be noticed. Well, that was not so very bad: it was another reason to keep Renzo in his place.

But what chiefly struck him was the sheer daring of the woman. Having escaped once, she was determined to come back, to brazen it out, to defy him, to confront him, to show him she was not frightened of him. He was, he realised, impressed by her bravery, which was a rare sensation. Such a woman could be useful. He marvelled at his own inconsistency. He had wanted her gone because she had annoyed him and she had reminded him of his brother. Now, he was not so sure. As for Gino, perhaps he could be dispensed with; and it might be a warning to Renzo to be careful in future.

There was another thing. He had not thought that Alfio his brother-in-law, or rather the brother-in-law of his deceased wife, would have shown such an adventurous spirit. Well, it was not entirely Alfio, it was Caterina behind him, he was sure. To please her, he was sacrificing his supposed best friend. That was flattering for her, a testament to her strength of will. And this was the woman who was coming back for him! Less reassuring was the thought that he would be forever in the brother-in-law's debt. Alfio was presumably ambitious, even if not as daring as Catarina. Well, he would send Alfio to Africa. Catarina, he would keep. She was the more deadly of the pair.

He looked at his watch. It would soon be time to go down. But then there was another soft tap at the door. This time it was Traiano.

'Not with the others?' he asked.

'They are in Sandro's room, enjoying their cocaine,' said Traiano.

'All four of them?'

'I think so.'

'The idiots. Well, the boy Sandro can do what he likes, it is no concern of mine. In fact, I am glad to hear that he prefers cocaine to having other ambitions, such as working for me or for his cousin. But the other three. Renzo, we know about. How many times have I beaten the hell out of him?'

'Lots, boss.'

'Remind me when we get back to Catania to beat the hell out of Gino and Alfio as well. Gino takes a lot of stuff, doesn't he? The idiot....'

'How is Romano, boss?'

'The most asked about child in the history of Sicily, not that he knows it yet. Doing well, and so is his mother. We will all be back in Palermo next weekend for the wedding, and then perhaps she will come over to Catania for a few weeks with Romano, and then after that we shall go to Donnafugata for Easter. So much moving around. In truth I did not want to come to this party, but one could not afford offending Renzo. One spends so much of one's time pleasing other people.'

'I am surprised you are not going back to Palermo after this, given that the wedding....'

'We have to be in Catania for the girls to go to school. I prefer Catania. When I am in Palermo, I feel like a guest. Catania is home. My mother is there.... Yes, I know, since when did I care about her? But she has the great virtue of being familiar. Catania is where I am from. I am a boy from the slums; that is where I started and that is what I miss. I know, I know.... But you are the same. These spoilt upper class rich kids... Renzo. My God. My poor sister. Oh well, she is ambitious. Some women are, but she will pay the price for her ambition, won't she? By the way, how is Gino?'

Traiano had not been expecting this question.

'He's fine. His wife left him, as you may have heard, or he left her. Or he sent her away. But that is not our business.'

'He revolts me,' said Calogero. 'How curious that I should have Alfio for a brother-in-law and you should be lumbered with Gino. Yes, he and the wife are separated, presumably forever. Well, that is not our business, as you rightly say. But you know that nice English girl I have employed? Henrietta? My elder daughter, Isabella, said something to me the other day. She has somehow or another found out about Henrietta and Gino... I am a little bit shocked that a girl of eleven knows about these things. And I would have assumed Henrietta had more taste.'

'Boss, people sleep together, you know. The women are always talking, but I try not to listen. He has been talking too. And Ceccina is always on the phone to Pasqualina, and even she had heard about it.'

'Well, I am not pleased,' said Calogero. 'Now, let us go and see the others.'

Dinner was magnificent. Great attention had been paid to the wines. There were six bottles (one each, Sandro realised) of white wine from the Veneto, and six bottles of Barolo from Piedmont; and there were six half bottles of a dessert wine from Pantelleria. He had not believed that anyone could drink so much, for there had been at least a dozen bottles of champagne consumed that afternoon. But none of them seemed to turn a hair or seem the worse for drink, apart from his cousin Renzo. He noticed that the boss drank in moderation, and don Traiano hardly at all.

The food, by contrast to the drink, was rather pedestrian, he thought, the sort of stuff that people who had never left Sicily no doubt loved. He himself had travelled, and not just to the continent, but to France, to England and to America. So had Renzo, but he seemed to be happy to eat what these trolls from Catania liked eating. They started with spaghetti alle vongole, which was perfectly nice. Then there was a lamb, again nice, but nothing special, accompanied by the inevitable potatoes roasted with rosemary; the pudding, washed down by the truly splendid dessert wine, was a mille-feuille pastry with confectioner's custard. He thought to himself that these people knew little about food, and when it came to drink, they simply chose the most expensive thing on the wine list.

He listened to the conversation with close attention. Don Traiano had been to Verona, and spent time there with Gino's brother. He had never been to Italy in his life before now, at least not on holiday (there had been some business trips). Verona was beautiful, so clean, so tidy, so nice. They had eaten lots of nice things. They had stayed in a very comfortable hotel, and it had been bliss not to have all the children, just the eldest one with them. The result was that they would probably have another child before long, given the length of time they had spent uninterrupted in bed. These men were obsessed with sex, which did not surprise him, but they were even more obsessed with having children. The boss had just had another one, little Romano; Traiano was planning on having one soon, yet another one; Renzo swore his wife would be pregnant at the first opportunity. It turned out that the man at the gate, Costantino, had two children with his wife in Messina, and twins with his girlfriend in Africa, who were about two or three years old; and Muniddu himself was expecting a third. Someone, it was Gino, asked him how many children he wanted to have, a question that was posed with the utmost seriousness, and which he had heard before. It had, he said, never crossed his mind. He was eighteen. He did not think in those terms. As far as he knew, men of his age took endless precautions to avoid fatherhood, rather than the opposite, as was the case here.

'You will change your mind and soon,' said don Calogero. 'Your father had four, and your uncle don Carlo had many more than four. I mean he had his legitimate children, and then the other ones who were off the books, if you see what I mean.'

'On the books, you mean,' said Renzo. 'We pay for them. They are all on the books. One day I shall track them down and meet them all, the little bastards.'

Traiano considered this. None of them here were illegitimate. His own eldest son, Cristoforo, had been legitimised by his parents' subsequent marriage, he was glad to say. He felt sorry for the illegitimate.

'They say that don Carmelo in Messina has thirteen children,' said Alfio suddenly. 'By his wife and two or three other women. Three separate families. The official one in Messina, and two others. The wife does not mind.'

'And Costantino, who he had with a Serbian woman when he was a teenager,' said Gino. 'Don't forget him.'

'The wife may not mind, but the children will mind,' said Traiano. 'As they grow up. But thirteen children is a good number. I want at least ten. But all by the same wife.' He stopped himself. This was not discreet. The boss was a widower who had remarried a much older woman, who was surely now beyond having any more children. As for Alfio and Gino, neither of them would ever father a child. 'I want lots of children,' he continued. 'To inherit, to inherit the earth. And they will all be doctors and lawyers. Do you know don Carmelo's children?' he asked, turning to Sandro.

Sandro strained to remember.

'There is one studying in America, who is years older than me. I was a child at the time, but they came to our house in Palermo. And don Carmelo came perhaps to Castelvetrano years ago, and I seem to remember being surprised, because they were not the same children. But I did not ask questions. I think he is a shareholder in the Grand Hotel, isn't he?'

'We all are,' said don Calogero smoothly. 'I am glad you do not ask questions. It is a good habit to have. Is your father a great friend of don Carmelo?'

'No, don Calogero, he is not. I can say that with certainty. He is not really a friend of anyone. He is anti-social. He likes his own solitude.'

Renzo laughed. For a tiny moment, Sandro felt a stab of sympathy for his hated father. But then he joined in the laughter.

'Have you met any of don Carlo's children?' Traiano now asked, turning towards Renzo.

'I don't know the guy's name, but it was not Santucci,' said Renzo. 'I think his name was Ginori. Years ago, I was in the car with my father coming back from I can't remember where, and we had to stop at a motor mechanic's place, somewhere the other side of Montelepre. I was about fourteen. The guy who owned the place said hello to my father and looked through the window, as if he were curious about me. He must have been about thirty or so. Then later, my father said: 'Did you know who that was?' and I said I did not, but the implication was that he was my father's love child. I am not sure which one he is on the books, and the books are complicated, and I have never seen him again. He looked in the car window, and he had the look of my father, and he was cleaning his hands with a piece of lint. I have also heard that one of the chefs in that restaurant near the palace of the Normans might be one. But they all seem to be normal guys doing normal jobs, grateful for the cheques they receive every month, or their mothers receive.'

At two in the morning, the house was quiet. At least Sandro assumed it was two in the morning. He used his phone as his watch, and he had surrendered his phone to the men on the gate. He could not get to sleep. The girl next to him, on the other side of the wide bed, was no doubt grateful for the light duties she had had to perform, but her presence, the sound of her breathing, made it impossible for him to sleep. He quietly got out of bed, put on the heavy dressing gown the place provided, and silently left the room. Light glowed under the bedroom doors still; from one room he could hear sounds of what he assumed was vigorous copulation; and from another sounds of conversation, between, he assumed, Traiano and don Calogero. He made his way downstairs, thinking perhaps he would go into the sitting room and fall asleep on one of the sofas. But in the sitting room he paused. Looking through the plate glass of the doors that led out onto the terrace, he saw someone engaged in the act of flinging empty bottles off the terrace, in the direction of the leaf covered gully. Not very environmental, he thought. The figure was large, and he recognised Gino. He went out to him.

'What are you doing?' he asked.

'Tidying up, getting rid of the empties,' said Gino.

'It is freezing,' said Sandro.

'I am tough,' said Gino. 'I am getting back in the water, get yourself a drink, join me. I don't feel the cold.'

Gino, having established which bottles were not empty, and having placed them within easy reach of the pool's edge, submerged himself in the water. His huge hairy and naked form disappeared into the surging waters, which were now steaming. In the distance one could, even in this darkness, see the snow on Mount Etna. Sandro took off the dressing gown, shivered, removed his underpants, and then got into the hot water.

'You look like your cousin,' said Gino, in a not unfriendly manner.

'Am I as ugly as that?' asked Sandro. 'Shame.'

Gino laughed.

'How was your girl?'

'Like a librarian, as was promised. We talked about books. She is now sleeping it off. How was yours?'

'I didn't have one. Perhaps that is why I can't get to sleep.'

'Can't you take a sleeping pill?' asked Sandro.

'You can, more than one, but after a time they stop working. Here I am, wide awake, after taking the lot. I lost count. Do you want some coke?'

'Yes,' said Sandro.

He liked coke, he really did. They got out of the pool, into the freezing night air. Sandro began to shake, but Gino seemed not to feel the cold. They ran into the sitting room, where there was a table, and where Gino had left his dressing gown. He extracted the coke, and began to form lines. They snorted three lines each.

'We can't let the boss see us doing this, but he knows,' said Gino. 'What a farce!'

They returned to the water.

Sandro began to feel that he liked Gino.

'Do you get on with your brother, the little one, the one they were talking about?' he asked.

'No. He is a pain. I hate him. Everything he says annoys me. It is like he has this gift, this negative gift, of saying the one thing calculated to drive me mad. He is even too stupid to learn to avoid me. Whenever I see him, and no one is looking, I kick him. But even then, he does not keep away. He loves my father.'

'And you don't?'

'He is a drunken idiot,' said Sandro.

'I knew you did not like your father,' said Gino. 'I worked it out. You see, you were invited here because it would upset your father. His son and heir hanging out with the Catania scum. He won't like that.'

'Fuck him,' said Sandro.

Gino chuckled.

'Fathers and brothers are difficult,' said Gino, with feeling. 'They won't accept you for the way you are. My father did not like me when I was young, and he likes me even less now. They did not like me moving to Catania, they did not like me marrying my wife, and now my wife is no longer with me, they probably do not like that either. They are poor, and they refuse to accept anything from me, as if they enjoy embarrassing me. But they idolise my brother. He did well at school, I did not. I was the tough one, and I sure kicked him as much as I could, I mean he was never a weak boy, but he was a pain in the neck, a right little martyr. Everyone thought he was so sweet, so handsome and so good, but I could tell that he was in fact a hypocrite. He still is. He came to Catania, he decided to marry don Traiano's sister-in-law, and it was hard to tell who he loved more, her or him. You see, he hates me, but loves don Traiano. He has never invited me up to Verona. Don Traiano is good enough for him, but I am not. So, my advice is simple. Save yourself a lot of trouble and don't just kick your little brother, kill him. You won't have any trouble after that.'

'You are right. I wouldn't. He would be dead.'

'I don't mean trouble with him, obviously. Trouble with anyone else either.'

'Do you regret not killing your brother?' asked Sandro, with a touch of irony.

'Oh, very clever. As if I would ever harm anyone,' said Gino.

'My father tried to kill me. He shot at me. He was drunk. He missed.'

'You see, I would not miss,' said Gino. 'There are good boys and there are bad boys in the world. People like the good boys. But the bad boys know how to shoot properly.'

'With the exception of my father,' said Sandro.

'They are the worst,' said Gino. 'Bad men who are no good at being bad, who are not bad enough.'

He took a swig from one of the bottles, emptying it, without seeming to care what it contained. Then he stood up, his body glistening in the cold night air, and threw the bottle into the darkness. There was silence, no sound whatever of smashing glass. The bottle, a heavy champagne bottle, had entered the void.

'It seems a pity to waste anything,' he said, reaching for another of the bottles, not looking at what it was, but seeing by its weight that it was half full at least. 'Tell me when you want to do some more coke. Or more drink?'

'He is just an innocent boy, don't try and corrupt him,' said a voice from the darkness.

It was Traiano, who laughed softly as he said this.

'I wondered who was out here, who were the other insomniacs.'

'Why aren't you asleep?' asked Sandro.

'I have spent years up all night. After a time, it becomes a habit. Hey, Gino, cheer up,' he said, noticing the look that Gino was giving him. 'Anyway, everyone else is asleep, except you two. I am surprised. You were having fun with the girl, were you?'

Sandro nodded.

Traiano pulled off his shirt, kicked off his shoes, and undid his thick leather belt. After a moment's hesitation, he stripped entirely and got into the water. Gino still looked almost angry. Traiano extended a hand and pulled him by the earlobe. Gino scowled.

'You see,' said Traiano to Sandro, 'He is jealous. I know how he feels, as I have small children. He thinks just because I love others, I do not love him; but the truth is that I love others and I love him too.'

'I don't see why you had to go to Verona to see Corrado,' said Gino bitterly.

'Ah, that is what it is. I went to Verona so my wife could see her sister. And to see your brother, naturally. And yes, I like him, I like him a lot. So do you. He is your brother.'

'I hate him.'

'So, the rest of us have to hate him too? He speaks very warmly of you, by the way.'

'You discussed me?'

'Of course. Why not? He is your brother, and I am your best friend after Alfio and Renzo and the boss. I was once higher up, but I have been demoted, but do I complain? How long have you known me for?'

'Since I left Bicocca. I was about fourteen or fifteen and you were seven or eight. I think. It is over ten years.'

'You and Alfio were both friends of my mother, if I can put it like that,' said Traiano.

'Boss, don't bring that up. We were not to know…. Alfio was, I wasn't, if the truth be told. How is the signora?'

'Very well, enjoying her life. I bring it up to show that I do not hold grudges or get silly ideas. Besides, we are related. Your brother is married to my wife's sister. So…'

Gino relented.

'Sorry, boss, you know how I feel about these things. In the old days we were happier. Well, I was happier. My wife …. She was Alfio's cousin, and Alfio takes her part. Not that he says so. It's just a feeling. And Alfio is jealous because don Renzo prefers me to him. The sooner I move to Palermo permanently, the better. I need to get away.'

'We all need to get away,' said Traiano sadly, with sympathy. 'Is that what you want to do, move to Palermo?'

'Renzo has suggested it.'

'We need someone sensible in Palermo.'

The next day the house was silent as a tomb until ten thirty, when a taxi arrived to take the girls away; then at eleven, the caterers returned and laid out coffee and pastries in the dining room, where one by one the men came down and feasted themselves, moaned and complained of headaches. Sandro felt like death itself. His head pounded. He had not brought any painkillers with him. His stomach, now empty, felt delicate. He drank as much coffee as he could in the hope that, when the time came, he would be able to drive back to Palermo without killing himself. After that, he went to lie down again.

Only the boss and Traiano seemed to be unaffected by last night's drinking, presumably because neither of them had ingested anything other than drink. Gino and Alfio and Renzo himself looked seedy. But despite this, Renzo was determined to make the most of the day and night to come. The idea, as far as he was concerned, was to get as drunk and as drugged as possible and leave the next morning. After all, when he was married, these sorts of exploits would be a thing of the past. But the boss had other ideas: he announced that he would leave after lunch, though the others should most definitely stay. But he had work to do in Catania, he needed to see his mother and his sisters, and then he would see them all at the wedding.

Renzo was happy with this; after all, the presence of the boss was a huge honour, and it was great he had come at all; the fact that he was leaving early meant, though he did not express this openly, that the atmosphere would lighten considerably, and they would not have to hide the cocaine.

'Maybe I…' began Traiano.

'No,' said the boss. 'You stay. I do not want to drag you away or break up the party.'

So, he stayed.

His last words to Alfio, on leaving, were as follows.

'We need to get together with that Costantino and talk about Africa. It could be big, for you, for all of us. And that other thing. Go ahead.'

He shook his hand warmly and then left.

Chapter Ten

He had thought he would go straight to Donnafugata to join his wife and his children, but instead he drove to Catania, and found himself making for his mother's flat. Luckily his sister was not there: Elena was away having yet another fitting for her wedding dress.

'I thought you were away until tomorrow at least,' said signora di Rienzi, without betraying for a moment that she was glad to see him. 'That was what they said. That you would be coming back on Sunday afternoon at the earliest. You did not enjoy yourself in Taormina?'

'I got bored. I made an excuse and came back early. I said I had to see my mother,' said Calogero.

'And they believed you? They did not point out that you hardly ever bother to see me?'

He kissed her cold cheek. She surveyed him. She read his mind. He was unhappy. And he knew she read his mind, which made him feel unhappier still.

'Two wives,' said his mother in gentle remonstrance, 'And five children. The first wife I did not like, because you were too young to marry her; the second wife, well you were older, but she is almost my age; the children, the little boys seem fine for now, but those girls will cause trouble. They are spoilt. They have too much. Your father never spoiled you or your brother or your sisters. You are not half the man your father was.'

He looked at her in mild surprise. It was the first time she had ever, since his death, mentioned his late brother. Nor had she much mentioned his father, since the late Chemist had blown himself up.

'You are right,' he said. 'My father did not spoil me. He was tight with money, and he spent most of his time when he was here, which was not so often, whipping me with his belt, while you pretended not to notice. Not that I blame you or him. It did me no harm, it made me tough. But if he had lived a bit longer, I might have learned more from him, learned how to do things better....'

'You fell in with that bad woman,' said his mother.

'Stefania?'

'No. Anna the Romanian. She corrupted you. And her son, that young man, I do not like him.'

'That Anna corrupted me is a new angle on things. Listen, mother, it is the way it is. I had to make my way in the world, from an early age, and I made my way in the world. Do you understand that? And there was a price to be paid for that, by other people mainly, but also by myself.'

'I don't understand it,' said the signora. 'I don't understand why you cannot simply enjoy what you already have. Why are you always wanting more?'

He laughed.

'There is competition. There is always competition. To stay still is to go backwards. One has to go forward. Sometimes it is hard, but we have no choice. We cannot afford to stay still. We have to be alert, on the lookout, at all times. Vigilance is everything. Listen, tomorrow, I will take you to Mass, and then you can cook me lunch.'

This appealed to her. He kissed her cheek and left her. A few minutes' walk took him to the square outside the Church of the Holy Souls in Purgatory. Passers-by stopped to shake his hand and wish him good evening. It was already getting dark. Small children came up to him to wish him well, and to receive the usual tip. To one small boy he passed a ten euro note and gave him instructions to find Tonino Grassi and tell him he was wanted. He would be in the bar.

In the bar, he had a glass of Marsala, and stood in the middle of the room, to be regarded respectfully by all the patrons. Once more, everyone came and shook his hand, congratulating him on the birth of his latest son. There were two policemen who came over and chatted amiably for some time. Eventually, Tonino appeared. He made him wait, and then, after a suitable interval made a slight gesture that indicated that he might approach.

'What kept you? What were you doing?'

'I was at home, boss, asleep. Sorry to keep you waiting.'

He nodded to show that this apology was accepted.

'Take your scooter and go to the Furnaces and come back here with the one they call Omar. Bring him to my house. I will be there an hour from now. OK?'

'Yes, boss.'

Two hours later he was at home alone when the bell rang. He pressed the buzzer and heard the lift. He went into the study to wait. Presently Omar appeared, with Tonino.

He regarded Omar with interest. He was tall, strong, and had a determined look about himself. This was their first meeting, but he knew that Omar knew who he was. Omar was impressed, a little excited to be summoned, and perhaps perturbed as well. He was perhaps wondering what this was about, while sure it was momentous.

'Fetch the whisky, and some glasses,' ordered the boss.

Tonino went to the drinks cabinet and took out the whisky. He poured some for the boss, and then some for Omar, and then some for himself, seeing the boss's approval. Another gesture commanded Omar to sit. He held his glass carefully.

'How many men are in your camp on my land in the Furnaces?' he asked.

'One hundred and twenty-three, sir.'

'And women?'

'Seventeen, sir.'

'I see. It is like a military camp. Well, you have been paid well, and you have done well, but your part in the operation is now over.'

Omar was impassive.

'I gather you had a little trouble?'

'Twice, sir. Both cases men caught stealing. We dealt with them.'

'So I heard, and of course I do not interfere, as that is not my business but yours. But I like men to be disciplined, so I am glad you know how to deal with disorder. The thing is, Omar, one operation is ending, but another is beginning. And I want to explain to you what that is.'

Omar leaned forward to listen.

While the African was eager to take in all the details of the new plan, Tonino held his whisky glass, sipped from time to time, and was impassive. But he took in all the details, storing them up, knowing that in being allowed to hear this, he was particularly favoured. After a time, the boss had explained all: the people in Rome and Milan, the hotel in East Africa, the roles to be played by Costantino and Alfio, the money to be invested, the role to be played by the private army he envisaged. And above all, the huge amount of money that was to be made and the future projects that would ensue, should this one go well.

At length, Omar was told he could go, and that he would have further meetings, with Alfio and Costantino the Serb.

Tonino showed Omar to the door, and then returned to the study to ask the boss if there was anything else he could do. The boss looked at him.

'Go down to the bar. See if any of the boys are there, and invite them up. Order a few pizzas, and we can watch a film or two. I don't feel like sleeping, and as my wife and children are not here…'

He did not feel like sleeping, but to Tonino, this whim seemed natural enough. Most of them spent the night awake and the day asleep. So, when the boss said he wanted to stay awake, he did not attribute this to some secret worry. The thought did not occur to him. What did occur to him was the privilege of spending time with the boss, something that was rarely conceded. He rushed over to the bar, and before gathering the boys, he made straight to the telephone, and called Roberto. He found him at home, just about to go out. He was peremptory in his instructions. Whatever Roberto was doing, he should drop it, and come to the boss's house via the pizzeria. This was an opportunity not to be missed. Roberto hesitated, but only for a moment.

Within an hour Roberto was there, with the pizzas, whose arrival was greeted with delight. It was clear that this was to be something of drunken party. A dozen men of varying ages were there; Tonino was the youngest, though, when you entered the room, where they were all holding their glasses, and where the bottles were laid out, one could sense a hierarchy of power. No one paid him any attention, Roberto was glad to see, so he could study the way the others interacted. There was, at the centre of everything, don Calogero, remote, withdrawn but watchful. All eyes were, if not fixed on him, at least aware of him, of his every need, his every desire, even if no such needs or desires were articulated – but they might be. It was outwardly a relaxed gathering, but there was an underlying tension, they were all there because he wanted them to be there, and because he might want something of them; they were relaxed and at the same time on edge. Not at the centre of everything, but at the same time a centre of something, was Tonino, the youngest, but by no means the least important, and he knew it. Well, he understood Tonino by now, he thought, or he was beginning to; he understood his ambition and his thirst for power, largely because he shared them. Tonino was there, close to the centre of power, the source of wealth, and guarding his privileged position. They all called Calogero 'boss', and they dignified Tonino with no special title, but they treated him with a slight wariness, knowing he was the boss's favourite, and that he was potentially dangerous, as was the boss. He saw it then, as the pizza was handed round, as more drinks were poured. How many men had Calogero killed, and how many had Tonino? More, it was certain, than all the others. It was this that made them dangerous. They were like beautiful glistening snakes, from which one should recoil, but which mesmerised you by their perilous nature.

He was a law student, and though criminal law was not his speciality, he read the papers, he watched the television, and he was interested in it. Fools got caught. And the ones who never got caught, they made fools of the system. Well, the system deserved it. The system was what kept them all down. If someone could beat the system, they were to be admired.

It was the first time he had been in the flat that don Calogero inhabited. The furniture, the marble, the fittings, everything indicated money, a great deal of money. One could tell that everything was expensive and of the sort that was designed to hide just how much it had cost. In addition, there was the drink, bottles of wine, whiskey and champagne, all of which had cost a fortune. Wine, he knew, cost a euro a litre in certain shops, where you had to bring your own bottle and where they filled it up from a tank. But this stuff cost twenty, thirty or even more a bottle, maybe even fifty. This was the sort of drink that people who never had to ask the price of anything consumed. It tasted like the nectar of the gods, rather than the stuff that rotted rubber and made your eyes water. Until now, he had had very little; Tonino too had once had very little, but now, they both had a lot; Tonino, thanks to the boss, and he, thanks to Tonino. Now everything was changed, and he was damned if he was going back to the way things had been before. Now he had nice food, nice drink, and so did his mother and sisters, who asked no questions. He had a job and the prospect of a degree. He had decent clothes and underwear that had no holes in it. He had a future, he had prospects.

One thing he had always had, and from a very young age, was girls. As a little boy, they had loved to pet him; from the age of eleven to kiss him, and from the age of thirteen, much, much more. He may not have had any money, but he had been popular. And not just with girls either. And now there was Gabriella, not a girl from his own quarter, or indeed from any quarter, a woman of importance and beauty. The signora, Assunta, also adored him, which was nice, as did his mother and sisters; he was at last rising, escaping or the horrors of this poverty-stricken childhood. One day, he was determined, he would be like Calogero.

'What do you think?' Tonino whispered to him, as they stood by the table with the drinks.

'Everything is so beautiful,' answered Roberto.

'No, I mean, yes, we know that. I mean what do you think of him?'

Roberto considered. He gave his answer. It was obscene, and very specific.

'So, you like that sort of thing, as well?' observed Tonino.

'Why not? Wouldn't you? And with him?'

But there was no time to discuss this, as it was clear the boss was calling them over. He did nothing, said nothing, but his look was a command.

He smiled at them, then looked at Roberto.

'I have a little job for Tonino, on Monday. I want him to go to Enna, spend the night there, do something for me. You can go with him, to make it look more natural. It is something important, that requires discretion. Have either of you been to Enna?'

'No, boss.'

'No, sir.'

'It is a nice place. Most people just drive past on the motorway. You can go there on your motorbike, book in to a hotel and then carry out my instructions. Monday.'

He dismissed them.

The party broke up at about 4am. They had watched two films: the first was *Jaws*, the second was Luchino Visconti's *Senso*. Calogero had greatly enjoyed the latter. It was about an older woman being in love with a much younger man. He had never seen it before, and had admired the look of it, the music, the way that the Austrians and Italians had fought. Naturally, he was on the side of the Austrians. Most of the boys, he had noticed, who had been wide awake for the shark film, dropped off to sleep over the Visconti, with the exceptions of Roberto and Tonino.

After they all left, leaving the wilderness of empty bottles in the study, he went and lay on his bed for a few hours, and as dawn came up, he even dozed. Then he rose, had a shower, and went to collect his mother to take her to Mass. She was pleased by this attention, but at the same time, being the woman she was, suspicious. His wife was away, his children were away, so it was natural that he should pay some attention to his mother, and make the most of these unusual circumstances. But at the same time, she suspected something. She had not been married to her own husband, Renato, the one they called the Chemist of Catania, for nearly two decades without being able to read the signs that a man who led a secretive life nevertheless could not avoid giving out, almost despite himself. Of course, she had known nothing of Renato's other life; but she had known that he had had one; and it was the same with Calogero. Something was happening.

After Mass, at his suggestion, she went to his flat to make lunch and to tidy up (he spoke airily of a bit of mess from the previous night), while Calogero went to the bar in the square for an aperitif, in order to show himself, once more, to the quarter. And it was here, as he sipped in a glass of vermouth, that the news of the disaster unfolded. The television was on in the bar, and he watched with unbounded interest.

It started off quite innocently. A missing man in a holiday villa in Taormina, indeed, above Taormina; fears for his safety, as the night had been very cold. Film of carabinieri and dogs, and a hunt for the missing man, presumed dead. No names released, as yet. Talk of drugs and drink and prostitution. Arrests were being made. A bad story. He was so glad he had left early.

He went up to his flat, and his mother prepared to serve lunch. The opening course was artichokes, his favourite, and he was just starting when the buzzer sounded. He knew who it would be. He told his mother to let him in.

'Sit down, have something to eat,' he said to Traiano, who looked uncharacteristically flustered. 'What on earth has happened? Something major, clearly, otherwise you would not have interrupted me. Tell me.'

Traiano sat at the table.

'Gino's dead,' he said. 'They have arrested Renzo and the cousin, Sandro.'

'Madonna!' said the boss. He got up and closed the dining room door. 'They have been arrested for murder?'

'It was an accident. Gino fell into the gully, it seems, off the terrace. He was in the plunge pool on his own, he must have got up to have a piss off the terrace, he had drunk so much, taken so much cocaine, swallowed so many pills, that he must have fallen off. I thought that place was dangerous. At night, and someone like Gino….'

'Someone like Gino,' echoed Calogero. 'Where's Alfio?' he asked.

'He came with me. I came to tell you, and he has gone on to Agrigento to break the news to the family, before they hear it on television. I need to phone Corrado in Verona. They made both of us give urine samples, and when we had done so, they let us go. The other two refused to give samples, so they arrested them, and they have taken the off to Messina, I think. They have got lawyers. The Santucci family have lots of lawyers,' he concluded bitterly.

'They have recovered the body?'

'Yes. And taken that to Messina for drug tests.'

'The police will be here soon,' said the boss, studying his artichoke.

'That is what I think too,' said Traiano.

'Let them come,' said Calogero.

It would take the police several hours to arrive, because they needed a search warrant, indeed multiple search warrants, and those things always took time. But they came, dozens of them, maybe even over a hundred, and they swarmed into the quarter in the middle of the afternoon. Their arrival caused something of a quiet sensation. No one could remember a member of the forces of law and order ever coming to their quarter before, except to have a cup of coffee in the bar; and now, after years of neglect, here they all were, dragged away from whatever other duties usually kept them busy. They were watched from every window; little boys who had never seen a policeman or policewoman before stared with open-mouthed curiosity; and the whole place was absolutely silent.

They found nothing; almost nothing.

In the gym they went through every single locker in the secret room, and found nothing. Tonino had got there first and thrown everything incriminating down the shaft. The guns and the knives, these were carefully wrapped up in a waterproof bag, sealed, and thrown down the shaft as well, but with a thread of nylon connecting them to a nail a few feet down, so they could, at a later date, be recovered.

The police came to don Traiano's flat and searched that, very thoroughly; they went through every drawer, and looked in every potential hiding place; they lifted the lids on all the lavatory cisterns, they looked in the fridge, in the kitchen cupboards, in the deep freeze. They checked all the tiles for loose ones that might conceal something; they removed all the pictures, hoping to find spaces in the walls; they examined all the pills and medicines in the hope of finding contraband. They looked under the beds. It was just as they were admitting defeat, that one of them noticed the small devotional picture hanging over the double bed. These pictures were common, he knew, but this one was clearly a copy of an old master; then he looked closely and saw that perhaps it was not a copy after all. He drew it to the attention of his superior.

The story was a good one: it had belonged to his friend Ruggero Bonelli, who had inherited it from his friend Professor Leopardi, or some name like that. It was very old, but he liked it, and Bonelli had sold it to him for a very modest price.

The police heard this story and thought that at the very least it was worth a try. The picture was taken down from the wall, placed in a plastic evidence bag, and impounded. Traiano protested. The child in his arms, who had been screaming throughout the raid, continued to protest. Then, grateful to be away from the child and his parents, particularly the father, the police left.

Alfio was in Agrigento with Gino's parents, but he had stopped off at home first knowing what would happen and removed his collection of guns and knives, which he had placed in a bag and carried down to one of the many cellars and lock ups in Purgatory to which he held the key. Traiano had done the same with his weapons; everyone had; the lock ups and cellars of Purgatory were numerous, and packed to their ceilings with junk. No one would ever find anything there, however long and hard they looked.

The police came to Gino's flat and found it empty. They forced the lock, and conducted a thorough search. This time they were lucky. It was clear that there had been no sudden tidying up in expectation of a raid. They found what they were looking for: a gun, several knives, lots of pills, and other evidence of daily life, hurriedly abandoned. Some half way through this forensic search, don Calogero di Rienzi appeared and asked to speak to the officer in charge, who obliged. He explained the reasons behind the sudden death of Gino Fisichella. He had been drunk, perhaps drugged, and had fallen off the terrace into a gully covered with foliage. No one had noticed his absence. Three of the others had been watching a film (they did not say what sort of film) and one of the others, Trajan Antonescu, had been asleep in bed. It was only in the morning that they had realised he was missing and raised the alarm. It had been Alfio Camilleri, who they understood to be the widow's cousin, who had called the police. Gino Fisichella had died of hypothermia, they thought; he had lost consciousness and the cold had killed him. The body would be released when the toxicology report was ready. Alfio Camilleri and Trajan Antonescu had been let go, because they had freely given urine samples. The other two, Sandro Santucci and Renzo Santucci, had refused, been arrested and taken to Messina. They wanted to know where the widow was. Don Calogero told them that he was confident that she would return very soon, now that her husband was dead; they had parted of late, but she would be back, he was sure, for the inheritance.

He thanked the officer and left. Of course, they had not searched his flat; but they knew that would be a worthless enterprise. He did not keep guns and knives at home any more, and they knew that. Going home, he rang his wife at Donnafugata and told her what had happened. She should tell the nanny Henrietta, he said, and of course, the children. But they must make sure the television was kept off.

A quietness settled over the quarter that night, and the next day, Monday morning, the atmosphere was subdued. Traiano went to meet the train that was carrying Corrado from Verona. He took him straight home to give him breakfast. They hardly spoke. It was only after Corrado had settled into his bedroom, had a shower, changed his clothes, and emerged refreshed and ready for another cup of coffee, that they spoke. Ceccina and the children were out, as if she had sensed the two brothers-in-law would want to be alone.

'The truth is, I don't know what happened,' said Traiano. 'I was reading a book in bed, and had fallen asleep and slept soundly. The others were watching a film, Renzo and his cousin doped up to the eyeballs. That was why they have refused urine samples and been taken away. And he is supposed to be getting married next week, and Gino was supposed to be the witness. I don't know what happened, but Renzo did not kill him, that is for sure. They are doing a toxicology report, then they will release the body for the funeral. But I already know what was in his bloodstream: lots of cocaine and alcohol and those wretched pills. He may well have fallen off the terrace in the state he was in. Such accidents do happen.'

Corrado heard this and sensed what he was not saying. He sensed too that he was being let into a confidence. If Alfio, the cousin of Gino's estranged wife, had pushed him off the terrace and left him to die in the cold, he would not have done this without the boss's permission, tacit or otherwise; and if the boss had allowed him to do so, he had done so without telling Traiano, which was worrying.

'Where is the wife, where is the child?' asked Corrado.

'Gone, and gone forever,' said Traiano. 'We will not hear from them again.'

Shortly after midday they arrived in Enna. They had both come by train, but not travelled to the station together. From the station, they took a bus to the town high above, and after a walk to orient themselves, they found a trattoria for lunch. It was the same trattoria where some years before, don Calogero di Rienzi and don Antonio Santucci used to meet. The food was good, and one wall was dominated by a mural, the nature of which was obscure to Tonino. He asked Robeto to explain it to him. It was, he was told, the rape of Persephone, which had happened on the plain below the town; she had been gathering flowers with her maiden companions and the God of the Underworld had seized her and carried her off. But her mother Ceres, the goddess of crops, had negotiated her return for six months of the year, which was how the ancients explained the seasons.

Tonino was, Roberto noticed, almost amused by this story of a dead woman returning. As for himself, Roberto told himself that he did not care about what had happened in Sicily three thousand years ago, or rather what had never happened. But the story was an unpleasant one:

one moment you were picking flowers in the field with your friends, the next you were swept away to the underworld. Poor Persephone. But she had had no choice, and a mother to rescue her. But he, what did he have? He could not even tell himself that he was an innocent, swept away by something he did not understand and could not prevent.

He wanted to ask what was in the bag between Tonino's feet, and why they were here, but he dared not. He knew if he did, Tonino would refuse to answer, or tell him to mind his own business. And he knew he should not ask because if he needed to know, he would be told, and he should not even show the desire to know. One had to put curiosity, that very human trait, to death. They were here for something, that was for sure, and at the behest of the boss, and the boss had wanted him to go with Tonino. He wondered whether they were here to carry out a robbery, or worse, a murder. He wondered for a terrible moment if the boss had told Tonino to take him up here and kill him? But why? What had he done? Nothing, he was sure. But would the boss tell Tonino to take him up here and kill him, just to show his power, just to test Tonino's loyalty?

He told himself that he was letting his imagination overheat.

The food was good, but the tension was palpable. What could one talk about, apart from mythological events from millennia past?

'Are you seeing anyone right now?' asked Tonino suddenly.

'Gabriella, you know,' answered Roberto. 'But 'seeing' is not quite right. We meet up, and…. She is not my girlfriend, but she likes to see me from time to time. What about you?'

'Only your sister, and that is very different.'

He understood.

'She is young, but she is a nice girl,' continued Tonino. 'Just right for me. I am glad she and you are coming to the wedding.'

'Don't you think they will cancel it?'

'No. It is too important. Too much hangs on it. And it has all been paid for, and if the witness is not there, well, you can find another.'

'Don't you care about don Gino being dead?'

Tonino looked puzzled by this question.

'Why should I? I don't have feelings about things like that.'

'Wasn't he your friend?'

'In a way. But why discuss it? What is the point? He is dead, and that is all there is to it. I mean, some people might want to say 'Poor don Gino', but what does that change? There is no point to it at all.'

'I suppose not.'

'How much money have you got in the bank? You and your sisters?'

He told him.

'That is nice. We should buy a vineyard; produce some wine. It is enough for a small one, I would have thought. People are always looking to sell. Maybe near Bronte, where that gravedigger lives. One buys a little one, and one buys more; people are willing to sell, though some need persuasion. And you would do it for me. What do you think of this wine?'

They were drinking the house red.

'OK,' said Roberto.

'They could do better,' said Tonino. 'We should perhaps have bought something better. Would you like to own a vineyard near Bronte?'

'Yes,' said Roberto.

The search of Gino's empty flat had been quiet and methodical, and the police had not made a mess, and neither had they sealed the place. Catarina found everything more or less as she had left it, when she had left the quarter a month or so ago. She looked at the familiar things in the flat, realising that they were no longer familiar, for everything had changed, life had changed. She reflected that she would move from here, that she no longer liked it. This was the place where she had lived with Gino. She wanted to forget Gino now. Gino was gone. Everything that might remind her of him needed to go too.

The child was asleep, and she had carried Tino up the stairs without waking him. Lucky boy: he would have no memory of his pseudo-father Gino, and she too would cleanse her mind of him as well. The child was now in his bed, and the car was parked in the square. People would notice it, she only had to wait.

The first to arrive was Alfio, the man who had done her such excellent service. Alfio spoke to her about what had happened, and she sat and listened. She heard him speak about the release of the body in subdued tones. She wondered if anyone had spoken to his parents, his brother; she wondered if she would have to do that. She asked Alfio. He replied that he had already thought of both eventualities. He had been to Agrigento by car with the sad news. Don Traiano had undertaken to speak to Corrado Fisichella, who was already here.

'They will want to bury him in Agrigento,' she said, more to herself than to him. 'That was where he came from. That is where he should go.'

Later, as the gloom of the winter afternoon deepened, don Calogero went round to Gino's flat. It was, he sensed, expected, and would be unremarked, a call of condolence. There were lots of people who would soon have the same idea. He came into the room and saw the two cousins. Alfio stood up, and left. The police had forced the lock, so he went and stood by the front door, on guard, to prevent anyone disturbing them.

'Well, well, well,' said Calogero, looking at her. 'I suppose you think you have won, don't you?'

'Is it a competition?' she asked.

'Everything is a competition,' he replied, undoing his belt. 'I need to take what is mine. I have won it, after all. I may regret my win, but it is too late now.'

He extended his hand to help her to her feet. She moved towards the bedroom. Once there, he closed the door and pressed her against it. There was a brief preparatory kiss. Then, after some difficulty with her clothing, the two bodies were joined. To his surprise, and to hers, she climaxed noisily. Even Alfio heard it out in the hallway.

'Good,' he said, as he dressed himself. He managed a more tender kiss. 'I will be back later and give you your instructions.'

He left. As he did so, he gave Alfio a friendly slap on the cheek. After waiting a decent interval, Alfio went back into the flat, to find his cousin where he had left her, seated on the sofa in the sitting room.

'Are you happy now?' he said to her with a bitterness he could not hide.

He had sacrificed so much for her; he had sacrificed his best friend; he had sacrificed any chance of having her himself; and what would his reward be? Surely, she would cast him aside? Why was that plain only now?

'Yes, I am happy,' she said triumphantly.

Don Calogero had told them where to go, and that is where they had come, a big, garishly painted modern building in a square, not far from the cathedral of Enna, which bore the name of Balmoral, a name familiar to neither of them. They had never been in a hotel before, either of them, and the process was slightly intimidating. They surrendered their identity cards to the man on the desk and were given the key to the double room, and made their way upstairs. The place was large, empty and echoing, at the very deadest time of the year for tourists. The heating made the room less cold.

They threw their bags down, and looked at each other. They did not exchange a word, they only looked at each other. Later, much later, it was Roberto who was the first to speak.

'He knew,' said Roberto. 'Don Calogero. That is why he sent us here. He wanted to have something to use against us. Well, not against us, against you.'

'You are paranoid, Costacurta. But you may well be right. I am his favourite.'

'What do you mean?'

'He likes me.'

'He does not like anyone,' said Roberto.

'In so far as he likes anyone, he likes me,' said Tonino. 'He has always been nice to me, and to my mother. He's looked after me. Right now, the favourite is Alfio, but that won't last. He is using Alfio, and he will toss him aside, just as he tossed aside Gino, though not in the same way. And he does not like Antonescu as much as he did. He sent me here, not Antonescu. He trusts me.'

'Whatever he sent us here for, it may be he sent you because he did not want Antonescu to know, because Antonescu would advise against it.'

Tonino frowned.

'Look, whatever it is, you need to leave it. Just enjoy Enna for what it is. There is a lot I cannot tell you. Your sister never asks questions. I hope Gabriella never asks questions.'

'Girls are girls, whatever age they are,' said Roberto. 'They do not understand power. And you, are you enjoying yourself?'

Tonino now looked annoyed.

'Do you really have to ask that?' he said. 'If I were not enjoying myself, you would find out. If I were not enjoying myself, I would not be here, I would be somewhere else. I don't have feelings, at least not feelings I want to discuss. I love my mother. That is it. That is all I can say on the subject. And if you want to know more, you are going to be disappointed.'

Roberto sighed.

'Yes,' said Tonino, in a more conciliatory tone. 'It is going to be difficult for you. I am not that sort of person. The sort of person people like. The sort of person you can get to know. I am careful with what I say and what I feel. But there is this one thing: I trust you. You are the only one I do trust. When we first met, I read your character and I thought you could be trusted. You want to get on. Together, we can get on. We will progress. Your desire to get on is almost tangible; I sensed it; you hate your father, don't you? I recognise that. I hate mine, though I have met him only once. Luckily, he is safely in jail, at least for the moment; and your father has gone to Rome with his woman, which seemed like a disaster at the time; trust me, it is the greatest blessing. No one to tell you what to do, no one to beat you for no reason at all; instead, you are the master of the house, your mother loves you, your sisters adore you, and you bring home the cash.'

'Do my sisters adore me?'

'Petra says she does and the others too. We talk, you know….'

'So, you talk to her?'

'I am talking to you now, aren't I? Now? Be happy with what you have got, and stop lamenting what you have not got. Think of what I can give you, and do not concern yourself with what I cannot give you. You are supposed to be intelligent. Be sensible too. He took him up to a high mountain….'

'Who did?'

'It is in the Bible, stupid. It is what I am doing for you. Taking you up to a high mountain and showing you the kingdoms of the earth. Now, let us get up and get dressed, let us go out, and let us do what we are supposed to do here.'

The job was very simple, as it turned out; to take the cash in the bag that Tonino carried and to find a flat to rent for three months, and to sign the papers and secure the keys. The instructions were clear. It had to be ready for immediate occupation. There were several estate agents in the town, and they visited them all. They saw details of all the properties and went and looked at several. After much consideration, they whittled the list down to three in the city itself, all with nice views, all near shops, all spacious, all with parking places nearby; they said they would make their decision tomorrow and that they would pay cash. It was Roberto who said this, as he was the elder, and, they both thought, the more plausible. Then, as evening fell, they went to an enoteca to sample the local wines, something that Tonino was very keen to do.

The news that she was back spread very rapidly. The car was seen in the square below, and after a time various female friends appeared, shocked, surprised and in a way relieved to see her. Then her parents came, and soon the flat was full of people, mainly women. She had gone away, suddenly, and told no one, and now equally suddenly, she had returned. What had brought her back? The death of her husband, obviously. And what had driven her away, but the very same husband, now dead. The women of the quarter knew about mourning, they knew what to do when a dear husband or father, son or brother, died; but this was rather different, and an air of slight unease and embarrassment hung over them.

This sense of dislocation became momentarily acute with the appearance of Corrado, the deceased's brother. Alfio met him at the top of the stairs and conducted him silently inside. As he stepped in, Corrado felt all of the friends and relations of his sister-in-law study him with intense scrutiny; he felt like a criminal, as if he were somehow responsible for whatever had gone wrong.

It was a big flat, of course, and recently redone to high specifications; he wondered if people were noticing how Catarina had spent Gino's money on the marble work surfaces in the kitchen, for example, and in the beautifully appointed bathroom. His visit was an event, he could tell; he entered the place and people noticed him, making him feel like the outsider he was.

The grieving widow had withdrawn to the marital bedroom, with her mother; one of her female relatives went in to tell her that Corrado was there. One by one, the visitors were admitted for a few brief moments to condole with the widow on the tragedy that had overtaken her. And when this was done, they gathered in the sitting room, watching little Tino, sitting around gloomily, accepting cups of coffee, softs drinks or whisky from the attentive women of the family. The sitting room was like a first-class waiting room, where people waited patiently for a train that never seemed to arrive. There was no need for them to be there, except that grief, or rather the pretence of grief, attracted crowds. The atmosphere was heavy, and at the same time it was leavened with a sense of rightness. This was what life was like: tragic. This was what they expected of life, and that it had happened gave them the satisfaction of knowing that all their gloomy forebodings were justified.

Of course, these forebodings had never had a specific form; they had just been gloomy background thoughts, and no one had ever expected Gino to die in such an unexpected and accidental way. They had all sensed for some time that the young man had drunk too much, or taken too many pills and other things, but that it should go so far, this surprised them. The news, which had spread through the quarter that afternoon, was, in its way, shocking, as had been the irruption of the police into the quarter the previous day.

Having shaken hands with all the gloomy people in the sitting room, having accepted a cup of coffee, and having kissed both the small child Tino, who seemed blissfully unaware of the tragic atmosphere around him, Corrado was eventually admitted to the room where his sister-in-law was.

Alfio, for a man whose best friend had just died so unexpectedly, was remarkably composed. He, as the best friend, and as the cousin of the widow, had to handle things; it fell to him. And now, they all thought, looking at him, what else would fall to him now that Gino was gone? They all knew the absence of Gino was an opportunity for Alfio. He felt it himself. Doors closed; others opened. Catarina would ensure his continued importance, even though he would have liked to have her himself. He kept his position at the top of the stairs, unwilling to join the mourners inside.

Up the stairs, on quiet feet, almost taking him by surprise, came Traiano.

'Corrado is in there?' he asked softly. 'I thought I would give him a bit of time. Poor Gino, eh? It makes me sad. I know it makes you sad too.'

He put his hands on Alfio's shoulders, and drew him towards himself. For a moment he held him, savouring the scent of his aftershave, the texture of his clothes, and something else, something more important than any of that: his fear. He released him, and looked into his eyes. Alfio was trying to be a good actor, and failing. It was clear to them both that Traiano knew, and that deny it as he might try, he could not deny the fact that he had murdered the man who had been his best friend.

'I know you had your differences of late, but you went back to the days of Bicocca; indeed, all three of us go back a long way. I confess I am surprised that she is back, your cousin, and the child, though naturally I am glad of it. I had thought, well, never mind what I had thought, but she is safe and well, and that pleases me.'

'I had to protect her,' said Alfio.

'Of course, of course. That is understandable. And I am glad you did. Will she stay here?'

'I doubt it. There is no real reason. Too many unhappy memories. They were not suited.'

'She should have married someone else,' said Traiano. 'Any news about the release of the body? Or the release of our friends in Messina?'

There was news on both. The dead body was to be released very soon. The live bodies were also free. Without saying a word, they both knew that don Renzo Santucci's prestige might never recover from this, which was no bad thing.

And now the boss arrived.

'Dearest Alfio,' said the boss, affectionately tugging Alfio by the earlobe. He greeted Traiano with a kiss on the cheek. The demeanour of both of them changed in his presence. Traiano knew that Alfio had killed Gino, he was sure of it; he was also sure who had connived at the murder, and why. But he gave no indication of this at all. His face was impassive. He felt an overwhelming desire to kill Alfio, right there and then, but he hid this, as he knew he must. He was horrified by the boss's behaviour, but he showed no sign of this at all.

'It has been a long time since we three spent time together, hasn't it?' the boss now said. 'Of course, you know why that has to be, don't you? I hardly saw Gino either. I have to be careful not to embarrass my new best friend, our future Mayor, Fabio Volta. But you two and I, we go back a long time, to the time when I was stealing car radios, and we were all bad boys in the quarter who never went to school. Pity about them catching you and putting you in Bicocca, Alfio. Ah well; Traiano and I were the lucky ones, and you less so. But now... well, I have not forgotten that you are my brother-in-law, well, the late Stefania' brother-in-law, the children's uncle, married to their Aunt Giuseppina. You will look after Catarina, as she is your cousin; I will look after her too; the business interests that Gino had will now go to her and Tino. I hope that you will help her when she needs help, as will I. She is going to be quite rich. Just as you are rich. I made you so.'

'You can rely on me, boss,' said Alfio with fervour.

'I know I can. As for poor Gino, he had served his purpose. He was a little too violent. Those days are over, I think. We can do without Gino from now on. Well, in that we have little choice. And all the things that happened in the past, things like the murder of that horrid little man, my wife's nephew, maybe it was the guilt of these crimes that drove him to, well, be so careless with his life. Perhaps he had lost the will to live? Perhaps the night he died he was depressed, thinking of that crime, and maybe that was why he did it? What do you think?'

'It was suicide?' asked Alfio, for a moment confused.

'No. It was an accident, but… The case of Fabrizio Perraino may now be solved, don't you think? Now, let us go to the others. I won't see Catarina. I am sure she will understand. You tell her. I am going to Palermo, but I will be back for the funeral, whenever that is.' He paused. 'Did the police find anything when they raided yesterday?' he asked.

'In Gino's flat, yes. Knives, and a gun, and various pills,' said Alfio.

He looked at Traiano.

'They took my picture, the one of the Madonna, saying it was stolen. Bonelli sold it to me, you know, as a friend.'

'Well, you will know what to do, speak to our lawyers, and they will know what to do,' said don Calogero. 'Taking the picture, that shows how desperate they are.'

All three of them went into the flat. There were hands to shake, women to be kissed on the cheek, teenagers to be chucked under the chin. Corrado had emerged from his interview with Catarina and was eager to escape. He accepted a handshake from Alfio and from the boss, and a few murmured words of sympathy.

Presently, the priest of the Church of the Holy Souls in Purgatory, don Giorgio appeared. There were murmurs of appreciation from all, Calogero included, though the priest accepted Calogero's handshake with something like coldness. Almost all the women and the younger males bent low to kiss the priest's hand; so did Traiano, who loved the priest with an almost passionate intensity, something, perhaps the only thing, which he shared with his mother, Anna, the former Romanian prostitute.

Calogero frowned at the sight of Traiano's greeting. All his dislike of don Giorgio, a person who was so inexplicably revered, came back to him. As for don Giorgio, his loathing of Calogero was visceral. He had known Gino and his wife, separately, and then together, for some time. He had never liked Gino, or approved of him, and Gino had certainly never gone to church, except for the baptism of Tino, but, now that Gino was dead, and Calogero so insolently alive, it struck him that Gino was another of his victims. For if Gino had stayed in Agrigento, never met Calogero, he would surely still be alive. Calogero had destroyed him, but how could he say that?

And so, don Giorgio despaired. Now, meeting Calogero in the sitting room, he had the humbling task of accompanying him and Alfio into the dining room and talking about the funeral. Catarina had spoken to Alfio, and she had also spoken to Corrado, and made her wishes clear, confident that no one would contradict her. As soon as the police released the body, the funeral could take place, as early in the morning as possible, in the Church of the Holy Souls in Purgatory. That could well be Tuesday. But there was the question of the burial. Don Giorgio had the idea that it would be best to place the coffin in the crypt of the Church of the Holy Souls in Purgatory, given the state of the municipal cemetery. But don Calogero would not hear of it. He had buried his first wife in the crypt. Besides, Gino had not been a member of the Confraternity of the Holy Souls in Purgatory. He could go to the municipal cemetery. Alfio said that according to Catarina he should go back to Agrigento, but this depended on the family there wanting him. The parents, according to Alfio, would soon be on their way, and might indeed decide to take Gino back with them. Perhaps there was a tomb in Agrigento; perhaps the cemetery in Agrigento was more appropriate than the one in Catania. Don Giorgio realised that he would have to go along with whatever Calogero or the family or both decided. He sensed that Agrigento would be the final resting place; that Catarina would want her husband as far away as possible. That too seemed to be the position of the boss.

And then, as if summoned by some indiscernible conduit that carried the news of death, Pio Forcella himself was in the flat, and after a gentle knock on the dining room door, standing deferentially in front of don Calogero and Alfio and the priest, waiting until don Calogero should notice him.

'Piuccio,' said don Calogero, as if greeting an old friend, though he hardly knew the undertaker and had barely spoken to him before now, as far as he could remember, yet flattered that Piuccio should come to him, knowing that he was the centre of power, and pleased that Piuccio had come, for he had surely come for a purpose.

The black-suited undertaker spoke in low and sombre tones, as he always did.

'I heard the news,' he said. 'I made a few enquiries. The body is now with the police in Messina and they will release it sometime later tonight. Cause of death is not in doubt. It was hypothermia. But they have done a toxicology report, or are doing one, the police told me; it means a slight delay. But they wanted me to know, and that means they wanted you to know. The other thing is that we will need some proper clothes for him. Should I speak to the widow, sir?'

'There's no need. Speak to the brother. He is staying with don Traiano. He is the most sensible one to make arrangements like that. He lives in Verona, but he came as soon as he heard the sad news, and he got here first. The rest of the family is coming from Agrigento. I am sure you will know what to do. And I will pay for everything.'

Piuccio bent over and kissed the hand of don Calogero.

The boss emerged from the dining room with Piuccio in his wake, and now made a fuss of the little boy Tino, cuddling him with great affection. Then he prepared to leave, Alfio and Traiano accompanying him to the door. He gestured them to follow him out onto the landing and to shut the door behind them.

'Could Gino read and write?' he asked quietly.

'I never saw him with a book, boss,' said Alfio puzzled. 'And I never saw him write anything down either. In Bicocca, if ever we had a magazine, he only looked at the pictures. But he liked to keep quiet about it. I knew, of course, but…'

'We will rely on rumour,' said Calogero. 'Written evidence, a signed confession, would have been very convenient.' He looked at Traiano. 'Speak to that policeman, Andreazza. Tell him we know who killed Perraino, that it was Gino. Let's blame the dead man. Now I am going home. I will tell my wife that the man people say killed Perraino is dead. I wonder what she will make of that?'

Alfio nodded, as if to say that this was a good idea. Blame the dead man. No one would mourn him now. The boss looked at Traiano.

'That picture, the one the police confiscated. It could get you into trouble, and the rest of us as well.'

Traiano took this as a reproach.

'I went to see Bonelli about it, as soon as I could, to get the story straight. When they go round to the gallery, as they are bound to, they will find that he knows what to say.'

'It would be a pity for a picture of the Madonna to ruin everything for you,' said Calogero, and continued down the stairs.

Traiano was left alone with Alfio.

'Does Catarina know?' asked Traiano.

There was a pause. Traiano could almost hear the cogs moving around what passed for Alfio's brain, while he calculated the chances of bluffing it out.

'The boss told you?' asked Alfio at last.

'He tells me everything,' said Traiano, which was not true, for he certainly had not told him this. He wondered if Alfio was clever enough to realise he had not answered the question. 'Does she know?' he asked again.

'No. No one has told her, not me, not the boss. She would not want to know. That is the way they all like it. She is glad he is dead. But she is not asking questions.'

'Then she knows. She is not stupid. She is clever, your cousin. She does not assent to something, even retroactively, without securing her own advantage. What have you got out of this? What are you looking for? You had better watch out, Alfio. One day she may have no further use for you. Maybe that day has already come. When you told her the bad news, was she so grateful as to sleep with you at once, and give you what you have always wanted?'

'I am her cousin,' said Alfio. 'That counts for more.'

'Let us hope so,' said Traiano.

'The boss says that maybe Gino killed Perraino, and that we should say this so the police have an excuse to shut down the investigation. I say that we should claim that Gino killed Rosario as well. That makes sense. He slept with her, didn't he?'

'We cannot blame every unsolved disappearance on poor Gino. He was a violent criminal but not that prolific. Who else slept with Catarina, I wonder?' asked Traiano.

Alfio's face burned hot. He had slept with Catarina, but that had been years ago, though he had never forgotten it. Neither had anyone else. He had slept with his cousin, if that was what you called it, just once, and she had wanted him no more after that. It was humiliating.

'You are not sorry Gino is dead either,' retorted Alfio.

Traiano understood this: it was a reference to the supposed fact (which Gino had denied) that Gino had slept with his mother, Anna, the former Romanian prostitute. Alfio attributed to him a hatred of all his mother's former clients.

'Never mind me. He was your great friend. I wonder what his brother Corrado thinks of all this.'

'Nothing at all. Why should he? He fell down into a gully when he was drugged and drunk, and died of hypothermia. It was an accident. You were there. You will tell him so.'

'Very convenient for you,' said Traiano.

'Look,' said Alfio. 'You know what it is like to kill, and to kill a friend. It doesn't feel good, does it? But it has to be done.'

Traiano considered this and shrugged after a moment. It would not do to show anger. It was true he had never cared for Gino, and yet, and yet… he cared for Alfio, right then, nothing at all.

'What will be, will be,' he said easily. 'It is certainly not worth quarrelling about.'

Tonino studied the menu of the enoteca with great care. It was long, a good menu, he could see, and there were useful pairings. For someone who wanted to learn, such as himself, it was instructive. As it was winter, the place was almost empty. Indeed, the town was empty. This enoteca seemed to be the only place open, and they the only people in it.

'They have Vin Santo,' said Roberto with a note of awe in his voice.

'They have Passito di Pantelleria as well,' replied Tonino. 'Have you had that? No? Neither have I. But let us not give that away. We can end with that. It will be heavenly.'

Roberto pointed out the price.

'Then it must be good,' said Tonino, with a smile. 'And it's only a half bottle.'

Moreover, it was the last half bottle, according to the owner. To precede it, he suggested a bottle of local red, produced by a friend of his, now very old, the fifth or sixth generation of his family, and the last as well. He produced a couple of hundred bottles a year, and it was excellent, and hard to find, but.... He mentioned a price, and Tonino did not turn a hair, and Roberto took his cue from him. The dusty bottle was bought, and the label examined. It was opened, and a tiny amount was poured into a specially polished glass. Tonino tasted it and pronounced it excellent. Then they discussed what they should eat with it, and what they should have with the Passito. Tonino felt an undisguised sense of satisfaction at the pleasures to come.

The first taste of the wine coursed through his veins, and his thoughts were of the great pleasure that lay ahead in the drink, the food and the companionship of Roberto. And almost immediately, the opposite thought struck him, the ever-present idea of death, of his mother and her fragile happiness, and of his father in jail.

'Don Gino is dead,' he said reflectively.

Roberto nodded.

'A stupid accident. This flat we are seeking out is for the widow. She has been away; she is back, but she is not staying in Purgatory, she is escaping. Like whatshername, Persephone. Sort of escaping. He is going to hide her away here. That is why he sent me and you; we are here to do nothing but take our pleasures, if anyone asks, not that anyone will. If they do ask, it will be interesting. But as I say, he is hiding her away here. Her cousin Alfio has already arranged a new identity for her, a new name, a new card. And the boss is giving me quite a lot for doing this. Quite a lot. That, and the fact that he asked me, not the Romanian, well, that tells me a lot. Our boss is, for the first time in his career, taking an unnecessary risk. He should have had nothing to do with Catarina. I thought she had gone for good, been told to disappear. But it seems not; now she is to disappear but not quite in the right way; she is to become his hidden woman. The same old story. A man making a fool of himself over a woman. I had thought that he was not so crazy about women, but it seems he is. Of course there is her, but there is also the child. The child, the future children, that is what he cares about. Dottoressa Tancredi is old, but dottoressa Tancredi will not be pleased. That is why he is taking such precautions. So, you see, if this gets out, it put me in danger, and perhaps you too. That is why I am telling you. I ought not to, but I trust you. Lots of people would like to know about this secret relationship. I bet signora Assunta would. I bet his mother would. I bet his wife would. But we must not tell anyone. Understood?'

'Understood,' said Roberto. 'I can keep secrets. Trust me. Even the secrets that one keeps from oneself.'

Tonino smiled.

'Well, there are plenty of those,' he said. 'Don Calogero likes me, he likes me a lot, and he will be grateful and generous for what we have done today and for our silence. It is a big opportunity. I am going to ask him a favour. My mother wants another child, and my father is coming out of jail, and that is my cue to leave Catania, not just yet, but maybe after a few months. My father is a stranger to me, and I do not want to live with him. Don Gino is dead, and things in Palermo need firming up from what we have all heard. They can find me a job in Palermo; and as for you, when you have finished your degree… well, the Santucci office in Palermo will be waiting, if I ask them.'

He was in further than he thought, Roberto realised. He contemplated the life that was opening up in front of him. He felt the excitement of it, and at the same time, a frisson of fear. It was, perhaps, already too late to step back.

The funeral was going to be held on Wednesday morning, early. It was decided between the family from Agrigento and the widow Catarina, in consultation with Piuccio Forcella, the ever-useful undertaker, that the Mass should be held in the Church of the Holy Souls in Purgatory, and the burial should take place later that day in a cemetery just outside Agrigento, where the family had a tomb.

The police released the body for burial, as promised, on Tuesday evening, whereupon it was taken to the morgue at his premises by Piuccio, who then reported to Traiano's flat, where the parents from Agrigento were staying, along with Corrado Fisichella, the brother of the deceased. The toxicology report had been released, detailing all the drugs, legal and illegal, that had been in Gino's body at the time of his decease, and which had contributed to it. Piuccio accepted a cup of coffee, and spoke to Traiano, the parents and Corrado. His voice was low, apologetic, fit for the sad news that he had come to impart.

'The body of the late Gino is in the morgue, and I wanted to know whether you wished to give me some clothes for him to be buried in. The clothes he had with him at the time of his death are still in the hands of the police.'

Traiano winced. He did not like this. Corrado was impassive. He was still tired after his journey, and had been tired ever since his arrival in Catania. He was full of grief for his poor parents and what they had to suffer. He was full of anger at the thought of what Gino had done, through no fault of his own.

'Did my brother have a suit?' asked Corrado, turning to Traiano.

'I am sure he did. We can go over to his house and check. He must have done. Yes, he did. I remember seeing him in a suit. He wore one for his wedding,' said Traiano.

'If you collect a complete set of clothes,' said Piuccio, 'We can dress him and put him in his coffin.'

'We should do that, his brother and his friends,' said Corrado.

'Many families like to do that,' said Piuccio with approval. 'It is very traditional. It is the Sicilian way.'

The body had been washed and wrapped in towels, and lay on a trolley under a sheet in a room with the destined coffin. Alfio, for some reason, had not joined them, to Traiano's resentment, who found himself alone, when Piuccio left them, with the recumbent corpse and Corrado. Gino, in death as in life, was large, and it took strength to manipulate his corpse, which was cold to the touch, pale and waxy. The eyes were closed, but not quite closed enough, and you had the impression that the dead man was looking at you, even if you tried your best not to look at him. The hair seemed lifeless, and through it, one could see the porcelain whiteness of his scalp. The various injuries the body had sustained in the fall were covered with sticking plaster, which seemed absurd. The first task was to put on the corpse's underwear while keeping the towel around his midriff in place, something that did not quite succeed. Eventually, that horror was covered by the Calvins, after which everything became much easier: the trousers, the shirt, the jacket, the socks, the shoes, the tie. Traiano noticed that Corrado dressed the corpse as if he were dressing a young and unwilling child, as many a time Traiano had dressed his own children. Finally, the job was done, and between them they lifted the huge form into the waiting coffin, and then stood back to admire their work. Corrado leaned forward and kissed his dead brother on the lips. Feeling he should do something similar, Traiano placed a kiss on the cold forehead. Then Corrado took out the rosary beads his mother had given him and placed them in his brother's cold dead hands.

It was a relief to step out of the morgue, to leave matters in the hands of Piuccio. They got into the car, and Traiano looked at the face of Corrado, to see if there was any redness about his eyes. There wasn't.

'Let's go for a drink,' he said, heading back to the town.

They parked outside the gate, and he led the visitor into the square outside the Cathedral, and they sat in the bar opposite the Elephant. Drinks were ordered. Corrado seemed subdued, which was hardly surprising, given what they had just been doing.

'You like this square?' asked Traiano, by way of conversation. 'How does it compare in your eyes to Verona?'

Corrado shrugged at this attempt at small talk.

'Pasqualina thinks she may be pregnant,' he said. 'Otherwise, she might have come. She is feeling very sick all the time.'

'Congratulations,' said Traiano. 'Ceccina may be in a similar situation.'

'Congratulations,' said Corrado. 'More baptisms. Nice. Catarina and her child....'

Traiano noted the phrase 'her child', not 'my nephew'.

'The little boy, Tino.... Did Gino ever say anything to you about him?' asked Traiano.

'We never spoke about that, or much else, really,' said Corrado sadly. 'But... You were there, weren't you? When he died?'

'I was. I went to bed and read a book. The other three were watching some film in one of the rooms. Gino was alone on the terrace. The other two had taken a lot of stuff and drunk a great deal, as had Gino.'

'But not you, and not Alfio?' asked Corrado. 'Does Alfio drink much and take stuff?'

'He does, on occasion. More than me. I hardly drink and I do not take anything.'

'But not on this occasion,' said Corrado. 'Strange. And he was his friend, wasn't he?'

'Yes, more than me. They met in Bicocca, remember.'

'I was younger than him, and when he was a little boy, he was very nice. Then when he got to a certain age, about eleven, he became very difficult. When they put him in Bicocca, we thought that perhaps that might cure him, but he came out worse. I wonder if he led Alfio astray, or the other way around?'

'Gino had the fiercer reputation.'

'He killed more people?' asked Corrado.

'We do not talk about that,' said Traiano. 'But he killed the policeman Perraino. People will talk about that. Now he is dead, now they cannot arrest him for it.'

'He and Alfio were friends, you say. Some friendship. He did not come with us to the undertakers. Perhaps he felt guilty. If he had been with him, he would not have died.'

Traiano was silent.

Traiano did not like funerals, but naturally he had to go to this one, given his long association with the deceased. In addition, he knew that the boss was sure to be there, and he wanted to see how Calogero would behave. It was still too early, surely, for him to acknowledge by some public action that Catarina was his mistress, but it would still be interesting to see his attitude to her in the church. Moreover, Ceccina, the soft-hearted Ceccina, wished to be there, to show her support for the widow, even if this were hardly logical, as Ceccina would surely one day realise. The Requiem Mass was to be very early, and after the Mass, the body was to be driven to Agrigento for burial.

There was a strange silence that night in the flat and in the quarter. They lay in bed feeling the silence around them; the parents were in one of the spare rooms, and Corrado was in the room Cristoforo normally slept in. Poor Gino lay in his coffin, dead and unloved.

They were a gloomy congregation that morning in the Church of the Holy Souls in Purgatory. The women went into the Church to pray before the Mass began, and the men, as usual, hung around outside on the steps, waiting for the coffin to arrive. There were hands shaken, and in a few cases, kisses exchanged. The boss arrived, looking serious and business-like, having dropped his children off at school, and shook hands, and went into the Church. Gino's parents, looking very old and desiccated, as all poor people did, though they were neither of them past the age of sixty, went into the Church accompanied by their son Corrado. Traiano saw Tonino, and nodded distantly. Then he went into the Church to join his wife.

The coffin entered, led by don Giorgio and the altar servers, followed by Piuccio Forcella. Everyone stood up. Then the Mass began. Traiano looked around for Tonino once or twice, but only spotted him as the Mass was ending. He had been absent of late, and he wondered where he had been. There were no tears, he noticed, for the late Gino, not even from his mother. His parents looked so poor, even by the standards of Purgatory. Gino had spent his adult life in the supplying of drugs, prostitutes and violence, and they looked like the sort of people for whom all three were daily realities in the neighbourhood of Agrigento where they lived. But the mother's sadness looked genuine enough. He thought of Corrado kissing the dead man in his coffin; perhaps there had been some affection there after all.

As for the people from Purgatory who were there, the women were sympathetic to the sadness of the occasion, while the men were stony-faced. It had been an accidental death, but there were surely no accidents, and it was best to give nothing away. At the end of the Mass, the coffin was taken out and loaded into the hearse belonging to Piuccio, to be driven to Agrigento. Corrado got into Traiano's car, borrowed for the occasion, to follow the hearse and to drive the parents and the widow. Catarina was going to Agrigento to see him entombed, leaving Tino behind under the care of Giuseppina. And so, Gino left the quarter for the last time.

After these departures, the boss made his excuses and left, and the rest of them stood around in the winter sunshine for a few moments, and then, by unspoken consent, headed across the square to the bar. It was still early, so the women and children sat down at the tables and chairs and had soft drinks or coffee and ate pastries, while the men stood at the bar, many of them drinking whiskey. Traiano contented himself with some coffee and some mineral water, but Tonino had some whiskey, knocking it back and making a face as he did so. Traiano saw him wince.

'All OK?' he asked Tonino.

'Yes, fine, thanks, boss,' replied Tonino.

'Good. How is Roberto?'

'Fine, boss. He and I were away for a couple of days, tasting wine.'

'Was it nice?'

'Excellent. We had Passito di Pantelleria. It was wonderful.'

Chapter Eleven

'Calogero says you are a fool,' said Traiano.

It was the night of Gino's funeral. Traiano was in Palermo now, at Renzo's flat.

'I thought he would come himself to tell me that,' said Renzo, miserably.

'That would be a mark of favour,' said Traiano. 'And you are out of favour. He sent me instead. But do not worry. I have not been instructed to put a bullet in your head. I have different instructions: To get you into shape for the wedding this Sunday. You followed the lawyers' advice?'

Renzo nodded miserably.

'I did. Sandro refused. He said that he is getting his own lawyer and he is going to fight it. He does not want to get a criminal record as he says this would make it impossible for him to go to America and study after he has finished university here. But I did what the lawyer told me to do, as he was acting under Calogero's instructions. I don't want to upset Calogero more than I have already.'

'Sandro is a little fool,' said Traiano dismissively. 'He should have done what he was advised to do, plead guilty and accept the inevitable, a time in a facility to treat drug abusers. That he has not followed advice means that he has lost don Calogero's favour forever. He is a dead man walking. He is finished. Forget Sandro.'

A little of Renzo's misery seemed to lift at this. The idea of Sandro being removed from the scene had always been pleasing to him. He looked up. Traiano had a rolled up heavy leather belt in his hand. He was holding it as if weighing it and the damage it could do.

'I need a witness now Gino is dead,' said Renzo.

'You do. Ring up your Aunt Angela and tell her you want your cousin Beppe. He is young, but at least he is innocent, unlike his brother. She will be thrilled and so will Beppe be. Do it now.'

With an eye on the belt, Renzo went to the phone.

Everyone, it seemed, was invited to the wedding of Renzo Santucci and Elena di Rienzi: both families, close friends, and the people who worked for both families, which all together came to close on a thousand people; but the guests were graded according to importance. There were the select few, mainly relations, who were invited to the small and very beautiful ancient church in which the ceremony took place, where Renzo and Elena took their vows under the golden mosaics of another age and under the rounded cupolas left by the Normans; then there were those who came to the massive banquet held in the Grand Hotel, where some three hundred and fifty people sat down to eat a never-ending succession of courses. And finally, there were those who were invited to the evening party afterwards, which started at about 10pm and which was expected to go on until dawn.

Muniddu, as a middle ranking employee of the family, was invited to the banquet, as was his wife, and his children. Traiano had had sight of the guest lists, and had insisted on this; there had been some talk that Muniddu would be needed to oversee the security at the occasion, but this was left to other, lower ranking, but trustworthy men. Tonino too was invited, as was his mother, the signora Grassi being an old friend of the mother of the bride, the signora di Rienzi. Under his mother's supervision, Tonino had bought a suit and attempted to impose some order on his bristly hair; he and his mother were given rooms in the Grand Hotel for the night, as they had to come all the way from Catania; not suites, but two single rooms on the top floor. He was familiar with the hotel but had never stayed the night there before. His mother had never stayed the night in a hotel in her life. Both were looking forward to it.

The unexpected death of Gino had caused barely a hiccup in the plans for the wedding. With Beppe as the new best man, assisted by Traiano, who had come over to stay before the wedding, everything could now go on as before. Indeed, Gino was hardly missed. There had been no talk at all of postponing the wedding because of the unfortunate death of the best man; the wedding had been postponed long enough; and, round the dead Gino, had closed a silence, total and profound, like the waters closing over the head of a drowning man, leaving no trace at all. It was not just that Gino was dead; it was as if he had never existed. No one mentioned him, no one gave any thought to him at all. If Gino left a legacy, it was this: that the groom and the groom's cousin both had court cases pending, thanks to the way they had been forced to give blood, in Messina, directly after the unfortunate Gino's demise.

Traiano marvelled at it. Renzo Santucci seemed not in the least bothered by the fact that he was to appear in court and plead guilty for the offence of being found in a drugged state, or whatever the law called it; he was confident that, at the very most, he would be ordered to spend two weeks in a drug rehabilitation centre. Sandro was more annoyed, given that if he were lumbered with a criminal record, this might cause problems later in life, and determined to fight the case, hopeless as it seemed. He was also annoyed by the way his mother had reacted. She seemed to take her son's cocaine use as a personal affront, and had been weepy and reproachful on the matter. His sisters were philosophical: everyone took cocaine, in their view. His brother Beppe might have had a view, but he did not bother to think what it might be. He was not talking to his brother.

In fact, there was now a new family rupture. Sandro felt that the position of best man to his cousin was rightfully his, not Beppe's, and that the way he had been passed over was a disgrace. Moreover, he felt no guilt at all about being arrested, and blamed Renzo for that. Passing him over added insult to injury; he could not forgive Renzo for it, and neither could he forgive his mother. He was glad that his two sisters sided with him.

Traiano too had a court case pending, though he was confident that it would be years before the matter came to court, and even if it did, it would be most unlikely that he would ever have to face doing time for receiving stolen goods. The Mantegna, school of, Madonna was impounded, and they would perhaps not see her again; it was as if the police had kidnapped her. One understood why. They wished to use this case as leverage, to get him to admit to other things. But he could and would play the long game. The defence was simple. The Madonna had been inherited from the professor by Bonelli, and sold on informally to Traiano. The case for the prosecution was that it was stolen, but, being so generic a subject, it was impossible for the police to prove just which stolen Madonna, of the many thousands on file, it was. Still, the whole thing upset Ceccina no end. Traiano's own view was that it was annoying; though there was another aspect that was troubling. He did not believe in accidents. He did not believe that the police had taken the painting by chance. They had surely known it was there. And who had known about the painting? Bonelli, for sure, and Pasquale Greco. And Tonino. Had either Tonino told Roberto, or Bonelli told his sister? Had she discussed it with Roberto? And who had told the police? But these were minor worries compared to what Renzo faced and what Sandro faced.

It struck some of the more wily observers in that delightful church that Renzo Santucci was essentially being co-opted into the family of Calogero di Rienzi, which was in fact the case. It struck Renzo's uncle, Antonio, who watched with his wife and children sitting near him, that there was a strange parallel between bride and groom; both were creatures of Calogero, and both had fathers who had died in explosions; one thanks to a bomb he himself had made, the other thanks to a rocket propelled grenade hitting his yacht. It struck his sardonic mind that this was a pleasing parallel. He wondered what his wife Angela thought - the groom's aunt. What indeed did anyone think? Was he the only one who saw the whole thing as the grotesque and bizarre charade it was?

His wife was tearful, perhaps thinking of her dear brother Carlo, the groom's late father; perhaps thinking of her son Sandro's recent drug trouble, which she had convinced herself would ruin any chance of an honest career for the boy; his daughters, Emma and Marina, were sharp eyed and observant, conscious of their own dresses, looking at everyone else's and, he was sure, calculating how much everything had cost, and storing up all these details against the plans they had for their own eventual weddings. The question of dresses was complicated, as there had to be one dress, suitably modest for Church, and for the banquet afterwards, and then another dress for the evening party, when there would be dancing, and which had, therefore, to be a different type of dress. And a different dress meant different shoes. And then of course, in a separate but related concern, just as the girls were looking at each other's dresses, the boys would be looking at the girls (not that they cared about dresses) and the girls would be looking at the boys. Both girls, both Emma and Marina, were estranged from their mother, for her lack of sympathy, in their eyes, towards Sandro, and were embarrassed by their father, his mood swings, his drinking, and the cruel and outrageous way he too had failed to love their elder brother Sandro who was, in their eyes, so brave, so cool and so beautiful. But their father had criticised him first of all for dyeing his hair (the girls too both dyed their hair, so why shouldn't Sandro?), criticised him for his clothes (he was now wearing a Dolce and Gabbana tartan suit, which made him easily the most fashionable man present), and lost his self-control entirely when Sandro had started to act as an adult, which was, they considered, completely out of order. As for the drug charge now hanging over Sandro, it was time for their parents, both of them, to join the real world.

As for their little brother Beppe, now wearing the sort of dark suit that made him look like an adult, though a small one, which, in a strange way, he was, and whose hair had been cut in a new more grown-up way, they hated him. Their hatred reached a crescendo as they saw him perform his duties as witness. He was such a little creep, putting himself forward like this, and the only one who still spoke civilly to their father, for which they could not forgive him. But Beppe was oblivious of their hostility at this present moment, for his attention was fixed elsewhere, either on his duties as his cousin's witness, or looking across the church to where the family of don Calogero di Rienzi sat; in particular, he was looking at a girl of about his age, perhaps a little younger, who they knew was Isabella di Rienzi, who was now to be their relation by marriage, being the niece of their cousin's wife. They had all met that time when the Santucci family had been to visit the new baby of don Calogero and his wife. Beppe had subsequently seen Isabella and Natalia in Catania, and he now wanted to renew the friendship, not that it was a friendship, at least not yet, but he felt shy at the prospect of speaking to them afterwards, but at the same time anxious because if he did not speak to them this evening, when would he be able to do so again?

The two girls had also spotted Isabella and her sister and wondered if they should notice them at the party afterwards, or whether she was beneath them. Isabella was very young, very pretty, they both thought. They had heard that her dead mother had been pretty, and considering he was so old, don Calogero was handsome too.

The dinner, as banquets went, was very long and very dull, and they were all stuck at their places for a very long time. Beppe looked over to where Isabella was sitting, with her sister Natalia, under the stern guardianship of her stepmother Anna Maria; he longed to get up between courses and say hello, but he knew everyone would be watching him. He was glad to be away from his sisters, both of whom he disliked being with, and with whom he had no interests in common at all. They were on a table for the younger people along with Isabella and her sister, while he was with his cousin the groom and his new wife and other important people, as he had been the witness.

He had been placed next to Ceccina who was, he realised with a jolt, like her husband, only a few years older than himself, but already the mother of three children. He calculated from what she said that she was nineteen or twenty at most, so five or six years his senior, as was Traiano, a few seats away, who was the same age. She complimented him on his new haircut, which had replaced his previous little boy bowl cut; the previous day, a lady had come round to Renzo's flat and cut his hair, and offered to cut Beppe's hair too, as they had been there, he and Traiano, to offer moral support while Renzo had had his hair cut as well. As for the suit, which she asked about, he had had it for some time, and he had bought it, with his mother, on a trip to Milan. His mother was so nice, remarked Ceccina, with a smile. Then she spoke of his grandfather and asked after his health. Don Lorenzo, reported Beppe, was doing well, and he and his mother Angela were visiting most days. He was usually in bed, but sometimes was able to sit in a chair. It was only a matter of time, but the priest don Michele was visiting regularly with Holy Communion, and when they were there, they all said the Rosary round the bedside while don Lorenzo dozed. Ceccina was pleased to hear this. This was the way men, old men, were meant to die: surrounded by prayers and children and women and with a priest in attendance. She hoped that don Lorenzo would remember Beppe accordingly in his will, though she did not say this out loud. Beppe was now saying that it was sad don Gino could not be with them, but how glad he was to be the witness to his cousin's wedding, and how pleased he had been to spend time with him and Traiano beforehand. She smiled at this too.

Sandro had been placed with the adults, much to his relief, and was with some people from Messina, whom he did not know, who complimented him on his suit. His eyes surveyed the vast room, and the vast crowd, some of whom he recognised. These were the people who had been his father's friends, and who were now the friends of someone else. He disliked his father, but felt for him too. At the table, perhaps not knowing who he was, they were discussing the two old Santucci brothers, his grandfather and his great-uncle, neither of whom were here; one of whom was very close to death. He heard this discussed as if he were hearing news of remote strangers who meant nothing to him. This was not his world. Very soon he would finish his degree and then go to do a further degree, preferably in America, and escape, provided his coming drug case did not muck up his chances of getting a visa. His eyes looked at the army of waiters marshalling the plates of lasagne. His eyes began to check out the various girls in the room. Perhaps some of them had noticed his suit as well.

The bride and the groom were making their way down the length of the tables, shaking hands, kissing guests, smiling, being polite. On arrival from church, after the photographs, they had gone up to the suite that had been set aside for them, and there, with a minimum of undressing, had consummated the marriage. Elena accepted congratulations from all, and was told that she looked radiant, while a triumphant Renzo accepted the knowing looks and congratulations from his male friends, and the innocent felicitations of the women. Sandro watched his cousin with little interest, but tried his best to be polite and agreeable to the bride. Muniddu stood to embrace Renzo and pat him on the back, and shook hands respectfully with the new signora Santucci. The children, especially the girls, were keen to see the bride close up and compliment her on her looks and her dress, while the boys looked at the groom with a mixture of respect and embarrassment.

'They have already done it,' Traiano said, leaning over towards Beppe. 'You can tell by the way he is carrying himself. You can tell by the way she is looking.'

'Don't be vulgar,' said Ceccina, crossly.

'We did the same at our wedding,' said Traiano. 'All couples do. It is part of the relief of being married at last.'

'Don't be vulgar,' repeated Ceccina. 'Men!' she said, with a pitying smile, remembering how her own husband had done his best to rip her wedding dress off the moment they were alone, despite her pregnancy. 'You must not listen to him, Beppe,' she said, turning to the boy.

'I won't,' he said. 'But I am fourteen now, so I do know something about these things.'

'Well, that is more than I do, and I am older than you,' said Traiano with a smile.

Elena was surrounded by happy women, all her friends from Catania. The dress, the make-up, the hairstyle, the shoes, the party, the choice of church, the honeymoon: all were to be discussed. There was a little edge to Giuseppina's questions, given that the expenditure on this wedding was at least ten times that on hers had been. But Renzo Santucci was rich. Elena smiled to be among friendly faces from Catania, feeling as she did a little overwhelmed by all this grandeur. She looked at Ceccina, and said she would miss Catania. She looked at Giuseppina and hoped she would visit often. But she was very pleased, very happy. Her husband echoed this sentiment as he talked to the men: very pleased, very happy, and they knew what he meant. Yes, everything had gone wrong, the death of poor Gino, his arrest, his guilty plea, the sentence awaiting him for his drug use, but from now on everything would change, he would change. He was married now, married to the boss's sister, and he had the friendship of Traiano. He looked at Traiano, and tried to express what he felt. The moments spent upstairs when they had sealed the marriage; the moments that would follow; the birth of children, the baptisms, the other family occasions. This was what really mattered: family life, being married, being married to the woman you loved; and at that moment he loved her, he saw it all clearly now. He loved her. He felt madly, blissfully happy and, at the same time, relieved. There were no sad thoughts to cloud his mind.

Beppe had just made up his mind to go over and speak to Isabella, who was looking at him, aware of his presence, inviting him over, clearly, without looking as if she wanted him to come over, but wanting him to do so all the same – it was as if he could read her mind – when, towering over him suddenly was the figure of don Calogero her father, whom, in his distraction, he had not seen approach. He was a little taken aback, as he had been thinking of the daughter, and here he was confronted with the father.

He was smiling now, looking down on him, with a hand on his shoulder.

'How are the lemons?' he asked, smiling. 'You must visit my garden, the one at Donnafugata, soon. Well, it is my wife's really. But I get to enjoy it.'

'I would like to see it very much,' he said. 'Are your daughters well?' Beppe asked, feeling this was bold. 'And Renato and Sebastiano? And Romano?'

'Clever of you to remember their names,' said Calogero. 'The boys are still too young for this, so we left them at home with the new nanny. But the girls are here. Why haven't you spoken to them?' He noted the boy's hot blush. 'Come, I will take you over there. Come with me and we will see how they are getting on.'

The great banquet was coming to an end. Vodka sorbet was being served to the adults, and ice-cream to the children. Beppe had his ice-cream next to Isabella, both of them tortured by shyness. Marina and Emma, who had used their brother's approach to facilitate one of their own, found this quite amusing, and spoke to the younger sister, Natalia, with interest. They listened to what she said about her father, the woman she referred to as her mother, and their life in Donnafugata, Palermo and Catania. The party, having been rather formal, was now becoming rather ragged. The children having sat down for so long, were getting restless and were becoming noisy, and the adults were dispersing, the more energetic to go for a walk down the via Roma, to try and work off the food; others, the lucky ones who had rooms in the hotel, heading upstairs to sleep for a few hours before the evening party began; some, not going to the evening party, heading gratefully home. Others were heading up to the rooms and to bed for other purposes: Alfio and his wife Giuseppina had disappeared, and so had Traiano and Ceccina.

Tonino had spent an agreeable few hours, which had passed very quickly, with Roberto and Gabriella, with Bonelli her brother and his mother, along with the family of Muniddu, who had been placed at the same table with him. Also present was his official girlfriend, Petra, Roberto's sister, who had had permission from her mother to come, provided Roberto was there to look after her. Roberto, Bonelli and Petra, along with Gabriella, were now preparing to leave, to go back to Catania. In the mêlée as the dinner ended, he and Petra had gone to explore the hotel, and had exchanged some sweet and passionate kisses in a deserted corridor upstairs. He was pleased about that and he was pleased that Petra looked so beautiful in her dress, but at the same time he felt a pang of jealousy as he watched her go with her brother, and Bonelli and Gabriella, the latter not disguising very well her interest in Roberto. He and his mother were staying in the hotel, and his mother was now deep in conversation with Muniddu's wife, who was expecting a third child. He felt himself being drawn into conversation with Muniddu, with whom, so far, he had only exchanged pleasantries, and whom he had not seen since their trip to Rome; neither had referred to their previous acquaintance, but now there was no avoiding their shared past.

Muniddu asked about Petra. He explained as best he could, and was relieved that Muniddu understood: they were boy and girl, but they were not sleeping together, as that was, by agreement, not allowed. Muniddu nodded in understanding; it had been the same between his wife and himself before they were married. He asked about Petra's parents, her brother, and received enough information to understand that they were ordinary people. Muniddu nodded. There were such people, but he himself had not married one. His father-in-law, his brothers-in-law, they had all been in the same line of business as himself. One married in, one did not marry out. If one did, there were so many things the wife did not understand; but his own wife, like Tonino's mother, she never asked, never questioned. It made life so much simpler. He asked about his father's release from jail. No one was clear about this, but it was going to happen, and happen sooner rather than later.

Muniddu considered. It was clear that he was about to offer advice, and Tonino, knowing that Muniddu was a considerable man, was most intent on hearing what it would be.

'You may want to consider leaving home, leaving it to your parents, that is, and coming here. Now that poor don Gino is dead there is need for someone here. That someone is me, I feel; I have known don Renzo all his life, I can look after him; but I could use a clever boy like you.'

Tonino nodded, taking this in.

The children had disappeared, but now reappeared: the daughter Rosalia, who was about his age, and very pretty, and her younger brother, who approached with another teenage boy in tow, whom Tonino immediately recognised as the youngest Santucci, Beppe. The latter greeted Muniddu with great affection and kissed his cheek; he also kissed the cheek of the signora, explaining how he had had some trouble getting away from the other guests. It was clear he was an old friend of the family.

In an upstairs room, Ceccina and Traiano lay in bed together. Her dress and his suit were neatly hung on hangers, in case they became crumpled; so was his shirt; the floor was littered with various other articles of clothing. Her finger was tracing the outline of his ear, and he was giggling. Then he was serious, and she sensed it. She had great skill in sensing his moods and reading his mind.

'I miss Gino,' he said. 'I am surprised I do, but I do miss him. He was not my type at all: stupid, loud, he drank too much, he took too many things I disapproved of, and he, well, he had the wrong ideas. But I feel sorry he has gone. I miss Corrado, too, and it was nice seeing him, but it is sad he is so far away. I suppose we will go often to Verona. I miss Pasqualina. I need my wife and my children, but I also need the wider family. I wonder what the children are doing now? Are they missing us, as much as we are missing them? Or are they delighted to be with their grandmother, their cousins, their aunts? I like Bonelli, I like his sister, but I am not sure I can trust them as much as our own people. We need to look after our children, protect them. Look at Sandro, don Antonio's son…. We must look after them.'

'We will, we will,' she reassured him.

'Poor Gino, no one cares he is dead, except his brother and his parents. If anything should happen to me….'

'Don't say that,' she said.

'The money is all tied up with Anna Maria, but I think she is fair and she would not rob you. And you know there is money in other places, too, don't you?'

'You have told me.'

'That picture, dammit. We will get that back. How dare they?'

'The calmer you keep on that matter, the less you show you have anything to hide,' she reasoned.

'Bonelli and Greco will sort it out,' he said. He sighed. 'This time next year…?' he asked.

She knew this phrase. He used it when asking if she might be pregnant.

'It is too early to tell,' she said.

The conversation was an interesting one, Tonino felt. Beppe spoke to Muniddu like a devoted nephew, and he was clearly still a little boy, even though he and Tonino were roughly the same age, and the same too went for Riccardo, Muniddu's son. Beppe was asked about his grandfather, and spoke of his almost daily visits, about how his grandfather was faring, his tone hinting that the outcome was not in doubt, and not far off; mentioning that his grandfather had had the priest visit him and received the sacraments (Muniddu's wife nodded at this with great appreciation). But he avoided the more adult topics, such as his cousin's and his brother's arrest: drug addiction and the role of lawyers were not in his sphere of interest. It was as if he did not know these things ever happened. They were, of course, happening all around him, but he seemed oblivious of this. He was congratulated on his role as best man and witness to the wedding, and spoke of his affection for his cousin, and what a pleasure it had been to spend time with him before the wedding, along with Traiano.

'Papa,' said Riccardo, butting in, 'They came and cut his hair, as you can see, and they also shaved him. That is why he looks so different.'

'I told you not to tell anyone,' remonstrated Beppe.

This first shave had indeed taken place, but it embarrassed him. Riccardo's rosy cheeks and smooth upper lip were still unshaven.

'And they poured hot wax on don Renzo's chest and pulled it off to make him smooth,' said Riccardo, coming out with more embarrassing details.

'I would never allow anyone to do that to me,' said Muniddu. 'Would you?' he asked, turning to Tonino.

Tonino, who had seen Muniddu's thickly carpeted chest in circumstances he preferred to forget, replied: 'No, sir.'

'It is something they do for weddings only,' said Riccardo knowledgeably.

'Sir,' said Beppe, changing the subject. 'My mother is going to Turin next month. She is going to a conference there, and it is at the same time that Juventus is playing, and you know how Riccardo loves Juvé. She was saying to me that I could come too, and it is a weekend, so we would not miss school, and I could bring a friend with me. Well, I would like to take Riccardo.'

Riccardo's face lit up.

'Let me talk to the signora,' said Muniddu.

'Thanks, sir,' said Beppe warmly, knowing that it would be unwise to pursue the matter.

It was only later that Tonino got Beppe to himself. Before that Beppe, he was pleased to notice, had spent time talking to the signora Grassi, his mother, and he could tell, talking about him. He wondered about this. Clearly Beppe was a 'nice' boy, just like Riccardo: young, innocent, sweet, interested in football, with a pleasant smile and an open manner; polite, respectful, eager to please, all the things that a teenage boy ought to be, all of the things, he thought, that he, Tonino, was not. In addition, unlike Riccardo, he was rich and used to being rich, without being spoiled. He could fly to Turin and watch a football match, but only with parental permission. He was newly shaved, growing up, but clearly not wanting to grow up just yet. He presumably liked girls, as did all boys, but had never kissed one.

The trouble with this picture, which was so complete, was that Tonino did not quite believe it. It was not that there was anything fake about Beppe, it was rather that Tonino did not believe that there were any nice boys in the world. Not only from his experience, but also from his belief, his profoundly held belief, there were no truly good people in the world, apart, of course, from his own mother. Teenagers such as himself were greedy, violent, manipulative, cold-hearted and lascivious. It was difficult to believe that Beppe was not like this too; but it was hard to believe that he was, and successful in hiding it. Surely that was not possible?

He could understand that Riccardo was naïve and innocent, as it would undoubtedly be the case that Muniddu and the signora kept him away from the world, terrified that he would grow up to be like his father. Sure enough, as they left the hotel to walk up and down the via Roma, Riccardo revealed his other passion, apart from Juventus: the desire to be a doctor. He and Beppe, though not at the same school, often did their homework together, at Riccardo's house. Beppe had first been driven to school by Muniddu when he had been five years' old. Tonino could picture the joy Muniddu and his wife must feel at the friendship between their son and Beppe, child of the richest family in Sicily. What a step up for them! But didn't Beppe see this, or did he sincerely accept this friendship at face value? Could he really be so innocent as not to realise that he was in a tank filled with sharks and piranhas?

The four youngsters went, with parental permission, for a little walk. Riccardo walked with Beppe, and Tonino with Rosalia. Eventually, as they walked up and down the via Roma, Beppe and Tonino fell into step with each other and spoke. Perhaps he was oversuspicious to think that this had been carefully planned, arranged, and delayed till now.

'Do you support Juventus?' was his first question.

He replied that he did not, that he really did not have much time for football, and that if he did, he would support a local team, preferably the Elephants.

'But your mother supports Roma,' Beppe pointed out.

'She does, she does. She likes Francesco Totti.'

'Everyone likes Francesco Totti,' agreed Beppe. 'He is so beautiful, so they say. It is a pity he does not play for Juventus. You know don Traiano and don Calogero? All our friends from Catania are so nice. That is what my cousin Renzo says. And now I am related to them all by marriage.'

'My mother is a great friend of don Calogero's mother,' said Tonino. 'We have known each other all our lives.'

'That is really nice,' said Beppe. 'So, you know his daughters well?'

'Of course.'

'They are going to spending more and more time here, as the dottoressa Tancredi has to be here so much. Maybe I will get to know them better in future. I really liked Catania when I was there in December.'

'I am pleased to hear it.'

'Maybe next time you come here, or next time I go there…'

'I would be delighted,' said Tonino. 'I could show you around, if you like. I don't have a phone, but I can give you my mother's number.'

'That would be very nice,' said Beppe.

He put the number into his phone. As Tonino watched him do so, he wondered if he would ever use it.

As they returned to the hotel, they met don Calogero himself. He shook hands with all of them, and after doing so with Beppe, pulled him towards himself and hugged him, much to the boy's evident delight. At the same time, he did not ignore Tonino, but tugged his earlobe, as was his habit, and told him that he had given his mother something for him. Tonino knew what it was – payment for the job in Enna. He felt pleased, not just by the thought of the money, which he imagined would be considerable, but by the knowledge of the boss's favour, and that he was trusted with secrets. Beppe must have heard what he said, but gave no sign that he had.

'My daughters have gone home,' the boss was saying, 'But they will be back for the evening party. They need to rest and to change their clothes for some reason. You are staying for the evening party?' he asked, looking at Beppe in particular. 'Then you can entertain them.'

He smiled a smile full of goodwill.

The music for the dancing was starting to blare, and at the back of the hotel, Sandro was smoking a quiet cigarette in the open air. All he could hear was the thump, thump, thump of the music, nothing more. It was almost peaceful, out in the February air. It was a little cold, and he buttoned up his tartan jacket. After a moment, he realised he was not alone, but someone had joined him in this secluded spot by the dustbins. He looked. It was Tonino. He had a vague idea who he was; he had seen him earlier, talking to Muniddu and his family. One knew who these people were, with their bull necks, their broad chests and their suits which strained at the seams.

'Hi,' he said.

'Hi,' replied Tonino, taking this as an invitation not to go away.

He took out a cigarette of his own, and as soon as he had done so, Sandro leaned forwards and offered him a light from his heavy, expensive, gold-plated lighter. Tonino looked at it with something like envy, an envy which Sandro did not notice. The lighter was impressive, the suit was impressive, as were the shoes. The suit was indeed a beautiful thing, but it was a pity about the man in it, thin, skinny, rangy, all arms and legs, with those narrow eyes like his cousin don Renzo, in fact even uglier than don Renzo if that were possible.

'You are from Catania? You work for don Calogero? How's work?' asked Sandro.

'Hard. Busy. But it has to be done,' said Tonino, not that Sandro would know, he thought.

'How long have you worked for don Calogero?'

'Forever,' said Tonino. 'My father worked for his father; my mother knows his mother.'

'And you know Muniddu? Well, it is obvious that they like you. I mean, they invited you to this, didn't they? Quite an honour,' said Sandro. 'There are lots of people here whom I do not know. I know Muniddu because he used to be my father's driver.'

His tone revealed that he thought none of the people there interesting. Then why was he condescending to speak to him, wondered Tonino, but only for a moment.

'Have you got any cocaine?' asked Sandro.

'Why ask me?' asked Tonino.

'Because the people who used to give it to me are not giving it to me any more,' said Sandro.

He meant, of course, his cousin and Gino. One was dead, the other supposedly reformed. It had been very noticeable that the groom had been drinking water all night.

Tonino looked at him. He did have some cocaine, as it turned out; he had brought some, not for himself, but in case he met anyone who might like some, someone he wanted to make a good impression on. Perhaps Sandro was such a person.

'I can fix you up. I have some in my room on the top floor,' said Tonino. 'But aren't you in trouble enough already?'

'Oh, we have got lawyers, and I am just a young boy whose been led astray. I have just got to keep off it in case they test me again. Not that they will. I can risk it. My defence is that I had never tried it before, and Gino, the one who fell off the cliff, the idiot, was the one who persuaded me to take it. If he hadn't been stupid enough to fall of the cliff....'

'I don't think he did so deliberately.'

'These people,' said Sandro with distaste, as if they were always falling off cliffs, just to inconvenience him. 'If he had not died, the police would not have come; and if my cousin Renzo had not decided to admit it, something I cannot and will not do... The Americans can block your visa if you have a drugs conviction. Damn it, no one has a drugs conviction nowadays, so why should I? These people, it is all their fault.'

'They are your people,' said Tonino.

'They are not. They are my relatives, the people I have grown up with: my father, my uncle, my mother the religious hypocrite, but I hate them all. My own father tried to shoot me, for God's sake. I am not like them. Don't ever say I am like them. Anyway, what the hell do you know?'

'Nothing, nothing at all,' said Tonino.

'You were talking to my brother earlier. I noticed. What did that lousy little kid want?' Sandro now asked.

'Nothing. I was just talking to him because he was talking to Muniddu, and I happen to know Muniddu.'

They agreed to meet later for the cocaine. Having finished his cigarette, he went back to the party and sat with Muniddu, his wife and his own mother for a time, while the ones he thought of as the children were dancing. Tonino had no intention of dancing himself. Then don Traiano approached. Traiano spoke to Muniddu in a very friendly manner, was introduced to the signora, whom he congratulated profusely, and then said a few words to signora Grassi, onto whom he turned all his charm.

'Do you want to stretch your legs?' he asked, turning to Tonino.

'Sure, boss.'

'We will walk around,' said Traiano, as if this were the most natural thing in the world. 'Can I take your young man away from you for a bit?' he asked signora Grassi.

He took him away. Traiano continued smiling. His arm was casually cast around Tonino's shoulder, a mark of favour. Tonino could smell Traiano's sweat, which was repulsive; at the same time, he could feel his warmth, which was frightening, if he were inclined to fear, which he hoped he was not.

'The boss has rewarded you, hasn't he?' said Traiano, casually.

Tonino felt a prickle of fear, and the hint of a cold sweat.

'He told me that he had given my mother something, but I have not seen it, I haven't checked how much,' said Tonino.

'What is it for?' asked Traiano.

'He often gives me presents, you know what he is like, our boss. When I was a kid, it was a euro for an ice cream, or five or ten for carrying messages. It must have been the same for you, don Traiano. Now I am older…. He gives me presents. But he knows I give it to my mother; it is his way of giving money to her, and he does that because his mother tells him to.'

'Your mother is looked after by the Confraternity. And you are handsomely rewarded, aren't you? Well, if the boss wants to be extra generous, that is his affair. Who am I to question it? You have been smoking, haven't you? Don't lie. I can smell it on your clothes.'

'I can't lie to you, boss.'

'I don't think don Calogero would be so generous to you if he knew you smoked, would he?' asked don Traiano. 'He would expect me to discipline you, wouldn't he?'

They paused in the midst of the tables, where everyone could see them. Tonino knew this was deliberate. He knew too what Traiano was thinking: that this was deliberate.

'You like Muniddu?' he asked.

'Of course, and his wife, and the daughter and the little brother too. They are all so nice.'

'Good, good. You met Sandro Santucci? Yes? And his sisters? No? Just as well. They are here, as are our boss's daughters. But keep away from them, stick to your girlfriend, stick to Muniddu's family. Remember that we are the same sort of people, you and I.'

'Of course, boss,' said Tonino. 'I know my place.'

It was a warning, he knew. He had been spotted. Not only had Traiano spotted the boss handing the money to his mother, he had spotted him as a threat, a potential threat, as a person with ambitions. They parted; on the way back to join the others, there was Muniddu, looking at him with meaning. He knew his place.

The groom came downstairs in good time for the dancing, leaving the bride up in her suite to change into her second dress of the day. They had spent an hour or so together in bed, and he had done his duty once more, and no doubt would do it again before dawn came, he was determined. He felt the urgent necessity of fathering a child before it was too late. The death of Gino, a week ago to the day, more or less, had affected him that way. Well, he had done his best and she had been satisfied, he thought; though it had been hard work, hard dispiriting work. He felt that his limbs were heavy and his brain thick with, not drugs and alcohol, as in the past, but something entirely different, the lack of drugs, the lack of alcohol. He had not snorted a line or even had a drink since his arrest. His whole body cried out for the drug, and the only thing he could think of, or so it seemed, was cocaine, and after that drink. But he had promised his new wife, he had promised his brother-in-law, and more importantly, he had promised himself that he would not touch the white powder again, or drink again. From now on he would be healthy. In a sense, his own wedding was the very worst place for him to be: everyone was drinking, and people were constantly going upstairs to either make love in the bedrooms or to snort cocaine, or both. Well, he had done the first. But marriage was a grim business, as was life. The fun was now over. But if he had to lead a life of privation and suffering, then he would make sure others did too. He would deprive those he did not like of life itself, he decided.

He was joined by his cousin, his best man, young Beppe. On the whole he liked Beppe, but this was because of some rather twisted reasons. He liked Beppe more than the rest of the family of cousins. He hated Antonio, Beppe's father, who had killed his own father. He hated Sandro, who was making so much trouble about the arrest and was absurdly planning to pretend he was an innocent victim, and not plead guilty to the drugs charge. He was indifferent to the girls, as he was to all his female relations, apart from his Aunt Angela, his father's sister; but he quite liked Beppe; and Beppe had the supreme advantage at this moment of not being a drinker or a drug user, being too young for both. That made him tolerable.

'How are you?' asked Beppe.

'Married,' said Renzo with bitterness. 'It will happen to you one day, so watch out. Have you been speaking to don Calogero's daughters? My new nieces?' A thought occurred to him. 'How is your grandfather? How is Uncle Lorenzo?'

'Not well,' said Beppe. 'We have been seeing him every day.'

'We?'

'Me and my mother. Sandro won't go, as he says he does not like it, and my sisters are too busy.'

'And Uncle Domenico, how is he? I thought he was here earlier. He must have gone home.'

'He is fine, but he says he no longer likes late nights.'

'How things have changed,' remarked Renzo. 'There was a time when he was not frightened of anything, but now he is frightened of staying up too late. Where is Sandro?'

'He disappeared upstairs. He is supposed to be taking me home later on.'

'Was he with some girl?'

'He was with my sister,' said Beppe. 'Emma. Not Marina.'

'I can imagine what he is doing,' said Renzo.

It was what he wished he was doing, snorting cocaine. Something he had done so much of, but would never do again. As if on cue, Elena appeared, in her new outfit, and kissed her new husband's cheek with affection. He accepted this tribute, which he assumed was her way of thanking him for his exertions in the bedroom. It rather surprised him, but she was as desperate to have a child as he was, possibly more so. She looked at her new cousin, Beppe, with a smile too, and then left to circulate around the room, realising that her new husband was happy to be left alone for the moment. The whole of married life stretched before them. Her watched her go, wondering whether they would have a baby by Christmas. Traiano then came, leaving his wife to the bride and to Giuseppina, Alfio's wife; and Alfio joined them.

The feeling of depression was catching, and soon became severe, Traiano noticed. After coitus, every animal was sad, as Aristotle had observed, and they had all, with the exception of Beppe, been upstairs for just that purpose. In addition, Renzo was probably reflecting that by now he would normally have taken a great deal of drink and drugs, and there hung over him the knowledge that this was now a thing of the past. Moreover, all of them, though in different ways, felt the absence of their friend, Gino, who had been with them last week, but was no longer there and would be with them no more. Even Alfio, Traiano sensed, mourned him; so what if you had killed someone? You could still feel the pain of absence. The presence of Alfio brought the thought of Rosario to his mind, and how much he had loved him. But he had had no choice. But he was filled with sadness, though whether it was pity for himself or for the dead Rosario, he was not sure. This was why, he knew, he exercised the mental discipline of never thinking of Rosario, of never allowing his heart to feel anything for any human being outside his family. And yet, had he not already broken this resolution? He knew he had, aware of Beppe standing next to him, aware that he could not be indifferent to him.

Calogero joined them. He noticed their glum demeanour, at least that of Traiano, Alfio and Renzo, but not Beppe. He himself was exuberantly happy, and showed it with a subdued smile. His satisfaction at getting rid of Gino was immense. He had killed him, or arranged his killing, and now had taken his wife. That obedient boy Tonino had arranged things in Enna, the town conveniently half way between Catania and Palermo. In his various trips between Catania and Palermo, there would be numerous stops at Enna in future, he was sure. And she would be there, waiting for him. He thought of the child his brother had left behind, Tino. He thought of the children to come. And he thought of her and them, all utterly dependant on him. She would love him and fear him; she would fear offending him, fear losing him, fear losing his favour. But would he love her? Not in the least. Had he loved Stefania? Did he love his current wife? He thought not. Did he really care about the sexual act itself? It was very nice to have a woman desire you, but did he desire them? Not so very much. What after all was sex, when you had experienced the drug of power? Power over women, power over men, that is what really counted. As he looked around these three, he realised just how complete was the power he enjoyed. There was Alfio, unable to beget a child, who, having killed his best friend, would now not stop at anything to please his boss, for he had broken the last barrier. Alfio was not a genius, but he was clever enough to know what he had let himself into, surely. Renzo was stupid, and perhaps did not realise Gino's death had not been an accident. But even if he did, he could surely work out that he, Calogero, had the power of life and death over all of them. As for Traiano, he was surely clever enough to know exactly the way things stood. All of them were his men, his slaves. Renzo's need for drink and drugs was nothing compared for his need for the boss. That was surely the more harmful dependency.

Upstairs in what was Tonino's room, Sandro Santucci lay back on the bed and felt the sweet hit of longed for cocaine course through his brain, and the welcome numbness of his jaw. Oh, how he had longed for this moment. He savoured its intensity. For these few moments, nothing mattered, only the pleasure the drug afforded. For just a few moments, the hell of existence receded. It seemed that it did not quite matter so much now that his father hated him, and that he hated his father; that his mother preferred Beppe, and that he could not forgive her, nor she him; and that he hated Beppe with a deeply rooted passion; it did not matter so much that women would only sleep with him because he was rich. All these things receded, and his mind was fleetingly at rest. He closed his eyes.

He had come into the room with his sister Emma and with the boy from Catania, Tonino, who had supplied the drug. He was now aware even with his eyes blissfully shut that he was alone. Then he was aware of something else, low voices, his and hers, and then, from the bathroom next door, sounds which, as soon as he placed them, were unmistakeable. He managed a gentle laugh. Tonino thought he was being discreet, and the knowledge of what he was doing with Emma made Sandro smile at the thought of the way the boy would supply more and more cocaine.

In the ballroom of the hotel, there was huge excitement among the younger people. Even Marina Santucci felt it. She and her sister had felt that such an occasion as this wedding was a little beneath them, as the guest list comprised not the richest and best of Palermo alone, but people from all backgrounds from all over Sicily; but a dance was a dance and she was happy to let her snobbishness go for a moment. As soon as her sister came back from wherever she had gone, she would dance, but she had to wait for her, as she explained to several young men. Their parents, both of whom could not stand noise in their own differing ways, had left, charging the girls to look after Beppe, who was determined to stay. Giuseppina was there, keeping an eye on her nieces, Isabella and Natalia, which satisfied signora Santucci that nothing could go wrong. Beppe and the others could come back in taxis when they got bored. One person who was delighted with the dance was Rosalia. Her mother too had decided to go home, leaving her brother, telling Rosalia that their father would bring them home when the time came. Muniddu and his wife were ambitious for their children and did not want to pass up this opportunity for them to socialise with not just Beppe but the rest of the family.

Tonino alone of the youngsters, when he came downstairs, faced the prospect of the dance with a measure of dread. He had never been to a dance before, at least not on this scale, and while some adolescents had a natural ability to dance, and a love of it, he felt awkward and self-conscious. Luckily his girlfriend Petra was gone, so could not drag him to the dance floor. But fate was kind; even before he got to the ballroom, he saw don Traiano through the door of the bar, who gestured for him to enter. He joined the men. They were drinking, taking advantage of the absence of don Renzo, who was on the dance floor, and forever sentenced to drink mineral water. He sat down next to don Traiano, and when the waiter approached, asked for some red wine, his first proper drink of the evening.

A few moments later, Emma Santucci passed by and looked in, saw him raise the glass of red wine to his lips; he did not see her; she looked at him for just a moment, and then smiled, passing on.

'A lot of money, a lot of money,' the boss was saying. 'Much more than we have ever made. The risks are huge, but the opportunity even bigger.'

'But can we trust these Arabs?' Traiano was asking.

'It is not a question of trusting them, it is a question of judging them on their record. And their record has been 100% so far.'

'So far,' put in Traiano.

'So far, yes, but why would their interests change? So far there have been terrorist attacks everywhere, but not a single one in Italy. Why? Because of the agreement we have with them. They leave us alone, and we do business with them. They gain as much as we do. Look, I am flying to the Gulf, you can come, and you too Costantino, then we will talk money on the journey, and we will meet these people and get their guarantee, and the guarantee of the Africans. Then we get to run the resort on our own terms, a private fiefdom, and then, with the men we have, we will have our own private army to hire out, our own Sicilian Foreign Legion.'

'Do you want to go to work in Africa?' said Traiano to Tonino. 'Lots of killing, lots of back girls.'

'Sounds good, boss.'

'He has got his mother here, don't forget, and his girlfriend. We can use him here,' said don Calogero genially, who was sitting on the other side of Traiano. 'Anyway, we will not be short of takers. You watch. From the way he talks about it,' he said inclining his head towards Alfio, 'and the way he talks about it,' nodding towards Costantino, 'It sounds like an earthly paradise. To me, and to my wife, it sounds like a financial paradise. We stand to make billions.'

It was after midnight when the bride and groom made their final appearance together and left, to the cheers of the crowd and the throwing of confetti. After that, everyone started to say goodnight to everyone else, and began to leave. Sandro, forgetting his promise to look after his sisters and his brother, left as well, to walk down the via Roma and to find a suitable bar or nightclub. His sisters left too, to go home in a taxi. Beppe found himself abandoned, but Muniddu promised to take him home in his car along with Rosalia and Riccardo. They drove northwards to the outer part of the new town where Beppe was left at the gate of an opulent modern villa; they watched him enter and then drove back towards the Corso Calatafimi. As they drove, the children talked about who had danced with whom, and who had spoken to whom, and Muniddu felt satisfied. At the hotel, Tonino, who had seen them all depart, went upstairs on his own (his mother had gone to her room some time previously) to go to bed. He entered his room, locked the door, and took off his jacket. He opened the envelope and counted the money that he had been given earlier, but had not had a chance to look at. It was all in five hundred notes. There were forty of them. He was pleased, very pleased. He looked at the clock. It was just after one in the morning. He got undressed, got into bed, and slept.

In Catania, Roberto looked at the clock, noting the late hour. It was already afternoon. What had woken him was the sound of murmuring voices, coming from the kitchen, two rooms away. He had a lecture in a few hours, he was sure, but for the moment he luxuriated in the soft bed, the warmth of the room, so different from the discomfort of home. On returning to Catania late last night, he had left his sister at home, claiming he had to go 'out'. He had texted Gabriella and accepted her invitation to come round. The lovemaking had been intense, and he could feel the remnants of that intensity in his aching limbs. Of all the girls he had slept with, this one was the one to hang on to, he reflected: she was not a girl, but a woman, and he liked the fact that she was six or seven years his senior; she was perfectly beautiful, tall, long haired, long limbed. And she was educated and, he assumed, rich. Well, she was richer than most people he knew, and everything about her advertised bourgeois respectability. How beautiful it was to live a life where everything was beautiful, where existence was not a struggle, where one was not worn down by poverty and adversity. How beautiful, in short, to live the sort of life that up to now he had not been used to. His poor mother, always having to make do; their house, constantly needing repairs it never fully received; the dark dank communal stairs that stank of rubbish; the broken bulbs, the unpainted walls. No wonder his father had left, though he imagined he would be disappointed to find the life of the poor in Rome not much different to the life of the poor in degraded Catania. But maybe the woman he was with would console him.

Women were the great consolation, and he had been consoled regularly in his teenage years by various conquests, which had allowed him to delude himself that he was, even if only for a few moments, not an unfortunate creature at the bottom of the pile, but someone in his own right, someone desirable. Well, how lucky he was now to be with someone who clearly desired him as much as he desired her. And if that were not enough, there was Tonino as well.

Just as he could not believe his good luck with Gabriella, he could not believe his luck with Tonino. They had met by accident on the night train, after all, and that chance encounter had surely changed his life. The short, muscular, pugilistic boy was his way into that world everyone knew existed but which the blind never saw, the world of privilege and power and wealth. The alliance with Tonino filled him with as much dread and excitement as his relationship with Gabriella. The risks were huge, but he was going to become someone. He already was. He thought of the money in his bank account, his mother's bank account, his three sisters' bank accounts. Women were a consolation, but money, money in the bank, that was what really mattered, particularly when you had grown up not having any.

He looked at the clock by the bed, and he heard once more the voices from the kitchen, and resolved to get up. Before he could do so, she entered, announced that her brother was there, and told him to join them. He did as she told him, and in a few moments, he was with them in the kitchen, fully dressed, apart from his shoes, his bare feet proclaiming that he was now at home in the house.

A cup of coffee was waiting for him, and he took it with thanks, and shook hands with the brother. They politely wished each other good morning.

'We were talking about your friend, Traiano Antonescu,' explained Ruggero Bonelli smoothly.

'He is more a friend of a friend, if you see what I mean. I am sure you know him better than I do.'

'He doesn't have friends; he just has people whose interests coincide with his. People like me. We are both on the receiving end of the wrong sort of attention thanks to this picture. I have to give evidence in court on a future date that I inherited the picture from Professor Leopardi, whose works were never properly catalogued. Our friend Greco says that the picture cannot be traced, as it is too generic. Still, it is a pain.'

'Will the court believe you?' asked his sister.

'Maybe not, but it might be enough to get them to drop the case, and try to give our friend Antonescu a hard time some other way. Whatever happens, Antonescu will be grateful to me for helping out. But what interests me, and must interest him, is that there were not many people who knew that he had the painting in the first place. I mean, no one apart from family go into his bedroom, where it hung. So how did the police know it was there? By the purest chance? Did you know it was there, for example?'

'No, not at all,' said Roberto, in what he hoped was a smooth manner.

'The only person who was there when he acquired it, that I can think of, was that little short-arsed friend of yours,' said Bonelli.

'It could not have been him,' said Roberto carefully. 'First of all, he never ever talks about anything that is remotely, shall we say, embarrassing. And the other thing is he knows nothing about art at all. He has never looked at a picture in his life, though he sees them every day in the gallery, and he would not have known what this picture was, let alone that it was potentially valuable. He is not educated.'

'But I remember talking to him about Caravaggio. Or have I got that wrong?' said Gabriella.

'And besides….' continued Roberto.

'Besides what?' asked Bonelli.

'Why would he want to make trouble for don Traiano? I mean that sort of trouble? It does not make sense.'

'Then maybe the policeman saw it on the wall and thought it might be something… In which case he would be that rare thing, a cop who can think and who has a brain. I am sure that your Tonino is a good boy. I shall tell Traiano that, if he asks.'

'Will he ask?'

'Only if he is really thinking that little short arse is to blame. In which case he had better leave now. Indeed, it might be already too late. No, I am of course joking. Tonino and signora Grassi take excellent care of the gallery.'

Bonelli was a graduate of art history with a further degree in restoration; his main interest was, not the Renaissance, Roberto was glad to hear, for he found the Renaissance rather impenetrable, but the baroque, and the lesser-known masters of that age. He was something of an expert on Mattia Preti, a painter that Roberto had heard of and of whom he knew little. In addition, Ruggero knew a little about everything, though what little he knew was more than most people. The gallery had examples of everything, and he liked everything, and he and Gabriella and Roberto were able to talk about the paintings on display, and which were the ones they liked, which were going to sell, and which were wallpaper, destined to be there forever. Then the topic moved back to one painting in particular, the Mantegna Madonna and Child, the one that Traiano had hanging over his bed, the one the police had taken away.

'Well, it is not by Mantegna,' said Ruggero. 'It cost him two thousand euros, which is pretty cheap, and a real Mantegna would have cost ten or a hundred times that. It is a sweet picture, probably cut down from an original, by someone we have never heard of, and it is old. In fact, I was surprised that he saw it and took to it. I liked it.'

'You were surprised he had taste?' asked Gabriella. 'Well, you should not be. He has some taste, but this,' she handed the phone back to her brother, having examined the picture he had been showing her, 'this would have attracted him because of the subject matter. He is very pious in that strange way that some people have. He never misses Mass. I believe his mother is very religious too.'

'The one married to the photographer? The one who….?' asked Ruggero. 'I don't understand these people,' said Ruggero, meaning that he did not understand the lower classes, seemingly forgetting that Roberto was in the room, or perhaps assuming that now Roberto was sleeping with his sister, he had effortlessly ascended into the middle classes. 'But as they get richer, they will grow out of their religion, you watch.'

'I don't think they can get richer. They are loaded already,' said Gabriella.

'I wonder how much they really have?' asked Ruggero.

'They themselves do not know, because it is all tied up in things, but it is a lot, trust me.' She turned to Roberto. 'How much does Tonino Grassi have?'

Roberto considered. He knew exactly how much, because he kept a record.

'He's well paid,' he said at last. 'He is generous to his mother; and he lives rent free; he has got a fair bit in the bank, I mean several tens of thousands, I think.'

'And he is how old?' asked Ruggero.

'Eighteen,' said Roberto, knowing that this would be the answer Tonino would have given.

'He is a nice boy,' said Gabriella. 'He is good to his mother and his friends, and he has a nice respectable girlfriend, Roberto's sister. OK, the father is in prison, so he is the man of the house. A typical good Sicilian boy. Very polite too.'

'Very polite,' agreed Ruggero. 'I am sure he is all you say he is. You forgot to mention that he is short and ugly.'

'My brother is a harsh judge,' said Gabriella. 'How old is Traiano?' she asked.

'About thirty?' hazarded Roberto.

'His mother has a young child, so that is not possible,' said Ruggero.

'Twenty-five or so?' said Roberto.

'He is certainly a very successful young man,' said Ruggero enviously. 'Traiano is a little bit rough for me; don Calogero is in a different league. You can take him anywhere…. The Romanian has the stench of the sewers about him. Do you like him?' he asked turning to Roberto.

'A bit,' conceded Roberto. 'But I see what you mean.'

'You heard about that doctor being killed some weeks back? How did that happen?' he asked.

'No idea. Never knew him or heard of him,' said Roberto.

'They say it is some turf war with some new drug, some pill you take,' said Gabriella. 'It was very strange. A man walks in from the street, waits in the waiting room, and when he gets his turn, he shoots the doctor and walks out. And not a soul can remember what he looks like. Maybe it was something personal, a young man with a grudge, the doctor having done something for his girlfriend which he objected to. Revenge.' But this did not interest her, the death of an elderly medic. 'What will happen about Traiano's painting?'

'That is easy,' said her brother. 'We will claim it is a nineteenth century copy of an old painting. And they will not be able to prove otherwise. They produce an expert, we produce an expert, and so it goes on, until they give up.'

Shortly afterwards, Roberto had excused himself, saying that he had to go to lectures, and when that was over, to work in the office, as Assunta would surely be back by the evening and want to see him there. He kissed Gabriella's cheek, promised to text her, and then shook her brother's hand, and left.

In Palermo, it was the day after the wedding. Some, who had had nothing more intoxicating than Coca-Cola to drink the night before, awoke refreshed and rested. Others woke with the most banging headaches, and desperately tried to get back to sleep. One such was don Antonio Santucci. But at two in the afternoon, his wife came to rouse him, to tell him that they must go to the hospital at once, to which his father, Lorenzo Santucci, had been taken, having deteriorated in the night.

It had long been known that Lorenzo Santucci was unwell and that there was little to be done for him; but now, now that the end was so near, the death seemed unexpected, sudden and unjust. He was in a private room, surrounded by relations, the various women of his family, who now, once having been pushed into the background, were in complete charge. His brother Domenico, old and frail as he was, had made the effort to be there, as had his wife, as had his sisters, and his sister-in-law. Angela, his daughter-in-law, brought her husband and, after a few phone calls, her children, to say goodbye to their grandfather; they all dutifully kissed his forehead, but only Beppe had the grace to cry. Her sister-in-law was there, Carlo's widow, and Renzo came, and Renzo's sisters. Then the younger generation went, Renzo back to his new wife, the others back home to pass the day in doleful expectation. The women stayed, and so did don Antonio, the son, and don Domenico, the brother. As Antonio watched his father fade away, he felt terrible resentment at the way his father had pushed him aside in favour of don Calogero di Rienzi and his own useless nephew; waiting for a word of apology from the old man, or trying to summon a word of forgiveness on his own part, knowing both were impossible. A priest came to minister the commendation of the dying, to impart a forgiveness that would be far more efficacious; and then, as the day faded, so did Lorenzo Santucci, the once feared and terrible man, who died peacefully, in sharp contrast to the manner in which he had once lived.

The funeral was held three days later, and the burial took place at the hilltop village of Montelepre, outside Palermo, which had once been the family home, and where the mortuary chapel of the Santucci family stood in the local cemetery. The Mass was in the parish church in Palermo, and afterwards the cortege made its way several kilometres along provincial road number one, up into the hills, to the cemetery of Montelepre, to see the old man placed in the sarcophagus that had been waiting for him for years. The chapel was neatly kept, with an altar and candles, and bedecked with flowers. After the coffin had been put in its place, and the slab sealed over it, people stood around in the warm sunshine of early spring.

The family – don Renzo with his wife Elena, now indisputably head of the family, stood to receive condolences from the mourners. His uncle don Antonio had come to the Mass but as soon as the burial was over, left the cemetery, taking his uncle, don Domenico, with him. With don Renzo were his mother and sisters, and his aunt Angela, and her children, Sandro and Beppe, and their two sisters, Emma and Marina. In addition, present were his mother, and his grandmother and great aunt. Amongst all these women, all virtually indistinguishable except perhaps by age, in their black dresses, Renzo stood out, in his sharp suit and his dark glasses. He projected an air of command and quietly received the condolences of the black habited crowd that shuffled past him.

Also wearing dark glasses, with Traiano similarly shaded next to him, Calogero surveyed the family, or what was left of them. Antonio, he had noticed during the Mass, had been barely sober, and had been wise not to linger in the cemetery, and had no doubt by now gone home with the surviving old man and was finishing off the job started with the few glasses of whiskey he had had before breakfast. As for Renzo, those dark glasses told their own story: he, no doubt, had longed for, but not dared to fortify himself with a fair amount of cocaine before he could face the ordeal of the funeral.

The atmosphere was silent, serious. Beppe was trying his best to look serious, wondering how much longer they would all have to stand around for. When the crowd began to dissolve, when the murmur of conversation arose, and the cigarette smoke began (to Calogero's disgust) to rise in the air, Beppe approached Calogero.

Calogero realised that the boy knew; there was something in his look, in his approach. And Calogero knew as well, for his wife had told him. The day after the death of don Lorenzo, she had been informed, as his principal banker, that the entire fortune had been left *in toto* to this child, to be kept in trust until he reached the age of twenty-one; and in the event of his death before that, to pass to the Archdiocese of Palermo.

'My condolences on the loss of your grandfather,' said Calogero, caressing the child's cheek, speaking in the tones of one who was congratulating him for securing a fortune, right under their very noses, while none of them had been looking. But it had not been his work, but the work of the mother. But the boy must have known; surely, he had known and co-operated. All that sweetness masked a calculating mind. Or was he wrong? Was the boy really an innocent?

Beppe accepted the condolences. Then he turned to Traiano, who hugged him. Well, Traiano knew nothing. But soon everyone would know, and what then? It would be interesting to see how they all changed. Money changed people, both those who gained it and those who lost it, as he himself well knew.

'Would you like to see something interesting?' asked Calogero, speaking to the attentive fourteen-year-old. 'One of the most interesting things in Sicily, here in the cemetery of Montelepre? Yes? Follow me. You too, Traiano.'

Traiano knew that Calogero's father had been born in Montelepre, and wondered if they were going to see the tomb of his grandparents. They followed him down another avenue of mortuary chapels, each of which bore the name of the family to which it belonged. Carefully, Calogero checked the names, until they came to one with a pointed gothic door, in the main avenue of the cemetery, which was open. Inside, the altar had a white cloth and burned with candles. To one side, was a white marble sarcophagus. There were numerous flowers, even though the man in the sarcophagus had been dead for sixty years. His name was on the side of the sarcophagus: Salvatore Giuliano. They looked at it in silence.

'Last year, at about this time, at the end of October, they came and opened it up to check it really was him. They did a DNA test, or so they say. Because the rumour was that he had escaped from Sicily, and that the body of the person murdered in Castelvetrano was not his. The rumour was that he was alive and well and living in South America.'

'He would be, what, eighty-eight or eighty-nine,' pointed out Beppe. 'But I see what you mean. Like King Arthur, *rex quondam, rex futurus*. Our once and future king.' He looked at Calogero. 'Do you think he is alive?' he asked.

Calogero considered. Traiano watched him. Calogero placed a hand on the marble lid, then knelt to examine the photograph on the tomb more closely.

'Ah Sicily,' he murmured to himself, kissing the photograph gently. 'You are so beautiful, so very beautiful.'

Author's Note

While this story aims at verisimilitude, it is a work of fiction. The Purgatory quarter of Catania does not exist, though it may be taken to occupy the area between the via Etnea and Catania railway station. Salvatore Giuliano is a real historical figure, and the description of the cemetery where he reposes is as accurate as I can make it. The same goes for the cityscapes of Catania and Palermo. However, none of the other characters in the book, particularly the office holders, are to be equated with living people.

Printed in Dunstable, United Kingdom